When desire sets you free...control is a matter of perception.

I'm Devin Hill.

Darkness taints my soul.

I'm suffocating. Drowning.

The sweet promise of air? Pure illusion.

Tested as a genius at age seven, I hide my emotions, become what they expect...bury my secrets. At nineteen, I trudge toward a predestined path, blinders on, heart safeguarded.

Until I dare to be wild.

Until Alec Marquez crashes into my world.

Until all that follows redefines everything I've ever known.

What happens when you stumble into a world of spies...and discover you belong there?

the
ESPIONAGE
effect

the
ESPIONAGE
effect

Kat Bastion
with Stone Bastion

Cover Design by ©Sarah Hansen, Okay Creations
Formatted by E. M. Tippetts Book Designs

emtippettsbookdesigns.com
First Printing, July 2015

ISBN-13: 978-0996418102
ISBN-10: 0996418105

OTHER BOOKS BY
KAT BASTION WITH STONE BASTION

No Weddings Series
No Weddings
One Funeral
Two Bar Mitzvahs
Three Christmases
For Valentine's

BOOKS BY
KAT BASTION

Highland Legends Series
Forged in Dreams and Magick
Bound by Wish and Mistletoe
(a holiday novella)
Born of Mist and Legend
(Winter 2015-2016)
Found in Flame and Moonlight
(Winter 2016-2017)

Romantic Poetry for Charity
Utterly Loved
Foreword by Sylvain Reynard

To all those seeking their place in this world...

CHAPTER 1

The darkest lie was the one I conned myself into believing…

Cool shadows cloaked me with the soothing comfort of a familiar enemy-turned-friend.

On either side of us, lush vegetation covered the ground, broad-leafed vines snaked up palm trunks, and the eerie roots of banyan trees hung from horizontal limbs, as if probing to snag an unsuspecting passerby. We walked near a pale blue-gray palm, unique amid all the glossy emerald, as we negotiated down an uneven limestone path which threatened to turn an ankle even in the sturdy wedge thongs I'd worn.

The manmade trail was an average width of forty-two inches. Between our hotel suite's small building and our current position grew thirty-seven distinct species of flora, *thirty-eight…thirty-nine.* I paused in my mental tallying to glance up at a large tree's canopy that spanned directly overhead. A quick scan from left to right calculated that one thousand four hundred and twenty-eight leaves quivered above us in the slight breeze, plus or minus an acceptable margin of error.

"Well, Dev?" Anna, my college roommate and fellow vacationer, nudged a hip into me, knocking me off-balance. "What d'ya think?"

Startled at her rowdy interruption, I blinked back to reality, then shot her a deadpan look. "I think it's a damn good thing you didn't wear your Choos or Blahniks." Designer shoes were her weakness, to the point of impracticality.

In the middle of the manicured jungle of a swank boutique resort we'd arrived at only hours ago, the closest friend I had struck a defiant pose, hands propped on her hips, lips plumped into an impressive pout.

If a male had been around? The poor guy would've stumbled. Passing cars would've crashed. With sleek black hair, wide-set green eyes, flawless olive skin, and graceful legs accompanying perfectly proportioned curves, she wandered effortlessly through the world looking like an exotic supermodel.

"Don't dis designer, Devin. And you knew what I meant. Is Maroma Beach *the ultimate*, or what?"

"Nice alliteration." I struggled to restrain an eye roll.

And yeah, I'd known what she'd meant. But we'd only been on the ground in the purported tropical paradise for a short time, and she knew what ailed me couldn't be instantly cured by the pretty veneer of a beach locale.

My last-minute decision to go on my first vacation ever had been driven by a desperate need to escape: from a colorless preordained life, from expectations of those who'd held court over my destiny, from the suffocating knowledge in the deepest parts of me that screamed for more…

More justice. More choices. More control…

Maybe the climate would be conducive to soul searching. Then instead of running from a future that fit me wrong in every way, I could chase something that would make me as whole as one could reasonably expect.

"It's amazing, Anna." The easy lie rolled off my tongue slow and soft, a skill I'd sharpened over the years, long before I'd met her.

Her eyes twitched, subtly narrowing before she outright glared at me.

It seemed she hadn't bought into my subterfuge. Although she didn't fully grasp the extent of all that plagued me, she understood that I desperately needed a break from an abysmal reality before I cracked.

"Devin Hill. You are here on vacation." She clicked closer in her jeweled flip flops, her menacing expression intensifying. "Blend with the natives. Be a tourist." She spread her arms wide, raising them as she closed the distance between us. "Embrace the happiness and serenity." She stopped when we stood toe-to-toe, voice lowering, "If you can't enjoy yourself for the seven days we have here, will you at least fake it for me?"

I tilted my head and beamed her my typical smile. "Absolutely."

"Good. Now can we eat? I'm famished." The matter apparently settled to her satisfaction, she looped an arm through mine and tugged me forward, unrelenting as usual.

Both almost twenty, with birthdays only three weeks apart in February, we'd met at the student union two years ago when I'd needed a body to fill a spare condo bedroom. She'd hovered over my shoulder as I depressed a pushpin into a *ROOMMATE NEEDED* flyer. But instead of pulling off one of the dozen slim phone-number tabs at the bottom, she'd ripped the entire page out from under the pushpin and declared herself as the roommate I needed.

Matter-of-fact, succinct, efficient, and confident? I hadn't argued.

"Me too." I matched her strides step for step, if not to fully embrace the spirit of a Christmas holiday in the brightly painted tropics, then to at least act like it. Having her as a determined cheerleader at my side couldn't hurt matters.

We stepped beneath a stone archway carved with historical Mayan reliefs, through an entry building, and into a courtyard garden shaded by a dense canopy of trees. Turning right, we picked our way over stepping stones edged with lush green moss, passed a blue-and-yellow macaw preening a wing from a perch on a terra-cotta birdhouse, then continued down the narrow path alongside a two-story white stucco building with spacious balcony terraces. To our left, water arced from circular stone spouts built within a blue-tiled wall, then lazily splashed into a crystal-clear pool surrounded by unoccupied chaise lounges.

Two quick steps up led us into a limestone-tiled entry hall. Farther ahead, at the end of a forty-foot breezeway, a larger archway framed the brilliant turquoise of the Caribbean Sea.

We skirted an enormous round wooden table that stood in the center of the entryway of a spacious building that exuded a stately Spanish-mansion ambiance. As we reached the table's widest point, Anna nudged my shoulder, whispering. "Leave all that 'choose a major' shit behind." She referenced the most recent reason I'd voiced that I needed a break. "Live a little." She stared hard at me, a single eyebrow arched high. "Or a lot." She gave a pointed nod, gaze flicking forward toward the right.

A gorgeous man walked from an indoor bar into the breezeway, the target of her thinly veiled hint.

"Do you ever *not* see men as playthings?" I murmured on a headshake.

"When one doesn't want commitment, that's what men are. Need I remind you of your recent pledge to honor that philosophy?"

Right. On the flight over, I'd agreed to have wild sex with unknown men just to placate her. With a heavy sigh, already regretting my promise as my gaze rolled up toward the ceiling, I caught sight of two male staff members in white uniforms, both perched precariously on a ladder positioned ahead of us a quarter turn around the table. The man on the highest wooden rung held a delicate bell-shaped glass globe between his fingertips and leaned with a soft grunt while he struggled to reach a naked unlit bulb hanging toward the center.

Unable to stop the chain reaction, I paused midstride, predicting in a fraction of a heartbeat the disaster about to unfold. The distance between his reach and his target were

5

disproportionate. Already his short arm trembled from exertion as his muscles expended every ounce of energy they had toward their unachievable goal.

Focus sharpening, zooming in on every minuscule detail in an instant, my mind's eye saw the result before it happened. Without thought, I lunged forward, extending my arm. His fingertips flattened, causing the weight of the globe to part from his hold.

Its cool glass hit my splayed hand a split second later.

Then in continued fluid motion, I spun around, bracing the ladder with my other hand as the wild-eyed maintenance worker flailed his arms, nearly causing both men to topple to the ground.

"*¡Señorita! ¡Perdón!*" Additional incomprehensible Spanish words gushed from their lips.

When they'd stopped verbally castrating themselves and put their feet on solid ground again, I unaffectedly handed them back their globe with a nod and a gentle smile.

"*Damn.*" Anna grabbed my hand and yanked me forward. "I *never* get used to you doing that."

The odd superhero-like gift had become second nature. With a tested IQ of 162 and an eidetic memory, my brain worked like a supercomputer when triggered. Combined with a body honed by varsity volleyball and many other physical pursuits, I often thwarted accidents before they had a chance to happen.

"*Ooooph!*" My shoulder collided into a rock-solid wall before I'd fully spun forward again. "Oh! I'm so...sorry." Bumbling out words, I shot my hands up, nearly knocking a coffee mug out of a man's hand.

My breath caught when I registered my palms had landed on a hard chest underneath a blue silk shirt. Heat shot through my fingertips, seared along the skin where my forearm rested along his.

I exhaled a measured breath through pursed lips as my face tilted upward.

Black hair. Dark eyes. Tall. Muscular.

The breathtaking man—the gorgeous man who'd earlier entered from the bar—gave me a penetrating look for a beat longer before his free hand wrapped around my upper arm. He said nothing as his jaw clenched, thick-lashed eyes narrowing. Then he eased his grip, took a step back after he appeared satisfied that I wouldn't topple over without his support, and turned away, heading in the direction from where Anna and I had just come from.

Thoroughly disoriented, I stared after him while my pulse raced, my breaths shortened, and my skin tingled, like every cell in my body had suddenly become attuned to his presence. The breadth of his shoulders and his laid-back but confident gait held my full attention until he disappeared around the corner.

Blinking at the unexpected effect one man instantly had on me, I glanced toward Anna. Then my awareness broadened to the handful of hotel staff who'd gathered at a ten-foot perimeter and the sprinkling of guests who hovered in the corners beyond. Evidently my instinctual rescue, and the maintenance workers' subsequent reactions, had ignited an excited commotion enough to cause bystanders to linger out of idle curiosity.

"Mmm-hmm…" Anna continued, as if an entire hazardous detour hadn't interrupted her. "Maroma Beach *is* the ultimate. Plenty of…playthings." She smirked as naughtiness twinkled in her eyes.

Exasperated by her incessant prodding toward all things sexual, I roped an arm around her shoulder and we resumed our course, heading toward a young woman dressed in a rainbow-colored flowing skirt and four-inch wedge espadrilles. She stood at the podium beneath the archway with a wide smile on her face.

"*Buenos días,*" she greeted with a nod of her head.

Due to my limited Spanish—languages not being a desired skill until our flight over with brief audio lessons complements of Rosetta Stone—and to convey my communication preference, I held up my index and middle fingers, speaking in clear English, "Two."

"Very good. Right this way." The hostess's polished English, tinged with only a hint of an accent, bore testament to either a selective hiring process at the five-star resort or a dedication on their staff members' parts to blend with the guests.

After we were seated on the lower terrace of the patio, I settled onto the chair cushion and inhaled deeply, doing my best to "blend with the natives" in a very foreign world.

The locale had a certain undeniable atmosphere: ocean mist the perfect temperature of cool; gentle waves rolling between a stretch of tempting white sand and an expansive cobalt-blue sky; sumptuous food meant to seduce the palate brought by serving staff who had impeccable manners, yet attended to the table with warm graciousness.

Earlier assumptions about the staff and guests twisted into more complex facets. In every corner of the multi-terraced patio, near the thatched roof bar, and down onto the wide beach spanning to the shoreline, the cultural diversity broadened into a rich international tapestry. Tables within earshot spoke not only English and Spanish, but also what sounded like French, Japanese, Arabic, and…Dutch? Among those who spoke English, myriad accents danced into my ears, teasing my brain: Scottish, Australian…South African.

A father and son spiraled a football back and forth on the sand near the shoreline. Two teenaged girls perched on the edges of their barstools, trying to capture the attention of an attractive man in sunglasses at the end of the bar. He was surrounded by a half dozen men and women in T-shirts and board shorts, many holding professional cameras with long zoom lenses slung over their shoulders.

Daring seagulls fought for scraps of food, swooping down the moment a table was abandoned, fighting for hierarchal rights to a toasted piece of bread or the remains of a basket of fries. In the center of our table, dainty black-and-silver striped bees hovered over a square glass dish made of translucent green bubble glass, each choosing one of the four sectioned-off flavors of tropical jams. They took turns landing gingerly on the sloping glass perimeter, then edged toward their chosen spread until they extended their proboscis into the inventive substitute nectar.

How quaint. Yet all of them? Oblivious.

Man and beast alike played in the sun-drenched vivid

colors of the world, recklessly disregarding the dangerous reality lurking in the shadows just beyond sight, as if they were ignorant of it—or impervious to it.

I was neither. Even though, at times, I wished fervently I was both.

The vantage point from the cold, monochrome shadows had proved my wisest course—observing, going through the motions only when necessary, but never fully participating.

Yet cocooned as I'd been for so long, I'd reached a crisis of destiny.

In the last year, I'd swung one-hundred-eighty degrees from all-encompassing astrophysics to the painstaking minutiae of nuclear physics, incessantly nudged by my parents and counselors, yet I'd still found the stagnant air to be stifling. I'd never fully invested in the path most fitting for my intelligence level. In fact, I'd only ever halfheartedly participated from the start.

Aptitude did not equate desire. *Not even close.*

I needed more.

Needed to venture out into the real world.

That was the reason for the whole spontaneous vacation: to reassess my skills and desires. I desperately needed to find a balance of the unexpected amid the landslide toward the mundane. And I had cast aside every ingrained rule to do it, decided to finally *live* for once.

Seven days of so-called blissful paradise held only one purpose: Be wild.

"...Mayan ruins. Oh, snorkeling," Anna droned on, assuming I'd been fully engaged. "The world's second largest coral reef is only five minutes away by boat." She'd been tossing out activity suggestions from the moment we'd sat down.

"Sure. That sounds...*sanitary.*" Sucking on stale rubber after a thousand other mouths had slobbered over it.

"You can buy a new snorkel," she countered, shaking her head with a dismissing expression that I'd grown accustomed to.

Yet instead of entering into a subject ripe for debate, my gaze landed on a family of four who gathered at a table alongside the sand. Two little girls who'd just run up from the beach vied for their parents' attention. The older one held up a carved wooden boat with a linen sail. The younger thrust a red-and-blue monster truck in front of it. "Look, Mama. The man on the beach gave us these." The smaller girl turned and pointed southward. The parents both looked over their shoulders, expressions bearing only passive interest.

With sudden alarm, I snapped my head around to identify the potential child predator. I exhaled a relieved sigh when a hotel staff member smiled broadly and waved to the vacationing family.

My gaze drifted back to the little girls, hair light brown with shimmering gold highlights, just like mine...*just like ours*...had been. Long-buried memories attempted to surface. I fought them, trying to tear my gaze away, but the strength of the dark undertow was too powerful, and it pulled me down anyway.

Staring at the youngest girl, a burning pain grew in my chest as two realities juxtaposed. Would she kiss a boy

11

without a care in the world? Will she dream of a big wedding with a white dress? The older girl placed her boat onto the table for her father to examine, and my attention shifted to her. When faced with a multitude of paths in life, will her parents let her choose? Would they both grow up the way little girls should: nurtured, adored…safe?

When she transgresses, will she be forgiven?

Will she be loved?

A warm hand covered mine, drawing my attention back. I turned and stared at Anna. Her image blurred through tears I hadn't felt coming.

"Dev, it's okay, you know. To talk about it." Typically boisterous Anna had transformed into a calm pillar of strength.

On a slow exhale, I gave her a slight headshake, leaned closer, and wrapped an arm around her shoulder. "No, I'm good." Another comfortable lie. My gaze floated back to the happy girls. "Do I envy them? No question. My heart hurts to see their innocence and know there's evil out there watching them, waiting for the right opportunity to snatch them from their bright lives to color them dark."

She nudged me and gave me a pointed look. "Anytime. I'm here *anytime* you need me. I know I've said it before, but use me. Sounding board, counselor, friend…avenger. Whatever you need, never hesitate to come to me."

I gave her a weak smile. "Thanks. I do like the 'avenger' part."

Every fiber of my being screamed for vengeance for what had been taken from my sister, from me. Too many memories had been buried.

Enough time had gone by for me to move on.
Yet not enough had been done to help me heal.

Through the afternoon, from the cool shade under an enormous beach umbrella, lazy hours had drifted by along with an occasional tiny cotton cloud overhead. We lounged on a blue, canvas queen-sized cushion mere steps from the ocean. Cool mist from breaking waves fanned our faces every so often, forcing me to clean my sunglasses with annoying regularity.

Anna nodded her chin down toward the shoreline, her lips still wrapped around a straw that descended into a green coconut "drinking goblet" that she cradled with both hands. "How many margaritas?"

We'd been playing her invented game between reading and sunbathing. How many margaritas would it take to "do" whatever random guy had the misfortune to walk into our purview. So far, all we'd spotted were pasty men who'd clearly landed on the beach to escape sedentary indoor lives filled with excess calories.

My gaze followed her chin-gesture to land on the male she'd indicated. "Uhhh...ditch the margaritas. Ditch mixed cocktails entirely. I'd need a whole bottle of straight tequila." With equal parts revulsion and fascination, I stared at the middle-aged man sporting a carpeted chest and greasy comb-over. Nature had given him hair in disproportionate amounts in all the wrong places.

"I dunnooo..." She tapped a nail on her straw, sizing up

the quarry as he walked by. "Looks like he's packing."

In a slow-motion unavoidable train wreck, my gaze lowered from his furry reddish chest-carpeting to land on an obscenely brief man-kini. "No way that's real," I scoffed. "It's the dimensions of a Red Bull can."

A silent beat passed. Then another. I pressed my lips together. Then we both burst out laughing.

She shoved my shoulder hard, knocking my upper body over from its pillow-propped position. "Why the hell have we never done this before?"

"Done what? Objectify unappealing men with a crude system of coitus-by-drunkenness?"

She scrunched her face. "Don't say 'coitus' in front of me. It offends my filthy mind."

"Fine. '*Fuck.*' Happy?"

Her ruby-glossed lips stretched into a wide smile. "Immensely. And no. This is the most fun we've had together in two years at college. You've been holding out on me."

If she only knew.

I settled back under our umbrella's shade against my perfectly arranged white and blue pillows, pulled my sunglasses atop my head, and turned my Kindle back on with the swipe of an index finger. "Well, I'm here now, aren't I? Be satisfied I've decided to go wild for once."

A shot glass appeared in my view with clear liquid in it. "Not wild enough if you keep ignoring the beauty around you in favor of an electronic escape. We should institute an unplugged rule."

When I made no move to accept the shot glass, she

shoved it between the lighted page of the tense scene I'd returned to and my face. "Shots before smut."

"Alcohol dehydra—"

"No." She leaned closer, dragged her sunglasses down her nose with a curved finger, and narrowed her darkened green eyes at me. "No more commentary about dehydration. In fact, no scientific analysis at all. *Drink*."

After bookmarking the page of the "smut" I'd been enthralled by, I put aside the Kindle, pressed the rim of the shot glass to my lips, then tossed back the shot of Anna's favorite tequila, Patrón Silver. I sucked in a sharp breath as the liquid scorched over the surface of my tongue before blazing a path down my throat.

After I leveled my gaze back down, I stared straight ahead. Then blinked.

A beautiful man walked in from the ocean at the shoreline. Water droplets glistened on his caramel-colored skin like diamonds. Subtle shadows defined the muscles along his arms, broad shoulders, rippling abs...which led toward low-slung board shorts that clung to powerful thighs.

I recognized his face. The man I'd bumped into in the breezeway earlier. Only now the incredible body previously hidden by blue silk and linen had been revealed. Complete with scuba gear resting near his feet and sheathed knife strapped to his calf, he appeared to be a fantasy hero who'd emerged from the sea.

"He's staring at you." She released her coconut hostage, then nestled her tropical drink into the folds of the blue towel between us.

Yeah, right.

With a swivel of my head that induced a slight buzzy spin, I dropped her a hard look. "No, he's not. You've got the eye-popping bod. Any man looking at me is wondering why Plain Jane is hanging out with the supermodel." Which was fine. With mousy-brown hair and minuscule curves, I preferred invisibility from the comfort of my obscuring shadows.

"Pffft." She shook her head. Then she gave me an exhausted look and gestured her hand in a sweeping wave from the top of my head to my toes. "You need prescription glasses. Or a better mirror. I may be classic 'fashion magazine' pretty, but you're beautiful in a different way. Exotic."

Riiight. Exotic meant almond-shaped eyes and glossy black hair—like her. Not girl-next-door average like me.

She flipped over onto her stomach, baring her perfect ass for his scrutiny. "Look closer," she continued. "He strikes me as different too. He wasn't looking at me this morning. And he sure as hell isn't looking at me now."

Casually grabbing a beer from the ice bucket beside me, I glanced back toward the man in question for confirmation, but the moment had passed. He dunked the bottoms of the tanks once into the surf, then turned and headed down the beach toward the long thatched-roof *palapa* that coordinated the sporting activities for our strand of Maroma Beach.

"*That's* the guy you need to do this week," she murmured sleepily.

My gulp of Dos Equis shot down the wrong way, the act of swallowing competing with my shocked gasp. I nearly coughed up a lung as I struggled to inhale clear air again. "*What?*"

"You know you want him. He's your perfect guy. You wanted to be wild? Well, there you go." She waved a hand back in the general direction of where said guy had last stood. "One Latin lover to have a wild fling with."

"He's not there anymore. He left." I grabbed my Kindle and cued up the bookmarked scene which still had a dominant male commanding the page, a man who wanted to stay and show me a good time. Well, me and his heroine.

Anna propped herself up on her elbows. Then she put a hand on the top edge of my Kindle, forcing it down. "Trust me. He'll be back."

"Uh-huh." As I stared south down the beach, he disappeared into the crowd of beachgoers.

A velvety ink-colored butterfly swooped into my line of sight from behind us, then sailed above the sparkling sand to our left, vivid black against bright white, before it swerved off at a right angle and flew straight over the crashing waves, out toward the vast indigo ocean. Against a punishing headwind, it flapped its wings with amazing ferocity for its delicate structure. I stared after it, entranced by another creature in this world set on a predestined course, undeterred or unaware by the immense monotony that lay ahead for days, perhaps weeks—decades to a human.

Would the dark butterfly veer off course? Take a detour from what its preprogrammed DNA had in store for it? Would a rogue storm tumble it toward a different fate than forecast by the clear skies ahead?

Deep inside, a burning desire to go storm hunting flared to life.

CHAPTER 2

On a stuttered gasp, I jerked upright from a deep sleep into a pitch-black room. My heart pounded, its pulse echoing with matching vibrations against my eardrums. Disoriented by unfamiliar shapes, I let the darkest part of the room envelope me before familiarizing myself with images that didn't immediately make sense.

A strange sound broke through the confusion as the soft booming of ocean waves crashed in the near distance, triggering a reminder of my location. I'd gone on vacation— supposedly. *We* had.

I skimmed a hand over to the other side of the bed. *Empty.* Anna had gotten up.

After a quick visual sweep of the room again, scanning across shadowy shapes that grew easier to distinguish as my eyes adjusted, I confirmed she wasn't in this part of the room. My gut told me she wasn't in the bathroom behind me either, lack of sound and light affirming my instincts.

Unwarranted panic fueled my quickening pulse, and I lunged out of bed toward the door. When my hands flattened against its cool surface, I slid them down toward the handle on the right. My fingers grazed over a two-inch length of metal, and I paused; the interior bolt had been thrown open.

After a hard swallow, I took a deep breath and quietly turned the metal door handle down. A loud click sounded into the silent room. Then I eased back and opened the door.

Dim lights flooded the upper landing between our suite and the adjacent one, the only two rooms on the second floor of our four-unit building. Padding barefoot on the warm ceramic tiles, I rushed across the narrow hallway to the top of the stairs. Curving downward with recessed lights hidden in low white-stucco walls every few steps, they led down to the limestone pathways: heading toward the beach on the left; to the spa straight ahead; or meandering through the resort's jungle, passing other hotel rooms and suites, and eventually veering alongside the gift boutique until it ended at the property's main entrance.

As I paused at the landing, a flash of movement blurred off toward the right, where the pathway led toward the heart of the resort. But I couldn't be certain if I'd glimpsed a human foot or the tail of a ground-dwelling animal. And enough time had elapsed since I'd startled awake that I had no idea whether or not she had recently left, or if she'd ditched me long ago and I'd only now discovered it.

"Idiot," I muttered, turning on my heel and heading back toward the open door of our suite. The disparaging label had been meant for me, but I mentally widened the umbrella to cover Anna too.

My invincible roomie habitually went running in the middle of the night, something I'd gotten used to at college. But we weren't in the States. We were one thousand seven hundred twenty-eight miles south of there, in a country where we'd been advised to look like tourists straight off the plane so we didn't stand out as targets to their rampant kidnapping rings.

Common sense screamed that when an attractive jogging opportunity appeared before a marginally moral employee or a desperate local, all of Anna's self-defense training would be put to the test.

"Why tempt fate?" I shook my head as the answer came to me, even though the reason paled in the face of the risks.

Jogging to Anna nearly surpassed her need to breathe, like her muscles would twitch and she'd bounce in place if deprived until she was able to relieve all that pent-up energy. On occasion, she never came back during the night, choosing instead to watch the sunrise from a park bench overlooking the Charles River.

I glanced at our room's slender doorknob. The *DO NOT DISTURB* sign still dangled from a delicate fraying rope which was threaded through the top holes of each corner and strung with colorful beads. When I shut the door, my fingers hesitated over the throw latch. I couldn't bolt it from the inside, or I'd lock her out. But not securing the door meant I'd remain vulnerable to anyone with a passkey: a random employee...someone worse.

"Get over yourself, Dev." Old fears died hard. Demons from the deep reaches of my mind haunted me with far greater effect than actual reality.

I backed up toward the bed, never taking my eyes off the door handle, until the backs of my thighs hit the edge of the mattress. I sat down, then scooted backward until I reached the center. Out of habit, I bent my knees to my chest and wrapped my arms around my legs.

"Calm down." I whispered the low words, followed by a drawn-out exhale. Logic always pacified my spiraling anxiety. I simply needed to immerse myself into the reasoning part of my mind.

My gaze tracked from the door, scanning across the room to the french doors leading to the terrace. Through the left door's exposed mullioned glass panes, I made out the right end of a hammock fastened to the ceiling by a thick metal hook. The rest of the hammock disappeared, screened from view by the slats of a closed wooden shutter over a window. Faint light spilled over from somewhere, probably a patio light from the neighboring unit on the right. A noise scratched against the adjacent window around the open corner of the building. My educated guess was the tips of palm fronds lashed against the glass as the strong breeze whipped them about.

The cloak of darkness within the room soothed me, and my heartbeat began to regulate. When the shadows that existed outside matched my insides, my world settled into harmony. No more pretending with coconut drinks that sported colorful umbrellas. No more perfect talcum-sand beaches tempting my unsuspecting inner child out to play.

The dark of night hid nothing. The realness of the world

existed there: all the badness. Humanity's baser instincts crept out around the witching hour, predators stalking forth, embracing their true selves.

And yet, no matter how right it all seemed to be, even though I felt more at home letting the darkness that tainted my soul mix with the real shadows encircling me, fear still pulsed in my veins. Anger did too. And with every next heavy beat of my heart, the stark emotion transformed, deepening, until white-hot fury took its place.

Then calm descended, like it always did with enough steadfast patience. The inner shift happened in slow measure. Until no fear remained. Only vengeance.

With willful purpose, I entered that deepest place inside my mind and heart. Cold, hard, sharpened like the edge of a blade, the inner determination to fashion myself into a weapon to mete out justice, overtook me once again.

I remained fully aware of my surroundings: every dark shape in the room, each muffled crash of waves, the shift of filtered light through the wooden slats as palm fronds rustled.

The familiar inner power centered me. It guided me when I found myself lost. Strengthened me when I became weak. Gave me purpose when I drifted—which was rare.

Every day since that harrowing one, I remembered who I was, though details of that night were sketchy at best, thanks to my distant parents.

But even my parents didn't truly know me.

Years visiting world-renowned psychologists hadn't unearthed what lay inside either.

But I knew of myself the only two things that needed to be known. I was a survivor. And every step I took in life would make me the hunter.

All of a sudden, as I sat on the bed, ensconced in soothing darkness, the details of my calm environment changed in rapid succession. A low *pop!* was followed by a high-pitched tinkling. The faint light on the terrace vanished, leaving only dim illumination from an adjacent building across the courtyard. A dark silhouette glided beyond the slats, then edged into view through the left french door. The hammock flailed for an instant, then a low thud echoed.

I launched off the crumpled bed sheets and flattened my body against the outer wall between two windows, hiding in shadow. My pulse skyrocketed, firing a rush of adrenaline into my veins.

My genius mind sharpened further, assessing the situation, searching for a weapon—becoming one.

Could I have scrambled out the front door? Sure. It was my only escape from the threat on my patio. But I still hadn't determined what that threat was. Or if a greater threat lay in wait beyond a door I *couldn't* see through.

A drug lord could have decided to make base camp in my room. Or a seabird could have collided with the light, then crashed onto my terrace. Except, there was no flapping. And the movements suggested something far bigger than a seabird.

A low groan came from the patio. Definitely human.

I'd positioned myself at the wrong visual trajectory to gather further information. With measured steps, I moved forward, tracing a pattern along the shadowed portions of the room with sweeping heel-ball-toe footfalls, silent like a ninja.

The mystery figure on the terrace stood. Its dark shape moved closer, then reached for the door handle.

I eased down the two tiled steps that led into the sitting area, then slid my fingers around a ballpoint pen which rested on a notepad on the corner of the desk. Pressing flush with the outer window, I inched closer to the door, hiding as I gripped my newfound weapon tightly in my fist.

A gentle click preceded a low squeak, then the door slowly swung open into the room. I waited until the intruder cleared the door's edge. On a hard swallow, I raised my arm and aimed toward the exposed neck on a very tall frame. *Male.*

In a flash of movement, he spun. Before he fully turned, I compensated and plunged my weapon deep into flesh. An instant later, an agonizing vice clamped on to my wrist until I gasped and eased my hold. We remained motionless for long tense seconds, his dark glittering eyes staring, his tenacious grip…punishing.

Electric heat charged the air.

A familiar scent wound around me, paralyzing my thoughts.

But only for a moment. Adrenaline rocketed me back to my senses. In a split second, I shifted my weight, readying to knee his balls into his throat.

Before I could enact my plan, he crushed me back against the door, and our combined force slammed it shut. The steel cage of his body trapped mine.

Warm breath fanned over my face. He loosened his iron grip at my wrist, but only marginally. Then his fingers slid upward, dislodging the makeshift weapon from my grasp.

"A pen?" Amusement laced his deep tone.

Unwilling to admit defeat, but biding my time until another opening appeared, I gave a half-shrug. "The butter knife seemed cruel and cliché."

Humor. I had no idea why it tripped out of my mouth on instinct. Maybe to calm me. Throw him off guard.

His chuckle rumbled out. With a sudden burst of energy, he released me, and I stumbled forward a step. Then he walked deeper into the suite, offering me his back.

Okayyy…clearly not intent on rape or murder. Uncertain of what to do, I remained planted to the cold tiles where I stood, the memory of his solid heat pressed against me frying my brain.

Obviously he either wanted to demonstrate that he trusted me, or he was very stupid. Said butter knife was within reach. I could easily reconsider my weaponry. Yet I chose not to. And he hadn't stayed in the room long enough for it to matter. I watched as he disappeared around the corner and flicked on a light in the bathroom.

Confused beyond my limited-facts reasoning—about his unorthodox entry point into my room, his continued presence here, his disregard for common protocol of offering an explanation for the entire event—I followed him.

Curiosity overrode the fear I should've had.

Its glaring absence puzzled me even further.

Had instinct done that? Obliterated something that would've served as a healthy protection mechanism?

Maybe. The predator in me still quivered under my skin. The only problem was, the man in the bathroom acted nothing like prey, which began to deflate my fighting instinct.

Moving with mindful caution, I crossed the room, then eased forward, hovering along the opposite wall so I could peer around the corner from the farthest distance. When I caught sight of the reflection in the mirror, I blinked, stunned.

There stood the man I'd collided with before lunch, nearly knocking his coffee mug from his hand. The same man that had stood twenty feet away from Anna and me at the shoreline, wet board shorts clinging to his hips, water droplets glistening off his tanned skin.

Now he stood in my bathroom, shirtless, muscular upper body twisted toward the mirror as he examined his lower left side. A crimson stream trailed down from his lower ribcage.

"You're bleeding," I murmured, as if I hadn't just stabbed him elsewhere.

He made a low dismissive noise. "Just a scratch. Bullet burn." He turned further, trying to see beyond his shoulder. "Your puncture wound, however; that'll need stitches."

A twinge of guilt burned uncomfortably in my chest. Apparently, he'd fled from flying bullets, sought refuge in my hotel suite, and I'd graciously welcomed him by stabbing him.

His head turned, his interest shifting away from examining his wounds as his gaze locked on to mine. Dark eyes, black as midnight, stilled for a moment, unblinking and wholly unnerving. Then his attention drifted lower, his focus gliding downward as he perused my scantily clad body.

And my body reacted, as if his devoted attention had become a sensual touch. My nipples hardened, a dull ache began to intensify between my thighs, and my knees grew unstable, forcing me to widen my stance.

"…bottle of alcohol?" he murmured, tone low and even.

"What?" My gaze snapped back up to his eyes, which stared straight into my mine.

I hadn't imagined his full-body admiration. Or had I? My nipples remained almost painfully hard and the irrefutable sensual ache still throbbed. Regardless if his sexually charged attention was real or imagined, the man had an effect on me. And had from the moment I'd bumped into him near the restaurant earlier today.

"Grab a few, if they're those little bottles," he said.

I stared at him, attempting to process his words into meaning.

He tilted his face down a fraction, shooting a pointed look from beneath those dark brows. "Mini bar? Alcohol? To cleanse the wounds."

"Right." I spun around, relieved to be distracted by a task that removed me from his mind-blanking influence so I could unmuddle my brain.

"Nice shorts," he added in a dispassionate tone while I rounded the corner.

As I crossed through the darkness toward the sitting area, my face flamed the moment I realized what I wore. Not only had I been standing there in a thin cotton tank top—braless for his unhindered male enjoyment—but thanks to Anna's efforts to *Victoria's Secret* my wardrobe, I had the word PINK emblazoned in collegiate letters across my ass.

I blew out a hard breath and shook my head free of any lingering embarrassment. *Whatever.* Not like I got an announcement of his pending arrival.

Then I popped open the mini fridge, an entire room and a half away from the alpha male fuzzing my brain, and as the cold air rushed over my face, clearer thoughts began pinging again about the facts of my encounters with him.

First sighting: standing in the crowd when I'd prevented a light-fixture/ladder catastrophe. Second sighting: emerging from the water in front of the exact spot I happened to be sunbathing. Third? He just so happened to stumble into *my* room? *Riiight.*

Hell-bent on following the sagacious train of thought, I stormed across the bedroom and back into the beamed reach of the bright bathroom lights. I paused at the outer perimeter, holding him in my sights but keeping my distance.

He'd fully turned toward me in my absence, ass propped against the edge of the counter, hands loosely gripping the tiled edge on either side. His shirtless state continued to unnerve me; that darkly tanned expanse of skin emphasized his sleek muscles. A dusting of dark hair trailed in a faint line from his navel until it disappeared down into black cargo pants. Weathered black combat boots were casually crossed at the ankles.

Furrowing my brow, I cast aside everything about him

that distracted me and glared at him. "You do realize, I know the statistical probability of your being here as coincidence is so astronomically high, it's effectively nil. Three 'random' occurrences where we cross paths in one day defies the theory of Occam's Razor."

The corners of his lips twitched. "Do you kiss with that extraordinary mouth?"

I blinked hard, entirely thrown. My extraordinary mouth—with all the brainiac comments that spouted out of it—was exactly the reason I *hadn't* been kissed much. Guys got turned off when you took them out of their body and into their mind...then confused the hell out of them with your words.

"*Boys*, you mean." He quirked a brow up. "Maybe you need to be kissed by a man."

Holy shit. Had I just spoken my thoughts aloud?

"Relax." Amusement sparked in those midnight eyes. "I promise you don't have to kiss me. *Yet.* Bring those bottles over here."

Before I could challenge his prediction, or the tone of his command, he lifted two folded white washcloths from the counter and crossed over to the tub. Then he propped a hip on the wide tiled edge and reached up for one of the bottles.

I handed him the first of four tequila brands.

With efficient precision, he unscrewed the cap, leaned over the tub, and poured the clear liquid over his ribs. He hissed in a breath the instant the fluid made contact, but it was the only sound he made as he methodically moved the stream from one side of the two-inch-long gash to the other.

When I moved closer and stood in front of the opening of the shower stall, I noticed reddish-brown liquid splattering onto the tiles on the floor of the tub.

"Another." With the severe angle he leaned at, none of the liquid trailed lower than his waist; it flowed across the open wound, over his last two ribs, then dribbled straight down into the tub with the force of gravity.

With only two bottles left, I preemptively opened the next one. But instead of asking for it, he lined up the second empty bottle a quarter inch from the first, label facing the same direction as its companion in perfect harmony, then grabbed the top washcloth. Rather than dabbing the wound itself, he merely cleaned off the excess alcohol from the skin around the wound. Then he stared at the bullet graze intently for a full minute.

After a barely perceptible nod, he reached his other hand down. A soft ripping sound of separating Velcro permeated the pin-drop silence before he straightened with a slender metal book-sized case in his hand. His finger curled over the top corner, and a crisp click sounded before the lid sprang open.

Trying not to look overtly curious, I set down the remaining alcohol bottles beside his empties. Then in keeping with his OCD nature about the labels, I twisted each to face the same degree of forward before casually glancing back at the case he'd opened.

Nestled within hard gray foam, three fat syringes were displayed, their various barrels filled with pale-pink to deep-maroon fluid, plungers extended. In another slot, several straight needles gleamed, and yet another held a few curved needles with bright-blue suture thread attached into the base of the needles. A pen-like object had a spongy tip protected with a clear cap: tissue adhesive?

He plucked the pale-pink syringe from its far left slot, affixed a needle, and immediately injected a vein in the bend of his opposite arm, depressing the plunger.

"What is that?"

"Field Cocktail."

"And the darker colors?" I nodded toward the case, with the medium and darker syringes remaining.

"Stronger Field Cocktails." He replaced the used syringe into its former spot, needle and all fitting with its now-shorter length. "Each has bioengineered antibacterial and nanotech healing accelerators, the darker ones have more powerful pain killers."

"Ahhh…" I began to connect the dots. Although he no longer remained classified as a hotel guest. Military operative of some kind began to fit him much better. "So for a bullet burn, all you need is the Shirley-Temple level?"

"Exactly."

"And the others are for more serious injuries? The strawberry daiquiri?" I tapped a fingernail on the middle, appropriately colored syringe. "The bloody mary?" I tapped the darkest.

He choked out a laugh. "Only if I'm a bloody mess. It's more like a Hail Mary: when surviving the next few minutes is more important than remaining sharp…or conscious."

"That strong?" I marveled at the advanced technology.

"Exponentially fast wound healing coupled with a serious morphine dose."

My gaze trained on one of many faded scars he had. I cocked my head and traced the outline of the tornado-shaped paler skin. "Does the rapid healing cause this tissue distortion?"

He pulled something else from the case, then snapped it shut. "Yes. The more potent the accelerant, the tighter the cells band together in a coil, starting from the most severely wounded tissue, then flaring outward.

With a slight nod as if the subject had been closed, he turned, giving me more of his sculpted back to look at. "You're turn."

"Excuse me?"

"You stab. You stitch," he stated dryly and held up one of the curved needles as the bright-blue suture thread dangled from its end.

A twinge of guilt pierced through me again. But I shook off the annoying sensation, yanking logic back into the forefront: Intruders take the risk of whatever awaited them. My action? Had been the downside of his risk.

"Why does the puncture wound need stitches but not the bullet wound?"

Still processing what he expected of me, I watched as he folded the washcloth until the exposed length showed only clean, white terry again.

Without answering my question, he handed me the third opened alcohol bottle and a folded washcloth over his shoulder. Then he bent forward and tilted his injured

32

shoulder downward. "Pour it slowly, at first. Make sure the wound fills completely."

"You sure you're supposed to irrigate a puncture wound?" I'd had brief first aid training one summer as a prerequisite to lifeguard training, which was my only exposure to healing the human body versus unraveling the secrets of the universe.

"I'm sure." He let out a sigh. "May not be convention, but it works for me."

Unwilling to debate a subject I knew little about, I did as he asked, pouring tequila at the optimal angle to achieve a narrow stream with just enough force for consistent flow without allowing it to dribble backward down the bottle. When the alcohol hit his skin, he didn't react—not one flinch or altered breathing.

Unlike the bullet graze, very little fresh blood seeped from the puncture wound I'd inflicted. Clear alcohol filled the deep hole, welled at the top for a split second, then overflowed. I moved the washcloth to catch the reddish-brown excess streaming down.

"Be sure to flush it until you get clear fluid, even if you need another bottle."

I handed him my empty. "Need it now."

With a curt nod, he opened the last bottle, grasped the base with a finger and thumb, then lifted it over his shoulder, all without altering the awkward angle of his upper body.

I took the bottle from him. Silence weighed heavy between us in the long seconds that passed as I continued to flush out the wound, but too many questions whirled in my head for me to continue with it. "Why did you get shot?"

"Got in the way of a bullet."

As if an alternate causality could exist. "How very brave of you."

"Brave had nothing to do with it, Pink. Wrong place, wrong time."

"My name's not 'Pink."

An amused sound followed, like a strangled chuckle. Yet he didn't move a muscle. "The name suits you."

When the rust-colored liquid gave way to almost clear, I handed him the empty bottle. "I'm out." I blotted the washcloth on the skin directly beneath the wound. "Only a slight amount of bright red blood showing."

He held up the needle.

On a deep swallow, I took it from him. I stared at the puncture wound. Then at the menacing curved needle that gleamed between my fingers. "Okay. About to do this thing." I gently pressed my forefinger and thumb above and below the small hole in his flesh, attempting to stabilize the site... steady myself.

"Don't go easy on me. I can handle it."

After a fortifying breath and a preemptive wince, I pushed the needle forward, piercing his skin. He didn't flinch, which calmed me, though only marginally. When the needle appeared on the other side, I pulled it through with a steady stroke. "Why does the name suit me?"

Another hook of the needle and another pull-through of the suture thread passed in silence. Maybe he hadn't heard me. Or he needed all his focus to get stabbed a few more times without any painkillers.

By the time the fourth stitch had been made, he finally answered, tone low. "Because it's the color your cheeks turn when I look at you."

I blinked, pausing before pressing the needle in for the final stitch.

When I eventually found my voice, it dropped to a whisper, "I blush because of the way you look at me." After a slow exhale, I swept the needle in and out a final time.

"How do I look at you?"

I pulled my hand away, suddenly very conscious of my slight contact against his hot skin. While trying to formulate an answer, I pulled the thread taut and examined the stitches. Then I began to knot the end, satisfied the wound was as closed as it could possibly get.

Refusing to avoid his question any longer, I stared at the back of his bent head while facing the truth head on. "You look at me like you want to take my clothes off."

After a brief pause, he glanced at me over his shoulder. "I do."

I sucked in a sharp breath. There it was. My opportunity. The man attracted me, no doubt about it with the way my body reacted to him, how my mind blanked out in his presence. And having a wild fling was a smaller part of what my impromptu vacation was all about. Go somewhere I'd never been before. Have incredible sex with a man I'd never see again.

I knew nothing about him. Other than he'd been shot at. Not exactly a glowing résumé. Nervous, I voiced my concern from the opposite perspective. "You know nothing about me."

"Not a requirement." Intent edged his low tone.

Boys. I thought back to the word he'd used earlier. He was right. The few I'd ever been with had been inexperienced boys. Of the three times I'd had actual intercourse, two had been during my senior year in high school: once with a fellow chess club member, once with a fourth-period AP Physics classmate. Both events had been mutual experimentation, to verify the mechanics of everything we'd read and heard: foreplay, increased arousal, coitus, and orgasm for both participants.

College brought the third boy. However, then, I'd recklessly decided to step outside the parameters. Far from sober at a frat party Anna had dragged me to, I allowed myself to be led into a bedroom with one of the football players who'd been staring at me. Exactly six minutes later, after no foreplay, much grunting, and an orgasm for only one participant, the disappointing experience practically ended before it began.

The stranger in front of me? Did things to my insides with a mere look.

"Alec Marquez." He shifted, facing toward the decorative tiles that spanned the wall from tub to ceiling.

"I'm sorry. What?" Snapped back to the moment, I stared at the knotted end of my suture work. Then I glanced at his metal Field Cocktail case, but didn't recall seeing a pair scissors.

"My name. Alejandro Marquez. But everyone calls me Alec." His full name rolled off his tongue with a slight Spanish accent.

Distracted by undefinable tension in the air between us, I returned to the task at hand and a small dilemma. I hadn't packed cuticle scissors. No idea if Anna had. I continued to hold the needle, reasoning through limited options. I wasn't about to ask him if he had the knife I'd seen strapped to his calf earlier on the beach. The suture thread, although strong, also had a silken fragile quality to it. *Teeth it is.*

Recognizing that we'd begun to exchange conventional pleasantries, I played my accepted role in the conversation. "I'm Devin Hill. My roommate, Anna, calls me Dev."

"Devin. I like that name."

*Annd…*the way he said my name, with that hint of accent and a lowered voice, sounded sinful.

Flustered, I pursed my lips and blew out a hard breath. Better to get the inevitable over with. Holding the thread taut, I pinched above the knot with my fingers. Then I lowered my face toward his shoulder and clamped my front teeth onto the thread about an inch and a half above the knot. It took a few tries of scraping the edges of my incisors together, but I finally broke the thread.

"There." I backed away, distancing myself from the overwhelming effects of the shirtless temptation in front of me.

"Exactly." He straightened back to upright, then reached over his shoulder and brushed a fingertip over the stitched wound.

I stood there confused, unsure how his response applied to my one-word statement that indicated I'd finished my repair job.

When he turned, we locked gazes. Heat sparked in those almost-black eyes, and…something more. I couldn't quite place what flickered there. Hesitation? Hope? Everything about him exuded confidence; so it definitely wasn't doubt.

"Now we know more about each other than even remotely required for sex."

Oh. We were back to the whole clothes-off thing. And really, with the way his stare penetrated me on every level, I already felt stark naked in front of him.

"Right." Nervous to the point my hands began to shake, I spun around and fled toward the darkness of the bedroom, walking beyond the reach of the bathroom light, down the steps and into the sitting room.

Seconds later, the air stirred behind me. The heat of his breath coasted over my shoulder. A shiver tremored through me.

He didn't touch me. But his raw heat warmed my back even with the minuscule distance of airspace remaining between us. The gentle fog of his slow exhalation traveled along my exposed neck, up to my ear. "We don't have to do anything. Only if you want to."

My throat went dry, and I swallowed hard. The force of nature that had crashed into my room placed control of the situation into my hands. *Only if you want to…*echoed through my mind that was dangerously devoid of all other thought.

Damn. I definitely *wanted.*

"Anna will be back…any minute." She'd already been gone too long. Which worried me. We were in a third-world country, and she'd likely traveled outside the protected environs of the resort. There wasn't anywhere she could jog in the approximate hour I'd been aware she'd been gone that wouldn't have taken her off the relative security of the property.

"Then we wait," he said. The soft-spoken words held both temptation and promise. "We do what you want..." His fingertips barely touched my wrist, feathered upward over my forearm. "When you want..." He closed the distance between us, pressing the scorching heat of his chest against my back, the thin material of my tank top becoming insignificant. "*How* you want..."

Images flooded into my mind, unbidden. Alec naked, me naked, us writhing on the bed, switching from one erotic position to the next.

My heart raced. My held breath rushed out in a whoosh, lungs burning. Overwhelmed to the point of near-spontaneous combustion, I leaned away from him. Out of real estate in the room, I spun around and pressed my backside against the glass of the french doors.

His heated gaze met mine for a moment, then drifted down to my lips. He eased closer. "Maybe just that kiss, for now."

That kiss. The one he'd suggested would be different. "Will it be worth it?"

The corners of his lips twitched. "The kiss? Or the sex." He weighted that last word to such a degree, the intonation transformed it into statement of fact.

"Both," I whispered.

He bent forward. With near-nonexistent pressure, he touched the corner of my mouth with his. Then he slowly brushed across my lips. An enticing scent wafted between us, salty and hypnotic. Back again he swept, teasing, tracing with patient intent as if his sole purpose on earth was to learn the entire topography of my lips. The temptation to lean toward him, beg for more, was intoxicating.

Before I fully comprehended what was happening, he paused in the center and kissed me. But it was the softest kiss, a tentative taste. The bare action dissipated into heated breath that fogged over my parted lips. "You tell me. The kiss is your prelude..."

Oh, damn. My chest rose and fell in shallow breaths. Pulse racing, I swallowed hard and closed my eyes, trying to calm the insistent throb between my legs, needing to stem an ache that had suddenly become all I could focus on.

I'd lost the ability to think. And I'd never *not* thought about anything.

Hyperawareness zinged through me. Not in my head with cognitive reasoning, but of everything in totality around me: the muted crashing of ocean waves through the closed door; the soothing hum of the air-conditioning unit on the wall near the ceiling, blowing cool air over my heated skin; the infinitesimal distance between us, charged by sparking sexual tension.

Before I exhaled another full breath, his deadly lips crushed against mine, rough and dominating. At my surprised gasp, his tongue flicked through my parted lips. It touched the tip of my tongue before sliding along the side, then curving underneath as the heat of his muscular arms caged me against the cool glass of the doors.

A low moan rasped from my throat as my body seemed to melt against him. Filled with an impossible need to get closer, to sustain our molded contact, I slid my fingers over his hips and through the back belt loops of his cargo pants, then held his pelvis in a death grip against mine, causing his rigid erection to press against my lower belly.

Lost. One simple four-letter word: the only way to describe the undeniable bliss of being dragged out of my head and firmly into my body—a body that had burst into flames.

In and out. Forward and back. Plunging tongue. Sucking lips.

Insistent. Merciless. His mouth claimed mine with the relentless force of a hurricane lashing against me.

His deep growl vibrated into my mouth and pricked my ears, rippling shock waves of ache downward, pulsing... pulsing.

The room began a slow spin, and I fluttered my eyes open to find him pulling us away from the french doors. I clung tighter to him as we danced, him urging me deeper into the darkness of the room, me stumbling backward, yet holding on to his solid frame for stability.

One bare foot landed on a cool-tiled step. Then a second step as we climbed. After a few more backward steps, the edge of the bed brushed the backs of my thighs right as he swirled his expert tongue around mine.

A momentary pause followed before the longest, most

titillating kiss of my life slowed. Easing his mouth back, his lips closed on mine. With a tight, gentle suck, he tugged my lower lip into his mouth. Then sharp teeth clamped down on the tender flesh as another low growl rumbled from his throat. The sudden piercing pain made me whimper, but the instant I tensed, he sucked on the tiny wound he'd inflicted.

I clung to the heat of his strong frame, afraid if I let go, I'd fall backward, lose the incredible moment of sensation to the darkness that had always threatened to consume me even as it protected me. In the murky starless sky of my existence, he'd become an unexpected dark beacon, drawing me in without even so much as the promise of light.

Then without warning, the kiss ended. Cool air rushed over my lips. Subtle illumination from the bathroom cast shadows and dim light across the features of his face. His lips, glistening with moisture, curved into a wicked smile as he slid his hands up my ribcage on either side until, with a firm hold, he gripped my shoulders, then pushed, knocking me backward.

I gasped softly as I fell onto the bed, but by the time I bounced up from the impact, laughter bubbled out. My unstoppable grin surprised me.

Unadulterated joy filled my darkened heart for the first time since…well, since I was a little girl. A man who I hadn't expected had crashed over a barrier that I'd built to be impenetrable. But instead of launching additional defenses, I'd let my guard down a little.

And was rewarded. A lot.

"Well?" The sexy-as-hell man with a questionable,

unknown background dared arch a black eyebrow at me.

Blowing out a shaky breath, I admitted the naked truth out loud, for once.

"Devastating," I whispered.

I had no idea how I would survive *more* than his all-consuming kiss. But the grueling anger and relentless pain that I'd always carried with me had gone blessedly and unexpectedly silent the moment he touched me and for every heartbeat after.

Alec Marquez made every cell in my body vibrate with aching need to discover *more*.

CHAPTER 3

Alec stared down at me, gaze hungry, the muscles of his bare chest tense. But even poised as he was to lunge forward, he waited. For a sign from me?

In those seconds where his sensual touch didn't obliterate every torturous thought in my mind, logic seeped in. What was I doing with a complete stranger? How could I let him past my defenses when every other person had been relegated an outsider? Even my parents. *Even Anna.*

They were among the handful of people who knew the facts, in varying degrees. But no one knew everything about the horrific incident. No one held on to the images in my head, my eidetic memory becoming a curse unlike any could have imagined. I'd never let them understand the depths of my rage. Nor had I left any clues about the driving force of my need for vengeance.

To have done so would have painted a different picture about me, the brilliant mind who they'd predictably expected to be emotionally handicapped. They all saw what they wanted to see: the next Einstein or Gates—their finely honed world destroyer, or potential economic rainmaker. All my life, I'd portrayed the two-dimensional genius I wanted them to see.

Not one of them knew my real destiny.

But right in front of me, delivered by fate, stood a six-foot-two corporeal representation of all I'd ever wanted to be. Only he'd also shown me something else.

That I craved more than *I'd* ever imagined.

One word. All it would take to have him all over me. *Inside of me.*

Tension wound so tight in the negligible space between us, all it would take would be one word to ignite the newfound powder keg deep inside me that desperately needed to blow.

I opened my mouth, prepared to spark the fuse.

An odd sound penetrated the silence. I blinked, glancing over my shoulder toward the source. On the nightstand beside the bed, my iPhone vibrated against the wood surface, its screen illuminating a soft whitish glow.

"Anna," I whispered, recognition and common sense dousing my arousal. I flipped over and lunged toward the pillows, reaching for the phone.

The number that appeared was unfamiliar, but I swiped the screen and answered it anyway. "Anna?"

"Hey, Dev. Did I wake you?"

"What?" Mind frazzled, I dropped my forehead to my hand and scrunched my brows, trying to focus. "No." *Only interrupted potential amazing wild sex.* "Where have you been? No note? You've been gone awhile."

"Sorry. The plan was a quick moonlight run on the beach, and you were out cold when I left. I had a little…accident."

"Oh my God. What kind of accident? Are you injured?" I pushed upright and perched on the edge of the bed. The serious warnings about kidnapping for ransom flew into my mind, making a night of gunshot grazes and stitched-up puncture wounds seem insignificant. "Where are you?"

"The hospital."

Two words. No further information. "*Annaliese Brianne Johannsen.* You will give me every single detail about what happened, by whom, and where you are at this very moment, or I will rain hell upon this country you swore to me was a vacationer's mecca."

"You're slipping, Brainiac," she teased. "You forgot 'how' and 'why' and 'to what degree' and 'trajectory.'" In the background noise of the mobile phone, a muted rhythmic beeping sounded out accompanied by the murmur of a woman's voice. "I have to go. They want to take an X-Ray to make sure nothing's broken. It's not. I'm positive. It's only a little ankle sprain."

"Are you sure?" *Only. Little.* Trivializing words that a religious runner like Anna would utter. No coded phrases were given, not that we'd decided on any. But her barbed humor seemed like normal, everyday Anna. Besides, what choice did I have? It wasn't like I had a car to drive. "When will you be back?"

"Not sure." Her tone altered, and the pause that followed made me listen more closely to the background noises, analyze everything she'd said and what hadn't been said. "I want to see what they can do to get the swelling down," she continued. "I'll be damned if this ruins our plans. We've got snorkeling to do."

Over the phone, a tense male voice grumbled.

"Gotta go, Dev. I'm fine. Go back to sleep. I'll call you tomorrow or later tod—" A loud click abruptly ended the call.

Closing my eyes, I imagined single-minded Anna would insist our plans continue uninterrupted. Still, I scowled at the phone, irritated that I could do nothing to help her. Or confirm anything she'd said.

The bed dipped, causing my weight to shift as Alec sat beside me.

"Everything okay?" Genuine concern laced his words. His eyebrows were slightly raised.

"Yeah. I mean, I think so. My very brave but mildly stupid friend went running at night in a foreign country and twisted her ankle. She said she's at the hospital."

"Do you believe her?"

I turned toward him. Had he detected my doubt? Masking emotions to get others to believe what I wanted had been an art form I'd mastered over a lifetime. Yet being around Alec had thrown my world into a tailspin. And apparently my keen senses right along with it.

"I have no reason not to." There were plenty of reasons. But shielding my true thoughts had become second nature, and the minuscule control I'd found around a man who'd so far made me feel completely out of it gave me a small degree of comfort. "How far is the hospital from here?"

"Twenty-six kilometers," he replied. About sixteen miles.

Suddenly distracted as a stray thought coalesced, I stared down at the phone in my hand. "I'm from the States. Don't you have to activate your mobile phone with your communications provider to receive calls and texts here?"

"Yes," he replied.

I frowned. I hadn't activated my service for use outside of the United States. Anna had? And my service provider hadn't required account-holder identity verification?

"Would you like to go?" His tone had softened.

Confused on multiple levels, I frowned and glanced up at him. "What?"

His warm hand slid over my bare thigh until it rested midway between my hip and my knee. "Would you like me to take you to the hospital to see your friend?"

"No." I shook my head. "Anna said she needed to get X-Rays." And I doubted they'd let us see her in the middle of the night. Unless visiting hours weren't strictly enforced.

Clicking the phone's function button again, I checked the time: 2:07 a.m. Then I imagined milling about a hospital in a third-world country, germs and diseases sprouting like weeds on every surface. "Maybe later?" Postponement didn't make the idea more palatable, but it would allow time for Anna's condition to be assessed and for me to consider subsequent options.

"Sure. You let me know." The weight of his docile hand changed, the strong pressure easing as he spoke. His voice had lowered, growing huskier with every successive word.

On a hard swallow, I glanced down as his hand feathered over my upper thigh that had erupted in goose bumps. When his long fingers reached the hem of my cotton boxers, his slow advance stopped. He tucked them under the edge until the fabric pulled taut, then his middle finger began to draw tiny, slow circles on my skin.

He leaned closer, broad chest pressing against my arm, until his warm breath danced over the outer shell of my ear. "I'm at your disposal."

Why? Didn't he have things to do? Or had his plans been derailed with being shot at?

Now that he'd volleyed the decision into my court, dripping with heavy sexual innuendo, my head whirled with the implications of having a man "at my disposal."

Heart thumping harder with every passing millisecond, I abruptly jumped up from the bed. The sudden movement knocked him back and jarred his hand away from me.

"I…have to go to the bathroom." *Get some air. Think things through.* Take a breather away from a man who clouded my judgment, overwhelming typically logical thought processes by his mere proximity.

As I fled the darkness and burst into the brightly lit bathroom, I sucked in a deep breath. I raced across the cool tiles and sought refuge within the toilet area, the only place in the entire hotel suite with a door. That locked. The click of the throw bolt as it secured into the frame provided some semblance of calm in a raging storm of uncertainty. I backed up, then sat on the closed toilet seat.

The muffled deep rumble of his chuckling sounded out. "You hungry?"

Brows drawing together in confusion, I stared at the carved wooden panels of the door that separated us. Was his inquiry some kind of a prelude-to-meaningless-sex courting convention? Feed the woman to placate her? The only sexual frame of reference I had consisted of calculated mutual agreement and drunken lost inhibitions.

My traitorous stomach rumbled. Likely all of the excitement of Anna leaving, Alec appearing, and the temptation of mind-blowing sex at my mere command had burned through calories at an increased rate.

"I could eat," I replied loud enough for him to hear. Middle of the night snacking had never been a compunction. But on a spur-of-the-moment vacation that showed promise in rewriting my dull world into a sensual adventure, going with the flow of events seemed prudent.

I tumbled his casual words over in my head: *Sure. You let me know.* And somehow my mind twisted the offer into something more erotic. No pressure. Everything possible to gain me physical release, which he offered. And due to the way my body responded to the mere thought, I clearly needed. In fact, my pulse began to make itself known as a cadent throbbing ache between my legs, pounding the point home in demonstration.

I stood, took a cleansing breath, then lifted the toilet lid and sat on the inner seat, deciding to make use of it since I'd hidden on it; I was nothing if not logical and efficient.

Afterward, I washed my hands under hot water for a twenty-second count, turned off the faucet, dried my hands in the fluffy white towel hanging from an iron loop affixed to the wall, then turned and faced the darkness once again.

Every time I sought the absence of light, I reminded myself of what lay in wait there. Not the dangerous man who'd stumbled onto our balcony, although that too. No, a mantra had been carved deep into my psyche to remind me of my purpose in this world.

In the middle of the night, she'd been taken from me. Shadows had danced across my twin bed as figures clothed in black from head to toe had stolen our innocent childhood. Fairy tales had been decimated when the monsters materialized from the darkness.

I'd kicked when they'd grabbed me. Bit down when they'd covered my mouth with a bare hand that reeked of sweat and metal. Suddenly dropped onto the hardwood floor with a loud thud, I cried out when struck across the face. Coppery blood had trickled into my mouth right as a light down the hall had glared blindingly on.

Then they'd vanished. The monsters. With my little sister.

That was the night darkness had infiltrated my world.

On a centering slow exhalation, I snapped my thoughts back to the present, expertly compartmentalizing. My gaze fell to the open closet area, to my resort wear and Anna's. Then shifted to the center of the tiled bathroom counter where complimentary toiletries were neatly arranged in a small rectangular basket. *I'm on vacation.* With a strange man in the other room. Those two simple facts grounded me fully back into reality.

When I reentered the suite's bedroom area, Alec reached over and dropped the hotel phone's handset into its molded plastic cradle with a jostling clunk.

He glanced up at me. "Twenty-two minutes."

I tilted my head, observing the imposing man who no longer sat on the edge of the bed. He'd stretched out into the middle of it, rolling onto his back after ending the call. Still dangerously shirtless, he'd now gone shoeless. Only his cargo pants remained. My gaze scanned back up to meet his. "How precise. Not twenty or twenty-five, but twenty-two minutes. They've got that delivery down to a science."

"Precise is good. Gives me plenty of time." He flattened his hand and patted a spot beside him on the rumpled white duvet three times.

I stared at the golden skin on the back of his hand. At the loaded indentation beneath it.

A sensual invitation. Not an expectation.

I maintained control with a simple choice before me: agree to obey the unspoken suggestion…or not.

Every cell in my body hummed to life, wanting what the mysterious stranger who'd stumbled into my world seemed to want in equal measure right along with me.

Before a conscious decision filtered into my brain, my weight shifted to the balls of my feet. Cool sheets met my knees. My gaze locked on to his, and the sizzling connection affected me on a visceral level, like he didn't just see me—he saw right through me, down to every last dark secret and untapped desire.

And instead of his blatant stare into the very heart of me feeling threatening, I found the action soothing. One lost spinning soul finally stabilized by another. Drawn in by its undeniable gravity. Not wanting…not even trying…to escape.

With efficient movements, I settled beside him, feeling the heavy weight of his watchful gaze. It scoured over every inch of my skin, heating the surface as if he commanded my blood to rush there.

He didn't ask me to remove my skimpy boxers or thin cotton tank top, but his attention drifted to my breasts. My thoughts went along for the ride, prisoner to his, as if joined by unseen bonds. And as my nipples hardened under his perusal, ached as they scraped beneath the near-transparent fabric, my breaths shallowed, chest rising and falling.

"Do you trust me?" His measured words held no tone.

"No." The word flew out in knee-jerk reaction. But he was a relative stranger, after all. And trust had never come easy for me.

"Good." His reply volleyed back just as fast.

I frowned when he failed to elaborate.

"Care to make this interesting?" He arched a single dark brow.

Mentally thrown, I stared up at him, incredulous. "How could it get any more interesting?"

"Depends. How much do you like rules?"

Constricting shadows edged into my mind. "Lived my whole life by rules. Despise them."

"Good. Then I'll only give you three."

My mouth fell open, but I snapped it shut, biting back my instinctive protest. He'd said interesting. *Sure as hell better be.*

When I remained silent for a beat longer, he continued. "Much as I love that luscious smart mouth of yours whipping out million-dollar words, no talking."

Sure enough, I gaped again.

His eyes flared wider as my first challenge went tested one second after he'd uttered it.

I pressed my lips together in obedience, not for him, but for me. If the kiss he'd delivered earlier had been a mere appetizer, every vibrating cell in my body wanted to taste the next course.

His short nod followed. "Keep your eyes shut at all times."

This time I didn't obey. We hadn't begun yet, after all. And I wanted to use all the senses I had to watch him, gauge his reactions.

If my nonresponse affected him, he didn't show it. He kept going, "And no touching."

"No touching?"

"For you. You are not to touch: yourself or me."

My brow wrinkled in confusion. "Where's the fun for you?"

His lips curved into a wicked smirk. "Everywhere."

Then he flicked a glance at the faintly illuminated face of his watch. "Nineteen minutes…"

The countdown taunted me more than the tone of his voice. Curiosity prevailed. I closed my eyes and laid back, relaxing my arms at my sides. Mouth shut. Eyes shut. Hands…I loosely gripped the sheets, ensuring that they'd stay put.

Stripped of sight, I became acutely aware of everything… including the sight that I'd been robbed of. Hiding in the shadows meant watching, seeing the world for what it was, analyzing and assessing others. Only now, I'd freely given up that valued sense—in lieu of something in return.

When nothing immediately happened, I inhaled a slow breath.

His weight on the bed shifted, my shoulder dipping, then rising, like his upper body settled there. Heat prickled over my skin, detecting his proximity. Seconds later: a touch on my shoulder. His lips. No, the tips of his fingers.

"Stop thinking," he ordered, his low tone curt with warning.

Allowing someone this close to me both unnerved and exhilarated me. I'd never let anyone in to this degree before. And Alec was in, all right. In my head. Under my skin.

Eyes firmly closed, resigned to my fate if only for the next eighteen minutes and twelve seconds, I gave a barely perceptible nod.

Before my next heartbeat, the warm brush of a sensation returned. Only this time, blanked out my mind, only enjoyed…felt…accepted.

That's when it happened.

As his slight touch traveled down my arm, awakening nerve endings with a whispering tease, the rest of my body hummed to life. My skin warmed further. Ache flared hotter between my legs. My lips parted on a gasp as my breath caught.

And his touch had only drifted to the inside of my elbow, lingering there in a slow circle.

Maddening.

His "stop thinking" command had been an add-on rule, but it wasn't a hard one to follow. The feverish sensations zinging out of control spun my thoughts into a chaotic whirlwind.

Warmth bloomed over one of my nipples. Hot. Hotter. *His breath.* I held mine, wound tight with need. When coolness followed, I exhaled.

Relief swirled, then mixed with heady anticipation.

Firm pressure slid across the skin below the center of my ribcage, then lowered over my belly, light at first, then heavier. *His flattened palm.*

The sensation shifted, splitting apart into heavier pinpoints, rotating. *Pointed fingertips.*

Lower, lower…they dragged over my skin, abrading the thin cotton over my flesh.

My breath quickened, pulse thrumming hard, as his touch veered wide, seeming to part around the hot, swollen bundle of nerves that ached to be touched. Instinctually, I arched up, seeking…more.

And everything vanished. No touch. No heat. Well, not exactly everything: I remained a throbbing, quivering jumble of need.

Forcing myself to follow the three simple rules he'd dictated, I settled down and relaxed back onto the bedding.

My reward was his instant resumed touch. In different places than before.

Hot breath fogged near my ear. A chill skittered across my skin, firing goose bumps in a torrent down my entire left side as I shuddered.

The sensation continued, a warm trail teasing sensually down the column of my neck, across my collarbone, drifting lower...

The firm pressure of his palm pressed just above my knee, slid upward along my inner thigh, rising higher...

Stripped down emotionally, razed to a primal level of trembling desire, I swallowed hard, trying to focus on slowing my shaky breaths to calm the dizzying erotic tailspin.

Softness pressed just below my collarbone, pinched together, sucked upward. A duplicate sensation followed slightly lower: another branding kiss.

Teasing pressure circled once on the sensitive heated skin of my inner thigh. Then rose higher, catching the fabric that barely covered me and tugging it.

His hand continued upward, binding the fabric tighter against the apex of my thighs, right where I throbbed hardest. His mouth trailed downward, the sharpness of teeth nipping at my skin in shortening intervals, like a stone skipping over rippling water, until he gently bit at the skin along my upper breast. Lower...

The hard pinch that followed ripped a moan from my throat as he clamped down around my nipple. At the same time, he yanked the material between my thighs harder, spearing an ache there, firing it deeper. My moan dragged out as the sweet torture wore on, long seconds of need coiling ever tighter.

A distant thump. A closer tinkling clank.

A loud knock echoed into the private space around us.

"Room service!" a voice called through the closed door.

My eyes flew open as cool air rushed over the wet fabric covering my nipple. When he eased his hold on my boxers, my hand shot to his wrist and gripped it hard. "Don't you dare."

"All three rules broken at once." One corner of his mouth lifted in a smirk. "Impressive."

He gave me a hard stare before it sparkled with both mischief and taunt. Then he placed his hands on my knees, spread my legs, and dove downward. His mouth crashed onto my clit, and he sucked hard on the sensitized nerves right through my boxers.

Pummeled with sensation, ache snapping into painful need, the buildup crested in seconds. In a fogged state of awareness, I turned my head and muffled a scream into the pillow that cradled my head. Wave after wave of pleasure coursed through me as he continued to rhythmically suck, wringing every last ripple of orgasm from my body.

When the intensity subsided, he lifted his mouth and stared at me with a satisfied expression.

Well, damn. That made two of us.

I blew out a controlled breath, mind still dazed, body still reeling.

The next moments flew by in a blur as he yanked the bedcoverings over me, answered the door while shielding me from view, signed the ticket, then closed the door before settling a large tray onto the center of the bed. Five dishes covered every square inch of the tray, some overlapping others. The burger platter loaded with fries competed with a massive chef's salad. But neither was to be outdone by a rosemary roasted half chicken, Bolognese spaghetti, or the full lobster tail.

"Wow. Hungry?" I asked.

The look he leveled at me sizzled every nerve ending to back to life. "You have *no* idea."

I blew out a hard breath. "Agreed."

Because as satisfied as he'd made me, I'd never been more filled with stark want in my life.

CHAPTER 4

When I woke, the remnants of an exhausting dream kept a sticky hold on me. Heavy eyelids prevented me from taking in my surroundings too quickly. After several minutes of opening then shutting my eyes, two slow yawns, and one lazy stretch, awareness of someone else in the room pricked at my senses, and I finally pushed myself upright.

Alec. I inhaled his scent before I spotted his silhouette across the room.

At some point, he'd turned off the bathroom lights, swathing the room in darkness once again. Only a dim blue-white glow that emanated from beside him cast light into the suite.

He sat at the large desk. His features, focused in concentration, were bathed in the soft illumination from a penlight affixed in some way to the top corner of an open laptop. As I couldn't recall any baggage thrown over the balcony with his unorthodox means of arrival, the laptop had to be Anna's.

Curious, I pushed off the bed. My bare feet landed toe first onto the cool floor tiles. I padded closer in silence, not wanting to distract him.

"You slept like the dead." His comment came without inflection of judgment, merely statement of fact. And he didn't move from his studious position. Nor did he attempt to hide what he was looking at.

My pulse accelerated as I smoothed my hands down the thin cotton tank top and boxer shorts I still wore, my thoughts drifting over the reasons I'd slept so soundly. "I suppose orgasmic endorphins followed by a meal heavy in carbs and fat will do it."

At that, he swung his gaze my way, arching one of his brows. "Orgasmic endorphins?"

I paused. The toes of my right foot slid just over the edge of the first step that led down to the sitting area. I curled them down over, rooting myself as I swayed under his sudden scrutiny.

Even in the dim light, I could see the heat in his gaze. I certainly felt it, my skin beginning to warm from the second his attention had shifted toward me. "Well, actually, many chemicals accompany orgasm: endorphins, dopamine, testosterone, norepinephrine, serotonin...oxytocin."

The muscles at one corner of his mouth twitched, tugging his lips into a sinful smirk as his gaze drifted a few inches lower. "That sexy mouth of yours keeps spouting intellectual factoids. I keep wondering what it'll take to render you speechless."

My mind froze. "Speechless?"

A full smile now played at his lips. "Oh, yes. I'm taking it as a personal challenge to blow your mind to the point you cannot describe an event that happens between us with mere words."

"Oh." I didn't know what to say. Couldn't fathom it. Then, I began to want it...

"See. You get the idea. We'll leave it there for a while."

Why? To let the anticipation build? Already, my heart rate quickened, my breath shallowed, my...mind analyzing the possibilities of orgasmic chemicals once again.

He turned back toward the desk with an unaffected expression, carefully smoothing his hands over a large, thin paper he'd spread across the surface—as if he hadn't just dropped a nuclear bomb between us and set the timer for detonation.

With a soft snort, I shook my head and eased my feet down the two tiled steps. If he could ignore the sparking chemistry between us in favor for something clearly more important to him at the moment, then so could I.

And right now, the mysterious man before me held my rapt attention. "What are you studying?"

"Blueprints."

I hovered behind him, mere inches from his bare shoulders, able to feel the heat radiating from his skin. On a heavy blink, I sucked in a deep breath. *Focus.*

When I opened my eyes, I leaned forward only enough to take in more of the white paper that had blue lines bisecting across it. "Of a house."

His head bobbed down once. "Down the beach from here."

A second page lay canted beneath it, corners askew. "What's the other sheet?"

He peeled back the floorplan layout to reveal a page bearing many more lines, arrows, and a few fine-printed paragraph blocks in the margins. "Mechanical schematics."

As he revealed the second page in its entirety, I leaned to the left to get a complete view, then bent closer to examine the handful of paragraphs. When he released the top page to drop back down, the vellum paper settled with a soft crinkle. I rested a hand on the corner of the desk, and in as nonchalant of a manner as I could pull off, scanned the entire image from top to bottom.

Then I turned and negotiated around a wicker chair and small table to gain access to the armoire beneath the TV. On the topmost surface sat a wooden serving tray that held two coffee mugs and two smaller espresso cups in matching brown earthenware. I opened the wooden doors below to reveal shelving that held shot glasses and a closed container of salt, wine glasses, and squat handblown tumblers with tiny imperfect bubbles in their glass sides and rims tinted a bright emerald green. I grabbed two of the tumblers with one hand. Then I opened the fridge and wrapped my other hand around the neck of a chilled Pellegrino bottle.

"Why the great interest in a house down the beach?" Had the question sounded casual? I'd struggled to strip the extreme curiosity from my tone.

"It belongs to a target of interest. We're attempting

to ascertain how he's moving…product. And what communications methods he's using."

"Communications methods?" I twisted off the cap, and a loud puff sounded out as the compressed air released. I poured us each a glass of carbonated water, then carried them to the desk.

Without glancing up, he held his hand out. I placed the glass dead center in his palm, amazed at how attuned he remained to everything happening around him while he stayed focused on his analysis.

I turned around and retreated to the white slipcovered couch a few feet away, spun on a heel, and plopped onto it, crushing the blue throw pillow that had been so perfectly perched in the far corner. I stared at the slats of the shutters on the windows surrounding the desk, all of which he'd canted into an upward position, screening our nighttime activities from view.

"We've tapped his landlines, cloned the mobile phones and computers. Nothing. Yet every instinct I have tells me he's operating from this house."

Should I ask? Would he tell me?

What did I have to lose? So far, he seemed forthcoming. "What exactly is the 'product'?"

His head shifted up slightly. Like he stared at an unidentified spot on the dark wooden shutters, trying to find the answer.

"A deadly virus."

"Deadly?" My voice strangled out on a breaking squeak. What would a "target of interest" want with a virus…other than to hurt someone?

"And highly contagious."

Correction: *someones*.

Dissatisfied with Alec's innocuous tradecraft label of a man capable of doing something so evil, I asked, "What's his name?"

He immediately answered, "Escobar."

Escobar. I rolled the name over my tongue as my mind tucked away the information.

I took a sip of the cool fizzing mineral water. "Doesn't seem that difficult to transport a virus. Couldn't he, or someone, just carry it within a case into the house?"

"We're not concerned only with the virus in its dormant state. It's the active contagion that has him as our highest priority."

"Who is 'they' and 'our'? The CIA? Some black ops organization?" The question of Alec's origin had been teasing my brain ever since he'd crashed onto the terrace just a few feet away and not so many hours ago. Every instinct I had told me he'd been honest so far, and that he operated just this side of the same darkness I cocooned myself in with familiar comfort.

At my last voiced speculation, he turned around to fully face me. With the light behind him now, his features were hidden completely in darkness. His deep chuckle rumbled into my ears. "Far more cloak-and-dagger than that."

I flattened my lips into a line, fighting a smile. "Impossible. You can't get more cloak-and-dagger than black ops. There are not degrees of obscurity."

"Ahhh, but there are, Devin." His voice softened,

deepening into a rich silk that caressed, mesmerized. "When no one knows we exist but those who work for us. When membership means becoming a shadow, permanently. When we fly under the radar but out in plain sight for all to overlook. We're the whisper of air that chases what goes bump in the night."

My breaths grew shallow. The hairs on my arms stood on end.

I wanted to whisper. *I* wanted to chase.

"But you're revealing yourself to me." My voice sounded thready to my ears. "Does that mean I'm expendable?"

I heard a soft breath of air from him. "No. It means I trust you."

"Because I stabbed you, then stitched you up?"

His soft laugh made the tension in my shoulders ease a bit. "There is that. But it's more with me. I'm trained to read others down to the slightest nuance. It's a gift I have and excel at in greater degree than anyone they've ever tested. I'm both a human lie detector and a fairly accurate predictor of someone's future actions—with varying percentages of certainty—based on their past actions."

Well. Wasn't that disclosure mildly disconcerting? Did that mean he saw through me? Knew that I preferred the dark because darkness was an intrinsic part of me?

Silence stretched between us, a palpable, heavy thing that grew, pregnant with the weight of what he'd said and what we hadn't extrapolated from it. If he'd been willing to reveal this much, did that mean I had carte blanche at the moment?

To test the waters, I asked a direct question. "What do you call yourselves?"

"Ethersphere One."

"Is there another?"

His black silhouette moved in a slow headshake. "Only the one. Meant to signify cohesiveness below all, above everything, holding the world as we know it together."

"Not for a single government?"

He leaned forward. I'd already edged from my slouched position in the far corner of the couch to perch on the last inches of cushion nearest him without consciously realizing my movement. Warm breath fogged over my lips. I closed my eyes and inhaled deeply, trying to calm my racing heart.

"Not for any one. *For everyone.*" He paused, another smooth exhalation brushing over my skin, past my defenses. "We are the last, the most important protection humanity has."

"To balance the ego of man." I'd often thought it. Those in power believed they were above it all. Made decisions based on greed and misguided motivations.

The warmth of his steady breath fanned over my chin, my mouth. I inhaled his enticing male scent, salt and earthy spice. So close, his lips were one slight shift away from touching mine.

Instead, I rocked backward a few inches. Coolness rushed between us from the air conditioning current overhead. The long, narrow unit's fins moved in lazy oscillation upward as I settled against the cushions of the couch. Even with the adjustment, he remained so near he took up all the air space, crowded out every other thing that I vaguely sensed I needed to focus on.

The minor distance cleared my head enough to realize that he'd straightened too. He watched me. Waiting for some move I'd yet to make. I dropped my head back onto the pillow and stared up into the darkness that clung to the ceiling. The air conditioning fins paused when it hit their maximum radius in the upward position, then began their gradual descent.

A puzzled piece clicked in my brain. "The limestone passages."

"What?"

I snapped my fingers and pointed behind him, toward his blueprints. "Hydroelectric energy. There's a generator, transformer…turbines."

He spun back around, facing the desk. "Where? Show me."

I leaned back further into the couch and stared up at the black void of the ceiling canvas, visualizing the mechanical schematics of the house blueprint. Imaginary phosphorescent lines glowed into existence, weaving a detailed tapestry in my mind's eye.

"Bottom right quadrant. It's disguised as an enormous wine cellar. Part of it probably is. But the mechanical room on the blueprints is too large for electrical purposes only. And the width in your schematic spans that entire side of the house. Underground rivers exist in this area, carved through the limestone. Anna was prattling off about one earlier today, the one at *Xcaret*."

"How did...you stood over my shoulder for only a couple of seconds."

"Eidetic memory. Mine delivers key pieces of data once my brain relaxes enough to see the bigger picture through the information gridlock."

The light in front of him adjusted, and my imagined diagram disappeared as I turned to watch him. He'd unclipped his tiny penlight from the laptop screen and swept it over the blueprints from the bottom right corner toward the top. "You're right. It goes straight through the house toward the inlet side."

"There's your delivery method." I pushed up from the couch.

He let out a drawn-out sigh. "Do you know how long we've been trying to figure that out?"

When I stood beside him, I crossed my arms and gave a one-shoulder shrug. "You've been focused on standard communications. Typical transportation." Although I would've thought a cloak-and-dagger spy organization would've had better intel. "You just obtained these blueprints?"

He leaned back in his chair, resting the penlight onto the center of the blueprints before glancing up at me. The diffused light from below illuminated his face, making his features appear almost menacing. He arched a thick eyebrow. "I did. Was shot 'obtaining' them."

My gaze drifted down his uncovered back toward his side, although his position obscured the bullet graze from my view. He'd risked his life, put himself in peril, all for the greater good, against a man who wanted to harm innocents.

"Take me with you." The quiet words were uttered before I could stop them.

"No." With swift efficiency, he gripped the pages at the corners, aligned and folded them in half on a preexisting seam, then rolled them. "What makes you think I'm going inside?"

"You were studying the layout. Your attention was focused on the lower portion of the blueprints, the subterranean floors. And your gaze swept from left to right, repeatedly. Like you were memorizing the layout."

His jaw tightened. "No."

"Admit it. You need me. No need for blueprints or the risk of a wrong turn."

He stood from the desk, scraping the chair legs back across the tiled floor. "I've worked for years without you. No way in hell am I risking you, or this operation, on some vacationing girl's whim for adventure."

"It's not a whim." I didn't know what my motivation was. The urge hadn't been there until I'd met this mysterious man who'd stumbled into my world. But now I became acutely aware that what he did, who he was, was something I'd yearned to do...to be...for a very long time. "And I'm not a girl." No idea why I felt the need to emphasize that point. But the woman he'd touched, the pent-up desires he'd freed, could no longer be denied.

"You're not field ready." He grabbed a thin white cardboard tube from the back corner of the desk, slid the blueprints into it, then plugged the end with a plastic cap.

I edged closer, leaning into his space so near that the heat of his chest began to make my pulse hum again. "So train me."

His dark brows drew together into an imposing scowl. "In a couple days? Impossible." He turned away, jogged up the steps, and went into the bathroom, flicking on the bright lights again.

I followed close on his heels, refusing to give up on an idea that energized me to a level I hadn't expected, beyond anything I'd ever known.

Not feeling even an ounce of remorse, I stared up at his shoulder, to where my untutored stitching burrowed under his skin. He pulled his black T-shirt over his head, hiding the evidence we both knew existed. "You know I've got combat skills. Try again."

In a sudden whirl, he was on me, crowding me back until we crashed against the wall. Both of my hands were suddenly pinned over my head, my wrists locked into the iron grip of one of his, then he grasped my chin with a firm hold. His fierce gaze arrested mine.

I stood there, frozen.

Why hadn't I fought him? My body betrayed me—it wanted this. *I wanted this.*

And as I tensed against the unyielding grip around my hands, my excitement ratcheted up with my pulse, thrumming a steady aching heartbeat stronger and stronger between my thighs.

His eyes widened at whatever he saw in the depths of mine. On a hard headshake, my chin broke free of his hand and I lifted it defiantly.

His chest rose and fell. His nostrils flared. His jaw clenched and released once, twice. Whatever he held back took incredible willpower to restrain.

Then he let out a low growl, tightened his grip on my wrists, and released me. As I stumbled forward, he took two robust steps back toward the center of the square bathroom, increasing the distance between us.

He stared at me, a vibration trembling through him until his gaze shot to the floor. "*Fuck*," he bit out. "I want to see you again. But I'm not training you. Not risking you."

An odd flip happened in my chest, and I frowned. My thoughts blurred. I wanted to see him again too. Sexual chemistry had only been something I'd read about, researched, but I'd not experienced it before. Now its exhilarating tension hazed around us, thick in the air.

When his gaze shot back up to mine, mild panic flickered there. Like he was afraid to stay, to give more than he'd been prepared to.

I moved to block his path, but he was too quick and brushed past me before I anticipated the move.

After a step, he turned, glancing over his shoulder. "I have to go. If you want a ride to the hospital, meet me out front at noon."

Then the door was opened. And he vanished.

Right as the heavy wooden door slammed shut behind him, I blinked, stunned. A split second later, the magnitude of the night's events crashed into my brain with the force of an avalanche.

CHAPTER 5

In the early-morning hours that followed, I'd crashed hard after puzzling over Alec, my sudden overheated sex drive, and my unexpected desire to forge a new career path into spy games. A series of soft clanking noises woke me. Disoriented only for the seconds it took to remember my foreign environment, I yawned, stretched, rolled over, then drifted back off after vaguely recollecting that the noises were the delivery of the standing-breakfast order Anna and I had scheduled for every morning at 10:30 a.m.

After the fifth positional shift, when my muscles and brain finally gave in to being more awake than asleep, I pushed upright with a final stretch, then tumbled out of bed and stepped toward the door.

I twisted the metal lock and slid open the bar latch, both of which seemed necessary after the events of last night. Although, evidently, a coconut palm was the only access point Alec had needed.

Two trays waited outside, one on a corner shelf built into the white stucco wall, the other sitting atop a large wooden trunk that resembled a treasure chest with its arched lid. With a grunt, I lifted the heavy tray from the shelf, bracing its weight with the filled coffee and tea carafes against my breastbone, and carried it to down to the small mahogany table in front of the couch. Then I transported the other tray laden with two plates of eggs, bacon, and toast; a basket of assorted pastries and breads; a platter of sliced melons and strawberries; and two glasses of juice, one the mellow orange of guava nectar, the other pink grapefruit.

Not caring where I put the even heavier tray, I took two steps into the room and lowered it onto the foot of the bed. My gaze drifted beyond the food to the center where only a crumple of sheets existed, but where a bronze-skinned man had been not long ago as he patted the smoothed-out surface of the duvet in temptation. The spot may as well have been on fire for how the revisited thought heated me now, tempting me to wonder what would've happened had he given in to what he'd clearly been fighting and stayed… instead of bolting.

I let out a measured breath as my pulse began to thrum harder. Then I tore my attention away from the one spot in the room that seemed to glare at me in the brightness of the day. My gaze landed back onto the tray of food, but with the level of nervous anticipation vibrating through my body, the idea of eating anything turned my stomach.

Some hundred feet away at the shoreline, the gentle rhythmic roar of ocean waves crashed, providing the soothing calm of a natural soundtrack. At the far horizon line, a dusky blue ocean peeked through the french doors and windows...whose shutters had been opened wide.

When did that happen?

Last I recalled, the slats to the wooden shutters had been angled shut. Now they were fully open, letting all the brightness of the day inside. A sweeping green frond of the coconut tree at the corner of the balcony brushed against the windowpane directly above the desk. Had my mysterious spy returned before I'd woken? Opened the shutters? Watched me sleep?

An involuntary shiver tripped through me at the thought of anyone creeping into my bedroom while I'd lain helpless. The idea unnerved me to my core, where the deepest shadows lay in wait. To ease the spike of anxiety, I embraced them, welcomed them in, shielding myself in their cold comfort. Out of raw instinct developed from years of self-soothing, my gaze shot to the darkest part of a suite that had been raided by morning light: underneath the desk.

I walked closer as I stared into that narrow shadow, willing my ragged breaths to calm until they lengthened into deeper inhalations. Only if I kept the darkness close at hand, reminded myself of that which had been taken from me, did I hold power over anything else that lay in wait.

Only then did I have control.

When my pulse calmed to a steadier beat, I slowly lifted my attention to the surface of the desk, where Alec had planned his current mission. Blueprints of his target had been spread out, harmless on the thin vellum paper, as if they held no importance.

But the schematics of a house and its mechanical systems had been so much more to me. They were a roadmap to my salvation. And Alec had been the messenger. Yet he'd been... more. Not simply the one who'd shed light into my dark ignorance, but the very instrument I wished to become.

An instrument of vengeance.

Suddenly anxious to meet him at noon, I spun on my heel and rounded the bed. As I passed the nightstand on the way to the bathroom, I depressed the function button of my phone. The time flashed up: 11:08 a.m. Was that local time? I trusted the phones ran on a combination of the atomic clock and my GPS position, automatically adjusting to the locale.

Suddenly grateful Anna had hijacked my phone to get service here, I took a quick shower and slipped into simple green flower-print sundress. Then I brushed my teeth and stepped into a pair of flat sandals.

Another check of the time told me fifteen minutes remained before Alec expected me out front. Eight would get me there at a leisurely stroll along the meandering broken-stone pathway that led through their manicured-jungle gardens.

I let out a slow breath, then crossed down into the sitting room and poured myself a coffee, leaving the aromatic liquid black, while I used the remaining few minutes to reacquaint myself with the facts and formulate a loose plan.

Alec had been shot. Were the gunmen still after him? Would I put myself in danger? Anna?

And what was it about the mysterious man that drew me toward him in spite of those risks? We both wanted sex between us. Our sparking chemistry made that abundantly clear. My heart rate accelerated at the mere thought of his touch, the smoldering gaze he'd shot toward me, evident even in the darkened room.

A vibrating sound startled me out of my sidetrack. My phone sat on the corner of the table, lit up with caller ID.

My mom's mobile number. *Great.* To answer or ignore?

No love lost with us, because there'd only been distance between me and both of my parents ever since the tragic event, I slid my finger across the phone to answer the call.

"Hey, Mom. What's up?" Casual. Practiced.

"Devin. Just making sure you arrived safely. And to wish you an early Merry Christmas."

Sure. Because like so many other holidays, on the actual day, they'd be unavailable. Scarce. In years past, I'd had to make other plans. Fend for myself. Reason away that rampant shallow commercialism amplified the emotional trappings of all holiday celebrations. Corporate entities loved to capitalize on the natural human desire for the idyllic family—something nonexistent in my gritty realistic world.

"I'm good." I'd failed to check in. And no matter what they'd done or not done over the years, they'd always been overprotective of me. Drilled into me from the tender age of seven, they'd guaranteed not only that alertness and defensiveness had become intuitive, they'd also made certain my judgment remained sound, every risk assessed, and multiple escape routes calculated.

Subconscious defiance had most certainly played a role in my failure to report in. My entire trip here symbolized the fact that I'd gone off the painstakingly constructed predestined rails. But I'd been cracking, tiny fissures weakening the façade I'd spent years perfecting.

I didn't have the energy to pretend anymore.

"Good," she replied. Awkward silence lingered. Like in so many other conversations. Different from most other human interactions I'd witnessed. As if we continually played pretend to be the family we weren't. "Well, we'll be traveling again," she continued. "Europe. South of France. Italy. A week in Greece."

As I swiped up my room key card and exited the room, I silently mouthed her words with her as she spoke—because I knew them by rote.

I flipped the DO NOT DISTURB sign to its PLEASE SERVICE ROOM side and pulled the door shut. My father's distant voice sounded out in the background. "Tell her Merry Christmas for me. And make her teach those Mexican bartenders how to make eggnog."

"Merry Christmas, Dad," I muttered, replying to his perfunctory wish and commentary.

Every year we followed the same routine. I studied away at school. They worked sunup to sundown, both with government biophysics projects that often took them abroad. When school was on break? They traveled. Always. Made a daughter wonder if it had been in their work contracts to avoid family.

I'd stopped caring years ago. Latchkey kids were a common thing on my upper-middle-income suburban block, two working parents the norm. And after the initial trauma had worn off, my situation morphed into something vastly different than normal. But my parents hired the very best psychologists to ensure their gifted daughter didn't skip a beat.

I hadn't.

Also hadn't taken me long to realize what little love my parents possessed in the first place had been rescinded. And following their example, it hadn't been hard to fool my parents. Then the shrinks. Then the test administrators.

Apparently I'd been gifted with my cognitive ability in all the right places, enabling me to hide my emotions so well, it was as if they didn't exist. And for a child testing on the top end of the IQ spectrum, the experts not only had accepted it, they'd expected it.

I learned very well how to hide in plain sight.

"Give me the phone, Francine," Dad said in the background.

"Good-bye, Devin," Mom said. "We'll try to be home for spring break." A lie. But then, why give up the pretense now. We'd mastered the pretty-little-family-unit camouflage so well.

"You know not to have drinks with ice, right?" Dad inquired. Clearly my first vacation made them second-guess my intelligence.

I jogged down the stairs, shaking my head. "Watch it, Dad. I might mistake your advice for parental concern."

He cleared his throat. "You've never traveled before."

"You drilled into me the necessity for research when stepping into unknown situations. Remember the shopping mall?" Maybe I hadn't ever traveled, but before I'd visited an indoor mall the first time, I'd spouted off the stolen-vehicle statistics of various parking quadrants, health inspection reports from the eleven eating establishments, and the location of the security offices, the number of exterior exits, and the distance to police and fire stations.

His deep chuckle sounded out. "Yes. You came home safe and sound." Which was all they cared about. Not whether or not my friends had ditched me, only to suddenly reappear when I'd initiated a heated debate with last year's star quarterback over his choice of colleges and the odds of him needing the education over the draft.

"Then trust me. I got this." *Mostly.*

"Of course you do." An awkward pause followed, then a woman's garbled voice sounded over an intercom amid buzzing background noise. "Time to go. Our row was called. We'll send you a postcard from Switzerland."

Right. They hadn't gotten their cover story straight. France, Italy, and Greece for Mom. Switzerland for Dad? Maybe things weren't all they appeared on the surface.

Their call ended right as I passed the gift shop and reached the gravel-covered roundabout near the resort entrance. Beyond two of the resort's black SUVs, idled an unassuming open-top Jeep. *Alec's Jeep.*

Just the mere sight of him, even with his aloofness, roused my body to life. My scientific mind provided an analytic answer. He was the ideal specimen—and my biological match. His pheromones enticed mine on a primitive level. Not to mention, I found that dark penetrating gaze of his both unnerving and exhilarating. And the way his sleek muscles tensed the closer I approached not only appealed to me, but suggested that his body also physically reacted to mine.

He leaned against the rear quarter panel, watching my approach with a look of focused intensity. Like he tried to read me—see through me. Had he detected something was off after I ended my call by the way I carried myself? By my expression?

Good luck with that, Spy Guy. I'd patented the ability to be unreadable. Fooled everyone. He wasn't going to crack my code with one spectacular orgasm and the promise of more. Some things were designed to be indecipherable.

And again, for the second time since our encounters, staring back at him was like looking into a damn mirror. Lack of expression. Layers of walls. Secrets.

I tipped my head toward him in greeting, mirroring him back.

He replied with a short nod of his own, then pushed off the tire with his boot and turned, breaking our eye contact.

Relief coursed through me and out with a slow exhale. He rattled me. But instead of wanting to distance myself from the perplexing phenomenon, the intriguing man only drew me closer.

His Jeep's body had no shine to it whatsoever, the surface rough against my fingertips as I opened my door and climbed in. No bulletproof glass either. Nor ballistic doors. Only thing above our unprotected heads? A roll bar.

I glanced at the tops of the buildings around us, the

shadowy walkways, and scanned the dense jungle perimeter as I fastened my seatbelt. "So, am I gonna get shot at today? Am I a target by association?"

"Doubtful." He slid a pair of dark sunglasses over his eyes, then pulled out and accelerated quickly as we drove along the shade-dappled gravel road that led out of the resort. "But it's early yet. We'll see how the day goes."

"Oh. So a *funny* Spy Guy, then." A gut feeling pinged into my brain. "You're not a guest of the hotel." He hadn't outright said it, but instinct broadcast the fact in nuances: the way the staff responded to him, the very non-rental look of the Jeep, his air of confidence when moving about the place, like he'd made himself at home. Plus there was the whole Field Cocktail kit versus guest-toiletry-sewing-kit clue.

"No." Short. To the point.

A gate opened a few yards ahead, and the guard nodded at Alec as we passed through.

"But you come here for coffee. Use their beaches for water sports."

"Yes." He never took his attention off the road, didn't alter his expression.

Okay. Clearly he wasn't a fan of elaboration.

Different tactic: an open-ended question. "What did you do this morning that you couldn't pick me up earlier?"

"Errands." He turned south onto the asphalt highway.

Right. Master of the one-word answers.

I decided to test his resolve and clam up myself. I could remain aloof too.

The towering monotonous green jungle on either side

was only mitigated by enormous billboards that diminished in number and size the farther we drove from the resort area. The warm midday sun beat down on us, but the close proximity to the ocean and our speed with the open-air Jeep made the drive itself pleasant.

After cruising down the highway in silence for almost fifteen minutes, my natural inquisitiveness won out over intense stubbornness, but only after a fierce internal battle.

"So how does it work?" I blurted, sounding far from casual about it. Didn't care. I had nothing to lose by revealing my interest in his work.

"How does *what* work?"

"The spy stuff. Are you on call or are you always working on the mission?"

He negotiated around a menacing pothole, then glanced at me with an arched brow. "Are you asking if I'm on mission now?"

Finally. An eight-word sentence. I stared back at those dark sunglasses. "Maybe." Curiosity about his job overrode every other thought. Could his line of work be something I wanted to do? Would there always be a focus for the copious amounts of energy I needed to funnel? And yes, if that was true, if he was on mission right now, how did I figure into the equation?

Returning his attention back to the road ahead, he gave a nearly imperceptible shrug. "The mission is always in play."

"Even when you're driving a girl to the hospital to see a friend?"

He gave a single nod. Then after a large work truck

passed us, he made a right-hand turn onto a two-lane dirt road.

Feeling brazen, I added, "Even when you're occupying twenty-two minutes of room-service wait time?" My whole body flushed at the memory, warming my cheeks as I stared at him.

Without skipping a beat, he dropped a deadpan expression at me. "Even then."

"So I'm part of the mission?" I scoffed, uncertain if I should be offended. Excited? Yes. With the way my heart picked up speed at the notion, I had the excitement part down cold. On a deep breath, I attempted to tamp my heartrate down. "So how does that work...exactly?"

The deep sound of his chuckle at my repeated question amused me. I enjoyed seeing the intense man beside me smile. He didn't indulge in the act often, but when he did, tiny lines crinkled the tanned skin on the outer edge of his eyes. "Aren't you the inquisitive one?"

"And persistent," I pointed out. In case he hadn't noticed.

About a half mile down the long dirt road, shops and small restaurants appeared in clustered groups on both sides of the road. On the north side, carved from a dense jungle poised to reclaim its space once civilization paused to take a breath, a white-stucco shopping plaza housed individual shops that boasted awnings in a wide array of bold colors from reds and yellows to blues and greens. And just beyond, a modern three-story building covered in black glass from foundation to roof spanned almost an entire block.

"The simplest way to explain it is this: We're always

active. Who we are, along with the short and long-play objectives, stays in the forefront." He turned into a curving paved entrance and followed it around toward a small empty parking area in the front corner. "However, in between actual tasks, we remain alert but off-the-clock. We never know when a chance encounter may become ideal cover."

After we pulled between the white lines of one of the available parking spaces, he cut the engine. I blinked, digesting his words. "So that's what I am to you? Cover?" The scientist in me surfaced, undeniable. I needed to quantify what I was to him and how I fit into the bigger scheme of his mysterious operation. Only then could I make a case for him to include me.

Instead of answering, he got out of the Jeep, and I followed. Then he paused in front of me and removed his sunglasses. Amusement danced in his eyes as he stared hard at me. "You are so much more than cover, *Pink*."

Great. We'd regressed to nicknames again.

His gaze shifted beyond me as he clipped his glasses into his T-shirt collar. "Gimme a minute? I'll be right back."

While I pondered the revelation of being "more than cover," and how I might use it to my advantage, Alec jogged along a worn dirt pathway that led a short distance through tall grasses until he reached an adjoining parking lot. Curious what drew his attention so suddenly, I crossed my arms and followed to the edge of the asphalt, watching him.

Four dark-haired children hovered near the entrance of the lot. They resembled several other groups I'd noticed on the drive that seemed to congregate in front of every shopping area. The moment they caught sight of Alec heading toward them, their faces brightened and they moved en masse toward him.

The closer the children came, the higher their slender arms lifted. One held up colorful bracelets. Another showed Alec what appeared to be watches dangling from his forearm. Packed tightly from wrist to elbow, their shining metal faces flashed in the sunlight, leather bands circling below.

Alec slowly shook his head, reached into the pocket of his cargo pants, then pulled out a money clip. He pointed toward a food vendor near the curb.

All four faces drew blank expressions as Alec kept walking. Seconds later, they chased after him with eager steps. Gesticulating over the metal counter of the food truck, he spoke rapidly. After a few minutes of the vendor scrambling back and forth, containers of food were being transferred from vendor to Alec to each child. The paper containers looked to contain tacos, hot dogs, and tamales.

Each child carried their meal up to the sidewalk in front of the nearest shop and sat on the curb. When the youngest settled, she started devouring a taco, and the rest dug in to their meals. Pulling up the rear, Alec joined them with additional treasure in hand and their eyes widened the closer he came. He handed the eldest four churros.

Then Alec peeled an additional two bills from his money clip and held them out to the boy. The child seemed beside himself, shaking his head with widened eyes. Alec gave him a stern look until the child relented and reached up to claim the unexpected gift. Then the boy safely pocketed the money as Alec gave a satisfied nod.

Away from the cool ocean breezes and the glamour of the resort, crowded in on all sides by a jungle teeming with predators of all shapes and sizes, the air stilled into a thick humid haze, lending an ethereal quality to the poignant scene. Yet through the mist, the image of those kids seared into my mind, the tragic dark parts of humanity on display from the obscurity of shadowed corners. And Alec appeared to be their brief ray of light.

An undefinable ache panged through my chest as he turned and left them. Yet I continued to watch the children, wondering about their story. Oblivious to my scrutiny, they ate with surprising slowness. Even the youngest. Like they wanted to savor the unexpected gift they'd been given.

Alec returned along the narrow dirt pathway, and I shifted my gaze toward him as he crossed into my line of sight. For a fleeting moment, his expression seemed unfocused, trained to some faraway place in his mind. But when he lifted his gaze to mine, his features blanked, then hardened into the mask he wore.

"Spy *and* humanitarian?" I murmured, trying to categorize a man continually breaking free of the typecast mold my analytical mind wanted to file him under.

He veered to my right and gave a slight shrug. "Been there. No child should go hungry."

I blinked. *Been there? On the street? Hungry?*

Those instant unasked questions spiraled into countless more. But as I stared at his back, while he retrieved a black leather bag from the backseat, I found in my confusion I couldn't voice one of them.

CHAPTER 6

"What's in the bag?" Amid the sea of churning questions, the seemingly harmless appeared a good place to start with a man whose entire body language screamed closed off.

As we neared the automatic glass doors of the hospital's main entrance, they glided open with a soft whoosh. Alec kept pace beside and just ahead of me, his assessing gaze discreetly scanning left and right in a comprehensive arc as we walked.

Watching for threats?

A subtle warning pinged inside my head. Regardless of Alec's casual attitude about potential gunmen stalking us, the danger remained.

"Gear," he replied, curling his fingers tighter around the short black leather straps.

"Gear for what?"

He glanced over his shoulder at me, heat in his gaze. "For later."

Later? Us later?

Had I imagined the suggestive charge in his tone? The bag looked heavy.

Couldn't possibly have anything relating to the...well, what we'd talked about doing...

Oh, hell. Get a grip, Devin. It's called sex.

As we walked, my steps slowed, awareness of the vast space we'd entered taking hold. "This isn't a hospital," I whispered.

He chuckled, then slowed his gait and leaned closer. "Oh, it is. Obscene wealth sugarcoats everything."

A shiver tripped through me as his warm breath danced over the shell of my ear and down my neck. I gasped at the sudden intimate connection, then camouflaged my reaction by inhaling a bit more slowly, trying to right my center of gravity again.

While I analyzed the degree to which his rich voice tantalized my nerve endings, he walked the remaining ten feet to the reception desk, then spoke in rapid Spanish with a woman wearing black scrubs trimmed in lime green.

As if he hadn't just sent my body careening toward meltdown.

Taking a second calming breath, I turned and wandered toward the center of the main lobby, examining the muted visual tapestry around us. Black granite spanned the floors, silver and turquoise flecks within the stone flashing when my angle and the natural daylight caught it just right. The dark tiles spread up the walls thirty-six inches until they abutted a chiseled limestone molding. Cream-colored plaster walls stretched up to thirty-foot ceilings, and in the center, right above my head, suspended an elaborate blown glass chandelier in various shades of white from a milky opaque to glittering iridescent, some twisted spirals with textured surfaces, others smooth and oblong. A handful of clear lightbulbs nestled within the sculpture, difficult to distinguish from all the sparkling shapes around them.

"Ready?"

My whole body tensed at the surprising tenor of his voice, and I gasped in a short breath. He stood so close, his thin T-shirt sleeve brushed against my shoulder.

"You should wear a bell," I muttered.

"You should be more aware of your surroundings." The corner of his mouth twitched up for a split second. Then he turned and took long strides down a hallway that began to the right of the reception desk.

I hurried after him, half-jogging to catch up. "What did you find out?" I glanced at my watch. While I'd been distracted by the opulent furnishings, he'd been in a heated discussion with the woman at the front desk for just shy of two minutes.

"We're allowed to visit."

Uh-huh. More than a few words had been exchanged. "Not what floor? Or directions to a specific room?"

He gave a quick headshake and pressed the elevator call button. "Already knew that."

My eyes narrowed. "How?"

He fully faced me, humor flashing in his eyes. "I'm in the intelligence business. You provided her first name last night: Anna. All I needed."

My skin warmed at the mention of last night. Anna's call had interrupted the sexually charged aftermath of the most erotic kiss of my life. I swallowed hard, throat suddenly bone dry as a gentle throb hummed between my thighs. On a deep breath to calm down, my nipples rasped against the thin material of my dress, hardening to my dismay.

I had to take yet another deep breath to calm down as we entered the elevator. The perplexing man mere inches away suddenly had command of my body in a most disconcerting Pavlovian way. I didn't know whether to be irritated or grateful.

We exited the elevator on the third floor before I could formulate any other investigative questions. But once the intoxicating spell of his proximity broke, they flooded in. When had he inquired about Anna at the hospital: The moment he'd left last night or just prior to picking me up? And if he already knew her floor and her room, what other information had been exchanged in the front lobby? The weather? The political climate?...A date?

Alec didn't strike me as the dating kind. More like the... fucking...kind. Hard. Thorough. *Primal*...

After another hard swallow, I sucked in a sharp breath. My illicit thoughts rocketed my pulse up faster than anything Alec had *actually* done. Shaking my head at my wild imagination, I followed his lead down another corridor whose floor had been swathed in the same black granite as the lobby.

He paused at the nurse's station, a semicircle area in the center of the floor, and rested his arm on the polished cream-colored marble counter.

"Room 302," he said while nodding toward the room ahead of me without bothering to glance my way. Instead, his gaze tracked farther down the corridor, then swept across the open area, panning from right to left as he scanned the entrance to every visible room.

His hand remained securely wrapped around the handles of his leather bag, his other arm casually resting on the counter. To an untrained observer, his stance might've appeared relaxed, but I sensed he stood guard like a self-appointed sentry, watching everything around us, ensuring my safety.

But the moment I stepped into Room 302…everything spy? Completely forgotten.

"Anna!" I rushed over to the bed, astonishing even myself with my level of excited relief.

Lazing atop the covers, wearing an ivory cotton gown with her toned, tanned legs stretched out and one foot perched on a large pillow, she grinned wide the moment I burst into the room. "Dev!"

I landed a hip on the edge of the mattress and threw my arms around her. When a tiny squeak accompanied her shrinking away from me, I released her. "I'm sorry. Did I hurt you?"

By the time I pulled back, she settled against the pillow-mountain propped behind her and shook her head. "No biggie. Turns out when you sprain your ankle and *fall*—like a total flailing klutz—a few other things are bound to get banged up."

"Only a sprained ankle, then? Nothing broken?"

She lifted her foot off the pillow, rotating her leg to show me the outside of her foot. Her ankle was swollen, the puffy tissue sporting a purplish bruise. "Nope. And Doc says if I stay an extra day or two, devote myself to elevated rest and all their physical therapy staff has to offer, I can wear heels in a few days, snorkeling by the end of vacation."

I twisted around, dropping her a hard look. "Really? You're laid up and all you can think about is Louboutin?"

She gave an unapologetic shrug. "My legs beg for a designer shoe workout. I'm addicted."

"More like demented."

Her mouth curved into a winning smile. "Just how you love me."

I dropped my chin to my chest, shoulders slumped in my honest defeat. When I raised my head, I pressed my lips into a firm line, doing my best not to smile. "Great. What does that make me?"

She tugged me down, scooting over to make room for me. "It makes you delusional, twisted, and perfectly sane in our crazy imperfect world."

I let out a soft snort as I settled on the bed, cushy for what I'd expected from a hospital. Then again, nothing here was anything like I'd imagined. Her room was private, spacious with a sitting area that included a small beige leather couch and arm chair. The same black granite and ivory limestone covered the hard surfaces, and moss-green curtains framed a wide window.

"I can't believe you aren't coming back with us today." Even odder was the jovial attitude I'd adopted since seeing

93

her. Like we'd switched roles. In her absence, had I provided balance to the darkness, compensating with a modicum of lightheartedness myself? Or had Alec's presence played a role?

She let out a dramatic sigh. "It's only another day or two. With your library of digital romances and all those sexy Latin men ogling you, you'll find something, or someone, to occupy your time." Then she nudged hard with her good shoulder. "And 'back with *us*?' What's the story?" she whispered in a conspiratorial tone.

I glanced in the direction she looked toward. Through the open door, Alec stood in our line of sight, his back toward us. In order for him to be located there, he'd moved farther down, toward the end of the counter. A man wearing a black lab coat stood beside him, a scripted name embroidered on one side, two pens clipped in his upper pocket, a stethoscope hanging around his neck—a doctor.

"Don't know." I stared at the two men, so alike in dark features they could be brothers.

"Really? That's all I get?"

Oh. Right. She had no idea he'd stumbled onto our balcony, shot. Then stabbed. Then kissed…

"Um. Well, we kind of ran into each other." If you count his lips entangling with mine. For some inexplicable reason, I had no desire to share more with her. The moments Alec and I had experienced were important to me in a way I couldn't quite wrap my genius brain around yet. And I wanted to understand it. Long before I revealed any of it.

"He's…nice," I added. If nice equaled enigmatic and dangerous.

I turned toward her, expecting mischief in her expression, but instead, she seemed focused and serious as she stared out the doorway. I glanced back at the two men engaged in what appeared to be a deep discussion. Then the doctor threw his head back and laughed at something Alec had said.

"Well, if that's how we're playing it, then I sort of ran into the man standing next to him."

"The doctor?"

"Yep."

Narrowing my eyes, I slowly turned my head toward her until our gazes met. "You don't *really* need to stay for therapy do you?"

Amusement flickered across her face. She gave a slow, calculating smile as she pivoted her attention toward the doctor, then returned her gaze to me. Her tone lowered, loaded with clear innuendo. "Define therapy."

As I smiled on the outside, all the humor in my head faded away.

Her comment, meant to be playful, cut to the deepest part of me, resonating with haunting clarity in all its personal facets.

CHAPTER 7

After over an hour of visiting with Anna, I'd exited her room to find Alec waiting at the end of the hall, comfortably standing guard, absent his doctor friend. The actual time back to the resort took the same thirty-two minutes it had when we'd made our way to the hospital, but every second that ticked by on the return trip seemed to stretch infinitely.

He'd supplied one-word answers again to everything I'd asked him. "What's in the bag?" I'd pressed. "Gear." He'd repeated in kind.

Like a cat-and-mouse game, I chased, he evaded. And yet, the minor challenge proved entertaining. And it served as a welcome distraction to the ever-present sexual chemistry that charged the air between us.

When the backs of his fingers barely touched the skin high on my outer thigh for the second time in the last twenty minutes, I sucked in a slow breath. Just like the first time, he didn't react. Only this time, after a few seconds, he brushed his knuckles up a few slow inches, then drifted them back down. Up. Down.

Each slight movement ratcheted my pulse higher. Along with the hemline of my sundress.

My lips parted on a silent gasp as a sudden frisson of excitement sizzled through me. He paused, then continued. I finally exhaled through pursed lips, as the electric sensation settled into a low ache between my thighs.

All the while, his gaze remained concentrated on the road, sunglasses firmly in place.

I forced myself to mimic his unaffected exterior, watching the billboards zip by as my heartbeat raced right along with my mind. Regarding what came next. Concerning where we were headed. Knowing that our not talking aloud about the subject didn't mean we weren't both constantly thinking about it.

He turned east onto the gravel drive that led to the front of the resort.

Desperately needing to divert maddening blood flow from where it throbbed between my legs to send it anywhere else, I forced myself back into my head and switched tactics with my line of interrogation, deploying the question-bomb I'd been sitting on for almost two hours.

Don't get anywhere scratching at the surface? Probe deep.

"What did you mean 'been there' with the children?"

Silence.

Then he removed his hand from my thigh. Cool air whipped over my heated skin, and I whooshed out a relieved breath. Even though my body hummed with need.

I waited, refusing to breach the awkward tension.

For the first time in his rapid report of one-word volleys, he hesitated. Had he meant to reveal that loaded hint about the kids to me earlier, or had he slipped? Would he give in now and share a piece of himself...or distract and evade, as per his usual MO.

"I grew up on the street." His quiet reply was the longest sentence he'd uttered in the last half hour.

I frowned. "What about your parents?" Surely all those kids earlier in the parking lot, clustered in small groups as they sold their wares to tourists, had parents.

"Didn't have any."

The concept struck me as foreign and familiar all at once. The loneliness he had to have felt mirrored what I'd experienced in a house with a roof over my head and an official mother and father.

"Where did you live?" With every hushed word as I waded into more sensitive waters, the tension between us thickened into something far heavier than sexual.

Wordlessly, we drove across the wood-slatted bridge that spanned a wide swamp area. According to the driver who'd first brought Anna and me from the airport, crocodiles lived in that dark, placid water.

Ignoring the danger outside the vehicle, I turned toward Alec, watching his profile as he focused straight ahead with a stony expression.

When the road widened enough to let oncoming traffic pass, it opened into the circular entrance of the resort. A long rectangular fountain stretched on our left toward the resort's entry steps, stone sculptures spouting arcs of water into its shallow pool which was dotted with lily pads.

He eased off to the side and stopped the Jeep in the dappled shade of towering trees, about thirty feet short of the parked resort SUVs and far enough away from the attention of the valet staff. He cut the engine, then removed his sunglasses, but continued to stare forward as a muscle in his jaw clenched.

"On the street," he finally replied.

"But where did you sleep?" The outrageous concept wouldn't settle into my brain.

His hands clutched the steering wheel. "Wherever I found a safe place. An abandoned garage one night. Storage shed the next."

"Oh my God," I whispered. I failed to fully comprehend what he'd endured. I'd had to steel myself against a home devoid of love, but he hadn't even *had* a home. "For how long?" My tone remained soft. I was afraid any greater volume could fracture the fragile moment.

"A few years. I was eleven when I lost my parents. They'd been drinking at a party and drifted across the lanes of a highway. They overcorrected. The car flipped, then slid on its roof off the edge of a bridge." His voice cracked on the last few words.

It was the most significant disclosure he'd made so far. And I had no idea what to say. But the pain of his loss cut deep, mingling with my own. I instinctively reached out my hand and wrapped my fingers around his forearm. He didn't pull away.

A few slow beats later, he turned toward me, gaze fierce. "What I am was born that night. With no relatives, social services came looking for me the following day. But I expected them. Anticipated their arrival. Had already stolen away every valuable thing we owned that I could carry and hidden them in locations around the neighborhood. Later, moved them into hidey-holes around the entire city."

"How did you know what had happened?"

His gaze dropped to my lap in thought. "It was the first time they hadn't left me with a babysitter. I was too excited to sleep, so I watched television shows they'd forbidden me to see. When midnight came and went without them returning, I began to panic; they'd always come home hours before then."

He paused. I waited as his face tilted up and he stared out the windshield, gaze unfocused. "I grabbed my bike out of the garage. They told me what restaurant they'd made late reservations at after the show. I knew how to get there, had traveled our whole part of town on my bike as a kid. On my way, the flashing lights of emergency vehicles blocked the bridge. More lights came from below, and I went down to investigate. The drought had been bad that year, the water level a tenth of normal..."

I tightened my hold on his forearm. "*Alec...*"

Slowly, he turned toward me, expression blank—all except for stark pain that shone vividly in his eyes.

My brows furrowed. "It's okay. I..." No part of me wanted to rob him of this cleansing moment, but I'd been stricken by the depth of his kind of pain before, knew I needed to pull him back. "I understand."

"You do…" His tone fell flat, like my relating to him wasn't such of a surprise. His gaze searched mine until he gave me a sharp nod. Then he glanced away on a deep inhalation, not asking me why. As if the tone in the car weighed heavy enough. And we needed to be able to breathe.

He dropped his hand from the steering wheel, then gave my knee a light squeeze. "Anyway, I remained on the streets until seventeen. Someone from the organization stumbled across my path and recruited me."

Curious about what attracted their attention, I cocked my head. "Just like that?"

"Yes." He started the Jeep's engine again and shifted into drive. "Just like that." In the seconds it took to coast to the valet waiting for us on the resort's front steps, he added, "Turns out anyone who can steal the wallet of a field operative…automatically passes the entrance exam to be considered as a field operative."

Not skilled enough to pick pockets to impress EtherSphere One, I parted my lips as we exited the Jeep, readying to ask what other tests they might have.

"Hungry?" He tossed the keys to the valet who'd already jogged around the back of the vehicle.

"What?" My question about spy-organization entrance exams dissolved on the tip of my tongue as my mind searched back to the last time I'd eaten.

After he'd delivered me a mind-blowing orgasm…

My cheeks flushed hot as I blinked at him.

His lips curled into a devious smirk, like he'd known exactly where my dirty mind had traveled. And his had tumbled right down into the same gutter. "Food. Have you eaten since…" His gaze held mine while he reached into the back of the Jeep and pulled out his mysterious black leather bag.

"No!" I barked out a little too forcefully.

He chuckled and wrapped an arm around my shoulder. "Then let's get some food into you."

And even though I knew he meant actual food, I remained fascinated by how readily my body reacted to his voice, his touch, and how my mind seemed to inject innuendo into his words.

Oblivious to my mild distress, he led us toward the open breezeway, through the courtyard gardens, and into the indoor space where I'd literally run into him the prior afternoon.

I paused in midstride, below the chandelier, causing him to stop beside me.

His brows furrowed as he scanned the perimeter, instantly threat-assessing. "Something wrong?"

"No." I shot him a deadpan look. "This spot familiar at all?" Was it coincidence that we'd collided practically twenty-four hours prior?

He shrugged and tugged me forward. "Busy spot. Never know who you'll bump into."

I scoffed at his blasé tone. But my exasperation got cut short when the hostess greeted us, then immediately led us outside to be seated.

Down beside the sand, we found a table shaded by a large market umbrella. I ordered the duck tacos with tamarind sauce and a house-brewed beer. He held up his index and middle finger toward our food server. "*Dos.*"

"So what do you think of our silver stretch of paradise?"

He phrased the question as if he belonged here. And yet even with his dark past and darker secrets, he blended well, a secret operative mingling with guests amid blatant commercialism. But then, the commercialism had carved its way into existence from a tenacious ancient jungle filled with deadly creatures. Only the sparsest glimpse of bright light made it through, barely touching the surface.

My heart twisted at the horrific loss he'd suffered—how it mirrored my own. And how, just like the enduring, carefully crafted oasis around us, we'd survived in spite of our unforgiving world.

He and I fit better than any tourist.

I raised my beer bottle, then lightly clinked his. "Feels like I've finally come home."

CHAPTER 8

The late lunch stretched into an early dinner. Our two initial beer bottles had already been cleared. The delicious sweet and salty tamarind duck tacos we'd ordered had been devoured. The sun had just set behind us while we talked about random unimportant things like his love for soccer and my addiction to volleyball.

"The sports are similar in some ways." Alec poured more chilled Pellegrino into our glasses, causing my pulverized lime to dance around in the fizzing liquid.

"True." I lifted my glass while peering at him over the rim, musing about how Anna and I had once ogled him from our chaise lounges as we played our "how many margaritas" game. My answer then had been none. And even though my stomach fluttered with nervous excitement, stone-cold sober remained my answer.

He relaxed back into his chair and stretched out his long legs, crossing them at the ankles. "No holding the ball," he supplied as his gaze met mine.

"Hitting only allowed with arms and hands…"

"Feet and shins, in soccer," he countered, tilting his head. "Player count is different though. Eleven are on the field."

I gave a conceding nod. "Six on the court."

"Doesn't matter whether we're talking about a field or court though, each player is independent, and yet one." He lifted his water and took a few swallows.

I nodded, catching his uplifting gaze. "Part of a team, yet playing to an individual strength."

Like spies. I suddenly wondered how much communication Alec and his fellow operatives had with one another.

We'd been talking about two different sports, but our gazes kept colliding and holding for longer and longer seconds, as if a deeper meaning lay hidden beneath our observations. And our respective interest in sports was the third area of discussion on the heels of two minefield topics: religion and politics. The former, neither of us had any strong beliefs about. The latter, no faith in the current regimes, in either the US or globally.

I brushed my hand against the side of his, for the fourth deliberate time. When he glided the backs of his fingers up underneath my palm, I curled my fingers down between his, entwining them. "Want to take a walk down the beach? There's a path that leads back to my room."

"Other than up a coconut tree?" he teased.

I huffed out a laugh as he stared at me with one dark eyebrow arched. Then he picked up that black bag of his and pressed a gentle hand to my lower back, guiding me down the two steps and onto the cool white sand. I kicked off my sandals, then bent to scoop the leather straps into two fingers before we continued on toward the water.

A quiet comfort settled between us that I hadn't expected. For a man who'd been shot at and had a mission to complete for some clandestine global agency, he appeared remarkably calm. Maybe his laid-back demeanor when he was off duty balanced out the adrenaline-pumping occasions when speed and skill became the only thing standing between life and death.

Without further conversation, we headed straight to the edge of the shoreline. He positioned himself on the water side, just beyond reach of the foaming waves as they repeatedly stretched toward us. Then he switched his bag to his opposite hand and wove his fingers together with mine.

Hand in hand we walked, a perfect silence wrapping around us as night gradually began to cloak the world. The purplish gray of twilight gave way to deepening charcoal hues by the time we made it to the far side of the resort. We angled toward the sports *palapa* across the private beach area below our room. Where Anna and I had spotted him standing at the water's edge with his scuba gear. When she'd insisted he should be my Latin lover. Tonight, he would be.

Oddly, the earlier nervous flutter had vanished. I'd had few friends in my life. Had only ever allowed Anna to get close enough to know a portion of the real me. But inside of a few short hours strung between a couple of days, I found myself considering the man holding my hand a friend.

The easygoing vibe between us relaxed me enough to

ask another question without filter. "You're not a citizen of Mexico?" His growing up here didn't seem quite right.

We reached the foot-shower at the base of the sidewalk, and he rested his bag atop the granite pillar. "No." He turned on the faucet for me. "I'm a citizen of Spain and the United States."

Surprised, my mouth fell open. "How are you both?" Military came to mind. But with the way he talked about his parents, what I'd imagined didn't fit.

"My father was Spain's ambassador to the United Nations. My mother met him in New York on one of his trips to the US."

Wow. "Is that why the organization 'found' you?" I uttered the question under my breath, as if someone might overhear us talking about his employer.

When he didn't immediately reply, I grasped hold of his hand, balanced, then extended one foot under the water spray. Then I stepped on the edge of the wet stone with my clean foot and rinsed the other.

"Probably," he replied, sounding thoughtful. "They never said why at the time. And I was seventeen and didn't care. They wanted to offer me a job where I could steal, spy, and kill for a decent cause? I signed up, no questions asked."

"When you said you were on the streets…where did you…" Halfway through my blurted question, I realized I'd treaded on sensitive ground again. He'd gotten so quiet earlier in the car when he'd shared the loss of his parents.

But he answered without intonation or hesitation. "A town on the outskirts of Madrid." Leaning down, he turned

107

the faucet off, then grasped me under my arms, as if I weighed nothing, and swung me onto a higher and sand-free stone step.

Comfortable silence followed as we walked hand in hand again along the stone pathway beside a softly glowing blue-tiled rectangular pool. The meandering pathways, bordered by flickering candles nestled within small glass holders, led toward the abandoned spa in one direction and through the manicured-jungle grounds alongside buildings of the resort in another. We turned right, down a short secluded path that ended at my building. An illuminated staircase curved upward in front of us.

He slowed his pace, allowing me to take the lead and guide us up. With the building now sheltering us from the ocean breezes, the air grew heavy and warm.

And had the tension around us thickened again?

My pulse began to beat faster with every footfall placed on the next tiled step upward. Sandals still dangling from my free hand, I touched the white stucco wall with two fingers every so often, steadying myself as we climbed. His fingers that held my other hand relaxed between mine, then tightened, securing his supportive hold on me.

I clasped his hand harder in reply. I wanted this. And I wanted there to be no doubt in his mind that I did.

When we reached the tiled landing at the top, we crossed the short distance to my hotel suite in silence. I released his hand, then retrieved my room's key card from my dress pocket. My hand trembled slightly as I raised the key and inserted it into the slot.

His hand covered mine as the light flashed from dull red to bright green. When I glanced up, warmth and desire radiated in his gaze.

Assured by the sense that he continued to follow my lead, that he only remained because I wanted him to, I gave him a genuine smile that fell into a lopsided smirk when I dropped my hand from under his and depressed the door handle.

"So…" I pushed the door open, dropped my sandals off to the side, then stood beside the nightstand as I propped my hands on my hips. "I'm only asking this one last time. What's in the bag?"

He ran his tongue along his teeth, holding my gaze as he stepped inside and let the door slam shut. Without answering my question, he dropped the bag onto the floor. Then he removed his boots and lined them up beyond it, along the wall. "What are your thoughts about protection?"

"Condoms?" So we were diving right into the nuts and bolts of things.

He gave me a nod.

"I'm a fan."

So that's what's in the bag? A year's supply of condoms you're carting around?

"Any desire to go without?" His penetrating gaze held mine.

I frowned. The suggestion threw me. On a wild fling, with an unknown man, I hadn't expected anything but. Yet I knew *I* was clean.

"I am on birth control pills," I hedged. "Haven't had sex in a while…"

"How long is 'a while'?" His words softened.

"Almost two years."

His eyes narrowed for a split second. "Good." He turned and crossed the room, stepping down into the sitting area. "Shutters open or closed?"

"Wait!" I followed, shaking my head. "You can't just move on to lighting. We haven't finished with condoms yet."

"I'm clean. Get full medicals every six months: agency protocol. Use condoms religiously."

Confused, certain I missed something, I tilted my head. "Then why would you suggest going condomless with me?"

"This is your vacation fantasy. Tonight is about what *you* want."

I blinked. Truly? This larger than life man was willing to alter his pattern for my benefit? And although I'd hardly established a pattern with the three paltry sexual encounters I'd had, condoms had been used every time. What would it feel like?

My rebellious side won out. "No condoms."

He glanced at the dark wooden shutters, then back at me. "Open."

I'd existed in darkness all my life. And although night had fallen, the sky nearly black, some illumination still made it through to guide our way.

And that was the crux of it, wasn't it? No matter how dark my world got, nor how comfortable I made myself with the cold shadows, the anger—the hatred of my lot in life—I still welcomed a degree of light. In fact, the contrast of the two had always drawn my attention.

He opened one of the complimentary bottles of water that sat on the corner of the desk and handed it to me. Suddenly parched, I gulped down half of it before handing it back to him.

He drank a few swallows, then put it down. "Just to clarify, this is a one-time thing."

I hadn't expected much. Didn't have a problem with his rule, understood it with his line of work. "Agreed."

He closed the miniscule distance between us, stopping two feet away.

"Take off your dress." His voice dropped low, the words measured.

Nothing in me questioned, only obeyed. I slid my fingertips downward over the silken fabric and bent forward, causing my arms to pull inward and press my breasts together. He stared with rapt attention as I grasped the material just above the hem at midthigh, slowly lifted it up, then dragged it over my head. By the time the dress cleared my face, providing an unimpeded view of him again, he'd already removed his T-shirt.

His scorching gaze landed on my breasts which were hidden by the black lace of my bra. With every deep inhalation, I grew more aware of them, heavy and aching under his scrutiny. My nipples drew tight, peaking to attention for him.

Trying to calm my breaths, my gaze traveled down his sculpted chest, taking note of the faint spiral scars in the dim light and the thin dusting of hair that trailed downward in a line from his navel until it disappeared beneath the cargos that hung low on his hips. I reached a finger out, touched his heated skin just above his left hip, then traced the defined line of his oblique in an angle downward until my fingertip tucked under the rough twill material.

The right corner of my mouth kicked up. "Pants. Off."

He arched a dark brow. "You. First."

Power.

Control.

Clear and blurred. Defined, yet uncaged. We each had it, yet granted the other a slight measure of leeway in our erotic tug-of-war. Tension pulsed electric between us in the decadent give-and-take we slowly unfurled.

Defiance sparked through me, and I gave him a slow headshake. "No." Then I eased a bare foot back and climbed the cool tiled steps that led from the sitting area, one then the other, before inching farther back into the room toward the bed. He followed, watching my every move with unchecked hunger. Eventually, his hands moved forward and he unfastened his belt, then unzipped his pants.

Standing only in my matching bra and tiny scrap of a thong, I slid my hands over my hips and slipped a finger under each lacy thong strap. Taunting him while testing my own courage, I ran my fingers under the thin material, tugging it down a few inches, but no more.

As he watched, he hooked his thumbs into the waistband of his pants and lifted his leg, climbing one step. After he cleared the second step, he slid them over his lean hips, down powerful thighs, and then dropped them.

My gaze held his the whole time, until I finally got brave

enough to let it drift lower. He spread his legs, standing in a casual but confident stance, awaiting my inspection.

Yeah, he passed. Semihard, his gorgeous penis hung heavy between his legs, thick and long and curving slightly to the left.

I swallowed hard. Now what? I understood the mechanics. Had run through them before. But tonight promised to be different. Was supposed to be out of my head. Spontaneous. Carnal rather than mental.

He saved me from myself by arching a brow and crossing his arms over his chest. "The rest of it. All of it. Off."

My lips twitched at his commanding tone. "Is the striptease for your benefit or mine?"

"What do you think?"

I huffed out a laugh and reached behind me, unclasping my bra. "I think you're enjoying this. A lot."

"You're not?" He stared hard, challenge flaring in his eyes.

I sucked in a deep breath as an instant hot ache flashed between my thighs, pulsing there. Still surprised by the effect he had on me, the power of which spun my head, I blew out a measured breath through pursed lips.

"I am." My admission was soft-spoken.

He said nothing more as my arms came forward; he merely held my gaze. Like it was more important for him to gauge how every move I made—every single thing we did— affected me, not him.

I swallowed hard as the lacy straps of my bra loosened then fell over my shoulders. When I lowered my arms, the remaining bit of material that covered the heart of me fell away, sliding to the floor. But it wasn't enough. Standing in the shadows, I brushed my fingers under the last of it, the slender thong straps that rested securely over my hipbones.

And down it went. All of it. My underwear. The armor beneath. Every constructed wall and safeguard tumbled away.

Although he had no idea. Only someone primed with the right information would know what to ask. And I didn't feel any compunction to tell.

But what struck me was the knowledge permeating straight to my heart, that if he did ask, I would offer him up my darkest secrets. And he would protect them.

"Beautiful," he murmured.

The reverent word spoken under his breath held more weight than any other he could've uttered. Because the way his intense stare penetrated down into my soul, I knew he didn't just mean on the outside. He knew me bone deep on the inside, without ever needing to be told what dark things lay hidden there.

A shiver coursed through my body, sensitizing every nerve ending, as if the crackling air between us charged me to life.

"Lie back." His commanding words softened as he moved from the foot of the bed, pivoting toward the bathroom.

I sat down, then scooted back toward the center of the large bed before stretching out atop the white duvet, unashamed to bare myself in the middle of all the pristine white.

Above steadying breaths that I forced into my lungs to calm my turbulent pulse, the sound of a zipper nearby rent the silence. Finally. The mysterious bag had opened.

Seconds later, he stood beside me.

Beautiful. In my vast knowledge of semantics, only his earlier word came to mind. Sleekly muscular, his lean body moved with efficient grace. His semierection remained the same: primed, and yet, controlled. For him or me?

I reached out, wanting to touch him, wrap my fingers around his thick shaft. A yearning deep within me needed to feel his heat as he hardened for me.

"No," he said. Before I registered the movement, his hand clamped on to my wrist, gentle but unyielding. "This is about you."

My brow wrinkled in disappointment. "We aren't having sex?" Memories returned of the last time we were on this bed, his heated touch, the slow burn that burst into flames.

"Oh, we are. But I'm in charge." His voice fell gruff, barely contained.

Confused, I blinked. Everything he'd done to that point had suggested otherwise. And yet, the idea of surrendering control shot a thrilling shudder through me.

My gaze dropped to his other hand. He clutched a small, black item. Then he knelt on the bed. "Close your eyes."

I didn't. A portion of what he held in his hand dropped free. I stared at the black material and realized it was a blindfold unraveling open. The fabric appeared to be solid silk on one side, brocaded material on the other.

My gaze flew up to his. "I thought you said not to trust you."

"I said it was good that you didn't. Do you think I will hurt you?"

I shook my head, certain he wouldn't.

"Do you believe I will protect you?"

"Yes." The word was soft, but sure.

"Then close your eyes. This isn't about you trusting me. Don't. I haven't earned your unchecked trust." He stared hard at me, searching my eyes. "This is about you. Trust yourself."

His words hit me like a sledgehammer.

Trust myself.

My whole life I'd been holding myself back, becoming what everyone else wanted me to be, expected me to be. This spontaneous trip was about escaping my predestined life, derailing a train I hadn't boarded of my own free will that barreled at full speed toward some unknown and unwanted destination.

Trusting myself…meant letting go.

And in the short time I'd known Alec, I'd determined he would be the one to guide me.

I closed my eyes.

"Good girl," he murmured.

A wisp of material feathered over my cheekbones. In the shadowy room, the scant light that glowed through my eyelids disappeared, casting me into a total blackout. Slight pressure rested along my temples, secured along the back of my head.

I felt soft movement across my shoulder, then a gentle tug of the hair my nape, until the light touch of his fingers brushed down from my collarbone only to be replaced by a warm, light mass: He'd swept my hair to one side.

"Stop analyzing." Amusement laced the command. "Just feel."

I pressed my lips into a firm line, suppressing a smile. "I'm trying." I inhaled slowly, attempting to banish every thought from my mind,

His weight shifted, causing my body to list sideways for a brief second until he returned beside me, the warmth of his knee pressing against my hip. He wove his fingers together with mine, then lifted. A warm touch pressed against the back of my hand, the low sound of a kiss following.

Then something thin encircled my hand and slid downward in soft movement before tightening around my wrist. Snug but comfortable pressure followed. He grasped my other hand and pressed my palms together. In the span of a heartbeat, before thought registered into my brain, he repeated the process to the other wrist.

I tried to tug my hands apart, but they'd been immobilized, bound together.

Panicked, my lips fell apart on a gasp. Instinct ruled, driving a protest from deep in my gut. Fears buried long ago bubbled to the surface, rising with the adrenaline that coursed through my veins. Flashes of being trapped, being grabbed, being stolen in the night assaulted me.

"For you." His gentle words pierced through the cascade, breaking my fall. And the developing protest died on my tongue.

In slow motion, Alec raised my arms over my head. Then he covered me with his warmth from head to toe. But he didn't press his weight down, held himself only close enough to blanket my body, let me know he was there.

His warm breath fogged over my cheek. His mouth barely touched mine at the corner. Then with a languid pace, he brushed his lips across once, then back again. "Only if you want to."

Want. Body bowstring tight with anticipation, I arched upward.

Eyes closed, blinded to the room, bound by him, from myself, I kissed him softly at first. But then I opened my lips, beckoning him inside, wanting…needing…his help to set me free.

CHAPTER 9

Alec kissed me, but his touch was so much more than mere lips molding, tongues sliding.

Like a slow-building tempest, pressure increased, not only at the point of contact, but farther away, deeper down. It tugged at first on the fringes of my awareness, prickling my skin, drawing me in until the force of him enveloped me, spun me, controlled my quickening heartbeat, commanded my shortening breath.

All of a sudden, my center of gravity shifted, no longer bound by the spinning earth but aligned to him as his strong arms pulled me from the bed and up into a straddled position against his heated body. The light hairs on his legs brushed against my inner thighs as he broke the all-consuming kiss.

Einstein's general relativity flared to astonishing life as time itself seemed to warp. The mere seconds since he'd blindfolded and bound me transformed into a hazy incalculable perfect span of minutes, an enticing taste of the erotic hours yet to come.

My connected hands held above us, I lowered them, about to part my arms around his head to hold him while balancing myself. Yet his hands on under my triceps halted my action. "No," he whispered. "Let me see you."

Even though I'd been denied the ability to see him.

His callused palms continued down. The slight touch of the pads of his fingertips traced forward over my ribs, swept under the curves of my breasts. Gentle pressure lifted their swollen weight as he caressed the skin underneath as if smoothing on a trace amount of precious oil. Then the sweeping sensations drew shorter together, drifting higher.

My breaths shallowed as my focus, every ounce of awareness, sharpened into a pinprick of sensation. As my nipples drew taut in anticipation, his low growl vibrated inches from my lips.

Then warmth fogged over the column of my neck, danced over my chest, trailed lower.

A soft moan escaped my throat the second his mouth made contact. A kiss over my nipple, so soft and unassuming. Until it intensified: a wet pinching suction, the hard rasp of teeth. A tantalizing ache coiled tight there, then snapped a twinge of pleasure down through my center.

My lips parted on a gasp as my needy whimper resonated into the darkness.

I squirmed and pushed up from my kneeling position, craving more.

An instant later, his mouth pulled away. Cool air rushed

across my wet nipple, rippling a shudder through my body.

With his steadying hand on one of my shoulders, his weight shifted, once, twice, accompanied by muted thuds behind me. Then both of his hands drifted down my sides to cover my hips. His lips barely touched mine, warm, teasing. Then he gripped my hips and lifted. My mouth collided with his, and our lips opened for one another into an urgent, deep kiss.

But the kiss ended as quickly as it began. He continued lifting my hips with a sudden hard rotation, my legs dragging over his thighs. Thrown off-balance as the world spun around, my arms fell forward until my elbows and the outsides of my bound hands braced onto the cool sheets. As my arms slid forward with the inertia, a pillow broke the rest of my fall, its downy support cradling my chin.

An instant later, his bare heat brushed over the backs of my legs. His hands returned to my hips, gripping, then lifting, propping my knees directly beneath my hips. His thighs moved between mine, then pressed outward, sliding my knees apart.

He leaned forward, and the warmth of his chest covered my back. Another weight shift was followed by a second pillow worked beneath my hips until it nearly supported my weight.

A spark of humor twitched the corners of my lips. "Satisfied?"

"Not even close." His deep tone reverberated against my skin as more of his weight leaned onto me until I yielded from the pressure and sank onto the pillows he'd so carefully arranged beneath me.

With his knees solidly planted between my legs, his hips curved behind mine until his entire body molded around me. The softest touch pressed against my shoulder blade: a gentle kiss. Then the scruff along his jaw scraped across my back until another kiss brushed over my upper spine. Another followed a few inches lower.

"For you," he repeated, his gruff voice rasping into the silence.

Another kiss landed, even with my waist.

I swallowed hard, then inhaled a deep breath as a low ache shimmered through me.

His lips lingered there, hovering over my lower back, a languid touch back and forth, as if that spot required more attention. "You need to feel, not think. That's why the blindfold."

Pace slowing, he dragged his mouth another inch lower, then paused. With a gentle suck, he drew my skin up between his lips. "You need to let go, not control. That's why the bindings."

Let go... So completely foreign, and yet something I desperately needed.

On a slow exhale, I did as he asked, giving myself over to him. Trusting him, to a degree. Trusting myself, more than ever.

The warmth of his hands gripped my hips again, reminding me of their presence, drawing me the rest of the way out of my head and into my body. His flattened palms dragged inward, skating over the globes of my ass, down the backs of my thighs.

All at once, the heat of his direct contact vanished as his weight shifted backward, between my calves.

In the pause, silence reigned.

Nothing happened.

And yet everything did.

With acute awareness, I felt his gaze heavy upon me. The air conditioner hummed, cooling the room. But my skin flushed hot. Wholly affected by him and nothing else.

"*Beautiful*," he repeated, tone awe-filled.

His loaded word ricocheted through me like a whirling sparkler, sizzling me to brilliant life from my heart outward.

Vulnerable. How I felt. Arms extended above my head, legs spread apart, hips raised, all for him. Bound, yet set free.

For you. His words echoed within me.

His touch returned. Whispers of sensation traced up along my calves. A warmer touch pressed along the backside of my bent knee. *His lips.* They trailed upward, dotting an unhurried path while veering toward my trembling inner thigh.

Firmer pressure massaged the inside of my other thigh, circling higher...closer.

Ache knotted deep inside of me, reducing me to gasps of breath to chase my thundering pulse.

Lazy circles worked upward along one thigh. His lips nuzzled my heated skin on the other. Firm pressure kneaded up tensed muscle. Sharp teeth nipped sensitized skin.

Amazed, my mind spun, buoyant. Of the few sexual acts I'd had, none compared. Not one scratched the surface of the extraordinary event unfolding between us. Not even close.

Trembling, I exhaled a shaky breath. Lost in the overwhelming sensations, I focused solely on him, us, as I began to drift into a sensual haze.

A sudden warmth ghosted over my sex, growing hotter as it gradually moved from back to front. My pulse throbbed in my clit, harder and harder as the heat intensified. Seconds later, a firm licking touch dragged across the aching bundle of nerves. I gasped. Harder pressure followed, a great rhythmic sucking. My breath caught, the intensity building to such a degree, my exhalation stretched into a prolonged keening whimper.

Random brushing touches continued, a trace along my inner thigh. A grip around my calf. The entire time, his mouth ravished the sparking terrain between my legs.

Throbbing, quivering, my breaths reduced to shallow panting, his touch and every decadent thrill of pleasure whipping into my body became my only world. Yet I hadn't been reduced to only this one thing. Alec made me feel as if I'd become everything.

The relentless ache grew in strength, coiling tighter as an orgasm edged into awareness. Tiny moans escaped with every exhale.

As if sensing the direction I careened toward, his hands slid up the backs of my thighs, paused right beneath the crease of my buttocks, then gripped there. His rhythmic sucking increased in tempo and intensity.

Too much.

Not enough…

Mad with lust and need, a deep ache spiraling into

intense pleasure bordering on pain, I began to thrash about, bucking my hips, seeking...craving.

His forceful grip on my hips tightened, immobilizing me.

A single hard pulse ripped a gasp from my throat.

He stilled, the warm pressure against my clit present, but easing.

Absent the constant stimulus, the aching sensation hung there. My breath caught. Intense pleasure like no other hovered, vivid and all-consuming. My muscles quivered. I gasped for air, low eager moans escaping with each breath.

All of a sudden, my entire body snapped taut. I teetered on the edge.

Softer pressure dragged across my clit, followed by his low growl.

The vibration triggered a dense implosion, winding tight into itself, pain and pleasure melding together during one split second—until it exploded.

I screamed.

The piercing cry echoed into my ears seconds before I thrust my face down into the pillow, muffling the sound. Hard pulses overtook my body, wave after wave of pleasure coursing through me.

Overcome by the onslaught of erotic sensations, I was dimly aware of Alec shifting positions. One moment, he'd been behind me, face between my legs. The next, his hands gripped my hips as the solid heat of his legs pressed against the backs of my thighs.

Firmness glided through my slick folds, sliding over

my sensitized clit. A fresh pulse of pleasure fired through me, and I drew in a sharp breath. Then he eased backward, dragging across the pinging nerves once again.

Skin hot and pricking with awareness, I turned my head to the side to let cooler air brush over my face. My blindfold was securely fastened. My hands were tightly bound.

Yet in a lifetime relegated to darkness, I finally began to see. Felt what it meant to be free.

The broad tip of his erection pressed against my entrance and another pulse of pleasure lashed through me. I gasped, gulping for air as my senses sharpened.

Body wound tight, I arched my back, seeking, needing more of what this dominating man delivered. In slow progression, he pushed inside, stretching me wide. The foreign sensation ratcheted me up again, flashing me toward another aching precipice.

I blew out a shaky breath, trying to hold still, failing as my thighs trembled uncontrollably.

He pressed in a couple of inches, paused, then eased back. He surged in the same distance again. Pulled back. All the while, his blunt tip dragged against the nerves just inside.

"Stop thinking," he growled.

G-spot. The thought fragment shattered with a hard pulse.

I gasped as a tornado of pleasure spiraled tighter.

He thrust forward right as a second, more powerful, orgasm ripped through my body. No scream managed to escape this time, only low moans and gulps for air as his thick length filled me. Pulse after pulse vibrated through me, surrounded him.

"*Fuck.*" He bit the short word out. But it resonated deep with meaning.

He drew back, then drove forward.

Nerves raw and sparking, my orgasm continued.

Holding my hips immobile with a near-punishing grip, he dragged out, inch by slow inch, then thrust forward, hard and fast. A torturous easing back, a staggering plunge deep.

Entire body vibrating with every impact, my inner muscles quivered with unending pulses. Ragged breaths rasped into the room, his, mine. Cool air feathered over sweat-slickened skin.

My awareness honed sharp with each heated sensation, every humming nerve.

The thrusts slowed even as they intensified, jarring purposeful movements.

And as he did so, my pulses subsided. Then in a heartbeat's time, the tension began building again. Faster and faster. Higher and higher.

His upper body curled down over mine, his slick heat covering me as an inferno raged inside while he filled me, again and again.

Spinning in a whirlpool of ecstasy, I rode the current, clinging to the tether between us.

He let out a stuttered gasp. His hips jerked backward, held there for a moment, then he gave a shallow thrust once, twice.

A shocked, choked-off cry wrenched free from my throat as I hung on an aching precipice yet again. Then colors exploded behind my eyes, sizzling through my body, lighting up the darkness in a fireworks of sensation.

Alec thrust deep, then held there, body draped over mine as he filled me near-to-bursting. His body tensed and a hot whoosh of air rustled my hair as his loud growl reverberated over and through me.

Seconds stretched by as the pulses of his orgasm faded with mine. Our breaths slowed as our racing hearts calmed.

While our bodies relaxed, we began to sink downward and sideways, off to the side of the pillow-mountain. At some point, he gently slipped the blindfold off my face. Then the silken bindings around my wrists were tugged off.

But lost in a bone-melting bliss, I didn't bother to open my eyes. Kept my hands together as I curled my fingers toward my palms.

And all the while, Alec curved the warm strength of his body around me, holding me close, keeping me safe.

"Want to go again?" I asked. My next exhale dragged into a humming purr.

A low chuckle vibrated against my shoulder, before a gentle kiss pressed there. "May need a minute. Or thirty," he murmured.

A smile tugged at my face as I snuggled back into him. I'd been wrung out. Wasted.

Yet, I'd never felt so energized, so alive.

And at the distant periphery of my consciousness, a hidden part of me, one that I'd suppressed for far too long… began to rouse.

CHAPTER 10

Behind me, Alec stirred and the bed shifted. Even in the calming near-absolute darkness, I sensed he'd left the bed and walked across the room, distancing himself from me.

Too sated to care, mind in a blissful haze from hours of pleasure and two more orgasms, I stretched, every muscle in my body sore from the incredible sensual workout.

But then I blinked my eyes open, forcing them to adjust to the dimness, distinguishing the various shades of black from one another. More awake and aware than I ever remembered, completely attuned to my body in ways I hadn't imagined, I propped onto an elbow and stared toward the sitting room right as he opened one of the french doors. He stepped out onto the balcony, then sat in a cushioned chair.

He left the door cracked open, and the previous muted hum of the rolling ocean waves grew to a low roar, booming louder with each powerful crash. Distinct shapes emerged as my vision cleared: the cozy room, the foreign world beyond, the silhouette of a man in repose who'd I'd never expected. He'd both disrupted my mind-numbing life in the most chaotic of ways and set everything to order again—but different…better.

I pushed upright from the cool tangle of sheets and wrapped my arms around my bent legs, resting my chin on my knees as I watched his unmoving back and the endless nightscape beyond.

So much had changed in twenty-four hours.

Inching toward the edge of a cliff over the last months— really the last couple of years—all I'd ever been able to see was a bottomless chasm, an unknown massive void threatening to swallow me whole if I let go of it all and fell. But something altogether different existed over that edge now—something more.

And I wanted whatever *more* the world had to offer.

No matter the obstacles.

Regardless of the danger.

The fractures that had begun to splinter me apart, one hairline crack at a time, had eroded my confidence, blinded me to the possibilities. I'd been reduced to my fear and anger, to all the pain I'd buried deep inside in order to be able to function.

And all of it had been slowly killing me.

But now?

I've never felt more alive.

My entire body vibrated with such excitement, I leapt from the bed. The room's air-conditioned coolness rushed over my skin, causing goose bumps to break out. On the next step, my toes hit something soft, and I bent down to the clothes strewn haphazardly over the tiles and plucked up the nearest item: Alec's T-shirt.

Unthinking, I pulled it over my head and became momentarily lost in sensation all over again. Soft fabric glided over every nerve ending he'd brought to life as his masculine scent surrounded me. I drew in a shaky breath as the material slid over my breasts, teasing my nipples, before it fell to my hips and settled over them.

And still, Alec sat out there, unmoving, oblivious to my erotic distress. Only twenty feet away, the earth stood stable for him. In here, I struggled to find balance in the midst of an earthquake.

I raised my hand, drifted my fingertips over kiss-roughened lips, mentally reliving the way he'd ravaged them, taken my body, given me more pleasure than I'd ever expected from a sexual experience.

A fleeting thought made me wonder if I'd been ruined for all other sex. I shook my head, huffing out a laugh as I jogged down the two steps and into the sitting room. *No way.* I simply knew where the bar was set now. High. *Amazingly* high.

The moment I stepped over the threshold of the door, from the cold darkness of the room into the humid fresh air lit by waning moonlight, more than the physical atmosphere changed. Alec's body stiffened, like I'd startled him out of relaxation, and he straightened upright in the cushioned chair. He'd put on his cargo pants, which were zipped, but not buttoned.

I took the empty chair nearest me, assessing his body language: not completely closed off, but almost.

"How do you feel?" He glanced toward me. His voice rumbled out low, intonation flat, matter-of-fact. As if he'd merely asked about the weather on a blue-sky day, instead of having recolored my perception of everything in the darkness of night.

"Fine." I gave a one-shouldered shrug. As if the entire event had been no biggie.

"Bullshit," he chuckled.

"Yeah." What else could I say? Clearly, he was distancing himself. And really, nothing needed to be said—he knew. Each and every moan, gasp—and muffled scream—had broadcast loud and clear what words never would.

"You let go." His warm hand slipped into mine, and he gave it light squeeze. "You were incredible," he rasped out.

The deep, soft-spoken words resonated into my body, rippling from my head to my toes. Tension crackled in the air around us, undisturbed by the steady wind.

My breath caught as a deep ache cascaded through me, sliding downward.

I wanted him. Again. Even after hours of carnality, a dozen positions, and five orgasms, my body wanted more of the addictive drug he'd hooked me on.

Primal instincts had never ruled me before. But after a taste of what it did for me, how it made me forget, how it changed the very substance of the darkness so prevalent within me, the idea of drowning myself in feeling instead of thinking tempted me beyond reason.

Rattled on a visceral level to be left drifting in uncharted territory, I forced myself back into my mind, onto familiar ground. Scientists experimented. Maybe the occurrence was a fluke. Only further studies would prove or disprove whether or not the earth would tilt off its axis a second time. Then a third.

"Let's do it again." The words escaped before I could stop them. Before I realized that even logic had sided with my aroused body. And I couldn't be sure whether the one had influenced the other. Scientists set out to prove their theories, some with a bias toward being right and not wrong. I wanted to be right. *Very* right.

"No," he replied.

I gasped, as if he'd slapped my cheek, rattling my brain. "What?"

He withdrew his hand from mine and braced his forearms on his knees. "You wanted sex. I gave you what you wanted."

"You wanted it," I countered, unable to believe his cool detachment.

"I did," he whispered.

"You enjoyed it..." I hadn't been the only one moaning with pleasure not more than an hour ago. *This is a one-time thing...* The echo of his conditional words filtered into a brain stuck in denial.

"I did," he admitted. "But it doesn't change who I am."

"Which is?"

"No attachments. No commitments. We only have sex once. I refuse to take it further, let emotions get involved."

Before the slight down-tilt of his head, I'd glimpsed his eyes. Compassion shone in them.

I pointed to the bed in accusation. "You're telling me emotions weren't involved in there?"

"Nothing permanent. It's easier this way."

A sardonic laugh bubbled from my lips. "Figures. I get the best sex of my life and it's a one-shot deal."

"You knew anything between us would be short-lived. That's what made it appealing. For both of us."

The stinging truth of it all? He was right. "Great. So I have five more days of vacation and I have to endure knowing the highlight of my trip has already happened?"

He laughed and stood, ruffled my hair, then pressed a kiss to the crown of my head. "It's not as bad as all that. I'm going to be busy. Tomorrow night I'm needed in the field, with preparations to make before that. Go snorkeling. Explore ruins. Be on vacation." He stepped inside. Seconds later, the rumbling whir of the Nespresso machine overtook the gentle roar of the ocean.

I'd been casually dismissed.

I stood, leaned my forearms on the terrace railing, and stared out at the charcoal-colored ocean at the horizon where it met the glittering expanse of stars overhead, trying to make sense of the thought fragments dizzying my mind. Vacation hadn't even been on my radar a week ago. In a few short days, not only had Anna convinced me to entertain the idea of an uninhibited fling, I'd actually done it.

But prior to the notion of wild sex with virtual strangers, before the idea of a vacation even blinked into existence, one thing had fueled me more than anything ever had. And the dark giant who'd been slumbering deep inside me, craving vengeance for a child who'd been robbed of any semblance of a normal life, stretched, gradually coming back to life.

Alec hadn't merely awakened me sexually. He'd opened my eyes to an entire realm of possibilities I hadn't considered before.

In the past few years, I'd grown restless and unfulfilled, blindly led down a road I hadn't wanted, had never asked for. Yet now, I saw my path clearly, as if an undeniable shining beacon on the far horizon drew me in.

The air shifted, and the fine hairs on my body stood on end, sensing his presence. Without a sound, he brushed his arm against mine as he settled beside me, mirroring my stance against the railing. He cradled a small espresso cup in each hand and lifted one, offering it to me.

I took the cup, absorbing its warmth through the earthenware sides. "I'm going with you tomorrow night."

He let out a soft snort. "No, you're not."

"I have skills. I did stab you, after all." Not even a twinge of guilt about it. Hadn't realized then that it would become a negotiating point.

"Meager, at best. Nothing happens as anyone expects in an operation. You plan for a dozen contingencies, and the one you didn't think of has you scrambling for an escape route. We have a training facility, undergo months of intensive exercises, are subjected to every torture method known to man to harden us, prepare us. What do you have?"

Black belts in aikido and jiu-jitsu? Even that sounded weak to me compared to all he'd said.

135

"Determination." Which made all the difference in the world.

"Just enough to get you killed."

"*Hmmph.*" I wasn't convinced. Or maybe I didn't care. The risk of getting killed didn't sound as bad as not living. And what he'd done to me, what he'd accomplished? Was like a lungful of fresh air. And I was done suffocating. Through with drowning.

Stewing about his bullheaded obstinance, but understanding the reasoning behind it, I stared out over the ocean. An interesting shape of lights floated far out, at the horizon line.

"Is that a cruise ship?" As I watched, the shape drifted infinitesimally northward.

He nodded. "Yeah. They follow the inland channel between here and Cozumel on their way to Miami."

Another illuminated ship edged into view as it cleared the darkened peninsula to the south. A few minutes later, another appeared. Only four inches apart from our perspective, if I held up my fingers to measure, a line of ships silently glided from right to left.

"The average cruising speed of a typical ship is about twenty-two knots. How fast do you think they're going?" Idle recitation of facts and collecting more data calmed me further.

"Hmm…'bout that." He lifted his espresso cup, taking a swallow.

We watched for a while. Another four ships appeared, each roughly the same distance apart, all in a single-file line, as if pulled along by the same massive string. "Why do they sail at night?"

"It's the most profitable. They sail after passengers have returned from expensive land excursions, while everyone sleeps. Then dock at the next port of call to have them disembark and spend more money on tours and duty-free designer merchandise."

My mind rifled through the possibilities. I huffed out a laugh. "What a tourist racket. Smart businesses would have shops at the most popular ports."

He nudged my shoulder, then nodded toward our left where the land curved toward the sea. Lights glittered from structures built along it. "Like Cancun."

"Cancun," I repeated, holding it in my sights. A commercialized tourist destination. Over 700,000 in population, almost 100,000 tourists every week staying at the resorts that had sprung up like tall weeds on every vacant inch of beach overnight. In comparison, Maroma Beach was a lazy stretch of undiscovered sand.

"Just beyond the peninsula jutting out at the end of the bay. Those lights are homes located in luxury beachside communities between here and there."

Over the next half hour, we discussed various topics about Maroma Beach and her surrounding areas while we watched the long line of cruise ships disappear as they sailed northward, sipping espressos inadvisably late if we wanted any sleep, which was the last thing on my mind. No caffeine required to fuel the jacked-up excitement that pulsed through my veins.

And even though he'd taken sex off the table, with every minute that ticked by, I grew more certain that our bodies had misplaced that memo. Seemingly unaware of his actions, the back of his hand occasionally rubbed the back of mine. When I shifted my weight to the leg nearest him and my bare thigh brushed the canvas of his pants, he sucked in a breath, as if startled that my heat had seared right through the fabric.

To experiment, I leaned toward him, brushing my cheek along his biceps. The muscle flexed, and he blew out a slow breath, then swallowed hard.

Yep. He still wanted me. Even if he wouldn't admit it.

Good thing. Because my body was a riot of sparking nerves, attuned to his as if each one longed to be touched by him again. My nipples drew tight as I inhaled his masculine scent. An ache began to throb between my legs in time with my heartbeat, dull but steady, as if keeping me primed for the next round. A round that would never come.

I exhaled slowly, fully aware that I struggled right along with him.

Smug about having an undeniable effect on him, regardless of what he did to me, I shifted, testing my theory by rubbing an aching nipple against his arm.

"Where is your house?" I assumed he had one, since he'd admitted he wasn't a hotel guest.

He shifted his stance, increasing the distance between us by an inch, then nodded off right. "In a pocket community past the line of resorts to the south."

My lips twitched at his subtle defensive response, but I abandoned my taunting in favor of gaining information. "Is it on the beach?"

"Yes."

"What style is it?" I wanted to envision where he went when he left here, where he slept—know the exact location and description. "You know, in the event I decide to drop onto the terrace from a coconut tree."

"Style?" He ignored my quip and tipped the tiny espresso cup back to finish whatever remained, then turned toward me.

Shadows played across his ruggedly handsome face as the palm fronds behind me filtered the terrace lights from the adjacent building. His brows drew together, his confusion evident as he stared down at me.

I turned fully toward him and waited, enjoying the moment as I held his searching gaze. Me in his shirt. Him with his pants half-fastened. Both of us denying the electric chemistry sparking between us, out on a balcony where he'd stumbled into my world, mere feet away from where he'd rocked mine irrevocably.

I pursed my lips in thought. "You know, adobe, mission?" I couldn't think of the names of any others down in Mexico. It wasn't like I dabbled in architectural design or real estate sales. "Territorial…" The last popped into my mind, but by the time it fell from my lips, it came out slow, heavy.

His eyes widened a fraction, then he relaxed them. In slow motion, he shook his head, never saying a word, but chastising me nonetheless for my loaded tone.

He leaned closer, the heated skin of his arms brushing against mine, his chest inches from my face, forcing me to tilt my head up. "None of the above," he whispered. Then he dipped his head down, stopping his lips a hairsbreadth from mine.

I froze, waiting to see what he'd do, needing anything he'd offer, wanting all he had to give.

Only in this cat-and-mouse game we played, he'd had more practice than me. Instead of a decadent kiss, he pressed his mouth to mine, close-lipped, chaste. The brief contact only lasted a heartbeat before it vanished altogether.

Yet it seared me.

Before I processed anything further, I blinked and realized he'd left the balcony.

I rushed inside to follow.

He bent over the bed, scooping up the abandoned black blindfold and silken ties before dropping the items into his open bag on the ground. He finished zipping up his pants, threaded the button closed, and fastened his belt.

"A Japanese long house." He stepped into his boots, one foot, then the other.

"What?"

"The style." He glanced up with smug expression, clearly pleased with how he'd flustered me. His gaze dropped down to my chest. "Gonna need that shirt."

I fought the urge to narrow my eyes at him. He'd done nothing wrong. Actually, he'd done everything to me that I'd wanted and half a dozen things I'd never even imagined. And now he was moving on. Treating what had happened between us lightly, making the event exactly what it needed to be: casual.

"Fine." I pulled his shirt over my head, unabashedly

baring my nakedness. My nipples reacted to the cool air, hardening as I tossed his shirt across the ten feet that spanned between us.

His gaze swept down my body, expression pained.

That's right. Get a good look at what you're denying yourself. I didn't bother crossing my arms or hiding my body in any way. For some reason, knowing he wanted what he couldn't have, just as much as I wanted it, took the sting away from the inexplicable frustration that I struggled to tamp down.

"Will I see you again?" I knew the answer. He thought he held all the cards, but if I was to enter the world of espionage, I had to be resourceful, seize opportunity.

Or make it.

Confusion flickered over his face again before he pulled his shirt over his head. When the material fell to his hips and settled, he shot a hard look at me. He took two full breaths as we stared at each other.

"Sure." He shrugged. "Ever snorkel before?"

"No." I almost laughed. He kept throwing me off-balance. And yet, I was hungry to get started with my hidden agenda of covert spy training, eager to learn. "But I'm a quick study."

He gave me a curt nod. "It's pretty easy. Breathe. Float. Repeat."

Now I narrowed my eyes at him.

He fought a smile. "Get some sleep. I'll pick you up tomorrow afternoon at 2:00 p.m."

He didn't wait for my reply. Simply turned, picked up his bag, unlocked the two locks on the door, then left, letting the door slam shut behind him.

I grinned, jumped, and landed facedown onto the bed, thrilled at how powerful the tension remained between us. Slowly, I stretched, inhaling the scent of our sex that clung to the sheets.

I wanted more from Alec than what he'd provided in this bed.

And although he didn't know it yet, he was going to give it to me.

CHAPTER 11

After a 9:30 a.m. wakeup call, a shower, and a smaller breakfast I'd arranged, I had one of the resort's drivers take me to the hospital to visit Anna. And if I had my determined way, she'd be coming back to the resort with me, regardless of her therapeutic hot-doctor agenda.

"Back in ninety minutes?" That would give me enough time to convince her.

The driver gave me a puzzled look. *"¿Nueve minutos?"*

That sounded like nine, not ninety. I scowled, wishing I'd learned more than rudimentary Spanish in the last few years. Even with my eidetic memory, the two-hour crash course from Rosetta Stone on the last third of the flight over while Anna had slept wasn't getting me far. A mind could only remember what it was exposed to.

"¿Dos…horas?" I attempted.

He nodded rapidly. *"Sí, señorita.* I come back. Two hours."

I let out a relieved sigh. "*Sí. Gracias.*"

"*De nada.*"

When he drove off, I reentered the hospital lobby to the muted whoosh of the automatic glass doors opening and braced myself against an onslaught of unwelcome factoids that rushed into my head: In a 2011 study, over 722,000 hospital-acquired illnesses occurred in the United States that year, with approximately 75,000 deaths. In Mexico, Hepatitis A was endemic. Typhoid and rabies risks increased in rural communities. Their tuberculosis incidence is five times greater than in the United States. Noroviruses, influenza, Klebsiella…MRSA…my head spun with some of the most dangerous and common hospital pathogens.

Somehow that barrage of frightening information escaped me last time. I'd likely been too off-balance in Alec's presence and awestruck by the luxurious hospital to get lost in the minutia of a developing phobia.

Counting the floor tiles in an effort to inundate my brain with something other than mysophobic statistics, I made it to the elevator, pressed the 3 button with the back of my knuckle, got out the moment the doors opened, then beelined straight for the clear bottle of antibacterial on the nurse's station counter. I pumped a liberal squirt and fastidiously rubbed the entire surface of my hands. Twice.

Then I scanned the entire floor like Alec had done, taking note of every person, staff or not.

That's right, Spy Guy. I am *a quick study, even in your absence.*

I crossed the hall to Anna's room. Her bed was empty,

but I heard the sounds of running water behind the closed bathroom door. Suspiciously eyeing the leather couch and chair for sanitary soundness, I opted for her bed. It was available, and I only needed to touch the sheets that Anna had slept on.

As I settled myself atop the bed, a man rounded the corner, entering the room. "How's my gorgeous patient today?" The smooth baritone voice belonged to a dark head that stared down at a clipboard.

I crossed my legs at the ankles with a grin, recognizing the striking Latin doctor Alec had been talking to yesterday. "I'm fabulous, Doc. Thanks for asking."

He froze, blinked, took four steps back and double-checked the room placard. Then he tucked the clipboard under his arm, glanced at the closed bathroom door, then back at me. He cleared his throat. "We're a full service hospital: Flattery dispensed freely."

Humor. Okay. I liked him already.

The bathroom door opened and Anna came out. The doctor's face brightened several degrees as she stepped toward him with a wide smile. Then she turned and caught sight of me. "Dev!"

Hovering in the doorway, the doctor's eyes nearly popped out of his head when she bared her naked backside in the classic tie-in-the-back hospital gown she wore. She winked at me as she kept her "assets" in full view for a moment longer before climbing onto the bed next to me.

"No better bait than the accidental flash," she murmured.

"Cunning," I whispered.

She grinned, proud of her deviousness as she wrapped an arm behind my shoulder. "You're not the only one looking for a Latin fling." She kissed my cheek.

When said potential Latin fling cleared his throat again, Anna flashed him a winning smile. "So how am I looking, Doctor Escobar?"

Escobar.

My heart launched into my throat. His embroidered name had been partially obscured by a folded yellow paper in his lab coat pocket. Escobar had to be a common name, right?

Nice observation skills, Devin. I needed to step it up and be more diligent if I hoped to gain the attention of any covert organization. But Alec had been talking to the man while we'd been here. The connection couldn't be mere coincidence.

"You are beautiful, as always. I was about to ask if you'd accompany me to a party tomorrow night."

Party? An Escobar *party?* And Alec had mentioned a mission tomorrow night. A statistically improbable coincidence.

Thinking fast, I let out a soft whine. "But I haven't seen my best friend for two days."

He glanced at me. "I would be honored if you both attended."

Jackpot.

Anna gave me her patented fierce dare-to-contradict-her look, then shot him a beaming smile. "We'd love to go." Her brows drew together. "What's the attire? We didn't bring cocktail dresses."

"Let me take care of everything. You're staying at the Belmond, yes?" When Anna nodded, he pulled out a mobile phone and dialed. "*Elena. Sí. ¿Cómo estás? Muy bien. ¿Tienes dos vestidos para el baile? Mañana en el hotel, the Belmond, por favor. A las cuatro de la tarde. Perfecto. Gracias. Un momento...*"

He pulled the phone from his ear, covering the bottom portion with his other hand. "Ladies, what sizes do you wear?"

"Two." Anna replied. "Sometimes a four." Which covered both of us, even if we'd put on a few vacation pounds."

When he returned to the call to relay the information in Spanish, Anna nudged my shoulder and let out an exaggerated sigh. "I could listen to that sexy accent all day. All night..."

Her doctor's accent didn't hold a candle to Alec's—in my completely unbiased opinion.

Before I had a chance to reply, Doctor Escobar slipped his phone into his pocket. "It's all settled. My family has a seamstress who creates custom gowns for my sisters. I've arranged for her to bring a few selections to your hotel tomorrow afternoon at 4:00 p.m. Then I'll send a driver to pick you up at 8:30 p.m. and bring you to the party."

He gave a pointed look toward Anna, his dark eyebrows lifting a fraction. "And tonight?"

Anna glanced at me, then turned toward him. "With your sign-off, I'd like to be discharged this morning. Would you be willing to come to the hotel?"

"I would. My shift ends midafternoon. I'll call you afterward."

"Perfect," she replied.

With a satisfied nod, he exited the room. I watched him walk past the same spot where he and Alec had been standing and talking, laughing. Was that the reason why Alec had been so eager to drive me to the hospital yesterday? Because Escobar worked here?

The mission is always in play... The phrase Alec had used as he'd driven me to the hospital echoed into my head. Irritation at his not disclosing more about Escobar niggled at me.

"What's tonight?" I asked as I settled back against the pillows, mulling over how charming Doctor Escobar was. Note to self: charming makes great villain subterfuge.

"Our standing dinner date. He's been smuggling in Kobe beef filets and New York cheesecake instead of making me suffer through overcooked chicken and stale Jello."

Should I warn her about her doctor?

No. I didn't have enough information to go off of. And what would I tell her exactly? That I'd shacked up with a spy? That he thought her guy was a bad guy? The entire situation seemed surreal.

And then there was Alec. He'd forbidden me to participate in his mission tomorrow, and yet through a stroke of fate, I'd be attending the party he hadn't disclosed to me as an invited guest.

Did I feel obligated to tell him? No.

"It's okay, right?" She clasped our hands. "We can spend time together this afternoon."

"No, we can't. I've got a snorkeling date."

She puffed out a soft snort, but didn't argue. Apparently friends didn't interfere when it came to plans with the opposite sex. "That's fine." Her shoulder lifted in a halfhearted shrug. "I plan to be sprawled out on a beach bed sunbathing all afternoon." She angled a leg at the hip, rotating it inward. "All this hospital light has made me look pasty."

I choked out a laugh, staring at the perfectly tanned skin on the back of her calf. "Anna, you haven't looked 'pasty' a day in your life."

My thoughts drifted to Alec and his bronzed skin, and how I'd be seeing plenty of sun along with plenty of him all afternoon. How easy would it be to keep my new party-invite information from him? The master deceiver conning the master spy?

A smile played at the corner of my lips. I looked forward to the challenge.

CHAPTER 12

Water sluiced off my skin in tiny rivulets as oxygen flooded my lungs on a deep inhale. My body floated to the surface, weightless. On my back, ears just submerged beneath the gentle rolling waves, I heard muted sounds: distant high-pitched cracks, lower booming thumps.

On a slow exhale, my entire form sank with every lost gaseous molecule. With an effort to balance my breaths, I swayed in time with the rhythm of the sea, in perfect buoyant harmony.

I wondered at the discovery.

Had I swam before? Sure. When I was younger. I'd raced from one side of an Olympic sized swimming pool to the other for better time, to develop another of the many skills I'd been collecting in my armory.

But never to just...*exist*.

Eyes gently closed, sensations affected me from every possible avenue. A salty taste lingered on my lips. The roots of my hair tickled as waves swept my floating locks to and fro. Cool water lapped at my skin as the warm afternoon sun radiated down, heating the front of my body through the crystalline Caribbean Sea. It was as if the elements all vied for my attention.

Guard down, my thoughts diverted away from my goal of learning all I could in the short training time Alec had unknowingly granted me. I paused to let my new sensory world say hello.

The man who'd stumbled onto my balcony had awakened me in an unexpected way.

And I was overcome by all that my newfound perspective offered.

With a heavier exhale, determined not to miss anything while immersed in a rare nature-epiphany, I let my lower body sink and scissored my legs, catching traction against the water with my fins. I kept my head above water, mask perched above my forehead, snorkel dangling alongside my face.

All the while, through a pair of dark sunglasses, Alec focused his attention toward the shoreline, oblivious to my mini mental fieldtrip. Or simply not caring.

I waited until my forward momentum glided me alongside him, then coasted to a halt inches away. "So what changed your mind? What made you include me in your 'preparations' today?"

If he registered my question, not one facial muscle betrayed his reaction. His body bobbed upright, his stone face scanning the half dozen houses sparsely dotted along the beach a hundred and fifty yards directly in front of us. A barely visible cadence to his movement was generated by a methodic flap of his fins with a drag coefficient slight enough to keep his two-hundred-pound lean body perfectly upright.

"You wanted to come. It's proving useful to me."

Amused at his pragmatism, I tilted my head and fought a smile. "In what way?"

"You're the perfect cover."

How flattering. "Why? Because I'm a mildly attractive tourist, and you're a local, showing me the sights? Hoping to get into my pants?"

The corner of his lips twitched. "You're an incredibly attractive tourist. And I've already been in your pants."

My body flushed warm at the reminder. "Now, your sole focus is the mission?"

"Yes."

I floated onto my back again, baring my bikini-clad body before him. "And how's that working out for you?" I stretched my arms overhead, mimicking the position he'd bound and ordered me into, on a bed not so far from here.

Silence followed as an angling wave lifted and lowered us in unison. Had he ignored me altogether? I glanced upward to find him staring, eyes shielded by those sunglasses, expression unreadable.

"Harder than you could imagine," he groused.

"Good." Pleased with his answer, I blew out a held breath and kicked my feet, propelling me a comfortable distance away from him. "Fun as this snorkeling ruse is, I'm glad I'm not the only one suffering. I keep imagining all the positions

Kat Bastion with Stone Bastion

you took me in, how many others we missed..."

His deep chuckle echoed along the surface of the water. "Clever."

"*Mmm-hmm...*" Wasn't every day I had a man to tease. And now that I had one as a captive audience, I intended to take full advantage.

He removed his sunglasses and secured them somewhere below the water again. Then he spit onto the lens of his mask, spread the saliva over the inner surface to prevent fogging, and put it on, securing it over his eyes. "And the snorkeling isn't a ruse. Follow me."

Once I quickly repeated the same mask prep, I finned after him. It took about ten minutes, but eventually we reached the crescent shape of a secluded little-known section of reef that thrived about a dozen feet below the surface. Brightly colored fishes teemed all around us. Blue tangs darted in and out of skeletal coral. A sage-colored Queen triggerfish with electric blue stripes swam by, delicate side fins fluttering. One anemone had gossamer tentacles tipped with tiny glowing white dots, resembling oceanic baby's breath.

We swam along the curving arc of the hidden reef, stopping occasionally to watch a fleeting episode of nature unfold before our eyes, like when a white-spotted eagle ray glided by. We even paused to watch a critically endangered hawksbill turtle forage along the reef for sponges.

Alec suddenly grabbed my hand. I blinked and glanced at him, barely perceiving his dark eyes through the shield of his mask. My gaze drifted down to his lips wrapped around the mouthpiece of his snorkel. Instantly, my thoughts flew to images of his lips wrapped around...other things...

But then he pointed, and I shifted my attention, following his arm. A young luminescent blue-green Caribbean reef octopus hovered over the ivory sand, swirling up tiny eddies in its wake as it undulated beneath us before disappearing into a shadowy crevice in the coral.

Without releasing my hand, he led me forward through the water toward land. Only instead of beaching ourselves, we entered a sea channel and swam inland.

The warmth of the sun gave way to the cooler dappled shade of tree canopies. Dense mangroves with broad emerald leaves and gnarled roots lined the inlet. The mixture of fresh and salt water alternated in random currents, slick, then less viscous, cool, then warmer.

When we stopped entirely and broke the surface, I glanced skyward. Mouth slowly dropping open, I slid my mask onto my forehead as I scanned my gaze up...up.

A massive white marble house towered above us, perched on a rocky outcropping, blocking out the sunlight as it overtook the expanse of sky from left to right. "Let me guess," I whispered. "Escobar."

"Good guess."

Before I could voice any of the questions that sprang to mind, including the safety and wisdom of our presence here, so close to a dangerous man whose security would likely shoot the sitting-duck snorkelers who dared stare up at his house a moment too long, he finned ahead again with powerful thrusts of his legs. I rushed forward in pursuit in an effort to stick close by him.

As we progressed into the shaded inlet and toward the northern edge of the channel, a stronger, cooler current tugged at us. Before long, we struggled against a powerful flow right up against the limestone-rock foundation of the house.

He pulled down his mask, securing it over his eyes. I did the same with mine, then followed him as he dove under.

Even in the darkened shadows as I searched along the light-colored foundation of the house, I identified a dark, circular opening, three yards down under the surface. Irregular in shape, slightly wider than tall, it was the source of the newer current that buffeted us.

When we surfaced, we propped our masks onto our foreheads again.

"The underground river," I whispered with a stunned exhalation. It was one thing to imagine the natural phenomenon sustaining a hydroelectric engine, quite another to feel its impressive nonstop flow pulsing in real time around us.

He gave me a single hard nod, then grabbed my hand again. "Stop kicking."

In unison, we stopped fighting the current and floated, letting the water carry us back out to sea. I stared behind us, down the inlet, watching as the sun reflected off a meandering waterway that stretched far beyond Escobar's house while pondering the quiet power of water. The underground river had carved a path through limestone over millions of years to create the tunnel beneath Escobar's house. The seawater flowed with the tides against landmass to gain an indomitable foothold inland.

As we approached the mouth of the inlet again, the last tree canopy vanished and the sun bathed us in uninterrupted warmth once again. Yet another example of the world's irony: An idyllic afternoon on the outside—bright blue-sky day, glittering turquoise waters—concealed dangerous complexities that lurked just below the surface, detectable only if you knew what to look for.

The afternoon and I had a lot in common.

Without another word, we secured our masks back onto our faces and surveyed the coral reef once more. Minutes stretched by as the afternoon lazed on. We had donned our "spy" personas again, cloaking us in the believable cover of tourists exploring the second largest coral reef in the world.

Eventually we made our way back to the boat. By the lowered angle of the sun, I figured we'd only been out in the water an hour and a half. Plenty of time.

When he locked his hands on my forearms and pulled me safely onto the teak boards of the thirty-foot speedboat he'd supposedly "borrowed," I steadied myself.

I blurted out the question hovering on my tongue. "Come with me on a sunset cruise." Okay. So what had been meant as an invitation sounded more like a command.

His eyes narrowed. "A sunset cruise?"

"Sure. Like you said, I'm the perfect cover. And Anna bailed on the cruise we'd booked to have dinner with her doctor instead."

"Escobar?" He frowned.

Ahhh, so he's not thrilled about that tidbit of information. "So it *is* the same Escobar."

"His son," Alec ground out.

I blinked, utterly confused.

One second, I stood in the coolness of his shadow. The next, the glare of the sun blinded my eyes. I stumbled a couple of steps to the side with a rocking wave, then spun around to find his back toward me. He stopped at the console and flipped a switch. A low whirring sound emitted from the engine compartment for about twenty seconds before he turned the key and fired up the engines.

Intrigued to see the almighty spy who had it all figured out flustered by my inviting him to an event he hadn't predicted, I followed him, then grasped the handhold on the dash as he pushed the throttles forward, sending us skimming through the water.

"Well?" I prodded as we both stared forward over the bow. We had barely over an hour to shower and get ready. Which gave us just enough time to meet at the boat launch.

His gaze never wavered from the horizon as we began the ten-minute high-speed ride toward the resort. "I'll be at your place at 5:00 p.m."

The satisfied nod I gave was as much for my benefit as his. I'd convinced him to see me again, advancing the covertly obtained training I yearned to continue. And he gained more reconnaissance time for his precious mission, one he'd adamantly insisted I not take part in.

If only he knew just how stealthy I'd quickly learned to be.

"How *exactly* is this a sunset cruise?" I scanned the crowd of twenty-seven people who milled around, many holding complimentary pink rum punch that sloshed in squat clear plastic cups.

"It's a cruise. At sunset." His arm wrapped innocently around my back.

But the hand resting not-so-innocently on my hip taunted heated memories to the surface. I blew out a measured breath, attempting to exude his same cool demeanor. "Thank you, Master of the Obvious."

On were those sunglasses again, obscuring his dark eyes that expressed so much. He stared in the direction of Escobar's house once more. Although no amusement pulled at the corners of his mouth, I knew his dry sense of humor lurked beneath the surface of his steadfast persona.

"I checked with the captain as we boarded," he offered. "We sail out to sea, about half a mile, then run the coast until the sun sets over jungle to the west."

With how the concierge had described the experience to Anna and me, I'd expected to board a sailboat, yet was surprised to find us on an enormous double-hulled catamaran. I curved my fingers around the top portion of a railing made of rubber-coated wire cable that stretched along the side of the catamaran like a flexible split-rail fence.

His casual grip around me tightened with the increased movement of the watercraft, and I eased sideways against him, welcoming the support. Even though the heat of his skin permeating through our linen clothing made my breath catch. Even though it triggered more erotic memories of us connected together without any clothing whatsoever.

On another slow exhale, I forced my attention away from the lingering erotic images, and watched the jungle-fringed ivory beaches slip by before they faded away as we angled out toward sea. Gradually, the glow in the northeastern sky transformed into shades of peach, and Alec guided me to face toward the southwest. The coral sun shimmered over the slim landmass before it began to dip below the jungle-canopy tree line.

And as slow as the sun had always seemed when it inched across the sky during daytime, its speed of descent at the moment of sunset was remarkable, the fiery orb disappearing by degrees with every blink of my eye.

Once the sun became a mere pinkish sliver, threatening to slip into the shadowy expanse, Alec gently turned my body fully toward the ocean, his solid chest pressed against my shoulders. The rough stubble of his cheek scratched over my skin as he bent down, warm breath fanning over my jawline.

Caught off guard, I closed my eyes, inhaling a deep breath to try to calm my eager body. Which resulted in his intoxicating scent wafting through my nostrils, exciting me further.

"Look up," he whispered.

Lost in a freefall of sensation, I obeyed, tilting my face skyward.

An explosion of color radiated overhead. Wispy clouds I hadn't noticed earlier sprang to dazzling life, bright pink vapor forming heavenly shapes, like angels.

A cramp burned at the base of my throat and the threat of tears stung my eyes.

Raw beauty had snuck past my solid defenses. I'd relegated myself to cold darkness for so long, yet now I felt myself drawn toward the light—its attraction: undeniable. Without warning, thoughts of my sister flooded in as my gaze drifted off toward the faraway horizon. Was Geneva out there somewhere in the ether? Would she squeal with joy at the sight?

Unaware of the action, my hands had encircled the muscular forearm that Alec had wrapped around my waist to steady me. I tightened my grip, wanting more of his grounding effect than to merely hold me upright. I needed the man who'd awakened me to keep me firmly planted in reality.

He had no idea that he'd been instrumental in reintroducing me to a world that I'd shunned out of necessity. Purposefully lost, cocooned in the safety of sensory deprivation, I'd hardened my defenses for years, convincing myself the sheltered action had been necessary to prepare for some future battle.

More than a decade of sharpening mental skills like everyone had expected of me, accompanied by years of physical training that I'd reasoned would balance my mental-acuity trials, had led me to this pivotal moment: when a man I hadn't expected slowly removed all of my carefully placed armor, allowed me to ease the pain incrementally, helping me heal.

I sucked in a shaky breath as he brought the protective strength of his arms further around me, shielding me from the whipping wind. I leaned back into his hold, letting him take over and support us both.

All too fast, the cloud-angels turned orange, then grayed, fading into the backdrop of a darkening twilight sky. The catamaran changed course, and its giant sails billowed with captured wind, speeding us away from the fragment of beauty we'd been privileged to witness.

The choppy waves turned a steely blackish blue as nightfall descended. And with the transformation from day to night, my spirit gained in strength, fueled by the comforting familiarity of darkness.

Nature had its balance. Hot and cold. Bright and dark. Life and death. And in a momentary glimpse, on a cruise only meant to prolong my exposure to a spy to gain training and access to a clandestine organization, I'd gained more perspective, found greater equilibrium.

Left to my surreal thoughts, letting them take root into the integral, vulnerable part of me that I'd kept hidden from the world—from myself—for so long, the features of land grew in size and clarity. Soon we sailed past the reef again, angling toward shore in full view of Escobar's impressive white marble house.

With quick purpose, we commandeered a private section of railing. Alec stepped to my left, but kept an arm draped behind me, hand resting on the backside of my hip. He stared intently at the shoreline again, expression hardened to granite.

If he glared with enough intensity, would lasers erupt through those dark sunglasses and scorch his evil target from the earth? "How can you even see with those things on?"

The hint of a smile played on his face. He dropped his head until his lips brushed the top of my ear. "I see infinitely better with them."

They were the same sunglasses he'd worn when we'd snorkeled. In fact, he'd only removed them to put his mask on. "Are they prescription?" I'd noticed him squinting when not wearing the sunglasses, but maybe he needed them for distance.

"In a way." He pulled them off, then slowly positioned them over my face. I closed my eyes while he carefully tucked the thin rubber-coated arms over my ears.

When I opened my eyes, I gasped. An entire computer array flashed across the lenses. Data streamed to the left: coordinates. And as I moved my head, scanning down the beach, the feedback altered, providing longitude, latitude, and altitude. On the right, additional information appeared: air temperature and targeted surface temperatures.

Facing back toward Escobar's house, I focused on it. All of a sudden, the structure grew in size. And the more I focused, the larger it appeared, until my enhanced view allowed me to spy right through the large plate glass dining room window, revealing a chef in a white hat serving four guests at a long teak table. I assumed the man at the head of the table was Escobar. Experimenting, I concentrated harder, sharpening further. The sunglasses zoomed in on his dinner plate: rack of lamb, baby carrots, and tiny wild mushrooms.

"Oh. My. God," I whispered under my breath, easing back the focus to observe the house as a whole again. "These are astounding."

"Now you know what I used to occupy myself with while snorkeling—when trying to distract my thoughts away from you."

I fought a smile. "I'm never giving these back, then." When he chuckled and reached for them, I turned my head, leaning away. I grasped his free hand and threaded our fingers together to keep him from stealing them off my face before I was ready. Then I shrugged. "Shouldn't we test your willpower without the glasses? We wouldn't want basic instinct to win out over clear reason."

He bent down again until his hot breath danced down my neck. "Is that *all* you think it is? Basic instinct? Carnal drive? Primal urges..." His voice lowered, cadence slowing as he laced each successive word with heavier erotic undertones.

I swallowed, painfully aware of my nipples drawing tight against my thin linen top, attempting to ignore a taunting ache that seeped down through my body, sparking nerve endings as they sizzled to life. When I sucked in a shaky breath, he escalated things, sliding the hand that had been parked innocently on my hip forward. He possessively dug his fingertips into the tender flesh on front of my hipbone and pulled me flush against him.

His growing erection imprinted against my backside, making its presence irrefutably known from the upper cleft of my butt cheeks, over my tailbone, and up against the small of my back.

"Behave," I hissed, even though I loved the game as much as he did. And in analysis, the pummeling of willpower didn't only test him, it also steeled me.

He ignored my warning entirely and slid his thumb underneath the loose waistband of my linen shorts. He began to rub lazy circles over my skin, stoking a hotter ache between my thighs.

I leaned forward, interrupting his teasing. "Something's happening."

"What?" His hand froze, grip tightening as he mirrored my movement, leaning forward.

"Escobar left his guests at the table. He's only taken a few bites of food," I whispered. "He glanced at his watch right before he rounded the corner. He's vanished."

"Maybe he's making a phone call."

I panned the view out, gaining perspective of the entire house again. "There." A light turned on in the first room down the hall.

"His office." He squinted, watching the house but not asking for the binocular sunglasses.

I returned them anyway; I'd seen enough of the impressive technology. And Alec was officially the one doing reconnaissance.

Near enough to shore to see the house unaided by technology, I watched our target with him. I grinned at the instinctive thought. *Our* target. Another light flared on, in the adjacent room. The first one flashed off. Seconds later, a third one positioned two rooms over turned on. Then a fourth illuminated down below.

"Huh." I narrowed my eyes in thought. "Did anyone else leave the dinner table?"

He gave a slight headshake. "No. All three are carrying on

an animated conversation. The wives are laughing; Martinez excels at flirting."

Ah. So Alec knows the dinner guests.

Another few lights glowed on, this time on the lower level. I cocked my head, analyzing. "Must be staff going from room to room. Maybe they're lighting candles."

We sailed away, running parallel to the shoreline and heading back toward my hotel. Alec grunted in reply, unable to maintain a head-on view into the windows any longer. From our growing distance, all we could see was the occasional room light up.

Near-total darkness had fallen by the time Alec loosened his hold on me and pocketed his sunglasses. The magic of our heated moment had dissipated, lost in our focused observation of others.

Great. On our excursion, his spontaneous covert reconnaissance (and my spy training, unbeknownst to Alec) had only uncovered mundane staff habits. Not a golden nugget of information, but gathered facts nonetheless, filed away with the discovery of an underground river tunnel's position during our snorkeling expedition. All in all, a productive spy day—clandestine acts, his and mine.

"Don't suppose we're having dinner together," I muttered, suspecting the answer. His mood had cooled with the temperatures. Our cruise and allotted time together rapidly spiraled to a close.

"No." His tone flattened.

The perfunctory rejection didn't matter. Obligatory, with the rules he followed. A testament of loyalty to his employer and the almighty mission.

Even so, although our teasing each other all day had become a sport of sorts, we'd recklessly engaged in more than harmless flirting. We'd had a taste of the explosiveness of our chemistry. To tempt fate further would risk greater attachment, involve emotions, neither of which we could afford. And I understood the reasoning.

Alec had a mission to accomplish, one he'd been clear I could play no part in. But with subtle urging, he'd relented and allowed us this brief time together.

I'd formed my own mission: increase our time together, exponentially. Agenda hidden.

CHAPTER 13

"Okay. Spill it."

Anna's curt demand made me spin back around to face her.

I cast her an unamused look. "You first."

Doctor Escobar's promised seamstress brought over a third dress for me to try on from her rack of seven selections. And after Anna's five "mandatory" hours of primping in the resort's world-renowned spa—Swedish massages, exotic sugar scrubs, pedicures, manicures, and finally our hair shampooed with organic concoctions and professionally blown out—a simple dress in ice-blue silk glimmered like a bright light at the end of a long grooming tunnel.

And as the divine material cascaded down my sugar-polished skin, my fortified cynical walls weakened. In spite of the best efforts of the darkest parts of me, I began to feel beautiful, transformed in a way I wouldn't have believed if someone had told me a pretty exterior would have a soul-warming quality.

But the ball-gown-window-dressing hadn't been the only cause. Recent events had compounded the effect. Such as the enormous effort Anna had expended in making our impromptu girl's day momentous; we'd been apart for the entire first half of our vacation, after all. But even more important, my coveted disguise had grown more complete as pieces I hadn't been aware were missing had begun to fall into place—Alec...the enticement of espionage. As expert as I'd become in hiding behind my façade of civility and calm, opportunity had finally shone down, enabling me to take my needed subterfuge in the world to a whole new level.

I frowned, common sense jarring my mind. Fun and pretty didn't suit me. Forgetting my past, even for a moment, was a slippery slope. Cloaking myself by playing pretend, but actually believing in it—even for a second—risked me falling into a numbing state of oblivious denial.

"What do you think of this one, Dev?"

Jolted from my philosophical thoughts, I took a deep breath and stepped out fully from the temporary screen I'd been hiding behind. Anna pivoted in front of the trifold mirror, examining herself from every angle in her sleek ruby gown. As I watched her, warmth seeped back in, nudging me away from the edge of the dark abyss I'd teetered on a split second ago. "Looks like it was custom made for you," I replied with stark honesty.

The rich material shimmered as she walked away from the mirror, pivoted after a few feet, then returned to watch her trio of reflections as she approached. Our "dressing room" had been set up in the lavish dining room of the resort before they opened for dinner. The seamstress had insisted upon the bright wide-open setting; its natural light radiated in from the windows, and the small dance floor allowed enough room to strut back and forth.

"And mine?" I played the part, slowly twirling for her.

Anna's eyes widened as she shifted her attention toward me. Her mouth fell open on a drawn-out gasp. "Devin, you… you look stunning."

My gaze drifted toward the mirror behind her, and she stepped aside. Diminutive pale-blue ribbon straps skimmed over my shoulders, then attached to a matching draped bodice. The wispy silk clung to my breasts, hugged my waist, then slid over my hips before dropping in a straight line to brush over the tops of my sparkling emerald-painted toes. I turned and glanced over my shoulder to examine the plunging back and nodded, satisfied the material covered my "assets."

She pursed her lips as she circled around me. "Beautiful. And those shoes!" With narrowed eyes, she glared at me through the mirror. "I never want to hear another harassing word about the necessity of a separate suitcase for designer footwear. You never know when the occasion warrants."

I bit my lip to keep from laughing. With her smartass tone, she'd begun to sound like me. And as I pointed my foot out from the floor-length hem and rotated my heel up, revealing thin sparkling silver straps that braided over my toes, I had to agree with her.

"You're evading the topic," I observed. She couldn't have forgotten. We'd been talking about her favorite subject: men.

"Oh? How perceptive of you." With a flourish of shining fabric, Anna disrobed while I began to do the same. We still needed to eat a light dinner and apply makeup, neither of which would be getting anywhere near our borrowed evening gowns. The moment my dress settled on its hanger, Anna stole it from me. "We'll take these two, Elena. *Gracias.*"

"Tit for tat," I continued. "You tell. I tell." I gestured between our half-naked bodies before we put our sundresses back on. "How this whole friend thing works."

Friends. A foreign concept before Anna had barged into my life by plucking that roommate-needed flyer from the bulletin board. With her boisterous personality, it had been nearly impossible not to let her in to some degree, let someone in for the first time.

And yet, even though Anna was the only person I'd let past some of my shields, I still kept layers of protection with her. Hadn't ever wanted to completely open myself up to anyone.

Until Alec...

Shaken by the unnerving realization, I furrowed my brow.

"Fine." She shot me a secretive smile as she stepped out of her Oscar de la Renta shoes, lowering her height four inches.

"Wait." I stared at her ankle, which still had greenish bruising on the surface. "How the hell do you plan to walk in those skyscraper heels?"

"Ankle brace, if needed." She reached up and plucked

an item dangling from her corner of the dressing screen, showing me the beige elastic brace. "I plan to have my doctor's hands-on care most of the night, anyway."

I shot her a skeptical look. But then I shook my head, huffed out a soft laugh, and gave her my typical smile, sliding easily back into the persona I'd worn for so long. I needed her to buy into my continued ruse; a distracted Anna at the party would give me free reign to carry out my plan, whatever that turned out to be. "Just don't fall again. Our agenda is party only, no hospitals."

"Yes, Momma Dev," she lilted in singsong, rolling her eyes.

Good. We'd assumed our typical roles: me chiding her inadvisable actions, her bristling at my incontrovertible wisdom.

I gave her a brief nod. "Okay, back to topic. Why'd Doctor Escobar drop you off so early last night?" Exhausted from snorkeling and sailing in the warm sun while making my mental-chess moves, I'd been half asleep when she'd returned, my only response to her entering the room a pillow-muffled grunt.

I'd actually been surprised she hadn't prodded me about Alec during our day's primping. But then, we'd had no less than two spa attendants within a two-foot radius of us all afternoon. Now we had relative privacy as Elena packed up her creations, out of earshot.

"His name is Miguel," Anna offered.

Miguel Escobar. I mentally filed that factoid away.

She eased closer, resting a hip on the edge of a round

dining table that had already been set, crystal water and wine glasses arranged over a white tablecloth. "And I came home early last night because he was on call with the hospital and an emergency pulled him away." Then she leaned forward, voice lowered to a conspiratorial level. "But on the way home, we did get *busy* in the back of the limo."

"*How* busy?" I arched a suspecting brow as I slipped on my flat sandals.

"*Very* busy." Her lips curved into a devious smile. "But I left him wanting much more than a fifteen-minute ride." She bent down, hooked her fingers into the back straps of our designer shoes, then stood with a pair dangling from each hand as she crossed her arms, staring pointedly at me. "Now you. Spill it. I know something happened between you and that Latin sex god."

I huffed out a laugh. "Latin sex god?"

Now one of her perfectly sculpted eyebrows arched in accusation. "Well, is he?"

"First of all, he's not 'Latin' anything, he's a Spaniard." Then I let out a long sigh, roping an arm around my closest friend, my only friend, as we left the five-star restaurant to make our way back to our room through the winding paths of the tropical resort.

"And yes," I added. "He *definitely* is." Memories flared into my mind of positions…sensations.

My pulse jumped, skin flushing. I sucked in a deep breath, attempting to stem my instant physiological response.

Psychologically? I had the sudden urge to make Alec break his "one-time" rule.

CHAPTER 14

Three-and-a-half hours later, after a short ride in a luxurious Escalade sent by Anna's doctor, the driver assisted us from the vehicle and escorted us down a long stone walkway that had a black carpet running lengthwise. On either side, large opaque hurricane lanterns on iron stands glowed with flickering light every ten feet, marking the edge of where a vast dark nothingness began.

Uneasy about waltzing into a scenario with unknown escape routes, I strolled toward one side as we walked to get a better look. My stomach dropped when I reached the edge. We were on a narrow catwalk, the tiniest bridge over a yawning chasm. With a steadying breath, I scanned up the side of the expansive marble-and-glass house that I'd only observed from the water, both in it and on it. Instinctual fear took hold, seizing my lungs.

But then I forced in another deep breath. Common sense told me the drop could only be down to sea level, some thirty-five feet. But that fall could still kill a person. And if the owner was as villainous as purported, he'd probably trenched a moat. And filled it with crocodiles.

So no catwalk sprinting in four-inch heels to escape. And no jumping out of windows.

After taking measured steps backward toward the relative safety of the black carpet, I hurried to catch up to Anna and the driver while taking in the palatial structure towering above us that seemed infinitely more imposing up close and personal.

As we walked through an echoing entrance hall and entered a main gallery, I craned my neck upward through a massive atrium-like space. Open balconies circled around us, stretching several levels up. Polished marble floors and gleaming glass windows were interrupted in perfect ratio by an occasional exotic orchid on a pedestal or a delicate arching palm in a corner. In the center of the back wall, a three-story sheet of water cascaded down, shimmering over thousands of tiny iridescent tiles until it splashed into mist over jagged rocks that were artfully arranged in a shallow pool at the bottom.

Champagne glasses glided by, perched on balanced trays held by waiters in formal attire. The male guests sported tuxes worn in an endless variety of styles, including their matching neckwear. One wore a wide crimson silk bow tie. Another, an opalescent cravat. A third man's neck was graced with a diamond-studded triangular bolo tie, its two gleaming black braids dangling over a pintucked shirt that draped as long as his tuxedo jacket.

Women outnumbered the men two-to-one and outshone them in equal measure. Sleek colorful gowns swayed as they moved. Fabrics shimmered. Diamonds sparkled.

"Look, there's Miguel." Anna began weaving through the crowded room right as her doctor caught sight of her.

I remained where I stood, scanning faces, watching as tight political smiles battled for genuine laughter. A quick headcount projected two hundred fifty guests in attendance in the main gallery. A not-so-subtle security force lined the perimeter: black suits instead of tuxes, harsh countenances with no smiles and focused eyes.

My attention drifted to the security guards' suit jackets. The way they carried themselves and moved, I surmised they carried concealed weapons beneath. Had one of those men shot Alec? I swallowed hard, suspecting they wouldn't hesitate to shoot a spy, official or not.

A waiter paused in front of me, hovering his tray of Champagne in polite offering.

I shook my head. "No, thank you."

With Alec's mission unknown, I needed to stay sharp, not risk alcohol clouding my judgment. Remaining vigilant, I continued to assess the room, analyzing each guest, identifying every potential threat or asset.

Anna and Miguel had met together on the other side of the expansive room, crowding close in intimate conversation near a marble pillar. A pair of guests near them struck me as Indian dignitaries: the woman demure beneath flowing layers of shimmering lilac silk, her man proud beside her in a long dark-amethyst brocade overcoat.

Verifying a forming theory, I analyzed the crowd once more. Familiar faces began to register: the prime minister of Egypt, the sheikh of Dubai, the prime minister of Canada.

Tonight's function was no mere party. It was an assemblage of some of the most influential people in the world—all gathered under one roof, on one night. A distinction among the security personnel began to appear; not all lined the perimeter, many wore varying lapel pins, which identified them to their respective world leader. Those without lapel pins? Had to be Escobar's.

Notably absent, however, were the leaders of the world's behemoth global superpowers, Russia, China, and the United States. Not a coincidence?

With my growing awareness, the magnitude of the event pressed in even as it countered the heaviness with buoyant excitement. I blew out a slow breath. The stakes of a game I didn't yet understand the rules of suddenly ratcheted higher.

Then, as if to keep my whole essence in perfect balance, the darkness hidden deep inside me rose to the surface, cynical as ever. The people around me weren't good in all aspects, many not on any level. All held positions so powerful, corruption became inevitable. None wore masks, yet in the entire majestic room before me stood the great masquerade. Behind the shellac of outer beauty, lay the ugliness of inherent evil, where loyalties went to the highest bidder and human lives were expendable currency.

The cold tendrils of my darkest thoughts grounded me, reminded me who I was, set the pretty superficial world into proper perspective again—untainted by the falsity of rose-colored glasses.

All of a sudden, my wandering gaze froze. My train of thought derailed completely.

Alec.

He entered from a hallway on the far side of the room. A large dark-featured man walked closely beside him as they spoke rapidly. The man laughed, nodded, then composed his expression as nearby guests turned his way. A wave rippled through the crowd, in movement and hushed whispers, as everyone turned with accelerating swiftness toward the new arrivals.

All except me.

Stunned temporarily immobile, I stared at Alec. All logical thought vanished.

A heartbeat later, his gaze landed on me. His eyes narrowed. A muscle in his jaw tensed. The slight movement of his arms suggested he'd slid his hands into his pants pockets. Then he tilted his head ever so slightly.

Unable to stop myself, I drifted forward. Drawn to him in a way I didn't fully understand, the tether between us pulled taut, unrelenting. In those stretched seconds, nothing else mattered. He'd become everything. Addictive. Magnetic.

Dangerous.

A faint warning bell clanged at the edge of my awareness, but it went unheeded. Regardless of what little I knew about him, the daunting stature of the man beside him, the combined deadly power of all the rulers around me, I fell prey to him, undeniably attracted.

As the distance between us narrowed, when only twenty feet remained, then fifteen, ten, five, his imposing companion's attention shifted toward me, lips twitching as he stared at me. Then he swung his gaze toward Alec. A full-blown smirk curled his lips as he arched a heavy menacing brow. "Well, I'd introduce the two of you, but I haven't had the honor of meeting the goddess shining brightly among our sea of mortals." He stared hard at Alec, narrowing his eyes. "And I get the sense you've already met."

Alec never wavered his gaze from mine. Only gave the man a short nod. "She's a guest at the Belmond."

"We met a few days ago," I said. A smile played at the corners of my lips as I stared at Alec and taunted him with the memory.

"Bumped into each other," he added, playing the game.

"Crashed would be more accurate."

"Indeed." His face tilted down a fraction, gaze holding steady with mine.

As the tone avalanched into heavy innuendo, a hot flush crept up my neck. Amusement sparked in Alec's eyes, as if he enjoyed knowing where my thoughts had fallen. I gave him a smug half-grin, pleased his mind had landed there too.

The man beside him cleared his throat.

Alec immediately broke the connection we had, turning toward him. "Forgive my rudeness. This beautiful woman is Devin Hill. Devin, this is Alfredo Escobar."

The father. *Our target.*

I instantly chastised myself for not remembering the man we'd viewed through those high-tech sunglasses, not recognizing the physical resemblance to Miguel, and not picking up on the cues from the commotion in the room through my Alec-induced blinding haze. Then with as much casualness as I could muster, I reassessed the man beside Alec.

Tall and broad, handsome in an understated way, confident, yet unpretentious, Alfredo Escobar didn't appear evil. He didn't even seem unpleasant. Powerful? Yes. But in a charismatic way.

Damn. As the realization hit me, I let out a slow breath. His son seemed equally as charming. So was Anna in danger, or wasn't she?

Who was the real villain? Rifling back through my memories, I realized Alec hadn't clarified. He had reacted negatively to the mention of Miguel.

Could our target be both men?

Escobar reached his hand out toward me, his calculating gaze locked on to mine. Uncertain I wanted the man to touch me, yet willing to do whatever necessary to play the part in our charade, become the secret agent I yearned to be, I lifted my hand on a steady inhalation.

Flesh slid across flesh. His skin felt surprisingly warm, his grip solid. In grand gesture, he bent down and brushed his lips over the back of my hand in a kiss. Soft. Polite. Not in any way the repulsive sensation one would expect from a… megalomaniac—an astute extrapolation with the power of the world he'd amassed in one location tonight.

"Clearly our local resorts attract the most exotic of creatures." His tone had lowered, thick accented voice gravelly. "A true pleasure to meet you."

Engaging in proper social protocol, I canted my head

toward him as he released my hand. "The pleasure is mine." Not entirely a lie. Getting close to a man who would serve as a worthy adversary held a certain satisfaction.

None of my intentions or white lies mattered as I played my role in the great masquerade. Only my dark truths that I honored in recognition and faithful duty were of any significance, even if I couldn't quite define a purpose for them.

"I agree, Father." Miguel and Anna stepped into view from our right, his arm wrapped possessively around her waist. "Their beauty has no measure or equal. We are indeed blessed tonight."

Anna stared up into Miguel's eyes, joy radiating on her face.

Oh, yeah. Anna's in definite danger.

In spite of my misgivings, I still had no warning for her. Hadn't yet quantified the threat, identified their intentions. But I planned to gather as much information as I could tonight. With or without one handsome spy guy's help.

Before I registered the movement, Escobar, the father, spun around and sidled up next to my open side, leaning down as his gaze swept across the room. "I know the secrets of everyone here."

Oh, do you? That Alec is a spy? As nonchalant as possible, after mimicking Escobar's sweeping gaze, my attention landed on Alec. His focus remained on the crowd, expression inscrutable.

And what about enigmatic me?

I turned toward Escobar, challenge rising hot and fast

inside me as I narrowed my eyes. "Tell me a secret."

He held my gaze, staring down at me with intense calculation. Did he know things about me, or was he trying to read me? Unfazed, used to being analyzed and categorized, I held my ground. My vault was locked up tight.

Escobar's attention shifted to Alec for a brief moment, almost a beat too long, then rotated back out to the crowd.

Did he know things about us? About me...about Alec? Alec had been shot at, after all. And obviously they were friends, a pertinent fact Alec had decided to omit. Had Escobar realized who Alec was? Was Alec something other than he'd professed himself to be...to me?

Keeping his tone just above a whisper, Escobar nodded at a gentleman who was flirting with a woman in a glittering sapphire dress. "Our playboy prime minister? Despite public affection toward grown women, he has a predilection for playing with boys."

A creepy shiver chilled my blood at the thought. Escobar spoke of it as if divulging the weather forecast.

"And our prime minister of Greece?" He nodded toward a handsome man who leaned forward amid a crowd of five other men, as if telling a lurid story. "He's got a secret economic weapon certain to reverse the tides of power in the European Union."

Okay, there was an interesting revelation. "That's two secrets."

He pegged me with an unforgiving look. "I'm feeling generous tonight."

All of a sudden, a guard rushed up to us. Escobar

immediately turned away and walked with his security man, speaking in hushed tones.

Then Anna tugged Miguel toward her, losing her balance until the good doctor wrapped his arms around her. They broke out into soft laughter.

Alec wasted no time once those around us grew distracted. He pressed close, placed a firm hand at the small of my back, then guided us toward the sparkling waterfall. He slid his hand into mine, then he tugged me against him. "What are you doing here?"

I glanced up with an innocent smile. "*I* was invited."

"*You* are devious." His words drawled out slow.

My lips twisted into a smirk. "Guilty as charged."

"You're also exquisite."

His lips crushed onto mine before I had a chance to reply, before I could take in a shocked breath. He'd promised distance. This was *not*.

Completely unprepared, heat sizzled through me, charging every nerve ending, until it settled into a low ache between my thighs. I moaned softly as his lips parted. His tongue darted in, sliding alongside mine. Sparking warmth continued to engulf me in a rippling cascade as he pulled me closer. My nipples drew tight, rasping against the silky fabric of my gown, whipping a sharper ache deep inside me.

Overcome by the intensity, I gasped.

"You want to be a part of tonight that badly?" he murmured against my lips.

He kissed me again, rendering me unable to reply. He tugged gently at my upper lip, then my lower, until he fused his entire mouth to mine, claiming it with fierce possession. The tiniest whimper escaped my throat, and I finally nodded, not wanting to break the spellbinding contact.

Then all at once, it was over. Cold air rushed over my lips. He stared down at me, gaze fiercer than ever. "Good. Then I won't have to worry. You" —his eyes narrowed, as if daring me— "will stay by my side at all times."

As if there was any place I'd rather be. "Yes, sir."

His chest heaved behind a perfectly tailored tuxedo as he sucked in an enormous breath. He pulled away, releasing his hold on me, but a slight tremor shook his hand until he fisted it, like he held back a ton of pent-up energy that he struggled to contain.

Good. Sexual frustration. Only fair both of us suffered.

Escobar's booming voice echoed over a sound system. "Thank you all for coming here tonight. This is a momentous occasion. A gathering of like-minded people to do our part to take care of the earth's resources."

Uh-huh. Generosity? That's what he's still selling?

"As the world's largest dams flow with water; the most renowned scientists tap into solar, wind, and geothermal energy; and celestial explorers discover new fuels for us to harvest, we witness the dawning of a new age."

My face fell into a frown as I turned toward Alec, whispering, "'Celestial explorers'?"

His brows drew together. Then he gave me a short nod before a slower headshake. Space exploration had nothing to do with our mission. Got it.

Escobar droned on as he held the focused attention

of everyone in the cavernous room. Except me. Instead, I watched them all, puzzled by how enraptured they were. The density of the ego in the room likely depressed the surface of the planet in this one concentrated spot, yet they all seemed to have checked their self-centeredness at the door in favor of the man spouting salvation for our world as if he'd become their prophet.

"Did everyone drink mind-altering punch before I got here?" I whispered.

"Good idea. Let's get a drink." He'd either misheard or ignored my sarcastic jibe as he grabbed my hand and led us toward the other side of the crowd.

A fresh wave of waiters descended into the room right as we began working our way through the guests. Each waiter held a tray laden with a dozen Champagne glasses. They methodically worked their way before every guest, waiting until a flute had been accepted while Escobar continued with his mesmerizing speech.

I reasoned he had to be offering them something they all wanted. But his topic continued to focus on energy and resources. Although, for a man who'd harnessed the power of water beneath his own home, the idea of him being passionate about natural resources shouldn't have surprised me.

When a waiter blocked our path, holding up his tray of Champagne. Alec shook his head. "No, we're heading to the bar."

Intrigued by his refusal of bubbly, I grinned. "Not into the fancy stuff?"

He gave an impressive scowl. "Fancy because they pour it into a pretty glass from a bottle with gold foil? Tastes like piss." He spat out the last words.

I fought a laugh. "I hope never to taste piss. But I'm with you. Bitter crap."

We reached the bar. It had a curving mahogany top with maple inlay designs, a striking dark contrast amid all the paler ivory marble and shining clear glass.

He gave a short nod to the bartender, who moved aside when Alec stepped behind the counter. I slid one hip onto the black leather seat of a backless barstool.

"What'll ya have?" Alec asked with a horrific western drawl.

I pressed my lips into a firm line, then scanned the brightly colored top-shelf liquors behind him. "What are you drinking?"

He angled back, glanced below the bar top, then pulled up a slender bottle filled with amber liquid. "*Ronmiel de Canarias*. It's a Spanish honey rum from the Canary Islands. My father's favorite drink—now mine."

My heart warmed at the sentimental connection. "I'll try one of those."

He twisted and reached toward the back bar counter, slipped his fingers into the rims of two squat beveled crystal glasses, and slid them onto the bar top between us. Then he poured two shots of rum into each tumbler.

Right as Alec handed me my drink and raised his own, Escobar's voice boomed louder, moving from background noise into the foreground again. Alec paused, diverting his attention to our host. I half-turned, taking in the room and listening.

"Raise your glasses in a toast to our future," Escobar said.

Rising crystal waved up across the room in reply.

"May we set aside our differences and unite together in a cause greater than any one of us. To feed the nations, quench the thirst of their people, and power the world."

Cheers shouted out as glasses rose higher.

When I raised my glass for a taste, my gaze collided with Alec's at the same moment a caramel aroma wafted up. I held his solid stare as we took our sips together. "Mmm..." I licked my lips, pleasantly surprised. "It's sweet. Intense, but soft at the same time."

He nodded. "My father described it simply as 'smooth.'"

Then his ever-watchful gaze drifted over my shoulder. I sat more fully on the barstool and also turned my attention back toward the party at large.

As I observed while marginally participating, an intrinsic protective sensation rippled through me, part exhilaration from the combined power in the room, part familiar adrenaline from my dangerous personal darkness that I harbored deep inside. Like a jet aircraft, out of sheer survival, I'd learn to pressurize myself from the inside out, enabling me to function in the harsh conditions of the unforgiving world around me. I saw through the façade to the true nature of humanity and cloaked myself within its shadows, enabling me to blend into their environment.

And blending? Made me invisible. Without alerting them to my presence, I'd become one of them. Not corrupt. Not out to harm the innocent. But one born from the devastation of the world, all the same.

None of the concentrated danger in the room threatened me. Not the Iranian president. Not Escobar, father or son. And not the spy mere inches away from me.

I wondered at the wisdom of that. Then self-awareness struck a piercing jolt of fear through my bulletproof egotistical armor. No one was invincible. My gaze tracked back to the menacing guards. *One thing I'm not? Immortal.* I blew out a reassuring breath, then took another fortifying sip of my drink. A small amount of nerve-settling alcohol couldn't hurt.

A string quartet began playing classic standards after Escobar's speech concluded. Near the waterfall, couples paired off to dance, arms held at respectable distances, bodies swaying in perfectly trained steps.

"Come dance with me." Alec tossed back his remaining *Ronmiel*, then slid his glass across the bar top.

I put my glass down, only half finished, then slid my fingers across his callused palm.

My gaze flitted up to his, catching a mischievous spark in his eyes as he tugged me through the room.

I tilted my head. "What?"

"Nothing. Except I've" —his husky voice grew in strength as he murmured against the column of my neck with a brush of his lips— "been dying to put my hands on you."

I shivered from his scorching touch, the weight of his words, as he guided us toward an unoccupied corner, obscured from most of the guests by the fronds of two potted palms. Pulling me into a dancing position, he faced toward the room, then gathered me close, settling his spreading fingers over the bare skin of my lower back with firm pressure. A fingertip slipped under the edge of my plunging gown, dancing along the skin above my left butt cheek.

My breath caught, stuck in my throat. The minute sensation of his fingertip playing against my skin stoked the embers of a fire deep inside as a slow erotic heat unfurled.

I swallowed hard, throat suddenly parched. "What are you doing? I thought anything more between us was off limits." *Even though* no *part of me wanted it to be.*

"You've changed the rules. Surprised me," he murmured.

"Oh?"

His gaze locked on to mine, searching for some answer in the depths. Verifying whether or not he should proceed?

I arched a brow, hardening my expression.

My defiant action was all it took for him to capitulate. "I sense you can handle more," he said.

"More?" I croaked out. Wonderful. In our sensual cat-and-mouse game, I'd been reduced monosyllabic speech. Without qualm, I blamed Alec.

"More contact." His hand shifted, breaking the intimate connection of skin to skin, until he floated his entire hand over the silk of my gown…lower. Then he squeezed gently.

I shivered, his action rippling a sizzling heat outward, and deeply inward.

After a slow inhalation, that did nothing to calm the chaotic sensations in my body, I replied, "I'm good if you are." The sugar-coated lie tasted like sweet perfection.

No part of me cared whether or not I would be able to handle more of the delicious drug Alec Marquez dispensed. Not a single thought lingered in worry that I'd become addicted. No part of it mattered—because he had invaded my monochrome life with bursting vivid color. And nothing in the world would force me to switch it back again. I strongly suspected nothing ever could.

"Just a little longer." His hand remained in the position where he'd slid it, possessively gripping my ass through my gown, aligning the center of my aching body against his groin.

With purpose, I moved my hand down from his shoulder to his beltline, clutching him back. There would be no doubts about what I wanted.

"Why the wait?" I whispered. "Is there a plan?"

He lowered his head and murmured. "There's always a plan." His breath coasted over the skin on my neck in tantalizing tingles. "We can't talk freely everywhere. The waterfall and music cover us here, but when we leave, you're a guest, I'm a guest. No further talk unless I initiate."

"Done." I gave a barely perceptible nod, causing my cheek to brush against the scruff of stubble on his skin. He hadn't shaved, and as I pulled back and gazed up at him, I determined that I found him sexier this way. The dark shadows along his jawline accentuated his rugged attractiveness.

Another rule not to speak brought the erotic memory of a night not long ago filled with temptation and promise. And yet, tonight? The anticipation blazed infinitely hotter.

I counseled myself to be patient though, reveling in the

knowledge of what we *both* wanted.

Into the next hour, we danced several more songs, mingled as he introduced me to a few of the guests, then made our way back toward the bar once the crowd around it thinned enough to allow us access.

"Another *Ronmiel*?" He arched a challenging brow.

I gave a slight headshake. "Still water, please." On my first mission, I wanted all my faculties to remain razor sharp.

"Wise choice." He winked at me, then escorted me to the only empty barstool, along the wall. "Be right back."

As he ducked down, searching below the bar top, my attention drifted across the room once more. Escobar had gathered an attentive crowd around him. I spotted Anna and Miguel at a wall by the front entrance, her leaning against it, him bracing an arm on the granite above her, staring down into her eyes.

A few seconds passed before Anna glanced my way, and the moment she did, her face lit up with a wide smile. Without raising her hand from the relaxed position at her side, she gave me a tiny wave, then pointed toward the open double front doors that led to the precarious catwalk. She wanted to know if it was okay for her to ditch me.

I smiled back and nodded twice. And while my usual MO was to put on an act, feign happiness for the benefit of simplicity, I meant it this time. Although I'd wanted to warn her to be careful, it hadn't felt possible. All I could do was hope she'd exercise caution.

And really, what difference did it make to any woman if the man she didn't know well, but planned to sleep with, was a threat to the world at large or only to her, an international villain or an ax murderer, a con-artist player or a Rohypnol-wielding date rapist. We all had to use our common sense, vet the person we allowed into our personal space, and take a calculated risk if we allowed them to remain there, to get closer—to be in a position of power when we let ourselves grow vulnerable.

I'd only just begun to learn that, exercised cautiously, the dance between man and woman could be quite rewarding—thrilling even.

Alec interrupted my line of sight, right after Miguel scooped Anna into his arms and vanished out the front.

He handed me a tall crystal glass. "One still water. Smart Water, actually."

"Oh, good. I need a synapse boost tonight."

His gaze shot to my lips, then slowly raised to my eyes. "There you go with that smart mouth of yours."

"My electrolyte induced neurons are stimulated into hyperactivity," I drawled out.

He bit the right corner of his lower lip, eyelids falling as if he'd been half-drugged. "Tease."

"Provocateur," I corrected. I took a few swallows of the water, then slid from the barstool back onto the four-inch Jimmy Choo heels Anna had loaned me. Gifted dress, borrowed shoes, at a ball replete with powerful dignitaries from across the land in a glitzy castle atop a hill, it seemed on the surface that I'd stumbled into a fairytale. Awash with devious plots. And heinous agendas.

Curiosity got the better of me, and I led Alec back into

the noise-shielding vicinity of the waterfall so we could speak without risk of being overheard. Even so, I kept my volume to a bare minimum. "It seems like you're waiting for something."

"I am." His gaze held mine for a moment more, then scanned the room.

I turned slightly, analyzing the scene in fresh perspective. "What?"

"For the optimal time to leave." His hand slid around my waist, then he exerted slight pressure until I yielded, tucking closer against him.

Unsteady in the stiletto heels, I leaned into him, letting his solid strength support us both. "When will that be?"

He leaned down until his lips brushed the top of my ear. With his slow exhalation, warm breath feathered over the delicate skin, causing goose bumps to erupt. "Soon," he whispered.

A sensual heat flared, warming every nerve ending. I had to inhale a deep breath to steady myself.

To distract me from sensation overload and keep my Smart Water-charged head in the game, I focused on looking at the room before us through Alec's eyes. From the viewpoint of a spy.

The guests were spreading out, migrating toward the fringes. The same security who'd been posted along the perimeter and guarding the exit points remained. Only this time, the guards no longer held a relaxed vigilance, zeroed in on the center of the room where every guest had earlier been docile. For every guard, there had to be a couple dozen inebriated guests. The guards' focus had now been scattered, their energy somewhat drained.

"You're waiting until two more 'drunken' guests can stumble into a quiet corner, without focused attention."

His deep chuckle reverberated against me, causing a fresh riot of goose bumps. A gentle kiss pressed to the upper shell of my ear. "You were right. You *are* a quick study."

He'd just unofficially acknowledged my capacity as trainee, a different category than when snorkeling and catamaran cruising. Did that mean… "Am I no longer cover?"

At the question, he pulled back, his nearly black eyes staring hard at me. Then he narrowed them. A muscle clenched in his jaw. Like he'd allowed my participation in tonight's event to flow unchecked, but now a decision had to be made.

"You tell me." His expression was unreadable.

Before I had time to register the words beyond their basic command, he bent down and crushed his lips to mine.

The kiss fired hot at first contact, igniting every nerve ending to roaring life. His words tumbled somewhere into the far reaches of my mind, beyond comprehension or analysis, exactly where they belonged when hit with a 9.5 body-shaking quake.

When he broke away, nearly as fast as he'd hit me unaware, I sucked air into my lungs. The clear answer to the question I'd asked boomed into my mind. "No longer."

No longer. More contact. My words and his from earlier echoed into my thoughts, both weighted with innuendo. No longer mere cover. No longer held at arm's length.

We'd crossed the line he'd so vehemently drawn in the sand.

Was I an unofficial agent, then? More than a one-night stand?

My head swam.

The lines identifying *everything* had blurred.

CHAPTER 15

"Come." Alec bit out the short word against the column of my neck, as if his restraint was flagging and he needed me to do just that.

Soon... His sensual promise echoed back into my mind, rippled across already heated nerve endings.

My thoughts drifted back into the moment when he slipped his warm hand into mine, easing his body away. "We have just under an hour."

"Before what?" Fuzzed as my mind was, I furrowed my brow, trying to concentrate and follow along.

"Shift change." They were his last words before he guided me from the noise-cancelling domain of the waterfall and down a hall that led deeper into the center of the house.

We wouldn't be able to talk freely anymore. And since Anna and I had arrived shortly before 9:00 p.m., and a couple of hours had passed, that meant midnight would be shift change—a golden opportunity when the security coming off detail would be tired and distracted, having chased down one too many drunk guests wandering hallways they hadn't been granted access to. *Like we were doing now.*

I took full advantage of the sobering seconds without the sizzling heat of Alec's lips on my skin to focus on the task at hand: *our* mission. Again, I still had no idea what said mission entailed, but I wanted my mind to be sharp and centered—not fuzzed out by arousal.

"*¡Pare!*" A baritone voice shouted.

"Halt," Alec translated under his breath before he turned us around. Then his expression brightened, eyes widening as a broad smile stretched across his face. "Pablo!"

He clapped the guard on the shoulder before leaning toward him. Then in hushed tones, he spoke in rapid Spanish. Recognition flickered across the guard's face before he nodded once.

I eased my tensed shoulders and blew out a held breath through pursed lips. The guards in the main room of the party had concealed their weapons. However, the man speaking with Alec displayed an automatic assault rifle blatantly as it dangled from a shoulder strap with his hand comfortably resting on the grip.

Alec released his casual hold on the guard's shoulder and spread his hands out in front of him, glancing my way. "I explained to him we're retrieving a promised rare bottle of wine from Escobar's cellar."

The guard grumbled a few more low words meant for Alec's ears, then let out a belly laugh.

No translation required with his lewd tone, likely "enjoy your piece of ass."

No problemo, señor. I will. My lips twitched into an uncontainable smirk. Apparently in the face of danger, dry humor prevailed. Probably served as an instinctual tension diffuser.

And really, the alarming interruption helped cool my blood enough to think clearly, separate our task at hand from raging hormones—or blend the two. If we had an hour to kill and an itch to scratch, no better way to pass the time than satisfying intense sexual urges. All it was. Two secret agents playing the part.

Our romantic ruse camouflaged us.

Alec returned to my side and slung an arm around my shoulder. I glanced back to verify the guard still watched us with hawk-like intensity. Only now, instead of suspicion hardening his features, a hint of amusement and jealousy relaxed them.

We rounded a corner. Then a few steps down the long corridor, Alec turned toward me, hunching his shoulders as if about to kiss me. But instead of leaning down, he held a single finger over his lips in reminder of our need for silence, then pointed up and behind his shoulder.

I played along, reaching up on tiptoe to kiss him as I glanced in the direction he'd indicated. A camera mounted near the ceiling had its lens aimed in our direction, its red light on.

When our lips collided, the contact was warm, but chaste. With a brief nod, I communicated my understanding: Even in the absence of a guard, we were still being watched.

Then Alec deepened the kiss and urged me backward

until my shoulders hit the wall. He pressed in further, slid his hand over my ass, ground his pelvis against me.

I let out a soft gasp when his rigid length rubbed over sensitized nerve endings at the apex of my thighs. The startling sensation fired hot arousal from that point outward, lower, until a torturous ache clenched the muscles deep inside me.

"I want you," he growled against my lips.

Was he playing a part? Did it matter? His body wanted mine. Mine wanted his. Cover or not, romantic ruse or honest desire, in the midst of a mission important enough to garner the attention of an invisible shadow organization, two people whose sexual chemistry defied quantitative measure needed each other on the most primal level.

"I want you. *More*," I murmured with competitive qualification.

"Debatable." He eased back and stared into my eyes, both of us breathless, chests heaving.

Before I could process another thought, he grabbed my hand and tugged us down the length of the hall. I grabbed a fistful of my gown and jogged to try and keep up, my stilettos clicking lightly on the polished travertine flooring.

Since we'd left the main room where the party continued to wind down, we'd passed nine doors in the first hallway, four on the left, five on the right. But in our current corridor, no doors marred the butter-colored plaster walls.

At the end, on the left, one finally appeared. Stained a reddish-brown mahogany, the wide rustic door curved at the top with a gentle arch. Its matte-black iron handle boasted a single latch lever above its curving twisted handhold.

When Alec released my hand and depressed the lever with his thumb, a soft click sounded. Then he shouldered the door, easing it open.

Cool, humid air rushed over our faces, chilling my skin for an instant.

He shot me a quick look. "Ready?"

I drew in a steadying breath and stared into an unknown darkness beyond. "As I'll ever be."

Had he meant for him? Or the mission...

I'd meant both.

In the last few days, the world as I'd known it had turned on its ear. New experiences rushed over my senses, each more exciting than the last. And not one part of me wanted it to end. Having painstakingly prepared for situations my entire life—guarded feelings, anticipated dangers, assessed every probability until I'd mentally exhausted all likeliest scenarios—I'd never understood the phrase "flying by the seat of your pants."

Now? I vowed never to fly any other way. The exhilaration as I leapt into the unexplored? *That* was living.

Yet in knee-jerk reaction to an event more than a decade ago, I'd voluntarily relegated myself to be the walking dead my whole life. *No more.*

I grabbed Alec's hand and moved past him. A series of quiet snorts, resembling silent laughter, huffed out behind me as I tugged him down the stairs. He gave my hand a light squeeze. "Look who's suddenly in charge."

I paused midstep, blinking. I *was* in charge. For the

first time in my life, I'd begun to control things outside of myself, beyond my inner prison. I'd ventured into the world at large, where countless forces exerted pressure from all sides, ricocheting people like pinballs to bounce helplessly in reaction to the cruel, unforgiving environment around them. Only now, I manned the levers—controlled the timing, the speed, the moment of impact.

Pleased at the revelation, I continued down the shadowy staircase with a smile tugging at my lips. But the room we descended into gradually stole my attention away from the epiphany.

In the dimly lit stairwell, I slid my hand along the cool roughness of the stone wall, gaze pausing briefly on one of many small niches that glowed softly from a recessed light hidden in its upper arch. As we descended, each successive caramel travertine step expanded in size from the last, stretching wider and wider, curving into the room as we neared ground level.

Only when we reached the bottom, did the sheer vastness of the unique space take shape in my mind. In a matter of seconds, I counted upward to identify the angled necks of exactly sixty rows of wine bottles that spanned from floor to ceiling. I would've estimated how many in sum total by scanning right to left, however the wall curved from sight behind the base of the stone staircase before undulating forward and backward in a general rectangular shape. Had the waves been stretched farther into the room and narrowed, they would have resembled library rows. As they were, the increased surface area flowing along the room's perimeter, except for the staircase, had to cast the number of stored bottles in the vast cellar into the thousands.

Four giant logs, each easily three feet in diameter, stood like silent sentries. They sprouted from burnished rust-brown concrete, which resembled a forest floor with various botanical impressions in its surface, and reached upward until they disappeared into the ceiling. Soft beams of angled light along their trunks aiming upward brought the intricate tilework of the barrel-vaulted ceiling to life, making the tiny iridescent tiles in diverse shades of leafy green shimmer like a real overhead canopy as I moved.

Although the air was cool and humid, as I moved from one area to another, the specifics of both varied to the slightest degree, the atmosphere of each section tailored to the type of wine housed there. A faint fragrance seemed natural to the space, tinges of dust and a woodsy aroma from the support logs and furniture in the room scenting the air.

The entire space held a mass that I felt all the way to my bones, like the walls were alive, breathing right along with us, changing and reacting—as if each bottle of wine waited with patient anticipation, preparing on a molecular level to be called to service, to fulfill its long-awaited destiny.

"Wow," I whispered.

The breathless reaction was the only brilliant word to populate my stunned but impressed mind. Not in any way a wine connoisseur, I appreciated the artfulness and creativity that went into crafting the unique space we stood within.

And I shared an odd, deep kinship to those ever-patient wines.

The chill in the air stirred across my skin, and I shivered.

Alec immediately moved into my view and pulled his tuxedo jacket off, revealing a holstered gun in a black leather shoulder harness worn over his formal white shirt. He flared the jacket out and around before draping the warmed fabric over my shoulders.

Then his lips twisted into a smirk and the corners of his eyes wrinkled ever so slightly, amusement sparking in them. "Now that you've dragged me down here, what are you going to do with me?"

My flushed skin suddenly felt thin, transparent. Like he could see right through me.

As my mind spun with possibilities, I searched the open floor space, spotting the many tables in the center with stately carved wooden arm chairs tucked beneath them. Pools of yellow light dappled the simulated forest floor.

Instinct reigned supreme when all other faculties failed me. Without thought, I took small steps backward, moving toward the safer shadows of the room as my desires rang clear. "No." My voice came out gruff. "Not me to you. I'm the guest. You're the one breaking your own rules. You want me? Take me."

In truth, I maintained control. I knew it, understood the concept now. But I wanted him to take what I freely offered.

Alec tracked me, matching every step I took, predator to prey. The heat in his gaze intensified, unrelenting as his eyes narrowed.

Easing backward, I led us behind the staircase, into the darkest part of the enormous room. Before long, my jacketed shoulders hit the stone surface of the wall. Seconds later, his body pressed flush against mine, both arms braced on the wall above me, caging me in.

A shiver ran through me, stark need throbbing an aching drumbeat of arousal into my veins. Exposed, yet protected. Desired, yet full of want. Raw, yet comforted. In control, yet so completely out of it. A dizzying juxtaposition of emotions and feelings whirled together into magnificent chaos.

No other place I'd rather be.

My eyes drifted shut, and I inhaled deeply, drawing his intoxicating musky spiced scent into my lungs. My body reacted, our chemistry attuned.

His warm breath tracked down the column of my neck, blazing a fiery trail as it descended inch by slow inch. At the base, where it sloped into my shoulder, his lips connected. He sucked gently, drew my heated skin into his mouth, past the sharp edges of his teeth. With slow purpose, he pulled my storming blood to the surface as he marked me.

A low groan rumbled from my throat as he gripped me in the one small spot, yet caused an ache to spear lower, deeper, as if my two erogenous zones were bound together by a fragile cord pulled decadently taut.

When he released my skin, a low pop sounded. He blew gently over the spot, cooling the surface, then kissed it tenderly. "You all right with an audience?"

Eyes still closed, my brows twitched in confusion as my mind succumbed to a sensual haze.

When I failed to reply, he continued, "Another security camera. Above my shoulder in the corner."

He didn't turn to verify. He'd obviously noticed while I'd been distracted counting wine bottles and leafy ceiling tiles.

I opened my eyes and peered over his shoulder as his lips slowly ascended up my neck. Smaller sucks marked his path until he reached my earlobe studded with a simple diamond solitaire. His teeth surrounded the earring, front and back, then he drew the tender skin into his mouth.

Mind fogged with blissful acute desire, I exhaled a measured breath, attempting to concentrate. "*Exhibitionism...*" The whispered definition came out breathy as Alec twisted my earring in his mouth with his tongue.

Did I care if someone watched? I didn't know the security staff. They didn't know me.

A low whimper escaped my lips, as an ever-present ache hummed louder at the lascivious thought. In response, Alec ground his hips between my legs, his rigid erection gliding upward. The only things stopping us from connecting, becoming one, were the silk of my gown and the wool of his tuxedo pants.

I stared at the naked lens of the camera, eyes glazing over with want and need, as a better question floated to the surface. Did knowing that someone watched on the other end of those electronics excite me further?

Ratcheting arousal provided a definite answer to the root of his question...*should we proceed?* "Yes," I groaned out, arching from the wall as I curved my hips. I ran my clit over his rigid length, needing to increase the rate of friction before I melted into a puddle of need at his feet.

My affirmative response was a go on all things: to exhibitionism, to Alec, to sex in a wine cellar in the bowels of a purported villain's home, but more importantly—to me... to tearing down the walls I'd imprisoned myself behind, to letting raw desire set me free.

As if my singular word destroyed a barrier that held back an avalanche, Alec exploded into action. He bent down, breaking the delicious position we'd been connected in. Then from a squatting position at my feet, he stared up at me, dark eyes intent in an uncompromising gaze.

His fingers slipped beneath the hem of my gown until both hands wrapped around my ankles. A feathered touch slid up my shins, twisted slowly backward, then drifted up my calves. His fingertips lingered, drawing tiny circles behind my knees. In response, they buckled, faltering a little, and I grabbed his shoulders for support, my eyelids falling shut once more.

Seconds later, heated breath fogged over the sensitive, throbbing juncture of my thighs. I sucked in a sharp breath as my gaze shot downward.

A wicked smile tugged at the corners of his lips as he stared up at me. Ice-blue silk bunched along the white sleeves of his formal shirt while he smoothed his hands up the backs of my thighs. Holding my gaze, he leaned forward, hovering his mouth inches from my clit, teasing the aching nub with his long, hot exhale.

Intense ache sparked through me. I gasped, then bit my lower lip, attempting to hold myself together with unraveling threads of control as my legs began to tremble. I let out my own breath, then paused when all the air had left my body. Time suspended for the briefest of moments, a heartbeat, then another, a blink that yawned wide into a giant chasm, a shift in perception from all I thought the world offered for me and what it had now become.

As if sensing that I might implode, while I sucked in air before the black dots speckling my peripheral vision became lights-out entirely, he shot his hands the rest of the way up. He gathered the fabric of my gown with them until he bared me fully. His hands made contact with my ass and grabbed me, pulling me forward, crashing my clit into his open mouth.

I cried out as pleasure jolted through me. At the sound, his suction intensified, unrelenting. I gripped his shoulders harder, afraid of passing out from all the blood rushing downward. Then a slight pain pierced through me, followed by even greater pleasure.

"Did you just bite me?" I rasped.

My whisper, and any answer he may or may not have provided, got lost in the thundering pulse in my ears. Decadent sensations drowned out the analytical question, and I let go, allowing myself to be swept away. I groaned and writhed against him. But his erotic bite held fast, driving me crazy as it ramped me ever higher.

Then he began a sensual rhythm with his mouth, alternating those sharp bite-holds with strong lingering sucks. On the fringes of my awareness, an orgasm edged into view.

With every throb-inducing touch, each bite and suck,

and now slow licks and lazy swirls, my arousal sharpened, the ache spiraling as it drifted lower, fired hotter. The tension grew nearly unbearable, every gasping breath reduced to a whimpering moan. My fingers dug into his shoulders. My legs trembled uncontrollably. Ragged desire coiled tighter than ever, then held, as if stuck there.

Erotic sensations balanced right on the edge of pain so intense, I bit my lip, muffling a scream as pleasure sprang free, bursting into the most intense orgasm of my life. My fingers speared into his hair, gripping at the roots as he continued licking and sucking, wringing every last pulse of release from me.

When finally he ceased, left my body wasted, my mind reeling, he launched upright, never releasing his tight grip on my ass. The sudden movement jostled me away from the wall, then shot me farther up its rough surface as he spread my thighs wide and positioned his body between them.

His gaze locked on to mine, eyes wild with desire. Pinned by his upper body to a stone wall whose cold began to seep through his protective tuxedo jacket, I loosened my hold on his hair and raked my fingernails along his scalp. "Take me," I breathed.

I wanted to give this man pleasure. Needed him to drown in it, revel in its consuming nature.

His slight shift caused my hands to drop back to his shoulders as he angled one of his arms downward. *To his pocket?*

When he brought his hand up, pinched between his long fingers was a gold foil packet. Then he ripped the corner open with his teeth. "Put it on me," he growled between heaving breaths.

"Packing condoms now?" I teased, taking the opened packet from him and pulling out the soft roll. We'd made no promises of exclusivity, and he'd had no idea I'd planned to come tonight. Just because we'd decided to go without protection, didn't mean he'd risk himself with another. A surprising pang of jealousy twanged through me. I didn't like the thought of him being with anyone else—whether or not I had the right to be possessive of him.

I reached down between us and unzipped his pants. When his erection sprang free, I caught the heavy, rigid length in my hand, then slid loosened fingers up its generous girth, marveling at the silken skin that had stretched so taut.

"Condoms have other uses," he ground out as I reached the ridge of his tip, then brushed a finger at the sensitive point on the underside of the crown.

"Oh?" My reply was entirely half-distracted. I had no idea what he referred to, but didn't care in the least as I unrolled the soft sheath over him, using the fingers of both hands to be able to encircle him.

"No more talk." He grunted out the last word when my fingers hit the base of his shaft, then drifted lower to skim beneath his balls, lifting. In the span of the next second, my hands were nearly crushed between us as he dragged back, caught his tip at my entrance, then thrust upward.

I gasped, breathless as he stretched and filled me. My hands shot up, pressing against his chest. He eased back, then drove upward, fully seating into the very depths of me.

His head tilted forward, dropping until his forehead touched mine. I closed my eyes, savoring the tender moment. What we shared was primal: sex, need, and satisfaction in the most basic of forms. But behind the masks we wore, underneath the shields we'd erected but dropped only for one another, we were a man and a woman, once children who'd been orphaned from love, unable to fully trust—until now.

No matter how brief our relationship, no one on earth could take away the moments we'd stolen together for ourselves.

On my next breath, the poignant moment vanished. He gripped my ass tighter with both hands, rendering me immobile. Then he pulled back and thrust deep. Holding there, he ground his pelvis against my clit, firing a fresh round of sparking arousal along every nerve ending.

Slow and steady, he continued, pounding into me with enough force to build another powerful orgasm within reach. I arched away from the wall, trusted the strength of his arms, balancing myself between his hold and the unforgiving stone behind me.

"Oh my God," I breathed, dropping my lips into the crook of his neck. I softly bit into the tender skin there, afraid if I didn't occupy my mouth in some way, I wouldn't be able to stop my impending scream.

After another forceful deep thrust, he paused. Then his head dropped until his lips pressed against my neck, vibrating a low, pained groan there.

My skin flushed hot, every nerve ending sizzling. A

pulse of pleasure tore a whimper from my throat before my body began to quiver from head to toe, hovering on an erotic razor's edge.

Then slower than I ever imagined possible, he dragged his cock backward, inch by slow inch, as some distant part of my mind measured by ragged heartbeats, *eight...nine...*

All of a sudden, he slammed forward, and a fiery bolt of lightning flashed through my body. My breath caught as pleasure whipped, then coiled tight, the pressure nearly unbearable.

His entire body froze, every muscle strained.

We both jerked at the same time. I screamed into his shoulder as his low growl rumbled over my neck. The pulses of my orgasm washed through me, clenching around his cock as his own release surged free.

In incremental degrees, the tension in our bodies relaxed. Our breaths began to deepen, slowing with every inhalation. My erratic pulse lagged behind but eventually fell in line with the rest of my body. My hazy mind drifted down to earth last, having soared with a near out-of-body experience.

I heard his loud swallow as he eased back from the pinned position he'd nearly crushed me in when he'd lost control. Then he stared intensely at me, gaze searching mine. A flicker of confusion flashed over his expression before a hardened mask slipped back in place, like he wouldn't allow uncertainty—definitely not while on mission, possibly about me.

Unwilling to go there, needing him to stay on point, I

breached the distance and kissed him.

His lips instantly softened, molding to mine as he groaned.

Once we caught our breaths, he pulled away, waiting until my feet hit solid ground again. Then with efficient movements, while I straightened my dress and pulled his jacket from my shoulders, he slid the condom free, tied it off, then tossed it into a plastic-lined trash basket that rested under the corner of the nearest table.

Alec glanced at his watch as he returned, then pressed a soft kiss to my temple. "Ten more minutes."

Right. Back to business. I gave a quick nod and handed over his jacket. Then I blew a calming breath through tightened lips, willing my still-charged body to get back with the program.

As he slipped his hands into the sleeves of his jacket, then shrugged it over his shoulders before gripping the lapels to straighten the fabric, he began to peruse the vertical acreage of wine bottles. His open palm hovered inches from the down-sloping corks as he stalked the undulating wall. He concentrated on the inverted angled labels on each bottle as he passed column after column.

He paused midway into a curve, touched an index finger to the edge of one bottle's label, then slid his fingertip down toward the cork before he began to grip the slender neck.

"Wait!" I warned as a schematic diagram suddenly flashed into my head. "It's alarm coded!"

His hand froze, then he glanced over his shoulder. "I knew your being here was an excellent idea."

"Uh-huh," I groused. "Had I not ignored your protests and accepted a random invitation, you'd be going it alone down here, sp...bud."

My eyes widened. I'd almost said "spy guy" loud enough for any listening device to detect. Thankfully, anyone eavesdropping on us would only think I'd meant him going it solo about the sex. My lips twitched in amusement at the thought as I crossed over to the end of the row where he stood.

"Spud?" He shot me a teasing look, giving me the sense that he'd picked up on the near blunder. "As in...potato?"

I shook my head, lips curved into a smile as I ignored him and focused on the softly illuminated grid that I'd not made any sense of until now. Each section's outermost curve had faint markings on a metal support between two vertical columns. The left side of the grid had five circular depression areas with faint white numeric markings on the brushed-steel surface, numbering one through five. The middle had six through ten. The right: eleven through fifteen.

The wine cellar's security was digital-keypad driven. I scanned along the wall, floor to ceiling, counting the number of bottles within this section. Satisfied I had the correct number, I reached forward. But then I paused, uncertain. I stepped back, assessing the entire collection as a whole to determine whether the one I stood in front of monitored Alec's bottle or the section curving beyond us to my right.

Alec watched me intently, silent and unmoving, as I blew out a relieved breath and stepped to the end of the adjacent column to my left. Then I depressed the *3* followed by the *8*.

Almost instantaneously, a soft pneumatic release sounded and Alec's chosen bottle shifted up and forward by two inches, its neck sliding into his palm.

"Well done, Pink."

I gave a sharp nod. "Anytime, Spud."

About eight of those ten minutes Alec mentioned had passed. "So now what? We slam back a bottle of wine?"

"No." He cradled the bottle, then spun it over his palm, presenting its label to me. "It would be a shame to treat a fine vintage such as this with callous disregard. I have better plans for this bottle."

He grasped my hand and led me back up the curving stone steps. When we reached the landing, I glanced back down into the impressive cellar with fondness, certain I wouldn't be back, but grateful for the memory I'd always have.

As Alec reopened the door, leading us from the place where we'd killed time in the most amazing way, renewed anticipation thrummed hard and fast through my veins. Whatever his mission had originally been, I'd become a part of it. Pink to his Spud—Watson to his Sherlock.

I only hoped I could handle whatever challenge came our way.

CHAPTER 16

We exited the wine cellar through the same roughhewn wooden door and slipped back into the hall. Alec casually held the wine bottle in one hand as he wove his fingers together with mine with his other. Before we moved from our spot, he stared down the long corridor from where we'd originally come, flicked a quick glance toward both corners nearest us, then looked at me. He paused and took a deep breath as his eyes searched mine. His brows twitched together, and his lips parted.

I leaned closer, sensing that he hesitated, like he struggled to express something rare and important.

Suddenly, soft laughter chimed out from down the hall, then quickly grew louder.

"Bingo." His expression instantly blanked, and he gave a decisive nod. Then he tugged me toward the sound. When only two yards remained between us and the end of the corridor, a couple in their midthirties appeared. The man pressed her against the wall, then kissed her until her body grew lax and she groaned.

I nudged Alec, whispering. "Part of the plan?"

He gave a slight headshake. "Fortunate coincidence."

"Gotta love those," I murmured. My vacation had been sprinkled with plenty of them where he'd been concerned.

Alec cleared his throat as we approached.

The man spun around, then chivalrously blocked his woman from sight behind him.

"Care for some wine on your adventure?" Alec asked.

The woman pushed her man aside, peeking out from behind him.

Alec tugged on my hand again, strolling us a few steps forward. "We 'borrowed' this from the wine cellar. But my date insists she's had enough."

Deciding to play the part, I swayed on my feet, wrapped an arm around Alec's midsection, and nestled my cheek in the dip under his collarbone. "The world's still spinning."

The man barked out a laugh, then glanced at his companion who'd moved from behind her noble guard to stand beside him. She held out her hand, reaching toward us. "We'd love to have the bottle." Her Spanish accent was thick, her voice throaty in a sexy way. "*Gracias.*"

"*De nada,*" Alec replied, tipping his head in a nod as he handed over our pilfered goods. Then he gestured his arm out toward the right, and the four of us meandered down that direction together.

Alec edged closer to the man, whispering. "I believe if you keep going, Escobar's bedrooms are that way."

The man's eyes gleamed. "With as many rooms as he has, one is bound to be unoccupied."

"Save a room for us," Alec replied lightheartedly and gave him a friendly clap on the shoulder.

The couple snuck deeper into Escobar's home, laughing for a brief second before loud shushing, then giggles, then silence.

We encountered another hallway at the same instant deep-toned shouts echoed off the hard surfaces from an unknown direction. Alec swept me into his arms and spun me, ducking us down the corridor, out of sight. An alcove recessed into the wall on the right, and we slipped into its shadows. I pressed against another roughhewn door as Alec edged in, flush against the narrow wall adjacent to the hall, both of us barely camouflaged in the shallow space. His hand smoothed over my belly, then connected to my far hip, holding me back. I straightened and held my breath, gaze locked with his as I gave a brief nod.

An instant later, heavy footfalls thundered toward us until a dark blur ran past.

We waited.

Seconds ticked by while I counted and expelled my held breath. By the time I reached six, Alec relaxed his arm away from my body, and we edged into the hallway. He glanced both directions, canted his head to the side as if listening, then grabbed my hand and tugged us down the same direction from where the guard had run from.

At the end, another corridor stretched in either direction, but Alec led us left without hesitation. Our pace slowed as a bend approached, another wooden door appearing on the right. On an expansive wall around the bend spanned a darkened outer window; its single pane of glass was short in height but ran long down the wall, measuring about four foot by sixteen.

Alec depressed the lever to the door handle, but it was locked. "Keep watch in both directions. We'll have no more than ninety seconds."

Great. Visions of armed guards and bullets flying flashed into my head.

Positioned on the L-bend, I scanned the direction we'd come from, then down the windowed corridor. Where the long window ended, a fifteen-foot potted palm regally arched upward, before an identical window appeared, leading farther down the seemingly endless dimly lit hall.

I stared straight ahead, concentrating with relaxed focus at the rounded plaster corner across from me, engaging my peripheral vision to catch movement in either direction. At the sound of soft clicking noises behind me, I diverted my attention for a split second.

Alec manipulated two thin metal instruments inside the door's locking mechanism, jiggling, then twisting.

"What's behind the door?"

"Don't know," he replied. He closed his eyes, brow furrowing as he tilted an ear toward the lock. "The guard that ran past us usually stands post here."

I returned to my own guard duties, scanning both corridors before settling into peripheral vision once more. As I relaxed, the blueprints from the other night flashed to mind.

"The hydroelectric equipment. The underground river." Our explorations tonight had continued westward through the maze of halls, which led us to our position on the extreme south side of the house and made the theory plausible.

A heavy metal click sounded. Alec slid his delicate tools into a leather pouch, then pocketed them. Before I had a chance to check both halls again, he opened the door, grabbed my hand, yanked me through, then shut the door behind us. Another metal click followed as he locked us in.

Warm humidity brushed across my face, carried on a swirling current of disturbed air. The muted roar of rushing water echoed around us. A musty odor wrinkled my nose, pungent and foreign. A minute vibration rippled up through the floor, tickling down to my bones. Without releasing Alec's solid grip, I inched forward, assessing our new surroundings.

We stood on another landing, atop a staircase. Only this one wasn't covered with pretty travertine tiles curving downward in ever-widening steps. No carved niches with soft illumination lit our way.

Instead, functional concrete steps hugged the south wall halfway down, before a ninety-degree turn led to a second flight angling back in the opposite direction, then a third traveled north along the same wall as the door above, before landing us onto the main floor. Bulkhead lighting, with protective aluminum grid housing over opaque glass shields, illuminated the space.

My gaze followed a vertical steel I-beam upward toward the ceiling in the massive warehouse-like space, then traveled along the length of forty-foot girders that braced the ceiling crosswise. Along the same side of the house from where we'd entered, three glass-and-metal sectioned-off rooms curved along the wall.

The first two were darkened behind their glass walls, metal tables and shelving glinting slight reflections. The third room's overhead fluorescent lights had been left on, revealing what appeared to be a biological clean room, two sets of double-glass doors separating its protected environment from the larger warehouse section.

The continual rushing sound of water stole my attention, pulling my gaze across the main floor to land on another metal lab table that stood empty. Two folding metal chairs had been left standing open, positioned a few feet from an end of the table and facing one another, as if abandoned by their occupants in midconversation.

At the far end of the open space, the composition of the room's exterior structure changed—where the source of the water began. Flooring and walls transformed from polished concrete to rough limestone, manmade elements vanishing along a jagged seam. Thick limestone arched upward into an impressive cavern that stretched back into a black tunnel beyond the room. On the far side of the great opening, three vertical sculptures were faintly illuminated; the glittering surface of stalagmites stretched upward from the floor toward icicle-shaped stalactites, mere inches separating the two forms.

An underground river poured into our formed chamber from the unknown darkness, rushing through a channel carved by millions of years of natural erosion. A large nearby alcove on the manmade side housed the hydroelectric generator that powered Escobar's house, the source of the slight vibration beneath our feet.

Sudden movement blurred beyond the river, and my gaze darted left. My mouth fell open as shock rippled through me at a horrific sight. My heart seized, then shot into my throat, followed by a strangled noise.

On pure instinct, I lunged forward.

But I never moved. Alec's unbendable forearm snapped across my chest, just below my shoulders. My hoarse cry of protest died against the flat palm of his hand that he'd suddenly clamped over my mouth.

"No," his fierce whisper hissed against my ear. "There's nothing we can do here. Nothing can be done to save them. Not now."

"But…" My muffled whine came seconds before my throat locked up again. Tears stung my eyes, blurring my vision.

And yet I stared through it, burning the appalling image into my brain.

Prison cells had been carved into the limestone walls on the opposite side of the river. Iron bars, rust coating their surfaces into a reddish-black hue, spanned the ten-foot-square openings.

Within each cell huddled a handful of prisoners, young Caucasians who dressed in colorful tourist clothing. Two were sitting on the floor in the corner of the farthest enclosure, five more populated each of the other four cells. They couldn't be much older than twenty and looked like they belonged on a college campus, not in a dank prison in the bowels of a madman's house.

"Devin, listen to me," Alec whispered as he eased his grip on me by testing degrees. When I no longer fought his hold, he gripped my shoulders and turned me toward him as he searched my eyes. "We have a mission to complete. You wanted to be a part of it. Here you are. Help me. Help them. We can only do that by learning what Escobar's plans are. We can't rescue them; we don't even have an exit strategy for ourselves yet. And Alfredo Escobar doesn't do anything small scale. To save a couple dozen now could risk thousands, possibly millions, later."

Millions. Millions meant entire metropolitan cities. That ghastly thought cut through the hurricane of emotions hazing my logic. I snapped out of the sudden panic that had paralyzed me.

"He has a dungeon," I whispered back, galled at the concept, unable to digest the level of insanity.

"Help me find out why." His words came out gentle, an urging plea.

For a tense moment, I struggled against the fresh agony roiling inside me. Then I sucked in a shaky breath and harnessed a survival skill I'd honed long ago, erecting an impenetrable wall and shielding the most vulnerable part of myself behind it. I blew out a strained breath, fighting to keep things compartmentalized—no small task, given my level of past trauma and the scar tissue that had just been ripped wide open.

Yet through sheer will, I ignored my screaming internal

needs. The mission at hand wasn't about me. I stared hard at the twenty-two unfortunate souls. Tonight was about them. *And potentially millions of others.*

I drew upon every bit of angered strength and vengeance that I'd held back for far too long, gave Alec a determined nod, and turned back toward him. "Tell me how to help."

"What do you see?"

I narrowed my eyes at the occupied cells, committing to memory the features of the kids trapped inside whose faces were downturned, eyes shut, as if resigned to some dire fate. They either hadn't sensed our presence, or had experienced enough disappointing visitors to believe no one would be coming to rescue them.

Bolstering my courage by focusing on our mission, convincing myself regardless of any supporting evidence that we would save the purported millions *and* these twenty-two, I focused on the room at large. "You don't happen to have those glasses, do you?"

In a flash of movement, they appeared in front of me. "Never leave home without them." From behind, he carefully slid them over my face, guiding the slender rubber-coated arms over my ears until they were secure. Then he grasped the right outer frame edge with his index finger and thumb, depressing a silver button on top. A faint chime sounded in my ear as the computer array appeared across the inner surface of the lenses.

Readings of temperature and humidity, altitude, and coordinates of longitude and latitude appeared on either side.

The image adjusted as I swept my vision to the hydroelectric station. Nothing remarkable or unexpected there. A simple housing, basic engineering to harness the natural power of water.

Next, I focused on the clean room. As I concentrated on the objects within, the binocular feature activated, enlarging each detail as I centered them, one by one, into view.

Narrow glass test tubes were lined up in a metal rack on one side of a gleaming stainless steel surface, all empty. On another table, two unused syringes were lined up perfectly parallel to one another on a blue cloth. A third expended syringe rested beside a mushroom-shaped cork. Two additional corks rested on their rounded sides in the center of the table, haphazardly positioned as if they'd rolled there.

On the far wall, a bulletin board hung above a desk. Pinned to its surface were pages of molecular diagrams, mysteriously beautiful and complex constructs of DNA strands. I zoomed in further and concentrated on each page individually, committing them to memory. It suddenly dawned on me that EtherSphere One would want copies to examine, I leaned closer to Alec. "Is there a way to take snapshots of what I'm seeing?" I murmured.

"Already happening. The images you see upload automatically to live satellite feed, then into our servers to be disseminated by electronic processors and human analysts."

I gave a curt nod as I multitasked, continuing to view and catalog during our conversation. Common sense warned me we didn't have unlimited time down here, and a growing sense of urgency churned in my gut. I blew out a measured breath as I continued to scan.

While I gathered information, Alec remained tense and alert, constantly scanning across the room, occasionally glancing up toward the locked door. I got the feeling that door was our ticking time bomb.

I blinked to clear my vision, then scanned downward from the bulletin board to a desk with papers strewn across its surface. Odd to have such scattered chaos in an otherwise orderly room. Two disheveled stacks of bound reports towered high on the desk's far left corner, occasional loose papers sticking out randomly between them. Unable to see the blue covers of the two bound reports on top, I stepped forward, unthinking.

Alec's solid grip clamped on to my right upper arm. When I glanced up, the sunglass lenses blanked out for a brief second, then a glowing blue grid appeared, mapping the topography of his face: cheekbones, orbital bones, jawline points, distance between his eyes. "Facial recognition," I whispered, amazed.

He gave a sharp nod, then pointed up toward the ceiling. A security camera perched above us, in the corner over the uppermost landing of the staircase. "We can't leave this area. We're in an approximate two-foot blind spot to their security cameras. Everything needs to be gathered from here to remain undetected."

And undetected was a top priority. No way to save the world if we got caught and imprisoned. My pulse quickened as that growing sense of urgency returned, and I hurriedly refocused on my task. Done with my examination of the clean room, I scanned over to the two darkened rooms.

With the aid of the ever-adjusting lenses I wore, the shadowed environment suddenly illuminated before me with night-vision technology. Beginning my sweep from the left, I spotted direct access from the first clean room: two sets of glass sliding doors separated by a four-foot space in between. Round, metal pressure knobs were mounted on the glass wall outside of each set of doors, three feet up from the floor.

The room held no furniture. And a darted scan to the right confirmed the last darkened room resembled the first: no furniture, no structures in the center of the room whatsoever, only empty floor space.

Along every square inch of wall space, however, from floor to ceiling and side to side across, stood refrigeration units. Through their glass doors, metal shelves spanned their three-foot widths. Each of the units held uniform contents, and a green digital reading displayed the temperature on the upper left corner of each door. When I focused into one of the refrigerators, my ingenious lenses blinked back a temperature reading in bright glowing red. Both temperature readings matched: *40*.

Deep voices broke my concentration.

Confused, I looked around. With the rushing sounds of water echoing off the hard surfaces, the clarity and close proximity of the intruding sounds startled me. An instant later, understanding dawned as another male voice spoke, clear as a bell…into my right ear.

Brow furrowing, I turned and glanced up at Alec. "The glasses pick up conversations?"

His expression hardened as he turned his head and stared at the door above us, our only exit point. "They're programmed into alarm mode. Picks up anything breaching the silence of a fifty-foot perimeter. Activates the sensors I secretly planted in the hallway."

"Sensors?" When the hell had he planted those? I buried the question. No time.

Not yet finished with our reconnaissance, I focused back on the refrigeration units, zooming in on the contents of each as I scanned inside from top to bottom. One held test tubes, another vials, a third, larger beakers. Two entire units contained what appeared to be upright Champagne bottles. All were scanned into my brain and the lenses simultaneously.

"We have to go." His urgent tone throttled any further exploration.

I tore the glasses from my face, folded them, and handed them back. He tucked them into the inner breast pocket of his jacket.

Panic boiled to the surface as I glanced up at the door we'd been locked behind. Then I stared across at the prisoners we were helpless to do anything about.

Alec gripped my hand and pulled me toward the underground river.

"The cameras," I hissed. "You said we had a two-foot perimeter of nondetection."

"Not absolute," he countered as he pressed his body flush against the wall, dragging me behind him. "Didn't want to risk a margin of error."

"And now?" I followed his example, doing my best to become one with the wall.

"We risk it."

Connected by the strong clasp of our hands, we edged around the corner. My size seven feet, even with their shortened footprint in stilettos, barely fit, with only two inches to spare on the ledge between our wall and a sheer three-foot drop into the river. His size thirteens hung over by a good quarter length.

Our lateral movement caught the attention of one of the five captives in the endmost cell, almost directly across from our current position. A girl no older than me with scraggly blonde hair and dirt smudged across her cheeks gravitated toward the iron bars, her eyes widening. She wore a Kelly green Fighting Irish T-shirt that had a ragged hole torn from the upper chest to one shoulder, half-decapitating the faded leprechaun mascot.

"Help us!" Her hands gripped the bars until her knuckles blanched. "Please, help us!"

The emotional dam I'd hastily constructed mere minutes ago burst. On instinct, without regard for the vast distance across the river that I'd never make, I lunged away from the wall. A hard band struck across my chest, knocking the air from my lungs, as I was yanked backward. Fabric ripped, but held, as Alec's hand fisted into my silk dress just under my arm.

"We barely have time to save ourselves," he growled into my ear. "Us now. Them later."

A deep, soft boom sounded out, almost inaudible over

the constant rushing hum of the water. The entrance door at the top of the stairs had to have just opened.

Resigned to the grim circumstances, I nodded, then stared down at the water whooshing by just a few feet below us, its flowing surface deceptively smooth. Scanning left, my gaze froze where water met the wall. "There's a grate blocking the tunnel." I pointed toward our only escape.

Ten yards down the span of the river's exit point, only the top arc of a metal grate was exposed above the waterline, riveted to the wall by a trio of heavy-duty brackets.

"Did you see a switch for it?" he asked.

I scowled. "No! I was watching the room."

There were no lights down the short passageway we stood in, so only the far side's wall and half of the river were illuminated. The stone wall we pressed ourselves against fell into the oblivion of shadow.

I dug deep mentally, flashing back to the blueprints and mechanical schematics Alec had stolen. "It has to be on the wall, back around the corner. There were junction-box markings." Which indicated the position for a switch of some kind. "About four feet up, three feet in."

"Be careful," he warned. "I'll hold you. Lean out and wide."

Before I had a chance to clarify, he slid his hand up my forearm, and I gripped his, locking us together as he guided me back toward the corner. Understanding dawned as basic geometry came to mind. Instead of continuing straight to the corner, I paused a foot from it, then leaned out over the river, craning my neck while angling my upper body toward the corner. All the while, my gaze trained toward the upper stairwell.

The technique allowed me to slice a greater part of the visual pie, exposing only a portion of my face instead of my entire head. I registered a dark shape hovering at the stairwell's uppermost landing before I darted a glance at the wall. A sleek metal button, the diameter of a coffee mug, had been hidden in the wall's sprayed-concrete surface.

I inhaled a deep breath, then leaned forward, leveraging the hold Alec had on me while I stretched as far as my reach would allow. *Farther...a little bit farther...*

Sliding my hand along the coarse concrete surface, I finally detected a circular ridge with the tip of my index finger. I scooted closer to the corner, gaining another two needed inches. My finger glided over to the center of the button, and I tensed my entire arm, pressing down hard.

Seconds later, a loud mechanical motor growled to life. I spun around. The iron grate on the wall that barred our way through the water slowly bent open on its hinges. "It's working. It's lifting."

"We have to go now." The grim announcement held no inflection, only factual warning. "Ready?"

No. But I stuffed my anxiety down into that dark place inside of me and pulled out anger instead. Then I nodded and took a deep breath.

"Three, two..." Alec counted down.

One never came. We squatted, then in a burst of muscle fired by pulsing adrenaline, we jumped, even though the grate still moved—not yet fully open.

We landed dead center into our fifteen-foot wide section

of river, knees to our chest, cannonballing with a splash. Cool water surrounded me as we submerged, followed a split second later by the balls of my shoes touching bottom.

Alec never released my hand as he twisted forward and kicked his legs, shifting in front of me while the rapid current swept us out of the chamber and toward the aperture that led toward the freshwater inlet we'd explored only the day before. Pressurized currents pulled me under and bounced me around.

Something tugged at my dress before the tension slacked. Beneath the surface, I glanced up and made out the hard edges of the grate flashing by.

Seconds later, when we broke the surface of calmer water, I gasped for air. Then as I still gripped Alec's hand like a lifeline, I floated onto my back. Mottled shadows danced above us, the delicate branches of dense foliage blurring together. *Mangroves.* A canvas of twinkling stars followed as cooler air brushed over my face.

Another current pulled at us, sweeping us in another direction: eastward, out to sea. The floating peacefulness mismatched the riot of emotion clashing inside me. The images of the prisoners Escobar held, the girl pleading for help, assaulted my mind.

A cramp at the base of my throat choked me. My lungs burned, screaming for air. But I couldn't find it. Couldn't inhale even one breath. Barely escaped from the snapping jaws of danger, I couldn't taste freedom.

The walls of captivity closed in on me regardless. Surrounded by the sweet promise of air, I suffocated. Buoyant on the surface of an entire sea of turmoil, I drowned.

CHAPTER 17

Uncontrollable shivers racked my body, but no sensation of cold bit into my skin. Water swirled around me, but didn't carry me any longer. Dead weight, I slogged through wet sand. Fell onto my knees. Coughed salty water from my lungs.

Numb.

I'd been lost in the blissful haze of it, body and mind. Like I'd frozen solid, then fractured, then in slow motion, burst apart, every shard drifting away from its whole, no longer connected.

Fringing into my awareness, pressure tugged at my arm, at the elbow.

My knees gradually unfolded. My stomach sank as I distantly felt drawn upward. The dark, wet granular earth withdrew, fading away.

Solid warmth tucked under my backside, surrounded my arms, curved under my legs. A gentle crush enveloped me, and I curved into it, needing it, seeking the tight security it provided.

Weightlessness spun my mind, whirled the air around me. Nauseated, I closed my eyes and swallowed the bile back down.

A slight tilt forward. A metal click in the background.

Cool air danced over my skin. A peachy glow breached through the protective cover of my eyelids.

I pinched my eyes tighter shut. Burrowed deeper. Sought the confining, dark warmth.

All too soon, my cocoon fell away. Bare feet touched a cold, hard surface.

I cringed. A weak whimper filtered into my ears. My brain dimly processed that the odd sound had come from me.

"Shhh, it's okay, Devin. I've got you." The low tone soothed me. I clung to the voice, leaning forward, seeking its protection.

When I blinked open my eyes, Alec's face slowly crisped into focus. Even though we stood in a dark room, dim light from somewhere beyond illuminated the angular planes of his face. Concern shadowed his eyes, drew his brows together. But then his features softened.

"Don't..." He brushed his knuckles against my cheek.

I lifted my fingers, entwined them with his until warm moisture coated my fingertips. My vision blurred, and I rapidly blinked. Confused, I pulled my hand in front of my face while still linked to his. *Tears.*

"We could do nothing. Don't blame yourself," he urged.

The weighted realization of what we hadn't done crushed in on me. I collapsed into a heap right on the cold stone floor. But he instantly dropped too, catching me as I fell, softening the impact.

But none of it mattered, did it?

"I didn't deserve to escape," I wailed, voice threadbare. "It should have been me. They should have taken me." With every successive word, I slipped further into the dark abyss, my voice fading, sounding more and more detached.

"Of course you did." His body curved around me, solid thighs and bent knees bracketing me on either side. His arms followed as he tugged me off the floor and into his hold.

"No," I croaked. "They took her. She grabbed my hand. I tried to hold on. But then she screamed, and a light came on, and they ripped her away from me. Stole her. Took everything."

Alec's arms tightened, a vice clamping down on me. They remained that way until I had to push my arms outward, fight his hold, to take my next breath.

Silence followed.

My heartbeat gradually slowed with the breaths he allowed me. And the more they settled into a calmer rhythm, the more leeway he gave, until I had to move my arms infinitesimally outward to confirm he still embraced me.

I closed my eyes, secure in the knowledge of where I was, who held me.

"My baby sister," I whispered, voice growing hoarse. "She would have turned five the next day. A birthday party had been planned. Balloons hovered in the corners of our living room. An ice-cream cake sat in a box in our freezer. Shiny presents with brightly colored ribbons had already been piled in the center of the table.

"She was too excited to sleep. Crept from her room across the hall and snuck into my bed. We'd giggled and laughed with the covers pulled over our heads, until we'd finally fallen asleep."

I took a shuddering breath, vivid memories scrolling forward as I watched, helpless to stop them. "They took her, not me. Two men wore black ski masks. Even through them, I saw the confusion in their eyes. There was only supposed to be one girl in my bed." My voice cracked on the last word— confession complete.

The logical part of my brain, the one that was supposed to rule geniuses, render their emotions moot, knew the painful symptom I suffered through was survivor's guilt. But mine was more than a transference of my own feelings about making it through the ordeal alive when another hadn't. Mine was literal.

They'd meant to kidnap me.

But had taken her.

No one had ever heard *that* confession. No other soul had born witness to the testament of the scathing pain I'd endured.

Of course, my sister's captors knew the circumstances of the situation, along with my parents and the three-hundred-dollar-an-hour therapist—along with the police, the FBI, and any number of crime-scene professionals and investigators tasked with finding my sister within the twenty-four-hour window of highest probability of her being found alive.

Statistics. Cold numbers. Facts in the case.

As the days had ticked by, followed by weeks, and months, then years—the calendar cruelly indifferent to those governed by it—two undeniable things surfaced crystal clear. My sister was dead, evidenced by the bones of a partial skeleton that surfaced years later and two counties over, along the shoreline of a river. And the loving family I'd once known perished right along with her, pronounced dead at the scene of the crime, the very night she'd vanished.

Somehow I found my voice again, forced strength into it. "She's dead."

"You're not." His tone held a cutting edge.

Lost in a whirlpool of misery, I found myself tugged toward the side as he grabbed hold and pulled me from the downward spiral. Weak from the night's events and the freshly opened wound that had been too scarred to fully heal, my head lolled to the side until my temple rested on the wet wool of his tuxedo jacket.

He curled his arm up and cradled my head with his hand. "You're alive for a reason, Devin. I don't believe in coincidences. I didn't just drop onto your balcony by some random occurrence."

I let out a soft snort. "I hadn't thought so. If you recall, I'd commented on the statistical improbability at the time."

"It was meant to happen."

Confusion clogged the gears of my brain, surely he couldn't mean… "Fate?"

A slight wobbling told me he'd shrugged his shoulders. "Sure."

Comfortable silence followed, minutes ticking by until he finally broke it. "You're a scientist. Take higher-power ideology out of the equation. Before I met you, I was an operative stuck in his assignment—in need of a breakthrough. You had the skill set and unrelenting motivation to fill that need."

One corner of my mouth tugged up at his "unrelenting" comment. "And we were innately drawn to one another before either of us knew the other's situation."

His arms and legs gave me a quick full-body squeeze. "Exactly."

Before I registered what was happening, his weight shifted back, to the side, and then upward, drawing me up from the floor with him until I stood, barely. He settled his hands on my shoulders, then turned me around.

"No more talk of the past." He peeled the sand-encrusted stiff silk from my skin and dragged the material down my sides. "You focus on here. Now. Just keep breathing, slow, deep…steady."

His low, soothing voice came out in a rhythmic metronome, calling out a subtle cadence that demanded obedience. Exhausted on countless levels, I submitted to his ministrations, needing whatever I instinctually knew he would provide.

He slowly undressed me, pulling the ruined fabric away from where it had been plastered to my body. Once lustrous fabric now crackled, a stiff, beaten mess. Coarse grains of sand abraded already irritated skin, but I welcomed the minor pain.

Cool air rushed over the abused surface. But the uncomfortable chill would be temporary.

Naked in front of the man who'd tenderly bared me wide open, exposed me to a level I hadn't dreamt possible, I stood there in the dark room before him, waiting, unmoving.

He quickly undressed, and his warm, solid hand slipped into mine. A gentle tug drew me forward in the darkness. Then the tinny sound of glass hitting metal clinked out, echoing against hard surfaces. A soft squeak sounded, followed by water droplets splatting onto tile. He ushered me inside an obvious shower enclosure, his chest to mine, his body a shield to the sudden elements. The cool mist that rained down on my face and upper arms quickly warmed, then grew hot.

Without request, he'd left the lights turned off. Another method of blindfolding perhaps, getting me to feel, not see. Yet when emotion had overwhelmed me, he got me to think, not feel.

And now, without sight, brain too exhausted to think, I followed his instructions...and just breathed. His solid frame stood inches from me, not crowding, but not easing away either. In natural movement to steady myself in the unfamiliar place, without sight to guide my balance, I brushed up against him in places, bumped into his thigh with a knuckle, his chest with my nipple. Yet the touch wasn't overtly sexual, merely comforting.

Water, heated just below scalding, pelted my skin, washing away the sand, the grime. A pleasant aroma filled my nostrils on the next inhalation, earthy with a light herbal undertone. The fragrance triggered a memory of our first sexual encounter, his body covering mine, me inhaling his incredible male scent. Now I knew the source. It began with him…in *his* shower. The sudden knowledge that he'd brought me into his private domain comforted me.

Foamy suds followed, and he turned me, facing me away from him. His hands slicked over one shoulder, cupped over my arm top and bottom, then massaged down the length of it, to elbow, wrist, then fingertips. He repeated the process on the other side. Every so often, his touch would pause over a tender spot, then massage gently, as if he knew I'd been injured there, wanted to fix it.

Steam billowed up around us in the generously sized enclosure as he rubbed my shoulders, my back, working his way down to the uppermost cleft of my ass. Then he rubbed down my glutes, one, then the other, before his soapy fingers slipped down the crack in between, cleansing every hidden part of me.

Then he moved from the stream of water he'd been blocking and allowed the hot spray down as he turned me under it. After another momentary pause, he shifted in place again, and his soapy hands returned, this time to my front side.

Tingles of awareness and sparking arousal charged my nerves to erotic life from the drowsy sensual place I'd been floating in. Gentle pressure of his flattened palms and his rippling fingers caressed around the curves of my breasts, circled around hardening nipples, floated over the quivering planes of my belly. His hands skimmed outward, sliding down my hips, then trailed back inward, down the sensitive crease along the uppermost edge of my thigh.

I sucked in a shaky breath when his hard fingers glided through the intimate folds between my legs, gently forward and back, only enough to be thorough in cleansing, but plenty to fire me into a trembling hot mess. But then he bent before me, lowering into a squat, and soaped my legs, one at a time, cradling and massaging around the muscles as he worked his way down my thighs, over and behind my knees, my calves, shins, ankles, all the way to my toes. He continued to find various knots and bruises, gently lingering over each one in assessment.

Then he lifted one foot and dug his fingers into the narrow channels of muscle and tendon in my arches, stroking with steady pressure from heel to toe. He slid a fraction of an inch inward, repeating the process.

I groaned, leaning forward, bracing my forearms on his shoulders.

His deep chuckle echoed. "*This* is what you moan over?"

I bit my lip to keep from smiling, sensing his purpose here. We knew the sexual chemistry between us was off the charts. But this moment wasn't about sex. These minutes we shared were a rare gift of connection, therapy—healing. In a jarring situation, one I hadn't expected, couldn't have predicted, I'd been stripped bare, flayed raw down to my most crippling vulnerability.

Alec sensed what I most needed…and provided.

A deep pang of emotion hit hard in my chest, burning there; the sexual draw between us had been undeniable, but this…this was something more.

Before I had time to analyze the startling realization not yet fully formed, he stood, turned me, and rinsed me clean with caring but chaste movements. Then he placed his hands on my shoulders, guided me as we spun one-hundred-eighty degrees to switch positions, then handed me the bar of soap.

"Your turn."

Tilting my face up toward him, I barely made out his features in the darkness. Although amusement tinged his tone, not even the hint of a smile belied his mood. Not in the firm line of his lips, nor in the intensity of his eyes.

Yet I felt the weight of the moment, both thick and ethereal, like the ever-present steam coalescing in the air. Our cleansing ritual went far beyond skin-deep for him as well as for me. He'd already divulged that he didn't do relationships, had never let a woman close enough to have a second sexual encounter. Yet here we were: *post* second sexual encounter, third if you count the decadent pre-room-service appetizer.

Yet instead of being skittish or defiant about his sound no-relationship rule, he stood with me: relaxed, yet unmoving. Solid and sure.

I didn't question the precious anomaly. Only respected it and cherished the gift for what it was. As I soaped up my hands with the bar that had flecks of coarse material molded beneath its smooth surface, staring through the shadows into eyes that gazed down at me with unreserved trust, I settled into the rare slip of time we'd been granted.

And as I ran my hands over the muscular angles and taut planes of his body, learning, yet already knowing, my inner darkness took on a glimmer of light that hadn't been there

240

before. Both of us had become orphans by fate, souls drifting through life as we searched for our place and purpose in it, yet neither of us were those personas within these glass walls.

We'd been attracted to one another, not by providence, but by circumstance. Drawn together, not by mere physical attraction, but by the soul-deep essence of who we were, what we'd become in spite of it all.

With methodical strokes, I cleansed the imposing man who remained docile—larger than life in the tiny space, yet his carnal side restrained in favor of something infinitely greater.

Any sexual current that had sparked naturally between us, ebbed deeper as it flared warmer. A stark sensuality lingered, holding us in its tenable grasp.

When I finished, after the remaining few minutes had passed in wordless reverence, he turned the faucet off. He opened the door and guided me toward the right, until my toes hit a plush bathmat. The following instant, a soft towel surrounded me. He rubbed my arms with it, then found my hands and tucked the ends between my fingers as he pressed a gentle kiss to my forehead.

I inhaled a breath far calmer than any I'd had since arriving half out of my mind.

"Are you hungry?" He swept his own towel over his chest and arms before he whipped the end over the top of the shower stall and let it drape there.

"No." Wouldn't have been any way to keep it down, even if I had been.

"Let's get some sleep, then. Plenty of time to sort it all

out in the light of day." He grasped my hand before I had a chance to respond, then led me down a short hall and into his bedroom, leaving the door open behind us.

I let him pull me down to the bed, allowing the weight of all that had happened, everything that had come before, to draw me under without letting any of it penetrate the protective shield that Alec had wrapped around us.

His body molded behind mine as soft, cool sheets tangled between my legs, soothed my abraded skin. On an exhausted sigh, I surrendered to the sinking sensation, gave myself over to the darkness enveloping us, knowing without any doubt that Alec would protect me.

My last thought as I drifted from consciousness was the fervent hope that we would be strong enough to protect everyone else.

CHAPTER 18

Air disturbance brushed over my skin, but I couldn't identify the source. Eyes cemented closed, I stretched, then winced, groaning as pain lanced through my muscles in a rippling wave.

With measured focus and slow breaths, I tested each sore limb with a gentle flex, confirming everything still worked the way it should.

Before I opened my eyes, recognition edged in: flashes of me collapsed on the beach, Alec carrying me up to his house, us showering together.

The shower.

That last memory lingered, rich in substance. The event marked the most intimate experience ever to happen to me, sex or not.

Had it all been a dream? Or worse...an act? A mask over his true self: the spy?

Plenty of time to sort it all out in the light of day. His words drifted back, a fragment of last night.

Sort what out? Adrenaline spiked through my veins, and I bolted upright, blinking my eyes open. I sat alone, stark naked in the center of a low platform bed with a sea of white sheets swirled around me.

Beyond the foot of the bed, bamboo flooring spanned forward, disappearing at a glass wall. Just outside, a silver strand of beach met an indigo ocean as the purplish hue of first-morning twilight faintly colored the sky. A slow-rolling wave crested, then collapsed down, its muted boom permeating the silence.

My pulse hammered, at odds with the peacefulness of the room, of nature...of everything.

Out of sorts in a way I couldn't disseminate, I pushed up from the bed, needing to find Alec. And answers. To what? I hadn't a clue. Something to settle the chaotic emotions inside of me, for a start.

The air held a slight chill, fanning goose bumps over my skin. The only piece of furniture in the room was an unassuming bamboo dresser. I pulled open the top drawer, found a soft, black V-neck tee, and pulled it on over my head.

After exiting the bedroom, I detoured into the bathroom to pee. The ruined clothes that had fallen to the floor last night had vanished; only black slate tiles existed, not a speck of sand on them. The towels had vanished too, bathmat and all. But the darkness remained. I closed my eyes and took a deep breath, embracing its therapeutic nature. After peeing, then washing my hands in the dim light with another bar of Alec's earthy soap, I stepped back into the hall.

On bare feet, I padded past a large glass atrium where lacy ferns arched over a shallow stream that meandered in and out through denser foliage. Nearest the hallway, dark-brown soil was speckled with a few golden bamboo leaves. A single palm stretched toward the fourteen-foot ceiling in a far corner.

Continuing on, I stepped through the backside of an immaculate kitchen. Grayish-green soapstone counters topped simple maple cabinetry. A white country-style apron sink hung low along the back counter. The brushed stainless steel appliances gleamed, from the stove, with its smooth electric cooktop, to the refrigerator that had a digital temperature reading within the door's surface that glowed a bright turquoise *42*.

Beyond the open soapstone counters, Alec moved soundlessly, his arms arcing gracefully, legs lunging in fluid movement. Eyes closed, his expression remained relaxed as he moved in nothing but a pair of black cotton lounge pants that hung low on his hips. He resembled a powerful Samurai dancing through the air, muscles tensing and relaxing, body ebbing and flowing to some unheard warrior's cadence.

And even though I'd awoken with an urgent need to find calm for my inner turmoil, I settled back and said nothing. I wanted to blend into the background, stay the observer in Alec's world for as long as possible—learn from him.

Getting the sense that I witnessed a rare event, something Alec didn't readily expose to others, I crossed my arms over my chest, leaned against the curved hardness of the counter's edge, and focused on my breathing, something he'd told me to do last night.

Last night.

As I watched his fluid movements, the masterful control of a body honed into a weapon, I contemplated the paradoxes of the man who quietly restrained all that power into an art form as he performed his *kata*. How did he reconcile who he actually was with who he pretended to be?

Perhaps the answer was simple—he didn't.

Compartmentalizing took many forms.

For a man determined not to have any sort of relationship with me—with anyone—he'd broken his own rule with ease in the wine cellar last night. Yet minutes later, he'd been precision-focused on his mission, in spite of our heated encounter...or maybe because of it.

He'd even been able to handle the situation of the captives we'd encountered with cold factual calculation. Hell, even I'd known with the scant time we'd had that no rescue attempt would've been possible.

Yet my scar tissue had still flared painfully, blinding me. *Disabling me.* I'd been unable to handle the release of emotion I'd kept bottled deep inside that had been unleashed with the unexpected horrors of witnessing their dismal state, the resignation in their faces...the anguish on one.

On the verge of losing control again, I sucked in a deep breath. Then I blew it out to a measured count of ten.

Alec continued his meditative workout. The soft turquoise glow illuminated the defined lines of his muscles as I pondered a last puzzling facet he'd presented: how caring he'd been when I'd lost control. Patient and understanding, as if he'd expected the breakdown or had been there before, he'd played the gentleman last night. He'd fulfilled my only need when he'd pulled me to shore, carried me to his house, cleansed me...cared for me. And in doing so, he'd brought to life a part of me that I'd buried, an emotion I'd thought long dead—hope.

"Thought you were sleeping." His low voice slipped into the silence.

"Thought I'd been stealthy."

Without turning or breaking stride, he remained a dark silhouette against the ever-lightening gray sky. His next move began with a lunge and finished with pushing open palms outward from his chest. Then holding his right arm stationary, he swept his left outward across a horizontal plane while pivoting on his weight-bearing foot and flexing his extended foot as it rotated to rest on its heel.

"Help yourself to coffee or espresso." He turned forty-five degrees in the same direction again, leaning more weight on his back foot as he bent the other leg and propped it on a toe while arcing both hands toward his chest again. "On the far edge of the counter."

The mundane kitchen task he'd suggested became a welcome distraction out of my head. Beside a chrome Nespresso machine, four double-walled glass Bodum espresso cups were arranged in a line, resting upside down. A Cuisinart coffeemaker and two larger glass coffee cups sat on the nearer edge. Between the two, a stainless steel carousel held a variety of espresso pods. I turned on the espresso machine, chose a midnight-blue pod, and inserted it before securing the chrome latch. When I depressed the illuminated green button, a loud motor whirred into the peaceful silence, like I'd revved an aircraft engine inside a monastery garden.

On the off chance he might want one, I perched a second espresso cup on the chrome shelf, inserted another pod, then depressed the button again before walking away as a stream of liquid filled another tiny glass cup.

By the time I reached to the other side of the counter and took a sip of the rich espresso through its foamy *crema*, he'd finished his *kata*. He stood in a relaxed stance, facing away from me, toward the sunrise.

I gazed out toward the ocean, not wanting to disturb him any more than I'd already done.

Charcoal shapes smudged the ocean at the horizon line. They stretched long, appearing taller and narrow in sections; three were uniform in length. I stared harder, seeking to identify the vessels. No lights illuminated any cabins, so they differed from the cruise ships we'd spotted gliding by a few nights ago. Were they freighters? Maybe commercial vessels traveled on a morning schedule.

Seconds later, beams of fiery orange pierced through the unidentified images, casting bright color over all the monochrome. The shapes remained unidentified no longer: Dense clouds ruled the edge of the world. But they were no match for the power of the rising sun.

A beautiful scene unfolded as I cupped my warm espresso glass. Every second brought another facet to shimmering life, every millimeter of change, a new perspective. I sipped the hot liquid, watching intently as the thick clouds gave the sun a great fight. But in the end, the determined rays multiplied, bursting through.

In the span of my next breath, an epiphany crashed into me, pieces colliding into place. I straightened, tensing my arms, and bumped into Alec who'd apparently snuck beside me while I'd been entranced by the sunrise.

"*The ships...*" The realization came out on a breathless whisper. "The lights." My voice grew louder. "On the ships. On the house."

He paused, his espresso cup frozen in midtilt at his lips. He lowered the glass. "What lights? What house?"

"Escobar's." Brows drawn in concentration, I stared down at a bamboo knot in the floorboard right in front of my emerald-polished toes. "Remember on the catamaran? How I thought it odd that the lights in his house were going on and off?"

"Like the staff were going through the rooms for the night," he replied.

I gave a nod, then turned fully toward him. "Only what if it was something else? What if Escobar was sending a coded message?"

His eyes widened. "To the cruise ships."

"Right. One of the ships, probably. Or one of many sailing under the same cruise line."

His gaze dropped to the counter in thought. "The catamaran cruise. That was two days ago. A Thursday."

"The night before Escobar's light show, when we were watching the ships from my balcony, one had strands of green lights running from the high points, captain's bridge to bow." I rested my espresso cup onto the counter, then tapped my chin. "I remember the green lights blinked out for about twenty seconds, then flashed on again."

"*That's* their method of communication." He slapped a palm on the counter.

"And maybe more."

"Like they plan to transport their cargo on a cruise ship?"

I nodded, turning toward him.

"Brilliant."

His gaze locked on to mine, intensity shining there. I didn't know if his comment meant Escobar's plan or my discovering a piece of it.

I frowned. "But I'm sure customs keeps a lockdown on what cargo is unloaded from cruise ships." I paused, thinking it through, remembering the tourist captives, the very *American*-seeming captives. "What if it isn't cargo? What if it's a person?"

He turned and leaned back against the counter edge, arms folding over his chest. "Or a weapon." His tone held conviction.

"A weapon in a person..." I added to our unfolding joint revelation. "A deadly virus...you'd suspected it earlier."

At the slight turn of his head, he stared hard at me. "I didn't see the details of Escobar's laboratory through the same lenses you did. What are the statistical probabilities?"

"In the ninetieth percentile, given the first-glance clues in that dungeon: clean room, test tubes, centrifuges... syringes. The DNA diagrams on the wall could've been a weaponized virus. I'd have to do some research. Can I use your computer?"

"Sure. I have to check messages first, report in." He

tossed back the rest of his espresso and headed to the sink where he washed and rinsed the small cup. Then he ripped off a section of paper towel before resting the glass upside down on it with care.

Afterward, he turned to face me, faint worry lines etched into his forehead. "Listen, about last night."

I shook my head, dismissing his concern. Didn't matter if the topic was his rule slipup, my breakdown, or his unexpected tenderness. The regret on his face was clear.

I swallowed down a simmering uneasiness. "No need to mention it. I won't let it happen again." That covered it all. I forced myself to focus on what I believed I could control. The most important thing to me was getting Alec on board with my official involvement with EtherSphere One.

If any doubt had existed that I wanted to be a spy, needed to be an instrument for revenge and justice, it had vanished last night. I'd been thrust into the realm of absolute certainty about the path I wanted to follow.

Confusion warred across his features until finally those etched lines relaxed. He gave me a curt nod. "Good. Best to keep the lines clearly drawn."

Were we on the same page? I had no idea. But since all possibilities landed dead center in a personal minefield I was unwilling to traverse, I kept silent, intending for the meaning on my end to encompass them all.

"But you need to train me." There. I said it.

His head twitched infinitesimally backward, eyes widening for an instant. "For what?"

Oh, here we go again. My eyes narrowed. "I had

to surprise you at the party to convince you to involve me. I just connected the dots for you on how Escobar is communicating. You need me."

One dark brow cocked up in challenge. "I don't *need* you."

"You do. Get over your pride about it. Let me help you."

Amusement flickered in his eyes. A smile played at the corner of his lips as he crossed his arms over his bare chest and propped a hip against the counter. "No pride about it. Sound reasoning prevails. You aren't prepared to be a field agent."

"I know that." Exasperated, I threw my arms wide. "That's what I'm saying. Prepare me."

"Impossible."

"Bullshit." I rarely swore, but was willing to try any tactic to break through his dense objections. "Only because you aren't *considering* the possibility. How do you think I stabbed you?"

A muscle tensed in his jaw.

"Wasn't beginner's luck." I turned my back to him and went to the sink. I remained silent while I repeated his anal-retentive routine: washing, rinsing, paper-towel ripping, and glass upending.

By the time I turned around, his expression had changed. It was still hard around the edges, but the slightest bit of curiosity shone in his eyes. Holding my gaze, he uncrossed his arms and braced his hands along the counter's edge at his sides.

"Convince me." The quiet words held a note of challenge.

Sounded like he wanted an oral dissertation, not a physical display.

Fine. Hadn't told a soul in the world what I'd done, how I'd prepared, but if this was my résumé and job interview wrapped into one, I planned to leave no advantage unleveraged.

"After my sister was taken, not only did my parents train me to assess every situation—to anticipate risk variables, plan to thwart danger and deal with it, if necessary—I trained myself in various…skill sets."

I paused, gauging him for interest.

His expression was unreadable. "Explain."

"It began with archery. I threatened my parents that I wouldn't go into third grade until they enrolled me in lessons. Within a month, my instructor unofficially pronounced me a 'prodigy master archer.' I kept the skill sharp by joining clubs as I got older."

He remained silent as he held my gaze.

"Next came martial arts. Aikido, to start. I achieved First Don. Then I began training in jiu-jitsu until I received my black belt."

"What style?"

"Jiu-jitsu? Shorinji Kan."

He gave a barely perceptible nod. "Training for multiple armed or unarmed opponents. Focus is on awareness of the entire situation. All potential threats."

"How I've been preparing all my life."

"Anything else?"

"Volleyball," I reminded him.

He coughed out a laugh. "Looking to play spy as a team sport?"

"No." I arched an irritated brow, then lowered it, taking a deep breath as I willed myself to stay calm, focused. "It enhanced my ability to read people, both my teammates and the opponent. Plus it kept me in shape." I shrugged.

His gaze traveled down my body. Not that he saw much underneath his enormous T-shirt. When a spark heated in his eyes and a corner of his mouth kicked up, I knew he saw right through it, right through me.

"That it did," he murmured.

Determined, I pursed my lips and narrowed my eyes. Sexual chemistry off the charts? No problem. But I could ignore it. I wouldn't let him rattle me. Not when a goal I'd been working toward my whole life, but hadn't clearly identified until now, was within reach.

"Train me," I repeated. "Show me what I'm missing. Make me a field agent."

His tongue skimmed along his upper teeth. "To be clear, it's impossible to train you to be a field agent in a day, even a week. Remember, it takes months of intensive exercise in dozens of areas, including resistance to torture. Repetition until each skill becomes muscle memory is employed before EtherSphere brands an agent as field ready."

"But you'll train me," I insisted. I heard it in the tone of his voice; he was relenting.

"I'll begin. If I'm satisfied you can handle the basics, we'll see."

"And if I can, you'll introduce me?" I wanted the terms

set. Before I gave him one more ounce of help, I wanted to cement what I would receive in return.

"To EtherSphere?"

I gave him a nod.

He stared hard at me before answering. "Yes. If you can handle everything I give you, *and* if you prove yourself in a field situation, I will introduce you."

"Last night was a field situation."

"Which you failed."

I scoffed. "I supplied you with valuable information."

"You wore electronic lenses that captured everything for base command. A task I'd intended on and was fully capable of completing myself."

Riled, I took a deep breath. "You said you were glad I was there, 'perfect cover' you claimed, right before you fucked me against a wall."

He fought a smile, but then his face fell, relaxing. "I was. You were." He tilted his head, eyes softening further. "Then you fell apart."

The prisoners. Their presence—my trauma—had crippled me.

And I guess we were going to talk about one of the three potential topics after all.

"So *train* me. Consider last night my baptism by fire. At EtherSphere, a weakness like mine would've been used to torture-train me. In the dungeons, I compartmentalized off the cuff."

"True. But then you completely shut down." He angled his face a fraction downward, but his fierce gaze held mine

255

from beneath his dark brows. "A shut-down agent…is a dead agent."

"Then I guess you'd better harden me. *You* are going to get me that introduction with EtherSphere One. *I* am going to find something better to wear." With that, confident I had him on board, I walked past him and out of the kitchen, in search of something to train in *other* than a loose-fitting tee with no underwear.

A lot was riding on the outcome of the next few hours. *Everything* was.

CHAPTER 19

After rifling through all four of his dresser drawers, then wandering past the wall behind his bed into a large built-in closet, I came to a conclusion: Alec had expensive taste, a monochrome color palette, and believed in function over variety.

He owned five pairs of combat cargos, four casual cargos, seven pairs of jeans, two tuxedos, one suit, five white dress shirts, and seventeen V-neck T-shirts in black, gray, or some shade in between. No pajamas to speak of. I refused to count his boxer-brief underwear. Or socks.

"Finally," I muttered. On a shelf in the back corner of the closet, two stacks of black clothes were neatly folded: six soft cotton lounge pants on the right, seven matching tees on the left.

I removed the large shirt I'd confiscated earlier in favor of one of the newer tees. The fit was a bit snugger—still loose, but it would serve better for ease of movement. I slipped my legs into the bottoms, pleased to find that while they dragged five inches beyond my heel, the lightweight fabric easily rolled, with enough material in circumference for me to fasten them below my calf with a small knot. They also had a flat woven drawstring at the waist, enabling me to cinch them securely into place.

Satisfied that what I wore was appropriate to test my hand-to-hand combat skills, I retraced my steps back to the kitchen. Not finding Alec, I continued through the house, passing a closed door on the right before stepping through an open door on the left.

Alec sat at a desk positioned halfway down the right wall, facing outside to view the stretch of beach and ocean beyond. He furiously typed at a laptop's keyboard. "Just about done."

"With what?"

"The report from last night."

"Encrypted," I murmured, assuming it would be. My comment went unchallenged as his fingers rapidly clicked keys. As the tapping sounds blurred together, I wondered if typing an astronomical amount of words per minute was a vital part of spy field-operative training.

"What?" He paused, glancing up at me. "Oh, no. Well, yes. The entire system is on the Shadow Network."

"Shadow Network?"

"The darker Internet behind the Internet. And our communications are invisible, even there. No one could accidentally stumble into or hack our grid. You have to be given the address, know how to navigate the security layers, and even if you make it there, you have to fluently speak the language or it throws you out."

"Oh." So no exceptional typing skills needed. One only need be fluent in the art of secret programming.

"I have another message to send. Make yourself at home; just don't venture into the atrium. Deadly viper. Grab something to eat if you want. I'm about to make energy smoothies. We'll make eggs, bacon, and stir-fry vegetables later. Once we're done, you'll need it."

My stomach growled at the mere thought. But he didn't notice as he focused on another black window that popped up on his laptop screen.

Deadly viper? When I left the room, I eyed the once-harmless atrium down the hallway with suspicion, but paused in front of the closed door across from Alec's office. The only closed door I'd encountered. He'd suggested I had the run of the house except for said atrium, so I reached for the metal door handle. When it gave without resistance, I nudged open the door with my shoulder.

I stepped barefoot into a room colder by at least ten degrees as overhead lights automatically flickered on at my movement. The low hum of the fluorescent tubes became the only background noise.

I stood inside a nondescript three-car garage, pale-gray paint coating the blank walls, floor covered in a darker gray, speckled with black-and-white flecks.

His Jeep was parked on the opposite end. Another larger vehicle, a Range Rover, sat diagonally in the middle, its front corner leaving only a three-foot gap between front bumper and wall. Directly in front of me, two stout black containers made of heavy-gauge plastic were stacked, one askew atop the other.

Gut instinct—or possibly some triggered memory fragment—screamed these were weapons cases. Only one way to find out. The latches were also black plastic, and although stiff, were smooth to open once I leveraged the heel of my palm against the edge. Two successive clicks echoed before it popped open an inch.

Breath held, I lifted the lid and peered inside. My lips began to curve into a satisfied smile before I let out a low whistle. They were ballistic cases, all right. Protective pale-charcoal foam cradled a shoulder-style missile launcher on the far side. Two smaller pieces were snugged down into their own custom foam nooks.

"Impressed?"

Startled, I jumped so unexpectedly I nearly dislodged my hand propping the case open. I expelled a steadying breath before glancing over my shoulder at him. "Who wouldn't be?"

Alec had soundlessly entered the garage and crossed half of the eight-foot distance from the doorway. An instant later, he invaded my personal space, the mind-scrambling heat of his body hovering a mere inch from mine. I swallowed hard, then mentally shook off the disorientation. If I stood a chance at being trained by the man, I needed to be able to withstand the storm of sexual chemistry charging between us.

"Ever fired a weapon before?"

"Yes." Another part of my self-training. "Gun club."

"Which weaponry?" he asked.

"Various handguns. Seven days of sniper training, basic and advanced."

He fell quiet. Likely pondering why I hadn't disclosed that earlier. The only reasonable explanation I internally deduced involved instinctual secret keeping. Why reveal until necessary?

Reluctant to supply that personal tidbit of self-preservation, I swept a second gaze over the gleaming metal weaponry. "You collect military-grade weapons?"

"In a manner of speaking." He pulled out the missile launcher "These are EtherSphere One creations, modified for our purposes. The bluish sparkle of the alloy in the housing itself is nanotechnology, making the weapon traceable from our satellites."

"Oh, is that all?"

"No." He replaced the launcher into its foam nook and pulled out one of two football-shaped missiles. "The ammunition is crafted with nanotech too. Only, these babies also have a unique guidance function. If the bad guy aims and fires this at a target we don't approve of, we have the ability to redirect its trajectory, or destroy it…in flight."

"Wow. *Now* I'm impressed." A factoid pinged into my brain about the military's being either guided *or* reloadable, not both, as I ran a fingertip down the cold shaft of the weapon, impressed by its size. "I've never been this close to a handheld missile launcher." The note of awe in my voice surprised even me.

Okaaay. Apparently I like big sophisticated weapons.

Our gazes locked and held for a beat before his attention drifted down to the base of my throat. *Can he read me? Are my pupils dilated?* My breathing had shallowed and my pulse pounded in my ears. Not from fear, not quite arousal...but close. Adrenaline. Gripping a weapon was akin to holding unreleased lightning in the palm of your hand.

He took a deep breath, chest expanding until his skin just brushed against my upper arm. Then he fitted the missile back into its foam housing, grabbed a thin black cloth from atop another stack of cases I hadn't noticed, and wiped down the grip of the launcher, removing any trace of prints or oil.

Needing a distraction from the intoxication of his close proximity, I scanned the room, realizing there were *many* stacks of ballistic cases. The containers nearest us were the largest, with a handle at each end and needing two men to move, but others were more reasonably sized, some footlocker shaped, others like large suitcases, all the rest manageable by a single person. The entire cache? Enough to arm a small army.

"Planning an attack?"

"Supplies."

"For...?"

The deadpan look he gave me almost made me laugh. Like I was supposed to know what the weapons stash was for?

Then it dawned on me. "*Escobar*," I whispered. The ramifications of supplying weapons—such sophisticated weapons—to a madman blew my mind. "For how long?"

"Almost three years." He gave a nod, as if that covered it, then began closing the lid, forcing me to step aside. He secured each of the fasteners with a loud click.

"You're his *arms dealer*? *That's* your cover?" My mind spun, attempting to make sense of it all. I'd initially thought Alec had merely been a spy. But he'd also been chummy with Escobar, like they were great friends. My only evidence that either of them weren't ordinary people? Prisoners. And weapons. Both incriminating.

"What do *you* think?" he asked, tone edging into sarcasm.

That was just it. I didn't know what to think. Alec hadn't provided me any proof of EtherSphere One's existence. Only his word.

Everything else? Could be explained away on a wide spectrum. He could have been spying on Escobar, or he could have been playing me, luring me in for some inexplicable reason.

But one skill I did have, one I hadn't revealed to Alec? Advanced-level deception training. The classes were hard to obtain, only offered to law enforcement agencies. I'd had to falsify my affiliation with an agency that luckily backed out at the last minute to claim a coveted spot. The training incorporated one's innate ability to detect deception and sharpened it with inerrable methods in order to create human lie detectors.

I sure as hell hoped my instruction had been flawless. Because instinct and training both told me Alec was the real deal—not in league with Escobar, but truly a deep-cover spy plotting to stop him.

He stared at me, waiting for my reply, expression hard, like the next hours depended on my answer.

Yeah. I'd gone too far to cast doubt now—I was all in.

What did *I* think? "I think you've got nanotech-missile-proof cover."

The corners of his mouth twitched, but he firmed his lips into a hard line. Then he ruffled the top of my hair and pivoted, heading toward the door that led back into the house. "Let's go, Pink. Daylight's burning."

After we'd sat at Alec's basic dining room table and downed energy smoothies, my training had begun with methodical precision. We'd run through some rudimentary defensive moves I'd been schooled in, then moved on to more advanced techniques.

He conducted the entire operation like a drill sergeant.

"Again," he commanded, voice low, tone curt.

With measured steps, he circled me. This I knew from sound alone. Because once he'd satisfied himself that I knew how to defend against anything I saw coming, he wanted to test my abilities against that which I could not. He'd blindfolded me. *Again.*

Initially the silk falling over my eyes had caused an instant trigger, reminding me of the other night and all the pleasure he'd delivered when he'd instructed me so thoroughly.

"*You need to feel, not think,*" he'd repeated the same command as before, tone harsher.

And with a slight furrow to my brow, I'd concentrated to banish the sudden arousal.

I did so now. Yet so much in totality wove together, interconnected: the rush of sexual desire, adrenaline of a weapon in hand, the instinctual determination to win.

Only a slight air disturbance telegraphed his location. My mind flashed forth a grid-like image, predicting velocity and varying probabilities. I moved with fluid grace, stepping one foot back in tandem with where I expected him to be. The whip of an air current flew past my face. At the last minute, I jabbed an elbow out.

It made solid contact with what I'd estimated to be his ribs. A soft grunt followed.

Suddenly the world spun, and I landed on my back with a loud smack, air knocked from my lungs.

Not giving in, I snapped back up to my feet, tracking his whereabouts from my blacked-out world. Interestingly, even though I'd never fought from the darkness, I found the method easy to adapt to, almost comforting in a way. There were no unnecessary distractions: no collateral persons or objects, no escape routes to calculate. Only my target existed.

Tapping into an endless reserve of patience, a virtue I'd had to become well acquainted with over the years, I waited, listening. Observed. Assessed.

Every other sense awakened tenfold when denied one.

Only now, he'd been relegated to the status of deadly opponent. And I focused intently on him, my life hanging in the balance, even in this unorthodox training.

When I calmed myself, pulled my sense of awareness deep into the core of my body, I entered a unique suspended state. Like meditation in motion, I became part of the universe that surrounded me on an atomic level. Made sense, really. Comprised of pulses of energy, every single thing existed in a framework. And reduced to their most basic state, tapping into the essence of the energy itself—*becoming* energy itself—I distinguished the world around me better than any mere visual tapestry could provide.

I remained motionless in the sea of the cool air current that blew into the room from the vent on the wall. My breathing, barely audible, settled into a steady rhythm. Probing out with awareness, I located his breathing, now easily distinguishable from mine and from the barely perceptible whir of the air conditioning.

He stalked behind me, body lowered. An electric tension charged the air. I drew in a slow breath, relaxed, ready.

A wave of energy pulsed, and I moved, riding the current, becoming one until it crested. Then I punched an arm out, my fist making contact with muscle over bone for a split second before the contact point gave way. My mind computed that I'd hit his shoulder, knocked him off-balance. Not satisfied in the least, knowing the scenario was do-or-die, both in a real-life situation and for my ability to prove myself worthy, I crouched, then swept a leg out and around.

I impacted my target, hitting the muscled part of my shin against bones, one, then another. A loud thud on the bamboo floor in front of me was followed by his deep grunt.

Not risking any counterattack, I scuttled backward. Then I quickly assumed a ready position, knees soft, thighs flexing, then relaxing, breath calming to a steady rhythm as I pulled my awareness inward for a brief stabilizing moment before I reached it outward, assessing for threats once more.

Deep laughter rumbled out, vibrating against my senses. "Enough for now," he called out from the floor. "Take your blindfold off."

I slid the black silk tie up, resting it at the crown of my forehead like a headband.

He remained sprawled on the floor where I'd toppled him down.

I grinned. "Well?"

"Not bad."

"Not bad, as in, 'she'll do'?" I crossed the distance between us and stared down at him, propping my hands on my hips.

"Yeah. We've still got work to do. Don't make plans for today or tomorrow. But, yeah. She'll do just fine." Fire sparked in his eyes as he extended a hand up toward me, silently asking for my assistance. I clasped my hand around his forearm, gripping the muscle while he clamped on to mine, mirroring my hold. I dug my bare heels against the smooth bamboo flooring, lunging my weight back in counterbalance.

Energy still sizzled in the air around us, and I drew strength from it, charged in ways I couldn't put words to. No one on earth knew as much about me as Alec did. Not the whole of me. Not just the vulnerable girl, not only the trained weapon, nor merely the sensual creature. He certainly hadn't reduced me to an exploitable genius, like so many others had.

No. He saw all of me. And accepted me exactly as I was, without expectation or design.

And that rare and unexpected quality made Alec Marquez the most attractive person I'd ever been lucky enough to meet.

Oblivious to my revelation, he crossed over to the refrigerator and grabbed a plastic bottle with clear liquid in it. He shook it before splashing about a half an ounce of it into two glasses. Then he held each glass under a slender chrome faucet on the corner of his sink, filling them halfway with water.

"What's in the bottle?" I asked.

"Minerals: potassium, magnesium, sodium—electrolytes for replenishment."

When he handed me my glass, I clinked it lightly against his. "To our health."

He tilted his head in a slight nod. "To our health."

The water had a mineral taste to it, all right. My best efforts to restrain my reaction failed as my nose scrunched. "Uck," I voiced when he gave me a confused look. "Tastes like bitter ocean."

"It's good for you."

Uh-huh. Said the parent to the kid while force-feeding leafy greens. Holding my breath, I chugged down my medicine all at once. Then I refilled the glass with fresh water, swished it in my mouth to cleanse my palate, then swallowed it down.

He watched the entire episode with thinly veiled amusement.

"Mind if I use your phone. Need to ping Anna, let her know I'm alive."

"Sure." He turned and nodded toward the hall before heading that direction. "In my office. She doesn't suspect we've hooked up?"

He asked the question casually, like it meant nothing to him.

I followed him, speaking again when we entered the room. "She knows. I told her."

His gaze slowly tracked to meet mine. "How much did you tell her?" The words were weighted with innuendo as he stared hard at me.

My pulsed kicked up a notch. "Only that it happened. No details." No scorching, body-tremor inducing, lurid details. But my mind flashed there. My mouth went dry, remembering. Heat began to warm intimate places as I began to relive the erotic images.

I took a deep breath, then cleared my throat, suddenly uncomfortable under his unrelenting stare. "But she'd be wrong."

"About?" He arched a brow.

"Us hooking up *last night*." Not at his house, anyway. Yep. I went there.

He kept his gaze locked on mine. It was hard, penetrating. Almost assessing.

Feigning nonchalance about the entire subject, ignoring the fact my body was so on fire—so attuned to his and primed to go off that I'd probably explode with a single well-placed touch—I swiped the mobile phone off the corner of his desk and crossed the room to stop within inches of the glass wall, maximizing the distance between me and the temptation we continued to deny.

Through the sealed glass, the muted roar of the crashing waves soothed my agitated nerves. I dialed Anna's number and listened to the phone ring as I shifted my attention to Alec's faint reflection in the pane of glass, visible only where the darker ocean served as a backdrop. He was too far away for me to discern his expression, but after a moment, he sat at his desk.

"Anna. It's me."

"Dev! Dessert *and* breakfast?" she teased. "I was about to send out a SEAL team."

If only she'd had a clue that I'd been embroiled in an even more covert endeavor. Not that it would've helped paint a picture. Hell, I knew; but the more I learned, the more questions popped into my head.

"No drastic measures needed." I let out my typical rehearsed soft laugh.

After so many years of deceiving her about who I truly was beneath the normal college-student mask, one more casual deception helped maintain the cover I really needed. Alec hadn't explicitly told me not to reveal anything about EtherSphere One, or his identity, or my involvement, but I got the overwhelming sense secrecy was a given. Inherent trust lay coded in what Alec hadn't said, and I sensed a breach in that trust would be game-over on any notions I had for being brought on board.

"Good. When are you coming back?" she asked.

I turned around, staring at Alec. He'd busied himself at his laptop again, clicking away at the keyboard.

"Not until tomorrow night. You cool with that?" Some

vacation the week had turned out to be. Her at the hospital for two days. Me, squirreled away in covert training for a couple more, just down the beach from our resort.

But the original plan to temporarily get away from the pressures of college? Had all been a superficial ruse anyway. I'd been looking to escape—more permanently—from everything wrong in my life.

Her voice grew distant, like she pulled the phone away from her face. "Want to stay the night?" She'd spoken to someone else.

"Escobar?" A pang of worry lanced through me as I spoke the name. Son, father, I hadn't decided whether or not one or both were dirty. After seeing all the lab equipment, everyone seemed suspect.

Alec's gaze shot up, a brow arching at the name as well. I mouthed out *"Miguel."*

"Yeah, it's cool," she replied. "But that's it. We only have three days left of vacation. No more boys. No more parties. Only girl time."

"Only girl time." The words I repeated held conviction, even though nothing remained certain any longer.

In my mind, only one thing had solidified.

No longer would I be headed along the stifling predestined route of genius physicist. I'd veered far off course, down a path I'd been searching for all along, one that had fortuitously revealed itself when I'd least expected, when I'd opened myself to the universe in question.

The universe had answered loud and clear: *My* future lie in the dark shadows of espionage.

CHAPTER 20

Alec shifted his gaze toward the laptop as I ended the call with Anna. I crossed back to the desk, braving the dangerous erotic current between us, testing the waters. As I slid his phone onto the polished mahogany corner of his desk, nothing untoward happened. He didn't pounce on me in predatory strike, and I didn't melt into a puddle of quivering arousal at his feet.

But whether or not we acted on the sexual tension charging between us, it remained ever-present, at a low insistent hum, all the same.

"He's positioning to make a move."

"Escobar?" Not that Alec's intimation needed clarification. "How do you know?"

"An alert was sent through the network. ESO picked up on a sudden increase in stock moves from Escobar's shell corporations this morning."

"ESO?" I glanced over his shoulder, noticing several open

windows on his laptop screen. One had his organization's name emblazoned in the upper right corner.

"EtherSphere One," we uttered simultaneously. The acronym threw me because he'd often dropped the "One."

"They've begun shorting stocks. In the hundreds of millions."

"What kind of stocks?" I leaned in closer, scanning the information he'd displayed in the various windows.

He clicked on one of them, enlarging it. "Across the board. Mostly blue chip, corporate household names: Home Depot, Wal-Mart, Microsoft...GM...over a hundred different stocks."

I scrutinized the list, recognizing most of them. "American," I whispered under my breath, making the connection. "The stocks. The captives."

"You're sure?" He glanced up. "They were all American?"

Aided by my eidetic memory, I replayed the image of those prison cells again. The green Fighting Irish Notre Dame T-shirt. The cardinal and gold USC emblem on the baseball cap of one of the boys. "American college kids and sports fans. Like they'd been abducted from tailgate parties or local nightclubs." Maybe they had. Drunk. Easily manipulated. Easier to drug. "But they didn't seem to know each other."

"How so?" His head cocked, ever so slightly.

Forcing myself past protective barriers I'd relied on for so long, I risked revisiting the scene in more detail and focused harder on the minute specifics to back up my gut feeling. "No one in the cells huddled closer than necessary. No one touched, that I could see." No hands were locked together, gripping tightly to life and to their comrades by circumstance as they waited for what had to be certain doom.

After a sharp nod, he abruptly turned, pulled up a new window, and began typing a message.

Wondering how much he trusted me, I edged closer in. He didn't flinch at my bold action. Didn't question my involvement or my peering over his shoulder into my first focused glimpse of the covert EtherSphere One through the Shadow Network.

I remained quiet, observing. A certain peace descended over me as I gathered intel for my own personal agenda.

A deep-cover spy my whole life—*in* my own life—I finally stood at the towering precipice of realizing all I'd strived toward. To become the weapon the world had born and honed me to be.

The moment, the anticipation, the idea that I would seek revenge—if not for crimes against me and mine, then for those whose life currently teetered on the razor's edge between salvation or forfeit—vibrated through every cell in my body.

I let out a controlled breath through pursed lips, tamping down the energetic excitement as I watched Alec scroll through the screens.

"If not tonight, then tomorrow night." With lightning speed, he typed a missive to whatever authority he reported to on the other end, detailing our suspicions.

"So soon?"

"It connects to something Escobar said at the party. He wants me at his house tomorrow night. I've got a gut feeling about those stock shorts."

"Oh." Stock shorts were what the terrorists of 9/11 had done. They'd physically attacked while they'd financially attacked, a one-two strike at the heart of their victims.

Bored with staring at a screen that held no further new information, my gaze drifted to the right. An antique map-desk lined the wall behind him, its shallow depth but long width stretching to the room's back corner. Across the top, burled walnut had been polished to a high sheen, the center inlaid with a detailed compass rose, its faceted precise angles shaded in dark mahogany and highlighted with swirling bird's-eye maple. A solitary object on its surface angled toward Alec's desk: a picture frame whose glass faced the ocean and the world beyond.

I picked up the heavy frame, careful not to mar the flat polished silver sides with fingerprints. Its edges had tarnished into a beautiful smoky patina, but it was the aged picture behind the protective glass that most captivated me.

A younger version of Alec stared into the camera lens, pure joy radiating from his bright eyes and wide smile. His arms were wrapped around a young woman with long, dark, wavy hair. His parents, without doubt.

"Do you remember their love?" An odd question, even to my ears, but I needed to know.

He didn't reply right away, only briefly paused, then continued typing.

I didn't release the photograph. Didn't turn around. Entranced to a level I couldn't resist or deny, I remained rooted to the spot on his bamboo office floor, clinging to a fragment of someone else's joyous life, stuck in my admiration for those who'd been able to defy the choking darkness of the world for its breath of light.

The keyboard clicking ended entirely. But I barely noticed.

My heart pounded in my ears as I gripped the frame, thumbs slipped into place on the perfect silver surface. My fingerprints might as well have marred the perfect picture. Its image marked me. Indelibly.

How had one two-dimensional image branded my heart so fast?

On a shaky exhale, it hit me. It hadn't. The delicate aging photograph hadn't been the one thing, it had been the last thing, the proverbial straw on the camel's back—the catalyst to the fractures spider-webbing through an armored façade I'd so carefully constructed finally shattering apart, blowing to dust the once impenetrable fortress walls I'd imprisoned myself within.

"I remember." His voice slid over my senses, warm and soft. His heat came up behind me, wrapping around me as his strong hands ran down my arms, then covered my hands as they still clutched the frame.

For the first time in my life, I finally stood without my armor. Terrified, yet convinced I needed to take the leap of faith even if I died from the fall, I leaned back into his strength.

And he held me. As I began to shake, gripped the frame tighter for fear of dropping it, he simply held me.

"Their laughter is the greatest memory; I can still hear its echo in my head, feel its presence in the middle of the night."

An aching pang thumped from behind my ribcage. That he would be lonely in the darkness too, seek the memory of what he'd once had to lull him to sleep.

I'd done the opposite. "I can't remember mine." My voice croaked. Hands trembling uncontrollably, I clattered the bottom metal corners of the frame down onto the perfectly polished surface before I dropped it. "Their love, I mean." I sucked in a ragged breath as my arms drew against my middle. I hugged myself, trying to hold in the pain that I'd never let myself feel.

His arms followed, covering mine. A cramp burned at the base of my throat, and I closed my eyes, pinching back hot tears, afraid of losing myself to the scathing onslaught of feelings. As my breathing grew shallow, Alec tightened his hold, wordlessly providing his protection from the unseen threat.

"I don't know what happened." My voice sounded hollow to my ears. "When she vanished, the love stopped. All of it. Anger and hate hardened my parents. Hardened me."

His head dropped down and his lips brushed over my ear. "Your love is still there. Underneath your shell, deep underneath the bulletproof plating you welded into place to protect yourself; it's there."

Certain I'd misheard him in the surreal moment, I tensed, then stood straighter, testing his words, letting them wash over me, through me. And the moment I shifted, the unyielding cage of muscle and protection he'd clamped down around me gave way enough for me to find my own balance. But he didn't let go.

I turned within his embrace, slid my hands up his chest, and lifted my gaze until I opened my eyes and stared up into the dark penetrating depths of his. "How can you be so sure?"

Alec and I hadn't shared love. We'd had sex. I hadn't loved anyone since I loved my sister, since the love from my parents had been ripped away the night she'd been stolen from my bedroom a lifetime ago.

His intense gaze held mine, unwavering. "I know."

He said nothing more, only stared fiercely into my eyes. Like the explanation didn't matter. Like I could divine the meaning if I looked hard enough, delved deep enough. And maybe I could. He'd also barricaded himself in a prison of his own making. We'd both become survivors in the harsh battlefield of life, cast alone far too young. Neither of us allowing anyone too close.

If the theory were true... Then last night as he comforted me when I'd nearly unraveled...

Then he saw in me what I saw in him—what I hadn't recognized, because it was too foreign.

He loved. I loved. Maybe not in the conventional way. We kept our guard up, our emotions under tight lock and key. But in the right moment, when the battering forces of the world eased and all that was left after the hard layers had been stripped away was the vulnerable person we'd boarded up inside, we allowed ourselves to love.

I exhaled my first truly calm breath in thirteen years. Then, rubbed raw by the sudden revelation, unable to handle too much too soon, I closed my eyes again. A lone hot tear tracked down my cheek before I pressed the side of my face into his chest. "Thank you."

His arms tightened around me in a gentle squeeze.

"Thank you for knowing," I elaborated.

Brief seconds stretched into solid minutes. We stood there, frozen in the space we'd stolen for ourselves in the midst of the world set to fall apart around us. Even though preparations needed to be made, all possible scenarios drawn, impossible last-minute training to take place, we settled into the rare moment absent of demands or expectations, yet so full of meaning.

We didn't know what tomorrow would bring. It no longer mattered what I'd been or who I would become through the ultimate trial that loomed ahead.

But now...now, I would revel in our only promised fragment of time, grateful Alec Marquez shared what little love he could afford—that he recognized that same sliver of love in me too.

CHAPTER 21

sucked in a deep, shaky breath. Alec did the same. In the next thumping heartbeats, we pulled away from each other in increments, him loosening the strong embrace he'd held me in, me standing on my own again, grateful for the support, but now ready to step back, reassess.

The tension in the air hung heavy, revelations swirling in my head. Vulnerability shone in his brief gaze before he glanced at his laptop, then at the blue horizon line out his windows, where sea met sky...the world exactly as it should be. Bright and vivid.

Come nightfall, another line of ships would cruise by, lights shining, one or more waiting to receive a message...or deliver one. "Will it be tonight?" I asked.

His brows twitched together as he closed the screen down onto the keyboard. "Don't know. Our analysts are reviewing the trade activity. They'll let us know if they find anything further."

"What will we do?"

"Wait. EtherSphere activated four additional agents to watch Escobar's house and the inlet." Reaching forward, he tucked a finger into the waistband of the soft pants that I'd stolen. He tugged lightly, pulling me forward.

My breath caught. Tension crackled between us. Would he give in? Instead of denying whatever was solidifying between us, would he accept it?

Over the next endless seconds, numerous emotions flickered over his face until his expression hardened. "And train." Before I could form a reply, his hand left my waist, grabbed my hand, then tugged me out of the room and down the hall.

I expelled a heavy breath, stomach dropping in relief, or disappointment…likely both.

And train we did, both of us compartmentalizing like the masters we'd become. Having proved myself earlier, no blindfold was used for the remainder of our training. More combat scenarios were run through, creating every situation we were able to simulate, then repeated until my reactions became automatic. Although he'd talked about a heavier meal, lunch was a hearty greens-and-protein smoothie packed with calories before we resumed a grueling training pace again.

Alec bounced onto his heels from the body slam I'd just delivered to him, gave me an approving nod, then exited the room. I took the pause in action like every other: I paced over the thin tatami mats we'd laid out to protect his bamboo floor once the beads of sweat had started to fly. I stretched my muscles by rolling my shoulders, scissoring my arms in front of my chest, and kicking each foot up behind me to grip my ankles and lengthen my quads.

Without warning, he attacked from the side. Catching the blur of movement peripherally, I lunged backward, grabbed his arm at the wrist and above the elbow, then pushed into the building momentum before arcing his arm around. But I misjudged the torque I had from my hand placement.

He spun into my body, knocking me backward.

On instinct, my hands shot up in front of my chest, counterbalancing my center of gravity as it reeled backward. My mental grid burst forth the possibilities, chose the one with the greatest probability of success, then fired an electrical impulse to my leg, instantly lunging it backward.

I spun, changing my backward momentum into coiling energy, then fired out an arm, knocking him off-balance.

At the last second, he swept my feet out from under me with his left ankle.

We both went down to the mats with a hard thud. I closed my eyes, head smarting with pain for a split second. I sucked in a lungful of air right as I heard him do the same. After a long silent pause, we both burst out into rare laughter.

I rolled over onto my side and propped my hand up under my head, staring at him.

Lines crinkled at the corners of his eyes. White teeth flashed in the middle of his broad grin. Dark stubble covered his strong jawline, framed his chin, encircled his lips. I stared at those lips, heated memories flashing into my mind.

"So, you've never had a relationship?" The blurted question felt surprisingly natural.

"Not one."

"Not even a fellow agent?"

"No." He rolled to his side too, facing me, eyes narrowing as he whispered, "Not even an asset."

My head jerked back a fraction. "Is that what I am? An asset?"

He gave a slow headshake. "Not even close."

"What am I, then…a fellow agent?"

"Not exactly. You don't work for EtherSphere. And I've never worked with an agent like you."

"Female?"

He fought a smile. "Attractive. Intelligent." He cocked his head. "Worldly, yet not fooled by it. Educated, but untaught, even with all you've learned. Alive, but only barely…and now for the first time, finally living."

My gaze drifted down to those lips again, where the hint of a smile still played. "But you have had *sex* with agents." I arched a brow as my gaze met his.

"I have."

"And assets." Something within me needed to quantify this, push to define whatever was developing between us.

"Yes." He gave a slight nod, then propped up onto an elbow, looking down at me. "Assets too."

"But I'm neither."

A slight headshake. "You, Devin Hill, are a great mystery to me. Not an acquaintance. Not a coworker."

"A friend," I offered. I hadn't had many. Anna was really the only one who qualified by time and depth. He'd become my second.

"Friend is too casual a word, don't you think?" His gaze held mine. "Friends are kind, confide secrets, grant favors. Friends don't have sex."

"Not repeatedly, anyway," I teased.

"True. Because if we'd kept it to just the once, then we could remain friends." Mischief sparkled in his eyes as he mocked right back.

"Lovers, then," my tone deepened, heavy with suggestion. I pushed my body off the mat. "We're done here, right?"

His brows drew together as he rotated onto his back again to stare up at me. His confused expression gave him a rare adorable quality. "With our conversation?"

I half shrugged, then grabbed the borrowed T-shirt I wore at the hem and dragged it slowly up over my body, allowing the material to rasp over my nipples, hardening them. Then I pulled it over my head and tossed it aside. "Our training. Surely, I've proven myself. And this body needs to rest if you want it to perform at its optimum."

He didn't reply. All he did was stare, his face stricken with fascinated wonder as I tugged loose the knot cinched at my waist and released my hold, letting the soft fabric of his lounge pants slide down my thighs to pool at my feet.

"You have a bathtub, I'm hoping?"

"A Japanese soaking tub." He blinked heavily. "Beside the shower." He pointed toward the bathroom area nearest his bedroom, where we'd showered so intimately the night before, chastely if only in body.

I had no idea what the "Japanese" part meant, but I had every intention of finding out as I counted seconds off in my head. *One one-thousand...two one-thousand...*

A distant low thump in the room behind me almost made me laugh. For all the grace the man had exhibited during his *kata* and the stealth he'd employed while sneaking up in attack during our training, after offering him my nakedness with no expectations, he'd suddenly become a clumsy kid.

My earlier blindfold-training served me well as I rounded the corner into his bath area. Deciding not the switch on the lights, I stepped into the dimly lit bathroom right as the air current changed in my wake, stirring as he closed in behind me.

Heat followed, a subtle warmth teasing the fine hairs on the backs of my arms seconds before he brushed his body against mine. He stood naked behind me, with me, bared on the outside, but the effect touched far deeper, even if neither of us was ready to admit just how far.

I stopped before the soapstone Japanese tub, a thick-walled vessel more vertical than horizontal, barely large enough for the both of us.

With a slight shift, his skin grazed over mine, his chest to my back, as he leaned over and grasped the faucet lever. He rotated it until a thick vertical stream of water flowed from a hole in the ceiling.

When he straightened, he rested his hands on my shoulders, then gently spun me to face him. Unsure of what to say, but never more certain of anything that held a glimmer of light in my life, I skimmed my hands around his trim waist, settled my fingers over the sexy depressions above his ass, and pressed a kiss to his chest as he pulled me close.

A single finger tucked under my chin, gently tilting my face upward. My gaze clashed with his and held. So much intensity shone in those depths. A thousand words that didn't need to be spoken. "Lovers, then," he rasped out. "But—"

Filled with sudden urgency, I bounced up on my toes and kissed him before he uttered another syllable. The impact of the intimate contact surprised me—even though we embraced naked—searing an ache from my mouth through my chest, then tingling lower, settling between my legs. His mouth softened under my pleading lips, opening for me with a low moan. The erotic sound reverberated through me, quivering into my bones.

When I eased away, I closed my eyes and relaxed, leaning more of my weight against him. Our labored breaths filled my ears. The corners of my mouth twitched, a smile threatening to break free with the raw joy of the moment.

"Lovers, then," I whispered, solidifying our classification. "No 'but' qualifying it, though. No expectations from it. Nothing more."

This time, he pulled back. As steam billowed into the darkness and splashing water echoed against the hard surfaces, his words cut through the hazy cacophony, loud and clear. "There is a 'but.' There *is* more." He let out a deep sigh. "That's why I never let anyone in. I could never afford to care enough about someone to risk their life."

"To risk losing them, you mean."

His Adam's apple bobbed as he swallowed hard. "To risk losing them," he agreed.

"Losing me," I clarified. In the weighted moment, we spoke of specifics, not generalities.

Anger darkened his expression. He gave a sharp nod, as if he couldn't bear to give voice to the idea.

An urgent part of me needed him to understand why his concern was shadowed by something greater. "Alec, you brought me to life. Don't you see? I *was* lost. You are the reason I'm not."

"But—"

I pressed my index finger to his lips, silencing him. "No. You don't get to decide. Neither do I. We lost control of whatever exists between us long before now. We only get to accept this rare gift or not. I'm done locking myself away in a prison. Freedom is too great a reward, no matter the risk, regardless of how brief. Don't you want to have what your parents had? Even if only for a blink in time?"

A cramp formed at the base of my throat as tears burned my eyes.

His expression seemed just as pained with emotion as he gave me a certain nod. Then his gaze sparked fierce. "Yes."

This time he gave no qualifications. No objections. No roadblocks.

No hesitation existed—from him or me.

"Then love me, Alec. No one is guaranteed tomorrow. *We* know this. Be with me now. Give me all of you. Hold nothing back, and I promise the same."

"It's yours." Gentle words, filled with power.

Honored to have a chance with him, I leaned forward and pressed a soft kiss to a faded spiral scar on his right upper chest. A faint jagged pink line curved under his left collarbone, and with a calming exhalation, I kissed that too.

Wrapping an arm around me, he rested his palm between my shoulder blades, holding there with tender possessiveness. Ever so slowly, he bent down until warm breath tickled over my ear, fogged down the column of my neck. The fingers of his other hand trailed over my shoulder, then skimmed down my arm until they tangled with mine, clasping my hand.

He expelled a long breath, as if the weight of the world had been lifted from his shoulders, as if he'd been waiting a lifetime for this moment—for me.

And I now realized...I'd been waiting for him too.

He meandered downward from my neck with a slow trail of brushed lips and dotted kisses. All of a sudden, he paused, his face mere inches from my breasts that rose and fell with ever-shallowing breaths.

On a brief glance up, his gaze locked with mine. Even in the near darkness, compassion and wonder shone in the depths, mirroring my own emotions. I squeezed his hand, wrapped the fingers of my other behind his neck until they slid up into his soft hair. His splayed hand still resting between my shoulder blades tensed, slight pressure urging me forward. And I gave in, drawn toward him as his lips hovered closer.

With the gentlest touch, he pressed a kiss between my breasts, right over my beating heart.

It melted.

And the only scar I bore began to fade.

In the dim light, we no longer remained hidden. Not from each other.

Gratitude overcoming me, I kissed the top of his head. Long seconds ticked by as we held each other. His face pressed to my chest, my lips resting atop his head.

When he shifted slightly, I eased backward.

He outstretched his arm over the tub and spun the faucet lever, cutting off the overhead flow of water. Then in a sudden burst of energy, his hands shot around my waist and he hoisted me high in the air. A wide smile stretched across his lips as he lifted then spun me toward the tub. I bent my knees, then unfolded my legs until they hit the slick bottom. I gripped his shoulders for balance and spread my feet until they braced against the sides.

Breathless from the sudden shot of adrenaline, I stared at him, fighting a smile.

Then his gaze raked down my naked body, and his boyish charm vanished. One corner of his mouth twisted up into a devilish smirk. "Room for me in there?"

In the tub? My body? The heart he'd just claimed?

Yes. *Yes.* And... "Yes," I whispered, certain of it all.

Gripping the edge of the tub, he put one foot inside, then another, maneuvering them around mine. He turned me until I faced away from him, put his hands on my hips, and squatted, pulling me down into the hot water with him.

I groaned as soothing heat seeped into my muscles. Water sloshed over the tub's edge as he wrapped himself around my body from behind, holding me half in his lap, half between his powerful thighs. Against my tailbone I felt a distinctive twitch. But he didn't move another muscle.

Time stood still. The world was no longer falling apart... not in here. Only we existed.

Our breaths gentled as contentment wove a spell around us.

A harder twitch pulsed against my lower back. He shifted and brushed another tender kiss on my neck. Then he gripped me tighter with his arms and legs and rocked his pelvis against me.

I gasped as a spark of heat sizzled through me.

Longing followed. I wanted him inside me in *every* way.

As if sensing my sudden need, he clutched my hips. Then he lifted me a fraction until his rigid erection grazed across my sensitized folds before it settled lengthwise through them when he eased me back down. I let out another low groan as I arched, then curved, rubbing along his length.

Languorous minutes passed in the darkness as I moved against him with barely discernible hip rolls as his hands gripped my thighs. Every so often, my ragged breath would catch as a jolt of pleasure flashed through me. On occasion, his steady exhalations fogging over my ear sharpened to a soft gasp as his cock twitched beneath me. In between, the only sounds were random drips of water echoing off the walls, the whisper of our heavy breaths escaping our lips, and my relentless pulse drumming in my ears—while it simultaneously throbbed elsewhere…deeper.

On the next firm kick of his cock against me, I gasped again, with him.

His strong grip on my thighs tightened seconds before I felt myself being lifted.

A sudden concern flashed into my mind, then tumbled from my lips before I could stop it. "Are you sure about this?

The eroding nature of wave currents and viscosity of water is detrimental to sustained lubrication."

He lowered his head with a sudden drop and growled against my neck. "*Fuck.* What that extraordinary mouth of yours does to me."

Then as if in answer to my apprehension, but without explanation, he began to stand. Jostled off his lap, I threw my hands up, but he grabbed my hips and spun me around. Off-balance, I flailed my arms until I clamped on to his muscular biceps, but the slick surfaces were no match against his powerful legs that he'd wedged against the high walls of the tub.

Before I had a chance to catch a full breath, he bent forward, gripped my thighs just under my ass, and hoisted me up as he spread my legs wide. Mouth falling open in amazement at his surprise action, I wrapped my legs tightly around him, gripping just over his hips.

With a grace I would never have imagined, he climbed out of the tub while gripping the globes of my ass in both hands. His strong arms bracketed around me, firm hands holding tight, as he took measured strides across the rough slate tiles of his bathroom.

His cock lay pressed between us, its rigid length sliding over the sensitized nerves of my clit with his every step. When an aching pulse sparked through me, I dropped my forehead against his shoulder and moaned. He hissed in a breath through his teeth as his cock twitched in reply.

Breaths ragged, he paused midstride just outside of his bedroom door and pinned me gently to the wall. Arms tensing, he lifted my body, sliding me up the length of his shaft, until the blunt tip caught at my entrance. My eyes widened. We stared at each other while he lowered me down, letting gravity aid his cause, as if the few remaining steps to the bed were too great a distance to wait one more second.

As he slid ever deeper, stretching me wide, filling me with the solidness of his heat, I clung tighter to him, not wanting this excruciating pleasure to end, never wanting to let go. His eyes slowly closed and his head drifted downward until his forehead touched mine. Our labored breaths rasped out. My pulse beat heavy against my eardrum. A torturous ache throbbed everywhere, through me, around him…for him.

All of a sudden, the grip he had on my hips tightened, then he jerked us away from the wall, spun us around, and after a few steps, lunged forward until our combined weight crashed toward the bed. But he shot out an extended arm at the last moment, bracing our fall. Then he stilled and we locked gazes for a few shallow breaths before he drove forward, imbedding completely inside me with one solid thrust.

Time slipped away into a dreamy haze, and I held him close as we began to move. He eased back, then drove forward. I undulated down, then arched up. Aching need wrenched a keening moan from my throat. Desire spiraled through me, white hot, a flash of gratification, yet wholly insufficient as the sensual craving for more stoked higher, burned brighter.

With a measured pace, he drew his hips back, paused

right before exiting my body, then plunged forward, sparking nerves along slickened inner walls as he stretched me, filling me once again. The ache deep within me coiled tighter with every meaningful thrust. Our breaths began to quicken.

When a forceful pulse arced through me, I gasped and closed my eyes, arching my head back as I strained for an orgasm edging within reach.

His cock hardened further and his body tensed. But he pulled back.

When I tilted my head forward, opening my eyes, I found him gazing down at me. A multitude of emotions shone in those mesmerizing eyes: astonishment, curiosity, gratitude.

As I hovered on the edge of the precipice, I sensed he teetered right there beside me, our bodies spent and ready to take the fall—hearts dragged along, to plunge in spite of the risks.

We didn't speak. Didn't nod our assent. Without any sign from either side, we both knew. He closed the distance between us until our lips brushed, then opened, molding into a passionate kiss. I gripped his hips, and he eased back and plunged forward one last time before our bodies tightened, then burst into blinding sparks of pleasure.

Our hearts? Already gone.

The rhythmic hum of breaking ocean waves became a hypnotic lullaby, shielding us from the realities of the world, cocooning us in a private one of our own.

In the quiet darkness of Alec's bedroom, we faced each

other, legs tangled together, warm breaths mingling. I smiled for the third time in the last five minutes. A record by any measure. Yet I couldn't help it.

His forearm rested on my hip while his fingertips brushed lazy circles over my skin, mapping the terrain of my lower back. My cheek rested on his upper arm as I skimmed my fingers over the scruff along his jawline, slid them over the outer shell of his ear, then clasped the soft lobe between my finger and thumb, tugging gently.

Which caused him to lean forward and kiss me. Again.

Tender lips molded with mine, coaxing, pleading… giving.

Every gentle touch, each sigh and shudder, painted the picture between us in vivid clarity. Gratitude filled our hearts. For all what we had with each other after being denied for so long. The immensity of that one raw emotion hung thick in the air around us.

When our passionate kiss slowed, he eased back and let out a long exhalation. The dark silhouette of his head cocked slightly as he raised his arm from my hip. His fingers touched my cheekbone, slid to my temple, then brushed through my hair before tucking loose strands behind my ear.

"Devin?"

"Yeah?"

Tones low, our words hummed out like an extension of the caresses, the kisses.

"Why?" he asked.

Despite the seriousness between us, I fought a smile. "Why…what?"

"I meant…you're in college, right?"

"Yes." Even though the answer no longer rang true in my heart. "I'm halfway through my master's program."

"Why do you want to get involved with EtherSphere One? You're brilliant. You could be anything you want to be."

In the shadowy room, I couldn't see his expression, but I sensed the intensity of his gaze. No pressure or judgment emanated from him, though. Instead, genuine concern and interest radiated through.

Needing space nonetheless, more to focus on my answer for me, as well as for him, I turned in his embrace, rotating until my back met his chest. The next silent seconds were spent adjusting together again, me shimmying backward, him curving forward, until his arms curled tighter around me. I stretched my arms under his, seeking his hands, then entwined our fingers together.

In the safety of the place we'd carved for ourselves, I drew in a slow breath as I cleared my mind before taking the plunge. Then I let the thought flow from my heart straight into my words.

"I want to be me." There. I said it aloud.

His only reaction? The tightening of his embrace.

I forged ahead. "Not who my parents expect. Not what some IQ test or aptitude scoring suggests. Not as a horrible tragedy paints me."

"No," he agreed.

"This trip. You. EtherSphere One. All of it made me realize I want the adventure—the adrenaline-pumping, puzzle-solving, world-saving, challenge to my body as well as my mind."

"This job can get you killed." His voice broke at the end.

"True." Another slow smile curved my lips. "But in the moments I control, and even those I don't, where I'm holding on tight, along for the ride…I get to live."

CHAPTER 22

After startling awake from a coma-like sleep, I settled back into Alec's tightening arms. Warm heat surrounded me as I gradually exhaled, relaxing into his embrace. His rhythmic breathing followed, chest rising and falling with mine, the cadence slowing with every deepening draw.

The pacifying effect almost lulled me back to sleep. Were it not for my brain rapidly firing its synapses on its own accord, working to fit more puzzle pieces together, I might've stolen another precious few hours of needed REM.

Instead, I waited several more minutes to be certain he'd fallen soundly back under, until his leg that was casually thrown over mine gave a slight twitch. Then I slipped out from under him with a held breath.

In the relative darkness, he lay peacefully on his side in the center of the tangled white sheets. Spoiling myself at the sight, reveling in what had happened—how my body and soul still sang from an experience I avoided giving a label to—I stared for a good two minutes.

Then I returned into his closet, stole another clean folded T-shirt, and slipped it over my head while I padded down the hall toward his kitchen. The muffled roar of crashing ocean waves grew louder as I walked, likely due to the increased surface area of windows in his great room.

When I opened the refrigerator door, I winced at the blinding light. Once my eyes adjusted, I realized it was organized into logical sections: ready-to-eat items on an eye-level second shelf; packaged meats, eggs, and deli items on two lower shelves; and brightly colored produce in two side-by-side crisper drawers. From the bins in the door, I grabbed one of an assortment of Evolution Fresh nutrition drinks labeled Sweet Greens and Lemon, shook the green-colored contents, then downed a few swallows of the bitter but sweet liquid as I headed toward the far end of the quiet house.

An unfamiliar peace washed over me as I entered his office. Maybe due to the fact that I no longer stood by myself in the darkness. Amid all the danger in our evil world, I no longer remained a lone cynic. Or maybe, I no longer remained a cynic at all.

Instead, I'd been given a reprieve from my self-induced banishment from the world at large. I'd returned from exile, ready to dance in the sunshine and defy the shadows—in spite of the threat of losing any unadulterated joy the millisecond I let my guard down.

Except I planned to never let my guard down.

Not completely. Nothing wrong with leaving some measure of protection up against the darkness that existed, whether or not I chose to vigilantly acknowledge its presence. Even a low hum of awareness served better than the naïve delusions held by the vacationers that shared this stretch of beach, occupied the rest of the planet. Which made me more safeguarded than most who simply lived in outright denial.

I flipped open Alec's laptop and hit the space bar with the side of my thumb, hoping he'd left it on and I didn't have to navigate any encryption or passwords to reach basic Internet—the good old regular kind, where search engines and email and online retailing nirvana existed for the rest of us plebeians.

Success. I grinned as his screen's background appeared, featuring a transparent white waterfall that sprayed over rock covered in lush moss and lichen. Even his computer exuded serenity. "Do you seek balance in your life, Alec?" I murmured into the comforting quiet. He had the Zen-thing going on in his private space while chaos threatened just outside his doors.

I quickly located his Web browser. His home page opened to the Google search engine. As the cursor blinked in the data-entry box, I tapped my fingernails absently on the keys without depressing them as I rifled through the whirlwind of information fragments spinning in my head.

Where to start? The DNA structures hanging on the bulletin board on the laboratory wall.

In rapid succession, I searched through the most well-known viral DNA. None matched exactly. Then I surveyed the lessor-known subsets. Nothing.

The screen faded to black as I stared ahead, vision

unfocused, diving deep into my thoughts. My eyes drifted shut, blocking out all external stimuli until the rhythm of the gentle breakers on the beach outside vanished, the hardness of the ergonomic chair under my legs fell away, my steady breathing dissipated into the background.

Utterly relaxed, the landscape of my mind unfurled into a multidimensional data-stream, sorting through pieces of random information at lightning speed, a biological supercomputer. Surfing the Internet had nothing on riding this internal wave of analysis, ebbing and flowing, cresting, falling, then rising yet again in rich color and texture: *my* version of a meditative state.

Every clue passed through a focused lens in pathways of both relation and disconnection. Escobar. His son. Anna. The party. The hospital. The lab. The prisoners. The dignitaries. A detailed image of the cruise ships floated by again. The pattern of lights replayed in Escobar's windows. Facts about the guards and their patrols.

The labs came into view again. The clean room. The centrifuges. The DNA sequencing. The...

"A hybrid!" The sudden intensity of my voice startled my eyes open to bright light. My brows snapped together, and I blinked at the fiery orange sun hanging high in the middle of a blue sky.

"A hybrid what?" A low voice asked.

I spun around in the chair.

Alec stood in the doorway, shoulder propped against the frame, arms casually crossed over his chest. A pair of those thin black lounge pants barely clung to his hips.

"A hybrid what?" he repeated as he pushed off the doorframe and stepped toward me.

"Damn. How long have I been sitting here?" The last time I'd blacked out while analyzing had been my first year of college. And it had been thoroughly unsettling. Traveling to the deep reaches of my mind occasionally resulted in time gaps. According to Anna, the longest one had been three hours.

"Don't know. I discovered you over an hour ago. Thought you were meditating. Or sleeping."

"A little of both, I guess." I scrubbed a hand down my face, clearing my head of everything but the one thing I needed to pluck free.

"A hybrid *virus*." I tapped the space bar with my thumb again, awakening the dormant computer. Then I quickly retrieved bookmarked pages of the viruses I'd scanned through earlier. "They spliced two viruses together."

"Which two?" His warm hands smoothed down my arms as he watched from over my shoulder.

I expelled a heavy breath, recognizing the pretzel-shaped virion. "Ebola." After a few more keystrokes, I pulled up a mottled, bumpy spherical image matching one of the diagrams in the Escobar's lab. "And rhinovirus." The common cold.

"*Fuck.*" His hands tightened on my upper arms, then released them altogether.

"Exactly." I spun around to find him pacing. Legs cramped from sitting for what I now realized had to be four hours or more, I stood and stretched my body, allowing blood to flow back into muscles sore from a good workout yesterday—and an amazing one last night. But I refused to dwell on anything happy for me. Not when lives were at stake—and not merely for a couple dozen college students. The threat could impact millions.

In a flash of movement, Alec sat in the chair I'd just vacated and began typing furiously. Seconds later, the Shadow Network where EtherSphere operated appeared.

"What are we going to do?" I was ready.

"*We* are doing nothing." He didn't turn away from the screen as he completed one short missive, hit send, then drafted another. "I am updating ESO on your suspicions."

"It's more than suspicion."

He gave me a short nod. "I'm not doubting you or your mental abilities, but ESO won't act without confirmation. They'll have all they need to decide."

"And we don't act without orders." I understood hierarchy and forced myself to respect theirs, no matter how badly I itched to act now. If I wanted to be a part of their organization, I needed to prove I could honor their rules.

"There are bigger forces at play here. Timing is critical, strategy everything. We need to make sure we don't pinch out the battle only to lose the war."

Made sense, but didn't soothe the anxiety boiling up from the pit of my stomach.

Alec handed me his mobile phone as he hit the control button, lighting up the screen. A text from Anna appeared with a time stamp of 10:14 a.m. My brow furrowed for a confused moment before I remembered calling her yesterday morning on his phone.

"Call Anna. I'll drop you back at the resort in a few minutes."

"What are you going to do?" Sudden panic welled in my chest at the thought of being separated from him. I'd only just found him, this man who'd become my counterbalance.

He reached into his top desk drawer, then held up a larger mobile phone. "Business phone. While you call Anna, I'll call Escobar to confirm our appointment tonight."

"Appointment?" My head spun, trying to remember details he may have mentioned before we'd lost ourselves in a night filled with passion.

"To play arms dealer."

"Oh. The missile launchers." I glanced toward the garage where a stockpile of weapons waited to be delivered. "And handguns. And probably grenades…" There were so many ways things could go south. Add lots of unpredictable and readily accessible things that go boom?

I frowned.

"Hey." He stood from the chair and gathered me close. He cupped his hand over my cheek and stared into my eyes. "This has been years in the making. I can handle it."

"What about me?" Had my voice sounded whiney? I scowled, suddenly irritated at damn female chromosomes.

He gave me a reassuring smile. "You can't come. Stay with Anna until you hear from me."

Tapping into the strength I'd somehow always had, I turned, pulled up Anna's text, then hit the CALL button. I refused to succumb to worry over what might happen if I lost Alec. After all, I'd pleaded with him to be strong for me, seize what happiness we could find now, even if we risked never having it again.

But for the first time in my life, I had something to fight for beyond vengeance. I had something to protect, to keep safe and cherish.

I had something to live for.

And although in some respects, I now fought for Alec and me, I also fought for those college students and their loved ones, I fought for my sister and the family her loss destroyed, and I fought for all the families in the world—whether they knew about the darkness surrounding them or not—that they wouldn't have to suffer at the hands of greed and cruelty.

Alec's call connected first, as he immediately spoke in fluid Spanish from behind his desk. To distance myself, I walked to the room's outer glass wall while the ringer chimed into my ear once, then again.

On the third ring it connected. "*¡Hola! ¿Cómo* the hell *estás?*"

I choked out a laugh. "*Muy* the fuck *bien. ¿Y tú?*"

"Must be 'very *the fuck* good,' Dev. You laughed. You never laugh."

"Do too," I countered. Albeit rarely. "And now we're slaughtering the native language? Sacrilege."

"No. Damn it all to hell, Dev. You better get your ass over here. This is our vacation."

"You telling me you didn't hang a sock on our door last night?"

Silence stretched on the other end.

"Uh-huh. Thought so. Playing doctor again?" Worry pinged into my brain, this time for Anna and her getting so close to the son of a bad man. Something had shifted irrevocably inside me the moment I entered into the light again, started living life. I began to care more.

Nothing to be done about my worries now, though. Later. Hopefully soon.

"You know it," she continued. "His patient needed a house call. A very detailed, very thorough house call."

"*Very* TMI." I scrunched my nose, not wanting to hear the intimate details. Then my thoughts drifted to last night, calming me as I relived my own. Caught unaware of my own bodily responses, I let out a dreamy sigh. Then I wanted to slap myself back into reality. Finding happiness amid impending catastrophe was doing a Jekyll-and-Hyde number on my emotions.

Anna sighed heavily. "You coming back here, or what? I've got beach time scheduled, and it has *our* name on it."

I turned to catch Alec pocketing his additional phone, his call apparently finished. The moment his gaze locked on to mine, he smiled, and I began closing the distance between us.

"Have Pedro snag us one up front." Our previous beach attendant to set up our beach-bed lounge. "I'll be there in twenty."

I disconnected, then slid the phone onto his desk, threw my arms around his neck, and lunged upward, crashing my lips against his.

A low growl reverberated from his throat, penetrating

my body straight to my heart, as he gathered me in his arms and kissed me with a restrained wildness. In those suspended seconds, we clung to each other.

I may have to let him go, wouldn't be able to control every little thing in the countless possibilities that lay ahead, but I did have the present moment—the only one guaranteed.

And for as long as I had him, I would make the most of it.

CHAPTER 23

After Alec had dropped me off with no sappy good-bye trivialities, simply a passionate kiss followed by an intense look that matched the blissful high I rode, I enjoyed a lazy day of crucial beach time with my best friend.

And even though she'd always been my only friend, the one person who I'd ever let close to me, I'd never allowed her to get too close. But now that Alec had chipped away at the protective walls I'd built, my perspective on the entire world had shifted, Anna included.

Did I regret not confiding completely in her? Sharing the extent to which I'd been broken?

No. Until Alec—until this vacation—I hadn't been ready.

I tossed a frozen grape at her. It lodged between perfect breasts restrained by her bikini top.

She plucked it out and popped it into her mouth, grinning. "What's with this new you?"

"You don't like me playful?"

"I *love* this new side of you." Pursing her lips, she sucked two long drafts through the straw sticking out of her green coconut goblet. "Who knew a fling would be so good for you?"

"Sure as hell not me." I grinned. The whole thing had taken me by surprise. Including the unstoppable feeling of elation after all Alec and I had shared last night.

A parasailer floated high in the sky, dragged like a kite by a canary-yellow speed boat that glided south. Following its direction, my gaze drifted farther along the beach, past Alec's place and down the coast toward Escobar's. My thoughts darkened, naturally gravitating toward the evil in the world that occupied the same airspace as so much good.

Then I forced the demons out of my head. Newly baptized into enjoying life, I would appreciate all the good I could get, like all the thousands of beachgoers on this silvery strand, ignoring the bad—until the time came to deal with reality.

"Well, your new side is coming dancing with me tonight." She sat straighter as a resort staff member walked by wearing a round drum container that dangled from a cross-body strap. He held a tower of empty ice-cream cones in one hand and a metal scoop in the other.

"French vanilla?" he asked.

"Two." She held up her index and middle finger, in case the basic number got lost in translation.

"Dancing?" Not remotely hungry for anything sweet, I didn't argue about the ice cream. Nor did I move from my reclined position nestled into the pillows.

"Dancing. The resort is having a beach holiday party.

Two days before Christmas, and we'll be shaking our asses on a sugar-sand beach with the trade winds blowing on our faces."

On a headshake as I huffed out a laugh, I grabbed a dripping ice-cream cone from the man's outstretched hand. Anna's mention of trade winds cast my brain on a warp speed factoid leap: our trade winds blew from the northeast, others swept across the globe from the southeast, the equatorial section where the two met was called the doldrums.

Then my mind flashed to the other meaning of the word doldrums: listlessness, despondency. How I'd felt before I'd come on vacation. What I'd been prior to meeting Alec.

Serendipity had an intriguing way of shifting the polarity of the world.

Sheer white screens spanned from posts that had been sunk into the sand, obscuring the resort guests from the south, the north, and partially from the west, save for a narrow entryway. Running along the uppermost line of fabric, strands of lights, some green, some white, twinkled against the night sky as they trembled in a slight breeze.

At least fifty guests gyrated to the latest dance music, writhing and bouncing to the pulsing beat as the ever-powerful ocean waves crashed to their own rhythm a dozen yards away.

Barefoot in the cool sand, a coral-pink beaded tank top clinging to my body over billowing gauzy pants, I laughed. At nothing. At everything.

Alec had texted me a few times throughout day. Once to apologize for the hasty drop-off after the incredible time we'd spent together...and that he missed me.

Then a second time, short and to the point:

Miss you.

I'd texted back:

Miss you too.

Then I'd fired off another, a split second after the first.

Spud.

His last replied almost immediately.

Pink.

We'd regressed into kids. Happy about silly things. Grasping at fleeting moments of joy amid a threat lurking just beyond our private intimate world.

Didn't mean we'd forgotten. Far from it.

But while Alec and I were stuck in a holding pattern waiting on EtherSphere and Escobar, I danced, soaking in music that had little to do with the holidays but everything to do with carefree celebrating. I would capture precious memories wherever I could.

Anna's smile brightened, her green eyes flashing. "You

dance like a deranged lunatic."

With added gusto, I jutted out an elbow into air to the right while swiveling my hips around left, ending in a jerky pop. "I've been saving up dance moves," I shouted over the blaring music.

All of a sudden, her eyes widened as a current of heat sizzled over my bare shoulders an instant before solid warmth pressed there. I gasped in surprise as firm hands gripped my hips, stilling my body in the middle of another hip gyration.

"We should have spent more time perfecting your dance moves, Pink."

I exhaled a shaky breath as he pressed closer, my body shuddering in sensual recognition of his touch as his soft lips brushed up the column of my neck.

My movements slowed in time with his, as he guided my hips into a gentle sway, back and forth. I closed my eyes and slid my hands over his, grateful to have him back.

When the rhythmic song ended and another began, I spun within his arms to face him as we continued to rock side to side in our own leisurely pace. "What are you doing here?"

Not that I wasn't glad to see him. I snuck a furtive glance at Anna, who'd been similarly waylaid by Miguel. They were bound in lip-lock, bodies pressed together, hands roaming as if no one else existed around them.

"Miguel insisted. Claimed he'd gone long enough without seeing his woman. I was in no condition to argue."

Thoroughly confused about Alec's plans with Escobar, yet unwilling to voice anything revealing within earshot of Miguel, Anna, and the rest of the dancing guests no matter how loud the music pumped, I furrowed my brow, attempting to harness a simple question. "Are you here for the night, then?"

He replied with a quick headshake. "No. Only a few minutes. We meet back at Escobar's at 10:00 p.m."

We: Alec and Miguel, two men thick as thieves, appearing to be friends to the two women they'd hooked up with. One a spy. The other…undetermined. I didn't even know enough to place Miguel into a category of foe or friend—warn Anna or rejoice with her.

I frowned at the time limit. Couldn't help it. Anna and I had been here for a couple of hours, and although the party seemed to be picking up speed, with the arrival of Alec, all I wanted to do was go somewhere private and curl up with him. Naked. Repeatedly.

No longer a product of the darkness I'd relegated myself to, I'd become someone who sought comfort from another. From him. I'd become more addicted to what he offered than I'd realized. And I understood the risk of wanting, of… loving. I'd had it cruelly ripped from me once before. But not one part of me cared about the risk.

I burrowed deeper into his embrace. On my heavy sigh, he eased back, touched a gentle finger under my chin, and lifted my face. He gazed down at me, his midnight eyes sparking with emotion. "I wanted to hold you again."

My heart melted at his words and the tension in my body dissipated. In the face of danger, before heading out on a mission where every time could mean life or death for an agent, he wanted to see me. Hold me.

And in my newfound world of happiness, I gave him want he wanted.

Standing on the beach, amid a blur of bodies moving to music I no longer heard, I returned his embrace, tightening my arms around him—well aware that a moment was fleeting and we lived in a world that was ever-changing.

CHAPTER 24

A choked-off scream curdled in my ear. Terror slammed into my chest, panic firing hot through my veins as I startled awake and jolted upright on the bed. Black-clothed figures towered in the darkness. One ripped my sister from my side.

She kicked, flailed her arms, but her puny size was no match for the hulking might of her captor. In the dim light, her panic-stricken eyes widened as her gaze collided into mine. Another man beside her stared hard at me, then her. My lungs burned, frozen in shock, before I released them to gasp in a lungful of air.

A ceiling fan whirled lazily overhead.

An air-conditioning vent blew cool air over my skin.

The muted roar of distant ocean waves crashed.

Wrong. All wrong.

Memories warped, transparently morphing, overlaid onto crisp reality.

A cloth suddenly slapped onto my face, hard pressure clamping down on my mouth, suffocating me. An arm banded around me from behind as I watched the man holding my sister back away from the darker shadows while her form went limp in his arms. Her silken black hair fell straight down over the man's muscular arm, exposing her face.

My mind stuttered. *Not* my sister. *Anna.*

Renewed panic fired another shot of adrenaline hot and hard through my veins. I held my breath and kicked against the bed while jabbing an elbow backward. A low grunt and an angry growl ripped into my ear. The band around my ribcage tightened, restricting my ability to inhale, even as I fought the urge to.

When my head yanked backward, and the arm around my ribs jerked me up from the bed, the cloth over my mouth knocked loose, exposing part of my lips to cool air. Shooting my arms and legs wildly in every direction, fighting with everything I had to break free, gain leverage against something to push away from my attacker, I parted my lips on the open side, sucking in oxygen before I passed out.

But my captor retaliated with renewed force. When the cloth slid fully back into place, I screamed with what little air remained in my lungs, terrorized by the sight of Anna's ragdoll body tossed over one man's shoulder.

Through tear-blurred eyes, I barely made out the other man in front of me. He stared at me with indifference, watching until I finally succumbed and inhaled deeply through my nostrils, unable to stop my body's automatic survival instinct to breathe. A heavy, sickly sweet odor assaulted my senses...familiar, but different.

Ether? That meant I still had time to fight. Yet my burning lungs gasped for a second deep breath. Then a third. And with every inhalation, my awareness faded as the chemical-soaked cloth made short work of disabling me. Had to be some kind of designer anesthesia.

Milliseconds of awareness remained as black dots speckled my vision, my lids dropped shut, and the last thing I heard was the sound of deep voices muttering incoherent...

"Welcome back, Miss Hill."

A bass voice, thick with a Spanish accent, slithered into my ear. I shuddered, recoiling instinctively, jerking my face away from soft material while shoving my arms at whatever pressed against my entire front side.

The world rapidly spun. My left knee smacked against a hard surface, the right onto a thick cushion. I yelped as pain lanced through the one knee and my hands collapsed onto more soft padding. A wave of dizziness overcame me, and I sucked in air, pinching my eyes tighter shut. When the vertigo calmed to a degree, I exhaled slowly and shook my haze-filled head. Then I winced as pain hammered from inside my skull with an instant headache like none before.

A low chuckle came from somewhere above me. "Go easy. You inhaled a horse's dose of our party drug. My guards said you put up an impressive fight."

My guards...his voice...

Escobar.

Lucent thoughts gradually began to coalesce around relevant facts.

Using the couch I'd apparently tumbled from as leverage, I planted my hands on the cushions and pushed myself onto my feet. My bare feet. My hand went to my throbbing knee and I felt the joint through the gauzy pants I'd worn dancing. Taking stock of my condition as awareness solidified, I bent the knee by lifting my heel up forty-five degrees, confirming it hadn't dislocated. With no increasing pain, it likely hadn't fractured either.

Buying time, maintaining whatever negligible control I had in my clearly unbound state, I leaned on one arm and rotated my body, falling into a seated position on the firm velvet cushion.

My eyes remained downcast as I assessed my surroundings with every sense at my disposal. Polished dark travertine flooring peeked out from a plush Turkish rug that spanned from just off my toes toward the opposite wall. Iron sconces mounted high on the ivory plaster cast soft pools of light onto the stone tiles edging the rug.

Black combat boots came into view from the right, soundless with each step on the expensive rug. "Do take your time, Miss Hill. Or do you prefer Devin? We were introduced to be friends, after all."

Bullshit. A deep breath filled my lungs as I bit back the sharp retort dangling on the tip of my tongue. No chance in hell.

But how to bide my time? Do I sidle up to the snake? Not yet. Too obvious.

Information. I needed to know where I'd been taken. Where Anna was. Only then could I begin to formulate a plan.

After another deep breath that did little to calm me, but at least cleared the last lingering cobwebs from my chemically dampened brain, I pushed up from the couch, hoping my knees held my weight. My legs wobbled a little, but I tensed my thighs, forcing them to obey.

Determined to face whatever awaited me, I scanned upward and met Escobar's piercing gaze. He stood in the middle of the large rug, his stance casual. He wore dark brown-and-olive camouflage fatigues and a black baseball hat pulled low on his head. His eyes peered at me from just under the curving brim.

"Glad you could join us for the festivities, Devin. The entertainment is about to commence."

Behind Escobar, and going deeper into an office filled with heavy furniture, treasured objects displayed on pedestals, and a semiprecious-stone-inlaid globe the size of a beach ball, other men stood in the same camouflage uniforms. Although I couldn't determine an accurate headcount with my view partially blocked by a large carved-wood bookcase that jutted from the wall to my right, at least a dozen soldiers stood in the room.

But my attention froze on one in particular.

Nearest Escobar, over his right shoulder and standing at relaxed attention with his arms clasped behind his back, stood Alec. His expression was stone. When we locked gazes for a fraction of a second, I fought my reaction, narrowing my eyes the slightest degree when instinctual impulse nearly widened them.

In warning, he gave a nearly imperceptible headshake, nothing more.

Escobar glanced over his shoulder, then smiled. "Ah, you see your lover. A good man. Alec's been invaluable to me. More so than to you, I'd say."

This time I couldn't hide my confusion. My brows drew together, and my gaze met Escobar's as he faced me again.

"How much do you know?" He quirked a brow. "Not much, I think."

Before I knew it, he lunged forward and grasped my elbow. Repulsed at his unexpected touch, I yanked back. But his grip held firm. "Come. I've something to show you."

Curious, yet distrustful of everything and everyone, I let him lead me to a desk on the other side of the bookcase. A bank of three shiny black monitors were mounted onto the ivory plaster wall, black against white. He depressed a silver button on a desktop keyboard and images appeared on all three screens. Within seconds, I made out the prison cells that I'd witnessed down in his underground-river dungeon. Each monitor showed split-screen images of the five separate enclosures: the college students slumped against the walls, crumpled on the floors behind the iron bars.

On the far right, one enclosure held a bright flash of turquoise. I blinked and leaned closer, staring at the monitor. Black, silky straight hair flew sideways as the woman threw her head back, bashing it purposely against the wall.

"Anna," I whispered.

"Yes. Your beloved Anna. Your best friend, no?"

I firmed my lips into a hard line, thinking about Alec, Anna. I didn't give a shit what this madman taunted me with, had no idea where the truth of anything lay, but I wouldn't give up any secrets. I could handle physical torture. Tested every other way possible, surviving one kidnapping only to fall prey to another thirteen years later, if those college students could endure, then so would I. For my sister, for Anna, for them all.

"Don't worry. You don't need to confess to anything. Your 'so-called' best friend already did."

Incredulous, a derisive snort escaped my nose. "What are you babbling on about, Escobar? There's nothing to confess."

The man was delusional. What had she coughed up? My catastrophic past? Not a weakness. Not anymore.

"EtherSphere One. Ring any bells?" he asked.

With every scrap of discipline I had, I fought the urge to spin around to see Alec's expression. I held an impassive one, forced my breaths to remain even, refused to give an ounce of reaction to the man clearly baiting me for one.

"Ahhh, guess not. She said it wouldn't."

She?

Again, my brow wrinkled. Confusion was okay. Went along with my needed role of playing dumb. But I *was* confused. "You're making no sense. I have no idea what you're talking about." *I definitely didn't.* What in the world could Anna have known…and why?

"Of course you don't, Devin." Escobar turned toward me. His hand lifted and cupped my cheek.

I jerked my face away, scowling.

He pinched my chin painfully between his fingers, yanking my head back to face him. "You've been a pawn in a game, my sweet Devin. Genius IQ from birth. Trained in martial arts, archery. Excelled in mathematics. Physics. Biology. Stop me if I get anything wrong."

My eyes narrowed, hate surging through my veins. I focused on the dark pupils of his eyes, wishing lasers would shoot from mine to incinerate his. Unfortunately, of all the correct abilities he'd listed, the god-like powers of Superman had not been among them.

"But what you didn't learn, what you've never known… is that Anna is a spy."

Stunned, my lungs froze midinhalation. Then I forced them to expand and draw in a deep breath; I needed that oxygen to clear my dazed brain.

"That's right, shocking, isn't it? To find out the best friend you've trusted, someone you've been living with for years, isn't exactly who she's made you believe."

I glared at him. "No way in hell I'd believe you over her."

An evil smile curled his lips. "The beautiful thing is you don't have to. We recorded her entire confession."

He reached toward the keyboard, clicked several keys, then forced my head to the right to face the center monitor. A blurred frozen image flickered into motion, video playing forward. Anna sat in a chair, her head lolled forward until a hand appeared and gripped her hair by the roots, yanking her head upright.

"What is EtherSphere One?" Escobar's voice came

through the monitor's speakers, from somewhere offscreen.

"I told you," she slurred, eyes drifting shut. "It's an international intelligence organization."

"And you work for them."

"Yes."

"But Devin doesn't."

"No. Not yet. Her parents didn't want her to know."

My heart plummeted to my stomach. Too much. Like a nightmare-come-to-life, the world as I knew it kept twisting into a different truth, some other version of the lie I'd believed.

"Her parents didn't want her to know what?"

"That they are a part of EtherSphere."

I closed my eyes, trying to block it all out.

The grip on my chin tightened painfully, then jarred my head with a brutal shake. "Look!" he barked, then took a slow breath before his voice calmed. "Listen to the truth of it. Of the lies they've told you."

"What part of EtherSphere?" Escobar's voice from the monitor prompted.

Anna swallowed, eyes fighting to open. Her brows drew together as she tried to focus on a point off the screen before her eyelids closed again.

"What part?" the voice demanded.

"The upper echelon." She paused, swallowing again. "They're a part of the High Council." The image froze, but a tornado twisted to mighty life inside my head, deadly, yet funneling to a focused point, searching for a path of reason.

Forced to watch a betrayal—of everything I'd believed to

be true, everything I'd ever known—I let my mind spin into chaos, allowed the logic to take hold, sifted through my past in a split second's time, trying to make sense of it all.

My parents *were EtherSphere One?*

Always had been?

No wonder they'd closed off and clamped down after my sister had been kidnapped. It was supposed to be me. Maybe someone had caught wind of their identities and wanted to steal one of their children as blackmail leverage. Or maybe someone within their organization needed to keep them in line. Possibly a counterpart decided too much power in one household put the rest of their group at a disadvantage, decided to even the odds.

"I hear the gears in your head turning, Devin. Does it really matter how or why it happened? It happened. And it shaped you into an even better instrument than any one of them could have dreamed. The anger. The vengeance. Wrath becomes the best tool, an instrument whose blade sharpens into an edge like no other. Trust me—I know this."

Muscles that had tensed in response to the shocking revelation began to relax as my familiar darkness wrapped itself around me, orienting to his voice and the meaning behind his words. He spoke the truth, the only one I'd ever known.

"Long ago you were simply the brainchild, the potential weapon." His vice-grip on my jaw relaxed too, as if he sensed my spine hardening while realization flowed into my mind, coursed through my veins. "Now you've become invaluable to them—worth orchestrating a vacation as a ruse to convince you to be a spy with them, according to Anna."

With the click of a key, Anna's image flickered into motion again, the video playing.

"Tell me more about Devin," Escobar's monitor voice urged. "Why is she here if she's not part of EtherSphere One?"

"Devin craved to be a part of something greater. She hated the idea of being cooped up, relegated to the indoor trivial life of being a scientist. Her parents pushed her toward everything she hated, suspecting it would rile her into fighting against it. Sooner or later, they expected she would break free. When she started showing signs of rebelling, and" —Anna glanced up at him, a crooked smile twisting her lips— "you started showing signs of movement toward whatever endgame you'd been heading toward, they saw the perfect opportunity to bring the two together."

"How?"

"I don't know. My mission was only to get her down here." Anna let out a heavy sigh, then scrunched her face, like the effort of disclosing exhausted her.

"That can't be all. Coincidence wouldn't be enough," he prodded Anna.

Coincidence. I agree. Alec played the other part in this grand scheme. He couldn't be innocent of it all. Yet Anna seemed unaware of his role in the mission. Why? Was Escobar not asking the right questions?

"It isn't all. I was told to get close to your son." Her face softened, then her smile widened. "And I got close to Miguel. *Intimately* close."

Deep laughter rumbled and Escobar edged into view for

the first time on the monitor. "*That*, my dear Anna, was your downfall. Women always let their guard down when a man shows them attention. Emotions and business don't mix. Your fairer sex struggles with the concept. My son does not."

The monitor went dark at the click of a button. Then to my left, from the ranks of his men, one stepped forward. Escobar's son, Miguel.

I knew it. Well, highly suspected it, anyway. Had no idea what I would've done to warn Anna—who was supposed to be my roommate and friend—about my concerns though. How would that have gone, exactly? *You're boyfriend's a villain and mine's a spy?*

Miguel edged into view, hovering as close to me on one side as his father stood on the other. He leaned closer, hot breath fanning over my cheek as his words whispered into my ear. "Anna played the part of patient well. A little too well. When she asked me one too many personal questions, something no mere resort piece-of-ass would be interested in, I gave her one too many pain killers to knock her out long enough to dig deep."

I held his gaze, refusing to cave under the pressure, even though standing between the vileness of the two Escobars gave me a skin-crawling chill.

Miguel cocked his head. "I'm not just a doctor, as you've guessed. I'm not only a scientist either. I'm highly trained in computer forensics and coding."

His father rubbed a hand over my other cheek. I couldn't stop the shudder running though my body at the repulsive touch. Only a forced breath into my lungs kept me focused.

My tensed legs were the only thing holding me upright.

Miguel caressed a hand up the column of my neck. "Anna's computer had a hidden coding behind the operating system. I didn't break all of it, but enough to know she didn't bring it down here to shop online."

The back of Escobar's hand trailed below my collarbone, then brushed against the curve of my breast. "You *aren't* innocent in this, are you?"

A lesser woman would have cowered. My former self might have shut down.

Yet I fought a reaction to their intimidation tactics with every fiber of my being. Tapping into anger I'd kept buried deep inside—that now boiled to the surface with the depths of the betrayals against me—I funneled rage instead of revulsion, harnessed the wrath I'd kept at bay for so long. Too long.

Barely restrained, I held my temper in check. Rather than act in rash haste, I channeled the blood thundering through my veins to give me clarity.

Escobar continued. "Anna swears under the influence of sodium pentothal that you knew nothing. Yet I think you did. You stumbled across something that led you to explore my house, didn't you?"

Uncertain whether his dungeon cameras had picked up anything when I'd lunged forward at the unexpected sight of his captives, I clamped my mouth shut. Apparently whatever my traitorous "best friend" revealed had satisfied Escobar enough not to truth-serum drug me too. And whatever role Alec played in all of this, good or bad, I wouldn't reveal what

I'd been told by him—didn't know how much of it bore the truth, anyway.

But whatever unrevealed secrets I still held, I intended to preserve, for now. Clearly those who maintained them and used them strategically gained the advantage. And to my knowledge, what Alec and I had done, and my suspicions about what the Escobars had planned were the only secret-cards I had left to play.

Course determined, my mind instantly dealt a reply. "You did say I was a brain child. An invaluable weapon. One would imagine an unfired weapon itches to be detonated."

Escobar twitched his head back at my rapid retort. Then a deep belly laugh followed as Miguel grinned wide.

"Oh, Devin." Escobar lifted his hand from where it hovered near my breast and rested it on my shoulder. "I think you and I will get along brilliantly. The weapon EtherSphere thought they had has turned against them—*because* of them. Little did they know, you would have the last laugh."

To reinforce the sudden turn of the conversation, Escobar gave Miguel a nod, and his son instantly backed away from me. Escobar also gave me more room, stepping away from the desk as he circled around toward his men.

I swiveled my head to track Escobar, then turned my body to fully face the room, not trusting any of them, not trusting anything. In a slow, calculated move, I landed my gaze on Alec, sized him up a moment, then scanned the rest of his men before aiming a hard scrutinizing stare directly at Escobar again.

Escobar's eyes narrowed, the same calculation and

mistrust shining from them. Adversaries at best, neither of us were willing to concede to the other; yet we each had something to gain.

"What do you say, Devin." His head tilted down a fraction. "Ready to exact revenge?"

Against whom? My parents for lying to me? Anna for deceiving me? Alec for not telling me any of this, for leading me astray, for conning me into caring about him…maybe even into loving him?

None of it mattered.

Only the truth deep in my heart did.

The world sorted itself into good and bad. Black and white. Lost souls drifted in and out of the gray shaded in between. But I was no longer lost.

Thanks to Alec, thanks to the divisiveness of my parents, of an organization I'd hoped to join—that had apparently been recruiting me—I'd emerged from the land of the lost.

Escobar edged closer, stepped into my line of vision to break the spell of the rage burgeoning within me. "Join me, Devin."

He flicked a glance at the Rolex on his wrist, then nodded to the soldiers that stood at ready alert toward the front. Two-thirds of them gave a sharp bow in return, then peeled away, exiting the room, including Miguel.

"Join the man who kidnapped me?" I scoffed.

"Only executed for effect. No better way to convince you."

"By subjecting a girl traumatized by kidnapping to more of the same?"

"Were you so traumatized? Didn't losing your sister to ruthless men shape who you are? One has to ask if they did you a favor."

"By killing my sister?" Reasoning with a madman incensed the logical side of me, yet I couldn't help myself.

Compassion washed over his expression and his head cocked as he took a step closer. "So certain she's dead?"

My mind froze, his insinuation not computing. I opened my mouth to argue, but no words came forth.

Escobar's tone softened. "With all the rampant lies, you have to wonder when they began, how far they went."

I had wondered. In fact, I'd investigated Geneva's supposed death myself. "I checked the records the moment I had the skills to break into their system."

"And what did you find?"

"They didn't exist. I was told they'd probably been sealed." And at the time, I'd written it off to bureaucratic bumbling. Never had I imagined that a secret agency—above the awareness of the government—had been at play.

He gave a satisfied nod. "And the police report?"

"Entirely redacted." Thick black lines had filled every boxed section, obscuring any trace of useful data aside from her name.

He reached his hand up and caressed the side of my face, his eyes searching mine. "We are more alike than you think, Devin. Betrayed by those we trusted. Out to seek vengeance on those who thought themselves above retribution. Help me deliver justice to the world."

The same promises Alec made, but a different side of the

coin altogether. Or was it? Who defined light and shadow, good and bad?

I did.

"Then let Anna go."

"Ah, my lovely Devin. Negotiating already. But no. She must be punished for her crimes. Were your parents here, we'd punish them too."

"The prisoners, the college students...set them free."

Before my plea had been fully uttered, the trio of monitors flickered on. The screens showed hidden steel bridges sliding into place above the underground river, providing access to the prison cells across it. Soldiers armed with snub-nosed automatic assault rifles slung over their shoulders opened the five enclosures and motioned the prisoners to cross the bridges.

"I intend to. Once they're on American soil, they'll be free to run home to their mamas and papas. And their families—the ones that didn't deceive them—will welcome them with open arms."

He was goading me. I pressed my lips into a thin line, but then failed to keep my mouth shut. "With your Ebola running rampant in their bloodstream?"

"Aha!" He spun around toward Alec, then glanced back at me. "I knew the two of you snuck down into my laboratory. My guard discovered the river grate in the process of closing." He fully faced me again, expression dead serious as he stared me down. "Are you a spy for EtherSphere?"

"No." The half-truth rolled off my tongue, silky smooth like all the rest I'd spoken over my lifetime. "Alec and I were having fun. Part of it was breaking into a locked door."

"*Tsk tsk tsk*," he clicked with his tongue, shaking his head. "The curious often end up dead." His hands slipped casually into his pockets, and he turned around. "Alec, why didn't you mention this?"

Impassive from head to toe, Alec gave a half shrug. "Not my place to question your activities or motives. You don't pay me for unsolicited advice."

"True." Escobar got into Alec's face now.

The danger of the situation escalated, tension charging the air. The megalomaniac had a warped sense of right and wrong. Which made everything he did unpredictable.

My attention slid briefly to the remaining six guards. Plus Escobar, that made seven. We could take them. Assuming Alec remained on my side—or ever had been. But escape had never been the purported plan. Getting as close as possible to Escobar had. Ferreting out his master scheme had been the endgame all along, no matter how Alec and EtherSphere got there.

Escobar pressed into Alec's space. "Is she a spy?"

Alec's shoulders shook with brief silent laughter before a soft snort huffed out. "Not that I know of."

"Are *you* a spy?"

At the implication, Alec's face hardened. He leaned forward until negligible space remained between their noses. They were both equally tall, both dark haired and broad shouldered, both could have been brothers, or father and son, and appeared an equal match for the other by physical strength.

"No," Alec replied, tone absolute.

Escobar pulled backward, spun, and clapped him on the shoulder. "Good to hear. I'd hate to replace my best arms dealer."

Even though he'd been absolved of suspicion, Alec's fierce expression held fast as his chest rose and fell in controlled deep breaths.

"Now, about Devin." Escobar returned and wrapped an arm around my shoulder, but I immediately shrugged him off. Faster than I could blink, his arm banded back around me, gripping my shoulder painfully. I bit the inside of my cheek, refusing to yelp.

Alec finally allowed himself to glance at me. The intensity of his stare spoke volumes. The interpretation was tricky, however. If I gave his silent look the benefit of the doubt, he warned me to trust him, to hold on, to play along.

Trust in all things with me had been obliterated. But I remained a survivor and could continue to play spy no matter what anyone tonight had said or believed. I'd been the master of duplicity all my life—surrounded by it, actually—even if I'd never officially recognized what had been going on.

"She will be mine," Escobar commanded. "I'm sure you don't mind sacrificing your lover for her own safety."

A muscle in Alec's jaw clenched at the suggestion that had been laced with an overt threat. A barely perceptible nod was his only reply.

"Good." Escobar spun around, easing his grip on my shoulder. As if it had been decided. As if I had no say in the matter. Then, seeming to realize his social-convention blunder, he turned toward me and put one hand on my shoulder while the other lifted my chin, gently this time. "This is for the best, my lovely Devin. You'll see. *No one* had your best interests at heart, only their needs. Not your parents, not your 'best friend,' and not Alec, who didn't know the real you."

"And you do?" My tone bled sarcasm as I arched a challenging brow. Couldn't hold back the words or my cynical anger. And truly, amid the unbelievable events in the last few days, in my entire life, Escobar was the only one who hadn't tried to deceive me.

"You have so much unrealized potential. Let me be a part of helping you see that."

Pain stabbed into my chest, intimate memories with Alec flashing into my mind. I'd been foolish enough to believe in the glimpse of potential with him. Stupid enough to hope.

I stuffed the sudden pain down, unwilling to acknowledge it further. And the sleeping giant within me, the darkness I'd kept close but harnessed for so long, stretched like a cat from a nap.

Of course, I distinguished good from evil. I also knew my choices were limited, control at the moment—an illusion. And the right thing to do? It depended on one's perspective.

I could deceive right along with the rest of them. And as I knew too well, even lie to myself.

I glanced down at my gauzy delicate clothes, ideal for dancing on the beach. Then I twisted my lips into the perfect smirk, aiming it at Escobar. "I'm gonna need a better outfit."

CHAPTER 25

Fifteen minutes later, after Escobar guided me down two flights of stairs, into a spacious locker room, then turned his back to offer me a modicum of privacy to change, I snugged a black baseball cap onto my head, then pulled my hair through the tightened back loop. The long-sleeved shirt billowed around my shoulders but had been tucked into the smallest cargo pants available—a doable fit with the belt cinched up. The black combat boots worked once I'd rolled and stuffed an extra sock into each toe cavity.

When I caught my reflection in the mirror, I paused, taking in the new version of me. My insidious darkness had bled through to the outside. It showed not only in the mottled camouflage of the borrowed outfit, but in the ferocity of my gaze. My skin prickled, like the thousands of fractures that had been spreading in the last few months were solidifying, hardening to granite.

Escobar led me out of the locker room. Then, in tight

formation and resembling a tactical team, me, Escobar, and Alec, joined by six soldiers armed with automatic weapons, strode down the halls of the sleek modern mansion. After a few minutes of echoing footfalls, we pushed through a roughhewn wooden door and began climbing another set of stairs located in the southwestern corner of the house, adjacent to and above the underground river cavern.

Escobar's loose grip never left my elbow.

Irritated, I wrenched my arm away. But his hand followed my sudden motion, never releasing, until he gently guided my elbow midway between us again.

I scowled. "Don't trust me?"

"Would you?"

"No." But any advantage I hoped to gain, relied on him letting his guard down.

"Don't worry, Miss Hill. The suspiciousness on both sides won't last forever. I don't blame you. Your reservations are natural. You think you don't know me. But you actually know me better than anyone else in your life. You are who I was, many years ago. We'll give it time. Distance and perspective settles all things."

Did it? Had it been true for him? I wondered what his trauma had been, since he believed we were so alike. Time had certainly revealed many things to me.

And I sensed my time for discovery had only just begun.

After a blood-pumping jog up four flights of stairs and a determined march along a dimly lit corridor, a metal door appeared. Two pairs of guards ahead of us peeled away, standing at attention to our left and right.

Alec stayed silent for the duration. Yet I felt his presence, hot and insistent at my back. Nevertheless, I wasn't able to sort him out right now. My focus narrowed to each split-second moment, continually assessing threats to me, the only one I remained capable of looking out for—or cared to. At every next step, I chose the path of least resistance. For now.

Escobar slipped a key card into a slot above the metal latch. When a green light flashed on, he depressed the handle and opened the door. A waiting guard to our right shot a hand up and grabbed the door's edge, holding it open while the soldiers filed out ahead of us.

We followed and stepped out into the darkness on the roof of his house. Air currents whipped around, and I inhaled the cool mineral tang of ocean mist through my nostrils.

A sleek black military-grade helicopter waited toward the end of a circular helipad, its whirling overhead rotor the cause of all the air disturbance. A pilot sat in the cockpit, wearing a green metal headset over his ears.

With efficient order, our entire group climbed into the large bird, first the two lead pairs of guards, then after finally releasing his ever-present grip, Escobar. He immediately turned and reached a hand down to me. Outnumbered and temporarily resigned to my fate, I grabbed on to his forearm and climbed into the vibrating tin can, apprehensive about boarding something that seemed so...unstable. Laws of physics eventually prevailed against the ego of man. Create something to defy gravity? Gravity would find a way to defeat you.

Regardless of my theories, I swallowed down instinctual fear and played along, like a good little spy...or bad guy—I hadn't yet decided.

After Escobar tugged me down into the seat beside him, he drew a thick safety-harness down around my shoulders and up through my legs. He secured its metal buckle over my midsection with a click while Alec and the remaining soldiers split apart and took seats along the two benches in front of us that lined the bulkhead. Seconds later, my stomach dropped, then rotated as the helicopter took flight.

When I deliberately glared at Alec, he ignored me. Which only enraged my simmering anger toward a rapid boil. Common sense assured me that he couldn't do any more than he was under the circumstances. *But come on.* Even a fleeting glance would've gone a long way to settle my ragged nerves. All his callous disregard did was renew my faith that lying, betraying thieves of hearts had infiltrated my life.

My jaw clenched tight, and I forced my attention out the open door beside me as errant winds whipped at strands of my hair. Down below in the rough waters of the ocean, a handful of watercraft skimmed over the waves. Resembling hydrofoils, the boats were narrow with extended stability skids jutting outward on each side. Light and nimble, they hovered over the choppy black waters, smooth as a hockey puck gliding on ice.

Farther ahead, a cruise ship loomed into view, a dark silhouette speckled with white lights that overtook the horizon.

Against my hardening will, my gaze drifted back inside, toward Alec, who had casually sprawled on the end of the bench on the port bulkhead, across from and five feet ahead of me. The soldier beside him leaned his face closer to Alec's ear, his lips moving in some shouted conversation I couldn't decipher through the roar of the rotors.

I stared hard at Alec, willing him to glance at me.

In spite of all the betrayal, I wanted so badly to believe in him. In everything he'd said. Anger helped to quell the storming emotions I didn't yet want to face. But my feelings for him, the ones I fought valiantly to ignore, kept creeping forward.

Look at me, Alec.

As if sensing my urgent mental plea, he finally glanced at me. With a nearly imperceptible twitch, his brows drew together. Like deep concern lay concealed behind his impassive mask.

I blew out a measured breath, then looked away.

The minuscule sign didn't mean he was worthy of anything from me. Didn't actually mean a damn thing.

Yet the hint of more behind his façade was enough to keep me going for now.

The time to kick his ass would have to wait until later.

CHAPTER 26

The modified hydrofoils were surprisingly agile on the choppy waters of the Caribbean Sea. And the helicopter we flew in was more than mere transport, it also served as air support. The aircraft's open doors on each side were manned by two soldiers apiece, each armed with those snub-nosed automatic assault rifles. They guarded Escobar's lynchpin, the human weapons being delivered for the final leg of their journey.

Any questions Alec and I had had about how they would board a ship cruising at twenty-two knots were answered as the scene unfolded before our eyes. The five hydrofoils all fell into a single-file line, just outside the wide churning wake caused by the ship's propulsion.

Lights from the ship dimly illuminated the activity below. As the lead hydrofoil came within twenty yards of and alongside the ship, one of the two soldiers aboard moved to its bow, aimed a crossbow upward at a forty-degree angle, then fired a thick metal bolt. The bolt flew through the air with an unfurling length of cable attached to its tail before it pierced the white hull of the rearmost lifeboat that hung three decks above water level.

The line twanged taut as the hydrofoil eased back by slight degrees. The soldier clipped a rod-like apparatus to the line. Then he motioned one of the male captives forward at gunpoint until the prisoner grabbed the rod and leapt from the watercraft. For a brief moment he dangled from the cable. Then suddenly his body jerked before he zipped upward toward the ship, defying gravity. Seconds later, two figures in white uniforms appeared behind the deck railing. They pulled the prisoner over the polished wooden edge ten feet below the anchor point of the line. Then one of the crewmembers cast the apparatus back down along the cable.

In the hydrofoil below, shoved forward by the guards at gunpoint, the captives began leaping from the bow of the watercraft, one after another, grasping the same rod before they were propelled upward toward the deck of the ship, dragged to their fate.

As cumbersome as the method first appeared, all five prisoners and one guard in the first craft were offloaded and boarded the ship inside of a few minutes. Once empty of passengers, the lead boat held its position while the next one eased into the narrow space between it and the ship. A small crane-like device shot up from the bow of the second craft and hooked on to the existing cable. Then the lead hydrofoil peeled away once no longer connected. The process of zip-line loading five prisoners and a soldier repeated with the second batch, then the three remaining watercraft.

My gaze scanned up the decks of the towering ship as we hovered in midair portside, staggered back in a near-blind-spot angle. Oddly, no stray insomnia-stricken passengers wandered any of the half dozen open decks.

The surreal scene played out before my eyes in degrees of obscuring shadow and partial light, black water churning away from the whitish foam of the ship's wake. On the ship itself, the deep nooks and alcoves of every ascending deck spanned endlessly from stern to bow, dappled with occasional lights shining from portal windows. The white hull of the ship stretched up toward a velvety black sky whose stars winked, the only witnesses to our helicopter hovering in darkness.

The ship's stern boasted the vessel's christened name: *Phoenician Sun*. How ironic. With no small amount of derision, I turned toward Escobar, suspecting a symbolic meaning lay beneath his choice, as if he'd poetically risen from ash to shine brighter than any other in the darkness of night.

He angled toward me, amusement kindling in his eyes. "You're impressed," he shouted.

"Hardly," I muttered. Another smooth lie. No reason to break pattern now.

His face lit up with bellowing laughter that I barely heard.

Good. Keeping him entertained would work to my advantage sooner or later.

At the nod of one of the soldiers manning the open starboard side, the helicopter banked hard with such unexpectedness, I had grab the cargo netting that dangled behind my head—better to hang on than tumble into Escobar's arms. The situation was vile enough that our thighs touched.

Infuriated that I'd been forced into this position, I shot another scathing glare at Alec.

But his hard gaze had already been directed straight at me. It held mine a beat longer, before shifting to Escobar, then forward as the helicopter rose and my stomach dropped.

In silence, I shifted my attention outward, watching as we rose above the top deck of the cruise ship, rotated around behind the captain's bridge, then touched the skids down on a helipad.

With efficiency, everyone disembarked. Once we cleared the radius of the whirling rotor, Escobar tugged me close to his side once again, separating me from most of his soldiers, distancing me from Alec who gave me one last look before turning away.

Refusing to give in to panic, I delved deep inside, disconnecting from the events around me that I had no control over. All my life, I thought I'd had it all figured out. My own deceptive ego had veiled the truth for too long. Gut instinct now had me hunker down, preparing for my world-turned-upside-down to shift yet again.

I no longer wanted to be the last to know, the biggest fool.

We entered a utilitarian bulkhead door. Then, with ever-quickening strides, descended several levels into the ship by a stark back companionway before entering a barren, narrow passageway. I imagined the ship had more elegant trappings, lavishing guests with amenities designed to draw forth awe and wonder: shining glass and polished elevators, wide curving staircases, hand-knotted plush carpets to cushion their footfalls as they gazed upon rare works of art. Wealth and opulence shrouded what really happened behind the scenes, much like the oblivious passengers aboard the Titanic. They'd dined and danced, enjoyed succulent dishes on gold-leafed bone china and beveled crystal right before they sailed into their fatal iceberg.

After a turn down an adjoining passageway, my mental sidetrack was cut short when the soldier leading our breakaway party came to a halt. All I could see beyond the wall of men surrounding me was Escobar pulling a key card from the pocket of his fatigues and inserting it into a slot above the door latch. A light flashed green accompanied by a soft click.

In a swift shuffle, I found myself ushered inside. I watched as the lead guard swept the room, checked the bathroom, then exited back through the door and shut it with a resounding thud. Only Escobar and I remained. And a stateroom that I knew must've been spacious by any ship's standards instantly felt claustrophobic as the giant male predator circled around me.

"What do you think?" Escobar asked.

"About what?" I shrugged. *Feign unimpressed.*

Unsettled to a level I'd not yet encountered in my *mirage* of a life, I clung to the only comforting thing within my reach: my wits. Strategy and logic would be my weapons of choice in a constantly shifting battlefield.

Overwhelmed by Escobar's imposing presence so close to me in the tight quarters, I turned away from him, taking measured steps toward the perimeter of the room. I sucked in a lungful of air and shied away from a large bed to stare out a dark portal at shoulder height in front of me.

"About me," he replied. His voice resonated inches from behind my left ear. "About the opportunity I'm giving you." The heat from his breath slithered over my ear.

I shuddered. "What opportunity?" Logic stuttering to a halt with his menacing proximity, I didn't get his point. In spite of my need to remain sharp, survival instinct rose to the surface faster than any other innate ability, including lucid thought.

"To become allies. Lovers. Equals." His breath now chafed across my cheek, his heat emanating across the scant distance between my back and his chest.

Repulsed, yet intrigued that he would assume I'd side with him so easily, I glanced over my shoulder. "What makes you think I'd be interested in an 'opportunity' like that?"

"We are alike, Devin. Cast from the same mold." His hand caressed my cheek, pulled my hair aside, then exposed my neck.

Rough lips touched the skin below my ear. I closed my eyes, fighting the urge to shudder. "We are nothing alike, Escobar."

A low chuckle rumbled from him. "Ah, you are wrong, my lovely. Your parents deceived you. My family misled me. Yours hid the truth from you, as did mine. Both were for their benefit, not ours. The only difference is my father was daring enough to dangle his triumph, the way he used me to accomplish his goals, right in front of my face seconds before he opened fire on me and my young bride."

His hand skated down my neck. "You have learned, as have I, not to trust love. It always hurts you. But then the pain makes you stronger.

"You see, his spray of bullets didn't kill me. Oh, they almost did. Sonia died right beside me, bleeding all over the floor. But by some dumb luck, the five bullets that hit my body missed every artery and bone, didn't even nick a vital organ."

He paused, then leaned forward and gave a slight tilt to his head. "How did you get damaged inside? Was it when your sister was taken in front of your eyes? Or when your parents conveniently told you she'd died? Did the heart of you doubt their words even though you let logic prevail? Was that when it happened?"

Stunned immobile by his words, trying to make sense of what I'd believed and the shocking reality, I stood there, unable to digest it all.

He put his hands on my shoulders and turned me toward him.

I didn't fight his hold, only stared up at him, shocked that I stood in the same space as this vile, powerful man coupled with all the events that had led up to this unbelievable moment. Words failed me.

"No," he continued. His dark intense eyes stared down at me. "It happened tonight, didn't it? When I forced their hand.

Only under duress did your friend reveal the truth. And she didn't even share it with you. Your friend, your parents, no one who was supposed to care about you shared the truth with you. Because their loyalty lies with an organization— not with you."

The harsh reality of his words cut me to the bone. He spoke the truth, the only person who ever had.

"The lies told to us don't make us the same," I bit out.

And yet, I got his point. We were brethren in a war not of our making. But my goals never wavered. My need for vengeance still churned deep within me. To make those who stole my sister pay. And since I had no clue as to the identity of the mastermind of that crime committed so long ago, Escobar would serve as a viable substitute.

His hand shot into the hair at my nape, gripping the roots as he yanked my head backward, forcing me to stare up at him. "We are the same at the core. Denial will get you nowhere." His expression relaxed as his gaze drifted down toward my mouth. "But I understand. You need time. This is all new to you. A foreign perspective takes a period of adjustment before we give in to the truth, before we believe it to be right."

Was I susceptible to his manipulation? Or would it be my eventual acceptance of reality. Logic forced me to watch for the barely discernable barrier certain to exist between them. The fine line between genius and madness dwelled in the shadowy gray area there.

Even if what he spoke bore the truth, it had to be out of context in the bigger picture. In spite of the dark miasma churning inside of me, a small but strong part of me held on to that hope.

Before another thought filtered into my brain, his mouth crushed onto mine. When I gasped in shock, his tongue took advantage of the element of surprise, sliding into my mouth. Cold and wet, it was everything I could do not to vomit into my mouth at the violation.

Unable to pull back with his hand knotted in my hair, when his tongue darted blessedly away, I bit down hard on his lip. The tang of copper floated over my tongue as he yanked my head backward with a low grunt, breaking contact.

Cool air rushed over my wet lips, and I wiped the back of my hand across my mouth. A smear of crimson marred my skin.

Escobar's eyes were wild as a wicked smile curled his lips. He released me, then touched his fingertips to his mouth as I stumbled backward, falling against the hard edge of a table.

I gripped the wood, thighs tensing, preparing to bolt if he leaned even an inch in my direction. But to where? My gaze darted to the bed. *Not there.* A sudden floorplan of the room exploded into a grid in my mind, potential escape points flaring brighter: door, sure to be barred with at least one guard; portal window, with no visible latch and likely fortified with no ordinary breakable glass; balcony beyond sliding glass, but a possible plunge to my death; the bathroom, with a slim door. The last surfaced as the best possibility.

His deep bellowing laugh rang out in the room, echoing off the hard surfaces. But he didn't come closer. "I enjoy the fight in you, my lovely. That will make our aligning together much more adventurous."

Great. Staring at him, holding the definite predator solidly in my sights, I rescanned my mental blueprint for potential weapons as I heaved air into my lungs, pulse hammering a frenetic pace.

He held my stare while he slipped his tongue out, then sucked in his bleeding lower lip for a brief moment before releasing it. "Make yourself comfortable, Devin. There are matters that require my immediate attention." His gaze roved down my body, before shooting up to meet mine. "I promise not to keep you waiting long."

An instant later, he spun around, opened the door, and vanished.

I didn't move. Could hardly breathe. The ship barely rocked beneath my feet, but my whole world had tilted off its axis. My legs began to shake uncontrollably as I gripped the edge of the table, willing myself to stay upright and not break down.

A shut-down agent is a dead agent. Alec's astute commentary broke through the muddy haze of my mind.

Focus. Use your smarts, Devin. I added.

I'd been training my whole life for this moment, preparing for the chance to step from the shadows, to no longer be victimized by the darkness but strengthened from it.

My gag reflex kicked in with the bloody taste of Escobar still in my mouth. I spun toward the stocked bar, grabbed a crystal decanter filled with amber liquid, and rushed to the bathroom. With both hands, I tipped the heavy glass up until warmth touched my lips. I winced as the burning alcohol, probably some thirty-year-old scotch, filled my mouth, then tipped it back and swooshed the mouthful around from one cheek to another. I spat it out, repeated the process, then spat again, hoping whatever germs and other diabolical contagions the man carried were dead, at least on the surface.

Returning into the generously appointed cabin, I took a more detailed note of every item as I crossed the room and replaced the decanter onto the bar. My combat boots made no sound, but the loose fabric of my cargo pants made a muffled scraping noise.

My breaths calmed over the next minute until a natural rhythm resumed. Clarity followed, and I assessed my surroundings, taking stock of the immediate situation. Even if Alec still remained on my side—if he ever had been— no doubt lingered in my mind about the state of affairs. Thanks to Escobar's meticulous planning, I was outgunned and outmanned—at least at the present moment. That last qualifying bit was the only thing holding me back from slipping over the edge into hysteria.

Alec's training and my father's words superimposed in my mind as a single mantra: Always look for a way to escape. I embellished it further, making it my own: If a clear path doesn't exist, make one.

Yet the ship's decorator hadn't made the job easy by any stretch of the imagination. By design, everything that was heavy enough to do any damage on a moving ship had been bolted down. When I tore back the edge of the carpet, I confirmed the metal table legs had been riveted to the floor. Likewise, so had the artwork been permanently affixed onto the walls, the 32-inch flat-screen TV to the entertainment center, and the delicate stained-glass Tiffany lamps to each nightstand.

Only the barware and pillows hadn't been secured. With serious consideration, I eyed the decanter I'd just replaced. Could I empty it and heft it like a rock? Sure. But how close would I have to be? And what were the odds I'd nail him on the first try with a fatal blow? Low.

And did I want to kill him? I hadn't given the option any thought. His testimonial rang in my head. But I rebelled against it. We were nothing alike. Similar situations of deception and betrayal? Fine. I'd give him that. But what about the dozens of people he'd stolen from their families and infected with his hybrid virus? And what was his endgame smuggling them into the United States? Infect the population? Cripple the country?

Yeah. Escobar and I were nothing alike.

The bastard needed to die.

And I had no qualms about his ultimate demise being at my hands.

I turned my attention away from the leaded crystal decanter, however. I wasn't an idiot. If Escobar had hired Alec, and Alec could kick my ass in martial arts, and Escobar harbored the same deep-seated fury born of betrayal that I'd kept at bay for so many years, I held no illusions about his level of training. Escobar would likely be able to hold his own against me, at the very least.

"Think, Devin. Find what was missed," I muttered and glanced toward the ceiling, emptying my mind as I stared at the smooth white surface like it was dry-erase board.

Then I closed my eyes, imagining each furnishing broken down into its parts to be utilized as a weapon. Bed? No. Dining chair? I opened my eyes and examined the forest-green upholstered barrel chairs. Nope, not unless I hefted the entire thing at him.

My gaze fell on the drapery rod. Custom designed, it appeared to be hammered steel with a two-inch square-shaped circumference. And because the window was only a three-foot wide portal, the steel rod, just a bit wider, was about the length of a baseball bat.

Uncertain of what time remained before Escobar would return, I grabbed a dining chair and positioned it below the window. Although secured into the side brackets to prevent movement, all it took was unscrewing the steel-scrollwork globe finial at one end to be able to pull out my makeshift bat from the other end.

With a swift yank of my arm backward, I cleared all the square rings hanging every few inches and held tight to my prize as the drapery whumped to the ground. Then I stepped down from the chair, moved into the centermost portion of the room, and tested out the balance with some trial swings. After brief consideration of removing the remaining finial and using the rod as a short bo staff, I decided to leave it as-is; the weapon had good heft and a balanced swing with the added weight on its end.

Seconds ticked by into minutes as I tested my new weapon, moving through scenario after scenario, anticipating how the door would open and from what direction I would strike. With my stance braced wide to account for the gentle sway of the ship, I lunged and swung an arm. The whizzing sound of metal slicing through air hummed an unexpected satisfaction through me.

Once I assured myself I was ready with every trial run I could think of, I stood along the wall, right behind the door hinge, catching my breath and reserving my strength. That's when the dark thoughts crept forth, unbidden. My analytical mind couldn't let the disturbing puzzle rest.

I closed my eyes and thumped my head back into the wall, swallowing down the burning emotions, doing my damnedest to filter through only the raw facts.

I'd been betrayed.

My parents and the best friend I'd ever known had perpetrated the greatest crime against me. Greater than the one against my sister. At least with her attackers, there'd been a clear delineation between the bad guys and the good.

But the worst transgression? My entire life had been a sham. When I'd thought I'd failed my parents, somehow deserved to be taken instead of my sister, unworthy of the comforting love that had vanished—I'd been wrong.

They had failed *me.*

I inhaled deeply, trying to keep some perspective in a situation near impossible to do so. My parents had lied, about what they did for a living, where they went on their so-called work trips, who they were. They were spies? The entire notion seemed at once ludicrous, and yet, entirely fitting.

And what about Alec? I didn't know what to believe about him. When logic suggested the coincidence of his arrival, stumbling onto my balcony injured from a bullet wound that had seemed statistically improbable, gut instinct had me believe him. And I'd always been a dead-on read of people.

Except for friends and parents who were spies, it seemed.

Needing to quiet my mind, I gripped my bat and slid down the wall until I sat on the floor. Trusting my position to alert to any entry, I stared forward and focused on one point, entering into a zenful state of meditation.

Murmured voices outside the cabin door had me jump up from the floor, tensing my muscles. After a deep breath, I cleared my head and relaxed my body into a poised ready stance. My focused breathing matched cadence with the ship's rhythmic movement.

When nothing happened, and the voices went silent, I dropped my gaze to the door latch.

A low beep was followed a split second later by a muffled click, then the metal door handle angled down. I gripped my drapery-rod bat tighter and raised it to shoulder height, preparing to strike.

The door opened. An inch. Then a few more. The instant I saw a shoulder appear, I tensed and unleashed a powerful swing, aiming at the head about to appear in the airspace I'd targeted.

But my swing never connected with a head. A large hand shot up and caught the rod a few inches from the end, radiating a jarring painful impact-shock through my wrist, elbow, and shoulder joints.

Then the figure turned, revealing his face.

"*Alec,*" I whispered with astounded relief.

"After getting stabbed with a pen, I enter any room that you're already in with a plan to defend myself." He winked at me.

Great. Humor. In the worst possible circumstance.

"Open the door wider," he said.

When I gripped the handle and pulled the door open another forty degrees, Alec dragged an unconscious guard in by his shoulders until the guard's boots cleared the threshold. Then he grabbed the edge of the door and closed it. Another muffled set of clicks followed as the door automatically locked.

I stared at the guard, trying to confirm he was breathing. Before I could tell one way or the other, Alec grabbed beneath his shoulders, then hoisted him upright, facing me.

With a steely expression, he gave me a quick nod. "Take your swing now."

Beyond confused, I wrinkled my brow and stared at the guard. "I think you already got him."

He shot me a deadpan look, then grunted, "Hit the guard. Then *you* did the damage."

Ah, more subterfuge. "What if I kill him?"

"What if you do?" He gave a slight nod to the guard. "You want to be a spy? Be able to kill. You *will* kill as a spy. Don't doubt that." The guard's weight slipped, slumping his form forward, and Alec grunted again as he lifted him upright once more. "Hurry up. Junior here weighs a ton."

Ignoring the sudden queasiness in the pit of my stomach, I took aim, arced backward, then swung forward, landing a blow that first impacted the guard's temple until it carried through, glancing up over the top of his head as the body began to fall forward.

Alec quickly jerked back, out of reach of the metal finial still arcing through the air.

The body landed on the floor facedown with a loud thump.

Alec whistled low. "Damn. You pack one hell of a swing."

I nearly grinned, then fought it. Not a damn thing amusing about the situation. "Softball champion in middle school," I muttered as I tossed the weapon onto the bed.

Staring at the trace of dark red on the guard's exposed temple, I frowned. "His head's at an odd angle."

"Probably from the broken neck."

My gaze shot up to meet Alec's. "From the fall?"

"From the snapping action of my wrists."

I blinked. He hadn't done that in here. So he'd already…

With a deep scowl, I shook my head. "Why'd you have me hit him, then?"

He leveled a serious look at me. "Think of it as in-field training. And we need to buy time. If Escobar believes you did this, he won't be thinking what *I* would do next."

I gave him a curt nod. Made sense.

But when Alec outstretched a hand toward me, I instinctually flinched away from his touch. The automatic reaction caught us both off guard, my eyes widening as he let out a heavy sigh.

"Devin, don't do this. Not now."

A flood of emotion threatened to break free. With

incredible force, I dammed it back, determined to act the model student, the consummate field operative in action. Yet, I couldn't keep it all in. "You told me not to trust, back then."

My breath quickened, anger welling to the surface. He stared at me, several emotions flickering over his face in an instant before they vanished and his expression relaxed.

"Trust me now." His tone was low, his eyes softening. A plea lay partially hidden below the surface of the command.

Gathering a fierce resolve on a deep breath, I reached up, took a solid step, and slid my hand across his warm palm. "Don't let me down, Marquez."

Our gazes locked for a moment, and with a muscle tensing in my jaw, I burned a message through my stare. He gave me a nearly imperceptible nod. My words weren't an absolution for him, and he understood.

The blind faith I held in our temporary truce was a necessary evil.

Because first, we needed to get out of this predicament alive.

CHAPTER 27

Without discussion of any sort of plan, Alec quickly ushered me through the cabin door and closed it behind us. I glanced left then right, down narrow passageways that I now realized—after my tunnel-vision fog of arriving with Escobar had dissipated—had burgundy carpeting with a gold latticework pattern and ivory walls featuring door alcoves trimmed in dark woods. Recessed rectangular sections of the ceiling glowed with hidden lighting.

After confirming the coast was clear, Alec grabbed my hand and we broke left at a dead run. Thankful for the borrowed combat boots even with socks stuffed into the toes, I kept pace with him. Barely.

We rounded a corner and ducked into the first door on our right. The sound of metal echoed upward and downward as we entered a nondescript companionway.

Alec didn't break stride as he pulled me forward and raced us up the steps.

"Where are we going?" I whispered.

"Aft deck."

"What's there?"

"Helicopter."

Oh. Of course. He planned to steal the helicopter. But with quick mental calculations as we climbed the steps, I stumbled upon a problem. "Aren't we going about twenty-two knots? Does the helicopter have enough fuel to get us back to Maroma Beach?"

"We've been cruising over thirty knots for hours. And we're not going back to Maroma Beach."

My feet planted as I blinked. "Hours?"

"We've been onboard for almost seven hours."

He squeezed my hand and dragged us onward and upward as my staggered brain finally let an explanation surface. While waiting behind the door to clobber Escobar with my makeshift bat, when I'd slipped into my unique state of zenful meditation, I'd lost time. A lot of time.

"What has Escobar been doing?" He clearly hadn't had the time to return to his stateroom.

"One of the prisoners escaped. Took all the guards and assistance from the captain and a few crewmembers to track her down."

"So the captain's in on it?"

"Yes." His expression turned disgusted.

And I grew grateful. That at least when it was just the two of us, Alec had become more himself—at least the version I'd come to know. "So…" Reality dawned on me. "We're a one-agent show?"

All of a sudden, he paused with his boot hovering over the next step, half turned, and leveled a look at me. "Two-agent show."

I rolled my gaze upward before locking on to his. "Right. Because agent-in-training me will make all the difference in the world."

"Believe it and it will be."

Simple as that. In a world and life where everything I'd once thought to be true had been illusion, why not fool myself into believing I could make a difference.

Yet wasn't that what I'd left my stifling predestined life for? To discover what I'd been meant to do, unleash my true self to match a greater purpose.

Without warning, Escobar's words echoed into my head: *You have so much unrealized potential.* I blew out a hard breath, shaking off irritation. It chafed that a man who sought to do immense harm in this world would point out that I was destined for something great, support my innate need to fly.

Why couldn't that unquestionable support have come from my parents?

At least Anna's belief that I would find my way had been absolute, even if her identity and motives had been a lie.

After another ninety seconds and endless climbing, we reached a bulkhead door at the uppermost landing. Alec grasped the escape wheel handle, spun it to the left as metal dogs scraped free from the hidden framework inside, then pushed the door open.

Cool, salty air burst over my face as I stepped over the

bulkhead lip and onto the outer deck. A clear night sky stretched over us, black velvet speckled with bright pinpricks of light.

Dead ahead, Escobar's sleek black helicopter glinted in the darkness. I glanced up to where a light source emanated from. The backside of the captain's bridge towered over us.

Earlier when we'd first arrived, when Escobar held a punishing grip on my elbow and Alec had been surrounded by a half dozen guards, I hadn't taken note of the deck where we'd landed; I'd been focused on where we'd been headed, and we'd gone below deck in the other direction, toward the stern.

Now I realized that the helicopter landing pad was actually in the center of a converted promenade deck with half its lounge chairs shoved aside. When we rushed forward, the echo of our footfalls muted, revealing that the deck's substrate had been reinforced from its inception, likely to accommodate such dual-duty flexibility.

A large nautilus-shaped pool shimmered some distance beyond the helicopter with its adult play area sunken into the open deck a half-flight of steps below our position. As soon as we stepped under the helicopter's stilled rotary blade, a whizzing sound then a high-pitched ping jerked my attention toward the aircraft's fuselage. A round metal hole marred the surface.

Alec grabbed my arm and yanked me toward the skid. "Down!"

"Where's it coming from?" I shouted, scanning behind us.

He grabbed my hips from behind and shoved me upward. "Bridge tower. Guess Escobar left someone to keep an eye on his toys."

"*Toys*?" The plural threw me.

My question was lost as Alec climbed aboard, rushed past me, then took the pilot's seat as he put a headset over his ears. He gave a jerky nod to the other set dangling from the bottom edge of the instrument panel.

I slipped the leather-cushioned cups over my ears and watched as his fingers flew across the instrument panel, flicking switches. A vibration trembled up through the seat as the turbine engine began to warm up. After another switch was flipped, the overhead rotor began to spin.

"Please tell me you know how to fly this monstrosity." Flipping switches and piloting with skill were two totally different things.

The helicopter had to be the biggest I'd ever seen in person. Uncertain about his flying ability, I pulled the harness belt over my shoulders and clicked the fastener securely into place.

He shot me a smug grin as the rotor whumped faster and faster overhead. "We *built* this monstrosity. And yes. I should be able to keep it airborne."

We? *EtherSphere One.* It seemed arms dealer also encompassed the facilitation of aircraft acquisition.

A bullet ricocheted off the windshield. Then a dark figure appeared, running toward us.

"How long?" I shouted, panic taking hold. We'd been sitting ducks for almost a minute.

"Another ten seconds," his calm voice murmured through the headset. "No need to shout."

Ten one-thousand. My attention remained riveted on the armed guard raising the muzzle of his assault rifle as he ran. "Got a gun?" We'd never make it otherwise.

"Toys in the back."

Eight one-thousand.

Aha. *Toys.* Before my next heartbeat, I released my harness belt. As I rushed back into the cabin, I vaguely remembered seeing weapons cases between the soldiers' feet on our flight over. They still sat there. I clicked a smaller case open. The uppermost layer of dark gray foam held three weapons, but a semiautomatic threaded barrel SIG SAUER P226 caught my attention.

I grabbed it, ejected the magazine to verify it was loaded, then reseated it with a firm shove of the heel of my palm before I racked a round into the chamber. Then I ran toward the open portside door. The helicopter suddenly jerked as it caught air, and I slid but then recovered on my next footfall.

Three one-thousand. At the bulkhead, I pressed my body flush just inside the opening, then darted a quick glance outside while slipping my fingers through cargo netting that hung beside me for a secure handhold. The pursuing guard closed the distance, sprinting inside our launch zone, the wind from our rotors beating his long hair back. His body compacted down, muscles coiling tightly for release as if he planned to leap into the side opening.

On a smooth exhale through tightened lips, I raised my weapon, finger sliding over the cold metal trigger. His eyes widened, then narrowed as my gun fired with an orange flash. The weapon kicked, but I tensed, fighting to hold it steady as I depressed the trigger again, and again.

His upper body jerked, throwing him off-balance in his crouched position until he tipped over while the helicopter began to take flight in a steady vertical rise. His lifeless body grew smaller with every passing second. A pool of dark blood bloomed across the deck beneath his upper body.

A low voice rumbled in my ear. "You good?"

"All good." *For us, anyway.*

Gripping the cargo netting as we gained altitude, I inhaled a deep breath. Then with no time to freak out, I compartmentalized what I'd just done: *killed a man.* Thirty feet, forty feet, fifty...we rose into the night as I scanned across the visible portions of the deck and along the railings of the captain's bridge, ensuring no snipers or shoulder-mounted weapons had sights on us.

Cold air whipped around me, battering my face until my eyes teared so badly, I had to retreat from the opening. Careful to grip handholds and secure my footing lest I be tossed out the side with a jerk of unexpected turbulence, I worked my way back up to the cockpit.

Through the side window, I noticed a distant trail of cruise ships ahead to our starboard, a total of five in a line. We flew parallel to them, heading north as we surpassed them one by one.

"Killed a soldier," I admitted. Not that I needed counseling about it. Only to alert my fellow operative of the situation.

He glanced sideways and pinned me with an assessing look. A quick nod followed.

Guess I looked okay with it.

"Won't matter," he replied. "With the captain and crew working in concert with Escobar, they'll want to hide the body quickly before a passenger trips over it."

I refastened my shoulder harness, clicking it into place as we continued to fly northward. "And we've stolen Escobar's only means of chase."

"Exactly." He pulled left on the cyclic stick between his legs and the helicopter tilted in the same direction. "Grab the map and light from the storage on your left?"

Between our seats, a metal console was built into the fuselage. I pulled opened the top and did as he asked.

"Ready to earn your supper, copilot?" he asked.

I gave a quick nod.

"Estimate Escobar's time of arrival versus ours. Their ship is cruising at blistering pace of thirty-two knots with the Florida Current, which has an additional velocity of almost four knots. We're flying at one hundred fifty knots. We're both heading to the Port of Miami and we've just flown past Key West."

My mind spun with his spouted factoids. "You know the velocity of the ocean's currents? And how do you know the ship's speed?" I recalled he'd mentioned how fast the ship cruised as we'd fled up the companionway.

Without shifting his gaze from the darkness beyond the windshield, his lips curled into a smug grin. "I casually toured the bridge under the guise of curiosity."

"On behalf of Escobar, naturally."

He tipped his head my direction. "Naturally."

"And as soon as you suspected the cruise ships as a means of smuggling," he continued, "I researched and studied their routes and the ocean currents."

Impressed with his research, I clamped the penlight between my teeth, reached down to fish out a pencil I'd encountered in the console, then examined the map. I folded its dog-eared paper to expose only the section I planned to chart, then leaned forward and scribbled a few calculations on the pale-blue section depicting open ocean.

"You sure we have enough gas in this to get us to Miami?"

"How far do we have to go?" he asked.

I double-checked my calculations. "Assuming the cruise ship keeps her current speed, and she slows as she approaches the port, she should reach Miami in just under four hours."

"And us?" he asked.

"We should pass into Miami airspace within forty-five minutes," I replied, confident. "Assuming we aren't headed off by the coastguard or shot down by scrambled fighter pilots, we should beat them by a good three hours."

"Shot down?" The corners of his lips twitched. "You do realize I've got connections." His calm words flattened into statement-of-fact as he leaned forward and flicked a metal switch upward, then turned a dial. "And we've got enough gas. Per Escobar's specifications, we amped up the range of his custom Eurocopter to fly from his house to Miami."

Several clicks sounded in my headset, then low static, followed by brief silence.

"Echo Sierra this is Oscar. Mother Hen, do you read?" Alec called out into the silence.

A field of light static played before another click.

After a piercing squelch, the low tone of a female voice filled my ears. "Mother Hen reads you, Oscar."

"We need a flight plan filed from Cancun International to show us departing there two hours ago in route to Miami. We've just left the *Phoenician Sun*." Alec gave her a bullet-point briefing of the situation.

"Current position and bearing?" The woman asked.

Alec provided our coordinates to her. "We're skirting US airspace bearing northeast. We'd like to land in one piece."

"Roger, Oscar. Stand by."

Static resumed.

"Roger, Oscar?" I asked.

He chuckled. "Regina's sense of humor."

"And you're Oscar?"

"I'm One."

"EtherSphere One," I connected, mulling over what he meant, after the obvious phonetic alphabet *Oscar* for *O* meant One to Alec. So the agents were independent operatives? Was that why Anna mentioned she had no idea about anything else? Had Alec *not* known about...

Another squelch interrupted my train of thought. "Flight plan registered retroactively. We've got you on satellite. Continue your bearing for another ten minutes to avoid a plane crash investigation in progress. Stay below ceiling once you reach mainland coastline."

"Below ceiling?" I wondered aloud.

"For stealth," he clarified. "Even though we now look legit, we still need to be ghosts. No need to attract notice."

"Ah."

Alec adjusted his mic. "Roger that, Echo Sierra. Much obliged. Over and out."

Then he leaned forward and tapped a switch down. After a click, the static in our headsets disappeared.

In the silence that followed, Alec kept his focus trained forward. Occasionally, his gaze would sweep over the instrument panel, then stretch outward again over open water.

Our close proximity in the cockpit taunted me. Enraged by the betrayal of my family and best friend, uncertain of the role he played in it, yet knowing the few minutes we had in this cockpit together wouldn't come close to covering my vent-time, let alone any explanations, I did my best to swallow down the bitterness threatening to overcome me.

It wasn't easy. Deep breaths and heavy swallows kept the rising bile down. For every minute that ticked by, another question crept forth. But I added it to the list, then forced the lid closed on the overflowing compartmentalized box that had begun to resemble Pandora's.

Still, even with the minimal time we had, one tiny question kept surfacing, breaking free of the tenuous hold I had on my emotions.

"Did you know?" Uncontainable, my question came out on a whisper.

A pregnant pause followed as signs of civilization shimmered into view. At first, tiny dim lights appeared, then clusters along shorelines, as the islands of The Keys blurred by.

"It's complicated," he finally replied.

"Simplify it."

"I didn't know about them."

Them. My family.

"Anna?" I asked.

He shook his head. "No."

Okay. Good. At least he hadn't been involved in the greatest betrayals. "What's so complicated, then?"

He sighed, then dropped a heavy stare at me. So much flickered over his expression in a split second before he reined back, regaining control. "I knew enough."

CHAPTER 28

Before I had a chance to process what Alec had eluded to—his involvement in the betrayal of all betrayals—the tip of Florida's mainland peninsula glittered into view. Minutes later, we hovered along the southern Florida coastline, an occasional light glimmering amid a long dark stretch of land before the glowing exterior lights of condo high rises began to appear.

Regina's voice returned through our headsets. "Your navigation system will guide you to an available landing pad." As she spoke, a screen in the middle of the instrument panel activated, glowing green lines outlining the geographical landscape on a black background. A white dot pulsing from a pinprick to the size of a pencil eraser marked our current location.

"They won't be expecting you," Regina added.

Alec gave a barely perceptible nod. "Wouldn't want it any other way. What's the story this time?"

"A local media outlet needed an emergency landing."

He coughed out a laugh. "So, now we're paparazzi?"

"Is it so farfetched?" she asked, humor edging her tone.

"Mystery billionaire would be better. We look nothing like media."

"We've positioned you close to the docks," Regina continued, ignoring him. "You'll land on the unoccupied top level of a five-story parking garage to hide in plain sight. Helps with the paparazzi cover. The *Phoenician Sun* will dock in the slip nearest your position."

And yet, was paparazzi so farfetched? Not so different from spying. Both stalked, lay in wait, spied on unsuspecting clientele, used zoom lenses and predictable patterns to glean private information. My gut churned at the parallel of events. How had my parents and Anna ever thought spying into my life would be acceptable?

Alec leaned forward and depressed a button on the corner edge of the navigation screen. The view shifted into an actual satellite image superimposed with data fed from a camera that had to be positioned somewhere on the aircraft's nose, because the image shifted with our movements.

"Are you there, Devin?" Regina addressed me directly for the first time.

"I am," I confirmed, wondering how she knew my name. Might as well have smacked my own forehead an instant later. EtherSphere knew all about me.

"We were able to determine by the DNA and virion diagrams, coupled with fast research on our end and the aid of an agent in the CDC, that it would be possible to hybridize Ebola with the common cold. They're calling it a weaponized supervirus. Alec, based on Escobar's past MO, he'll be sneaking these kids back into the states right under everyone's noses."

"Not on my watch." His tone held no emotion, only the weight of fact.

"Good. What support do you need?"

"Call in a bio-team, but have their vehicles lined up outside the facility grounds. They are only to move on our command. If Escobar has any moles within the port itself, they'll know we're here. We can't afford to force him underground." Alec zeroed in on the makeshift helipad highlighted by the navigation system.

"Done," Regina replied. The sounds of rapid keyboard typing followed. "Anything else?"

Alec glanced at me right as our rotating motion slowed and we hovered over the helipad, seconds from touching down. His gaze pinned mine, fierce as his eyes narrowed for a split second. "Wish us luck."

Us. Regardless of what had transpired, no matter what he'd known or hadn't been privy to, at the moment, we were a team, attempting to save the lives of two dozen kidnapped college students and one captured agent. And in the bigger picture, if we could stop the weaponized supervirus from getting into the general population—saving the world.

"Good luck, you two," Regina replied.

With a slight wobble, the skids touched down, then with the flicking of several switches, Alec powered down the bird and the instrument panel.

We pulled off our headsets, hung them on the instrument panel hooks, then unfastened our harnesses. Alec stood, then paused, placing a hand on my shoulder.

I glanced up at him. Volatile emotion swirled in his eyes. A storm of activity was happening around us, yet for the briefest moment, we connected. Wordlessly conveyed, I got the sense that whatever had happened before, however complicit he'd been in the undefinable betrayal, we were together now, in every way.

"Ready, Pink?"

Choked up with emotion, I nodded. At the moment, I didn't trust my voice not to give me away.

I followed him to the back of the helicopter, and we began unloading the weapons cases. He handed me the SIG SAUER I'd used, then handed me a long, narrow case.

"Sniper rifle," he explained when I gave him a questioning look.

Then he opened additional cases and armed himself with a semiautomatic pistol, a snub-nosed assault rifle slung across his body, and grabbed his own long, narrow case.

"What about that?" I nodded to the handheld missile launcher case.

"Looking to blow up the ship?"

On a heavy sigh, I shook my head. All the anger in me wanted to blow up something into tiny little pieces, but a ship with innocent passengers wasn't it.

"Surgical precision would be better," I agreed.

On a curt nod, we left the cases with the heavier weapons where they sat, then he led the way off the helicopter. I squatted, planted the heel of my hand on the edge, and hopped down. An odd question pinged into my brain: If I'd wanted to blow something up, would he have let me?

After getting our bearings, we walked from the center point of the structure we'd landed on, but as we approached the elevated parapet edge, we crouched down until we belly crawled the remaining few feet, sliding the sniper rifle cases in front of us as we went.

Sunrise splashed growing light onto the bustling docks below. Alec sidled up beside me as we made ourselves comfortable. Regina had positioned us at the perfect vantage point. Obscured by other buildings at our flanks, we had a clear line of sight to where the *Phoenician Sun* would dock.

After we spent the next several minutes disassembling, checking, and reassembling our weapons, I sat down, knees bent in front of me, and leaned a shoulder against Alec who sat beside me. I yawned, then let out a long sigh.

"Sleep," he said.

I let out a soft snort. "I lost almost seven hours on the ship."

"You need it. You've been through a lot. I've got us covered."

I closed my eyes, unable to argue. The emotions of the last ten hours had drained me. And I still had a ways to go.

A slight jostling startled me awake.

The sun had risen higher in the sky. I scrubbed a hand over my face, blinking heavy sleep from my mind.

Alec still sat beside me. He pulled out those high-tech glasses from his pocket and put them on, then stared over the hundred-yard distance between our location and the side of the ship, whose gangplank had already been lowered and was filled with activity by crew members.

As Alec surveyed our target with stony seriousness, I stared at Alec's lenses.

"Got any more of those—"

Without a glance or a word, he pulled a folded second pair from his front shirt pocket and handed them to me.

"How…?"

"Each of the long-range weapons has a pair in their case. Thought you'd want one."

"They sync with the sniper rifle too?"

"Yes."

All business. Which, under the circumstances, I was more than all right with.

From the ship, bins were wheeled out, so enormous, it took two deck hands leaning forward and pushing with dug-in heels to maneuver them. With each twosome of personnel, I engaged the binocular feature of the glasses, zooming in. But none them were of the kidnapped college students or anyone else recognizable.

Additional crew members disembarked in larger and larger groups. Most in gray uniforms. Others in blue. Customs officials in black uniforms at the end of a roped-off line checked documentation in rapid succession as the crowd of people funneled together. In the last group, the workers wore civilian clothing, duffel bags slung over their shoulders. One held a dual-handle sport bag at his side, the contents stuffed so full the seams looked ready to burst.

"There!" I called out in fierce whisper. I pointed the muzzle of my sniper rifle toward a tight-knit group among two hundred plainclothes crew members.

In the middle of and around our college students and Anna, workers appeared hungover. Some seemed to be singing a song. Others leaned toward each other, arms slung over shoulders, eyelids drooped over their eyes, as if they were still drunk from an all-night bender.

But those workers held themselves a little too well in their "drunken" stupor. And several had a hand stuffed into a jacket pocket that had been conveniently pressed up to their captives' sides.

The captives themselves could barely stand upright. They stumbled along, propped up by a corresponding "fellow crewmember."

As if this were an everyday disembarking occurrence after a voyage at sea, the customs checkpoint didn't even slow when our crewmembers and college students passed, either used to half-baked ship employees or bribed in on the situation.

"Why not call ahead to have the customs officials detain them?" I kept my high-tech sunglasses and weapon trained on the group as they cleared the checkpoint bottleneck.

"Many reasons. We needed to know Escobar's plans. He didn't fill me or any of the guards in prior to our boarding. Our orders were to make sure the prisoners stayed below decks, nothing more."

"Then what?"

"The moment we boarded, Escobar briefed us. After the ship docked, half of us were to scatter through the shipyard and take up sniper points, guarantee the kids made it through."

Blinking in shock at the suggestion that we weren't the only ones with a high vantage point in and among these buildings, I scanned the visible rooftops around us. But nothing appeared out of the ordinary. "Why didn't you alert Regina? Couldn't she have warned customs?"

"EtherSphere won't interfere in local law enforcement. And we don't expose ourselves. Our organization has remained cloaked from discovery for a reason."

"Are you sure you're not careful to the point of ineffectiveness?"

"We are silent. Until it's time not to be." He paused, then shot me a sidelong glance. "Then we speak in ways others can't detect, but will still readily understand."

"Still, this all seems so…elaborate. Why not smuggle in the actual serum versus people? Infect them within US borders? Why not cars or trucks, a means of transportation with less eyes watching?"

"Elaborate to Escobar is the beauty of it. He basks in the elegance of a plan. And he especially enjoys taking advantage of the ego of any democratic government who believes they're untouchable. Vacationing families? No more perfect ruse to slip in right under their impenetrable noses."

I chewed on that for a moment, staring at the group that began to congregate around four white panel-vans. Instinct tightened my muscles. "They're getting ready to disperse. It's now or never."

He shook his head. "I haven't seen Escobar."

Alec was right; Escobar hadn't yet emerged. I identified a few soldiers disguised as plainclothes crewmembers, but had yet to sight Escobar. Although Miguel came into view from the far right, dressed in full fatigues.

An analytical web played out in my mind: soldiers previously scattering to vantage points, bold arrogance in believing they wouldn't be stopped by customs, his son stepping into view, seemingly from nowhere.

"Alec, there's more to this. It can't be all about smuggling them in. Escobar kidnapped me. Then it was so easy to escape. *Too* easy. Even if that was coincidence, he would've discovered me missing hours ago. Us missing. He would've employed counter measures."

Cool steel slid over my cheek. "I did."

Escobar.

I didn't flinch, although it took a deep breath and incredible focus not to. Alec didn't respond either.

"Letting you go was the first." The hard muzzle of a gun slid along my jawline toward my ear until it pressed against the back of my head. "Seeing how you'd respond? The second."

My mind reeled. Had Alec been in on this? Was he a double agent: working for EtherSphere to spy on Escobar only to spy on me while he worked for Escobar? And where did that put Alec on my map?

Didn't matter. Immediate logic reigned, blocking out

any further questions, overruling all emotion.

Fleeting seconds remained. One, maybe two. Coupled with the element of surprise and focused determination, they were the only advantage I'd have before all was lost.

Never taking my attention from the group gathering below, the prisoners already being loaded into the unmarked panel-vans, I lowered my head, but not my gaze.

"Put the weapon down, nice and easy," Escobar commanded with a pointed jab of the muzzle against my skull. "Alec, it seems you were playing for the other side all along. Well, I may have just lost an arms dealer, but I'll be damned if I lose the asset EtherSphere had worked so hard to attract. In the end, it hardly matters. Your bitch is mine now."

Good. He's not looking to put a bullet in me...just yet.

I couldn't see Alec in my peripheral as Escobar dug his gun muzzle against the base of my skull. Years of anger suddenly sharpened into this one moment, the weighted space between one heartbeat and the next.

A subtle shift was all it took, enough to feign compliance. Then a dance began, multiple moves all choreographed into a split-second chain reaction.

One finger on the trigger, I locked on to the electronic bull's eye in the high-tech sunglasses, then I took aim and squeezed, firing a single round at the most powerful target before releasing the sniper rifle.

Without breaking my movement, I continued to lean left, feeling Escobar's gun slide away from my scalp as I reached up over my right shoulder. Cast off-balance, his weight fell forward. He shot a bracing leg out, but I grabbed the barrel of the automatic assault rifle that he gripped with both hands. Flexing my thighs, harnessing their crouched power, I lurched forward, yanking the weapon over my shoulder and out over the rooftop's escarpment. And in basic instinct's truest form, Escobar didn't release his grip on the weapon until his brain fired signals of impending danger—too late to save him from it.

With my heightened awareness, I also perceived my target's reaction: Miguel clutched his chest and fell to his knees while a dark spot spread across his camouflage shirt.

A gasp sounded out as Escobar cleared the airspace over me. His rifle drifted away from him as he clutched at air. I stared hard at him as he plummeted, memorizing every feature of a man truly terrified: the widened shocked eyes, the mouth agape, hands clawing, reaching, searching for salvation that exceeded his grasp.

Muscles in my jaw clenching, I watched with grim satisfaction as an evil man fell to his death. My sister's terrified expression had haunted me for too many years. Now I had a better memory to replace it.

No part of me cared that it was a statistical improbability that Escobar was the one responsible for Geneva's kidnapping. All that mattered were the lives that he'd put at risk now.

My gaze held fast as his body slammed onto the pavement below, landed with his limbs unnaturally askew, lifeless, broken.

The wrongdoing carried out so many years ago had been avenged my way.

I scanned upward, and time sped up again as additional

guards began to fall. One backward. Another while running for cover behind a white panel-van. One of them grabbed Miguel under the shoulders and started to drag him off, before he too was shot.

Blinking rapidly, my brain caught up with an instant adrenaline rush to the task at hand. Alec had returned to my side, firing off round after round as he neutralized the opposing force.

Remembering the rest of the soldiers who'd supposedly taken sniper positions, I touched a finger to the lenses of my glasses, switching to a thermal view to more carefully search for signs of life along the inert rooftops.

Reddish orange illuminated five hotspots, all spread in a semicircle perimeter within view of the vans. Thankfully all of the college kids had been loaded and were out of harm's way before the shooting had begun. I hoped they stayed there.

Readjusting the aim of my sniper rifle, I synced the glasses to the weapon, pointed at the target on the far left, and fired. Not skipping a beat, I repeated the process with the next closest target.

"I'll take out the right side," Alec offered.

As I took aim at my final target, I stared down the scope of his rifle. How long had it been pointed our way? Was he aiming at Alec or me?

With no time to spare, I fired.

As if all had been completed, my body collapsed.

An instant later, I stared up at a clear blue sky. My limbs fell back, my body seemingly sucked downward. I relaxed into the pull, not wanting to fight gravity. A burning fire lit up my hip, but I didn't care. The pain felt good—proved I was alive.

"Jesus Christ, Devin." Alec's words sounded hollow, like he called out from blocks away down a narrow tunnel. His handsome face filled my vision, dark features drawn tight with concern.

I smiled and reached a leaden arm up to caress his face. "We did it."

Was that my voice? It sounded tinny to my ears.

Mind detached from the images, sounds, smells…a coppery scent filling my nostrils, I watched absentmindedly as Alec blurred into action.

A metal case opening.

A dark-red syringe being assembled, held aloft, the barrel flicked with his fingernail.

I felt my other arm lift, then a sharp prick at the inside bend of my elbow. "Field Cocktail," I slurred out, grasping at the memory fragment.

"The good stuff," he explained.

"*Mmm*…morphine."

His low chuckle preceded black dots that fringed into my vision before the world funneled into a total blackout.

CHAPTER 29

A plane engine rumbled. Floorboards vibrated beneath my feet.

The world blurred back into existence…from my groggy consciousness strapped upright in the copilot's chair of a cockpit. A *plane's* cockpit.

"What…" My sandpaper throat locked up.

"Welcome back to the land of the living," Alec murmured, not far away, beside me somewhere.

I swallowed hard as my vision cleared by small degrees. Dozens of round gauges on a matte-black instrument panel sharpened into focus. Two control wheels moved in concert, resembling dual curving joysticks, complete with a black button on the inside stick and black and red buttons on the outer.

Turning my head to the right as far as possible, I stared over my shoulder at blue sky. The white surface of the fuselage glared so bright, I pinched my eyes shut, blinking away intense pain that instantly throbbed at the backs of my eyes.

"You stole a plane," I croaked out, master of the obvious. "You stole...me."

A low snort sounded to my left. "Something like that."

I swallowed twice more past the grittiness in my mouth as I scanned out the windows of the plane. Indigo-blue ocean waves rolled below us, all around us.

My hip ached. I pressed at the source, then winced. "What did you do?"

"Brought you back from the dead."

"Oh. That all?" A sense of impending gloom made me question my level of gratefulness.

Silence followed.

I couldn't determine our bearing by the position of the sun. Sluggish brain cells began to engage again as I tried to find coastal landmarks. *Nothing but water.*

"Which direction are we flying?"

"South."

Were we flying back to Cancun?

No, further south, intuition instantly replied. *To a silver strand of paradise: Maroma Beach.* Toward the deadliest man on earth: Escobar. *Correction: the* deadest *man,* my sparking brain provided, even though there were no degrees of dead.

Escobar's frozen horrified expression as he fell to his death replayed in my mind.

A heartbeat later, satisfaction thrummed through my veins, and I took a deep breath.

The world shone a little brighter suddenly. The only

colors in view were black and the digital reds and greens illuminated on the instrument panel and the shocking white and vivid blue visible from our altitude. But in unexpected consequence, the beauty that existed in the rest of the world down below interested me.

As my mind relaxed further, a hazy memory floated in:

Alec pulled me tight to his chest.

High-pitched shouts pierced my ears: Anna. *"Devin! Oh my God. Are you all right?"*

The world spun, dizzying. I burrowed deeper into Alec's strong hold.

"She'll be fine." His deep tone reverberated through me.

"But…all the blood." Terror laced Anna's voice. "She was shot!"

"Gave her a syringe full of Field Cocktail III. She'll live."

I straightened a little and turned my head, squinting as I zeroed in on the sound of her voice. "Anna?"

"Devin, listen to me." Her cold hand skated over my forehead, then cupped my cheek. "I didn't…couldn't say anything. EtherSphere, the mission, it was for you. But everything else?" She focused her intense emerald-green eyes on me. "The fun and laughter? That was us. Remember the laughter. Remember us. I'm still your best friend—if you want me to be."

Reality jarred back in and I narrowed my eyes, pushing aside the drug-induced fragment. Then I turned toward Alec. "Did Anna manipulate me?"

Instant tension hung heavy in the air between us. I sensed so much more lay unspoken.

"Yes."

Satisfied with his answer, I gave a sharp nod. "Good. No lies."

"I've never lied to you."

Uh-huh. "Just not offered the complete truth: the story behind the story." Even though I'd fallen prey to deception, I'd mastered the art of lying through distraction and distortion. Too bad the best liars made the worst detectors.

He finally glanced my way. "Wasn't within my authority to offer it."

"And now?"

"Anything you want to know."

"Because you've suddenly been authorized?"

He flicked up a switch. A green autopilot light glowed on. Then he unharnessed himself and bent his leg on his sheepskin-covered seat, fully facing me.

He stared at me for a few beats, dark eyes full of compassion, the features of his face drawn tight. "I'm here now because I choose to be, not because a mission mandates it."

The sadness of that gradually sunk in. "But before? When you…" Brought me to life, jump-started my heart—made me love again. The meaning behind my emotions bottlenecked into a choking cramp at the base of my throat.

"Everything between us was real, Devin." His hand slipped over my forearm, down to my hand until he threaded his fingers through mine and squeezed gently. "It *is* real."

Too much. The lies, the levels of deception, were all too much to process so soon.

Panic welled in my chest, and I jerked my hand away. With trembling fingers, I depressed the metal buckle securing my harness until it clicked and released the straps. I bolted up in my seat so fast, I knocked his upper body back against the buttercream-leather surface of the bulkhead.

His expression hardened as he pushed upright into his seat again.

"I don't know what's real," I hissed, my breath coming in short bursts as I began to hyperventilate.

Action. I needed to do something. Get out of my head that whirled with all the wrongdoings of my parents, of Anna…of what he'd done, no matter how he spun it now.

I climbed over the center console, then rushed into the lavishly appointed cabin, searching frantically for something, needing to push through the out-of-control state I found myself freefalling in.

"Whose plane is this?" I jerked open a large cabinet door at the back of the cabin. Parachutes were stacked. A medical kit and tool kit were neatly positioned in their own nooks.

"EtherSphere's."

My gaze landed on familiar black cases scattered haphazardly on random leather seats, in the carpeted aisle. "Those our weapons?"

The "our" slid off my tongue, smooth and easy. Because I considered myself an agent now? That had to be the reason.

"Yeah," he replied. "Anna and an EtherSphere field-response team helped me load them, got us to the airport."

Anna. The mention of her name pulsed anger hot inside my gut. I had no idea why it riled with greater fury than Alec's in-my-face presence did now. Betrayal was a funny thing. So was compartmentalizing. Survival instinct brought forth only the necessary, without obvious reason.

"Can you hotwire the plane?" Logic pinged strong into the forefront of my mind, and I clung to its familiar security like a life preserver.

When he didn't respond, I turned toward him. He stared at me, blinked, then narrowed his eyes and glanced toward the front of the plane. "It's already flying, Devin. You feeling okay?"

"Of course not." That was beside the point. "But I need you to splice the plane's autopilot function together with" —I bent down, fire flaring into my hip as I froze in a half-crouch before I growled in frustration and straightened— "That. What is that?" Instead of opening the case, I pointed and sucked in a deep breath, blinking back fuzzing vision, trying to remain conscious.

"Handheld missile launcher…theoretically, hotwiring a plane is possible."

"Well, make it *realistically* possible."

My command held a biting edge. Not one fiber of my being wanted to soften the harshness.

His penetrating gaze held mine, like he searched for unspoken answers somewhere in the depths of my eyes. Would they look wild, crazy? I didn't care. He would either cooperate, or I'd initiate an on-the-fly Plan B.

Thankfully, he honored my commanded request with a

curt nod, and he opened the case. In a matter of seconds, he disassembled the launcher's housing and pulled out a small circuit board, its short wires dangling.

"Got a plan?" He climbed back into the pilot's seat, resting the circuit board on the console between the seats, then reached around the control wheel and rapidly removed a few screws. Then he yanked the wheel off the top of the control column, pulled out a knife, and began slicing into the plastic coating covering the wires.

"Formulating one," I said. "Will you be able to program coordinates?"

"In a way. Since the tech sunglasses sync up with the weapon, we should be able to rig it so the glasses sync up to the plane. Will your target be by sight?"

"Yes." I almost smiled. *My* target. As if he was my agent and his actions were at my command. I didn't delude myself, however. His loyalty had been clear: to EtherSphere. His cooperation would only remain as long as his and their objectives aligned with mine.

A ribbon of greenery came into view to our starboard, and the plane gently turned on its autopilot course to fly parallel to the shoreline while he twisted the last set of wires together.

"No," I corrected. I leaned a supportive arm on the back of the copilot's seat. "Can you find coordinates that are stored in the glasses?"

"The target is something we've seen?"

Closing my eyes, I remembered when the longitude and latitude first populated my field of vision. "Back on the catamaran." It was when we'd first spied from afar, when I'd noticed the light pattern in Escobar's windows. "Escobar's house."

He stared at me a beat longer before his eyes widened infinitesimally. "You want to blow the house." The corners of his mouth twitched. "I love the way your mind works, Pink."

Pink. The endearing nickname jarred an aching pang into my chest.

His gaze held mine, like he realized his faux pas and my stunned reaction to it.

We treaded on thin ice, he and I. And still, we took tentative steps forward, feeling our way to safety, to solid ground.

Before either of us broke the silence, the plane course-corrected again, swaying us both.

He broke the intense gaze between us, maneuvered into a seated position, and grabbed his glasses from his front shirt pocket, then slid them onto his face. "This will take a minute. I'm assuming you wish to *not* be on board when this happens."

I pushed off the seatback, returned to the back of the cabin, and reopened the large cabinet. "Preferably," I muttered as I tried to remove the top parachute from the stack, but it seemed to be secured in some way. I growled in frustration, tugging on a belligerent strap that refused to release.

Pain flared in my hip again, and I groaned, hand instinctively gripping the site, as if pressure would alleviate the fiery nerve endings. It didn't.

"What happened to me?" I huffed out between controlled

breaths as I focused on mitigating the pain through sheer will. Logic had a funny way of funneling the order of what I worried about. My parents, Anna, Escobar, Alec, then me, dead last, as per usual. After this plane ride, I intended to seriously reprogram my brain about priorities.

"You were shot with a .30 caliber round." He depressed a button on the upper right of the glasses while simultaneously flicking the autopilot switch off, then back on. A faint beep sounded from both units. "Clean through muscle, in and out. Miracle, really. Only millimeters from shattering your pelvis. Had I not injected you with EtherSphere's Hail Mary Field Cocktail, you wouldn't be standing here."

He let out a heavy sigh. "I sold him those rounds. Thankfully, they weren't hollow point."

I nodded absently, grateful to be breathing, then frowned as I continued to wrestle with the parachute.

Angry at the injury that evil man had caused me, at his kidnapping innocent kids, at hybridizing a deadly virus, conviction fired through me. "Everything of Escobar's needs to burn. Dungeons. Labs. All of it."

Sudden movement caught my attention. I turned to see him climbing into the copilot's seat before putting on a headset. When I furrowed my brow, he pressed a vertical index finger to his lips, asking for my silence.

"Hold on," he said, still holding up his finger, gaze locked to mine. "Strap yourself in. I'm losing control."

Even though I sensed a charade being played, I obeyed and dropped into the nearest seat and quickly fastened the seatbelt.

The plane suddenly lurched, its movements erratic as Alec wrenched the copilot's wheel in one direction, then another. We began to wobble, losing altitude.

"Cancun Tower," he said, loud and clear. "Mayday. Mayday. Mayday. N511EE. Loss of pitch control. Attempting water ditch." He repeated the distress call in Spanish. Then he yanked his headset off and depressed the sunglasses still attached to the pilot's hotwired control column.

The plane settled a bit as he climbed back into the cabin. "Gotta make it believable. The temperatures after that ammunition explodes will obliterate any other evidence."

As the plane began to bank then climb on its own, and sensing that we had limited time, I punched my seatbelt release and lunged back to the rear cabinet.

With a hard yank, the unruly strap finally released its hold on the parachute, and I stumbled back, clutching it to my chest.

"Here, let me help with that," he offered.

Mind going blessedly numb, focusing on the task and nothing more, I handed him the parachute. He secured the harness across my chest, then more gingerly around my legs to protect my injury.

With a quick glance toward the front of the aircraft, he spun around and worked quickly to get his own chute on. We approached the northern tip of Cozumel and made our final course adjustment as the plane began to descend, rapidly.

"We have only a few more seconds. Ever done this before?" he asked.

I gave a firm headshake. "No."

"Piece of cake." He stared hard at me. "You got this." Then he grabbed my hand, squeezed gently, and slid my fingers over a metal handle then closed my fist around it. "Only, at this low altitude, the instant you jump, count a steady 'one one-thousand' then pull hard on this ripcord. We'll only have about ten seconds before impact. It could take half that for the chute to open. When you hit the water, release these buckles here and here, then swim away from the parachute." He moved the fingers of my other hand over the plastic harness buckles as he spoke.

"Half that?" My mind got stuck on those two words as we moved to the bulkhead door. My heart began to race. I watched numbly as he pulled the lever on the door and gave me a quick glance. When I nodded and grabbed the back of the seat, he released the latch and pulled the door open.

"Takes two to five seconds for chute to open, typically."

"Let's hope for two." I envisioned smacking down onto the ocean with an injured hip. Not cool.

"You'll be *fine.*" His stone-cold expression made me wonder if he was trying to convince himself or me. Before I had more time to question the plan, he gripped my shoulders, stared down at me, and kissed me.

Hard at first, then softer, as if he wanted to convey everything into the small action. My body melted instantly, molding to his. But just as fast as it came on, the kiss ended, cold air rushing across my lips.

Wind whipped around us, battering our faces. The ends of my hair lashed my cheeks with tiny painful pinpricks as I stared into his eyes that glistened with unshed tears. Had to be from the gale-force wind. Right?

"Remember," he said, dark brows drawing together. "Jump, count out one full second, then pull."

"Got it."

Then he shoved me out of the plane.

CHAPTER 30

The next ten seconds unfolded in a slow-motion series of shocking events.

Unprepared to be cast into a wind tunnel at over a hundred twenty miles per hour, I gripped the nylon straps of the chute as my body flew horizontal with the plane for a fraction of a second before air turbulence knocked my body about, my stomach dropped, and my body followed.

"Remember...count one full second..."

I blinked hard. "One one-thousand..." I couldn't hear the words with all the wind and the roar of the engine as the plane sailed toward the coastline. But I spoke the mantra Alec had asked of me aloud, all the same. I gripped the metal ripcord handle in my hand and yanked it hard right as Alec's dark form jumped from the plane.

A hard jolt rattled every bone in my body as the chute caught full air, snapping me out of freefall. I groaned, gritting my teeth as my healing hip blazed anew with pain.

Four one-thousand...

Alec's chute fired out above him, a neon orange splash of color unfurling against the blue sky as air billowed into every silken nook and cranny.

Five one-thousand...

I instinctively reached for the toggles hanging from the shoulder points of the harness and after a bit of trial and error, began steering my parachute in Alec's direction, toward the distant shoreline.

Six one-thousand...

Dangling in a harness as the surface of the ocean rapidly approached, a sudden thought occurred to me. I abandoned steering for a precious few seconds, and reached down. With fingers numb from cold, I fumbled with the belt of my cargo pants.

Boots! Damn.

I lifted my good leg, quickly unfasted the laces, gripped the toe and heel, and pulled off the boot, dropping it to the ocean. Gritting my teeth, I did the same with my bad leg, grabbing my knee with one hand to help support the weight, then yanking the laces loose enough before dropping the second boot.

Eleven one-thousand...

The ocean was right there, less than fifty feet away.

Twelve one—

The impact hit me hard. Fiery pain flared in my hip as my body plunged down into cool water. Clenching my jaw, I focused beyond the pain to the tugging of the harness as the parachute dragged somewhere behind and above me, on the surface.

I followed Alec's last advice and quickly pinched the hard plastic buckles, releasing the harness restraints. Grateful I'd had the foresight to rid myself of the heavy boots, I maneuvered out of the harness, then my heavy cargo pants.

A percussion boom resonated through my body, making my eardrums ache to pop.

The plane.

Lungs burning, I opened my eyes, located the faint glow of blue amid all the darker water surrounding me, and swam toward the surface, following the bubbles, scissoring my legs with the force they had to give regardless of the incredible pain in my hip.

The second I broke the surface, I gulped in a lungful of air, then another. I treaded water but was impeded by the loose fatigue shirt I still wore. I unbuttoned it halfway, dunked underwater, and swam backward out of the material. Then I swept my arms in two wide breaststroke arcs back up.

Bobbing on the surface, slowly up, then down on a rolling wave, I rotated toward land about a half mile away. A dark plume of smoke mushroomed up into the air off to my left.

I blew out a hard breath, unable to pull any immediate satisfaction from the destruction, survival taking precedence. After a quick three-hundred-sixty-degree scan, I failed to spot Alec. Only empty shoreline straight ahead and endless water all around.

Legs already tiring, and that incessant hip ache dulling from an attention-grabbing nine on the pain scale down to a more manageable throbbing four, I began a slow freestyle stroke toward shore.

Too many things hovered on the edge of my thoughts to dissect which ones to worry about, but first came my survival, which was all that remained in my fragile control.

And yet, burning welled behind my eyes as I searched across the surface of the water with every breath, alternating sides as I swam. Every so often, I'd stop entirely and rotate around in a complete circle, methodically searching every degree before me. To no avail.

Nothing. My chute had sunk, likely pulled down by the weight of the harness.

Had Alec's sunk too? With his weight in it?

I pinched my eyes shut and resumed stroking, refusing to give further thought to the notion.

Alec couldn't be dead. A man so alive, so vibrant—the one who'd taught me *how* to live—couldn't be gone.

Familiar agony assaulted me, ripping off old scars from the past. Of someone stolen away from me by circumstances beyond my control.

But had they been this time?

I was the one who'd suggested—practically ordered—the plane to become a weapon.

After another few strokes, a crushing weight began to press in on me.

The real world taunted me with vivid sensations. Salty ocean water coated my lips. The cloudless blue sky radiated warmth. A single gull's cry instigated half a dozen replies in kind. With the rise and drop of each swell, I caught glimpses of activity unfolding in lazy beach time. Although I couldn't see detail from this distance, my mind filled in the gaps: waitstaff carrying trays laden with drinks and bowls of colorful fruits, resort guests in bright swimsuits lounging on beach beds angled toward the sun.

The oblivious world kept on with the charade…

As if a global threat hadn't been thwarted.

As if a beach house a quarter of a mile south wasn't being engulfed by flames.

As if two evil masterminds, father and son, hadn't been killed, their plan destroyed.

"As if a great man hadn't sacrificed himself for them… for me," I murmured, disgusted by it all. That I still lived, in spite of the chaotic mess. That I still lived…

A choking cramp seized my throat. A sob tore free. Hot tears streamed down my cheeks as I mourned the incredible loss. Of my sister. Of my parents. My friend, Anna. Alec.

I was no longer oblivious. The darkest lie was the one I'd conned myself into believing. That I could swath myself in darkness and be the wiser wolf on a planet full of ignorant sheep. But I'd really been a sheep in wolf's clothing, kidding myself into being unaffected by it all. I suffered. I bled. And if I stumbled unsuspecting into a river too deep, I'd drown.

Heart heavy with anguish, I swam into a colder patch of water and stayed there, soaking in the deeper blue that soothed me like the darkness had always done. On a defeated exhalation, I let my strongly treading limbs slow, let the cold seep in, let bleaker thoughts take hold.

What if I didn't keep swimming? Would it be so hard to succumb to the pain? Could the satisfaction of vengeance be enough? What did I have to live for, anyway? Who waited for me? What new set of lies would I be buying into if I chose to go on?

Long seconds ticked by before I exhaled a heavy breath, ready. Nothing remained for me.

A colder current licked across my thighs seconds before something brushed against me.

A shark?

How poetic. I would die at the hands of a natural predator. But in the circle of life, I welcomed a species governed by pure instinct, a creature unable to deceive.

A splashing sound slapped the water. I closed my eyes and relaxed, bracing myself for impact. I tipped back, floating, submerging the backside of my head, my ears. Water lapped over my face. Sounds faded to the background, muted by the deep mass of the ocean and rushing blood that pulsed through my veins past my eardrums.

Another second passed.

Another.

Nothing happened.

Was that how life ended? Peaceful...but unremarkable?

Despair coursed through me. In a world where everything turned out to be against me, I couldn't even seem to die right.

"You okay?"

Am I dead?

No reply came to my mental question.

I startled upright, then sputtered out water I'd sucked into my lungs. A coughing fit followed. After my third lung-clearing hack, something hard thwacked my back. My teeth rattled from the jarring impact.

"Devin, are you all right?"

My eyes flew open. Alec's sharp features came into crisp focus. "Alec!"

I threw my arms around his neck. Then I tightened my grip, clinging to him so tightly, he had to pry my hold loose. "Easy. You'll drown us both."

Then I hit him upside the head.

"Ow!" He winced, then pulled back, ducking as if I'd raised an arm for another blow.

My arm hovered above my head. I slapped down hard on the water instead.

"You idiot! I thought you were dead."

"Close. Got stuck in my parachute and a mess of seaweed. By the time I worked free, a current had pulled me a quarter-mile farther out to sea."

Sudden anger replaced the anguish I'd been wallowing in, and I resumed my freestyle stroking toward shore with renewed vigor.

Alec kept pace with me. "So, I'm assuming you're okay, then."

"Define 'okay.'" I ground out. My hip killed me. Unfortunately only in the metaphorical sense. My whole world as I'd known it to be had turned upside down. And I wanted to destroy everything fragile and smash everything breakable I could lay my hands on. Literal...very literal.

"Still breathing," he continued as we swam. "No broken bones. Not in life-threatening danger."

Lucky for him, he didn't fit the category of fragile or breakable. "Then, I'm fine." Not even close, but passable by his definition.

Several long silent minutes later, diagonally flowing waves began to break parallel to our position and a few feet ahead of us. I tentatively stopped kicking and let my lower body fall. My feet hit sand just shy of vertical, and I bent my knees, letting the ocean flow pull my legs beneath me. Using the momentum, I pushed up and stood among waves whose lapping surface pushed against the back of my upper thighs.

I trudged forward, bearing the walking motion in my hip slightly better than swimming.

Once our feet hit dry sand, I glanced toward where Escobar's house once stood on the precipice. The structure proved to be one of those fragile things I'd been able to destroy. A column of thick black smoke spiraled up into the air before sheering off into the wind current. As I stood there watching the devastation, the distant sound of multiple sirens began to wail.

Without another word or thought, I headed north, leaving Alec to stand there.

Oddly, no emotion assaulted me. Only the absence of emotion.

Like I'd been bled dry and had nothing left to give.

Seconds later, he caught up, then kept pace right beside me, but respected the silence I'd initiated. When we reached the stretch of beach in front of his house, I continued walking, not breaking stride. Once I passed the far corner of his lot line, Alec disappeared from my peripheral.

On a sigh, I turned around. I couldn't do this. Not now. Things had been left undone, unsaid. After the crazy roller coaster ride I'd been consigned to without my permission, I needed answers.

"Do you have access to my parents?" A spike of anxiety pulsed through me.

He stared at me with his dark, assessing eyes. Hesitation shone clearly through their depths. The delay of our personal business bothered him.

But he gave a curt nod and outstretched his arm up toward his house.

I couldn't remember the walk up to his house. Not how we entered. Nor how the charcoal towel got wrapped around me.

My awareness flared sharp the moment a low motor hummed. Through an aperture in the ceiling of his office, opposite from his desk, descended a flat-screen TV as Alec's deep voice murmured from behind me. Once it reached its lowermost position, after several clicks on his laptop keyboard, a frozen image appeared on the screen.

On a sage-green background, an artistic infinity symbol stretched horizontally. The ivory narrow loops on either side appeared to be etched. In the middle, where the linear paths intersected, gold shimmered.

My legs trembled as I stood there: the fading effects of adrenaline. Why wasn't I pumped up now? Exhaustion. Irritation.

I'd had enough. Of all of them. Of the charade.

"Come, sit down." The air behind me stirred. A gentle hand pressed to my shoulder. "You look like you're about to collapse."

"No."

I didn't offer explanation. He didn't ask.

After a life filled with half-truths and duplicity, I intended to stand before those who'd enacted the travesty. Cold fury settled into my gut. The muscle tremors began to dissipate. White-hot determination surged a fresh dose of adrenaline into my veins.

They no longer held court over my fate. And in the wake of their inexcusable crimes, I would be their judge and jury.

The green background on the screen glowed brighter, then faded away into a live image. In the center of a round gleaming black expanse of floor space, stood my parents, expressions impassive as ever. Behind and above them, on a semicircle dais, were the shadowed silhouettes of a ten seated figures.

"The High Council," Alec provided as he gave my shoulder a firm squeeze before stepping away.

I still felt his close presence, the air charging electric between us even in the tense moment, but he stood behind me, in support of what I was about to do.

Hair likely plastered to my head, face itching from the dried salt and sand encrusting my skin, I pulled the towel edges tight into my fists as I straightened, lifting my head high.

I narrowed my eyes at my parents. Accusations flew in chaotic order in a brain ill-equipped to handle the barrage of information in the midst of the emotional turmoil, but I funneled them in. Only shallow temporary satisfaction would come from finger-pointing. I needed answers now.

Justice would come later.

"Why did you lie to me?" I ground out through a clenched jaw. "About Geneva?" *About the circumstances. About themselves.* "About it all?"

Dad had the decency to sigh. But Mom answered, hard as nails. "Wasn't our decision to make."

Duty above family. The words had never been spoken, but in our regimented excuse for a homelife, the message had been clear. Only their duty had been to the world at large, not some scientific corporation or government entity. Their loyalty had lain with EtherSphere One.

"You had no qualms about changing? About withdrawing into a cold, heartless shell?" Because, in truth, that was where the deepest betrayal lay. Not in what they'd done, but in what they hadn't.

"We dealt with the situation the only way we knew how." Mom's eyes held no remorse.

"Efficiently." My teeth ground together, anger rising.

"Without emotion," Dad corrected. "You should understand that."

"Really?" I shouted as my fisted hands exploded outward, yanking the edges of the towel until it pulled taut on either side of me. I didn't give a flying fuck if they saw me standing in my soaked-through bra and underwear. The time had come for them to take a good hard look at the real me, inside and out. "If you'd bothered to pay an iota of attention to the daughter you abandoned, you would've realized that I'm the exception, not the rule."

Both my parents seemed taken aback by that tidbit as

their eyes infinitesimally widened.

"That's right." My body trembled with rage as my tone lowered, each word forged with steel. I pulled my towel around me again, hugging my midsection. "I have emotions, and they run deep." My throat worked as I struggled with a hard swallow. "I suffered from that loss too. But Geneva wasn't the only one stolen from me that night. Your perfect little genius noticed the love you ripped away."

Miracle of miracles, their hardened façades faltered. Dad blinked, as if fighting back tears. Mom's gaze lowered, shame flickering over her features.

"I did nothing wrong." My voice flattened, some of its angry punch fading away. "It wasn't my fault they stole her instead of me."

Dad shot a sidelong glance at Mom. A couple of the shadowy High Council figures shifted in their seats.

"Tell me. I'm done with lies." I scanned my gaze across the semicircle of council members before landing it squarely on my parents again. "Anna said this entire thing was orchestrated by your organization, EtherSphere One."

Mom turned slightly, glancing over her shoulder. The shadowed council members leaned to one side, then the other, appearing to discuss a topic that didn't filter through to the feed. Then the figure on the far end gave her a slight nod.

When she turned back to face me, my parents leaned in toward one another, arms shifting as if they'd clasped hands. And her expression had completely changed. Compassion softened her features as she tilted her head to the slightest degree.

"They weren't after you, Devin. They wanted Geneva. She tested even higher than you did."

I blinked hard, confused. "Tested?"

Dad lowered his face, never taking his gaze from mine. "Both of you were tested. You were above a 160. Geneva's intelligence level was..."

"Immeasurable," Mom supplied when Dad faltered.

"Who is 'they'?" *The dark figures in my nightmares.*

"We don't know," they both said simultaneously.

No deception threaded their tone. "She isn't dead though, is she?"

"No," Dad replied.

I closed my eyes, unable to fathom what that meant. "Where is she?"

A silent beat passed. Then another. "We have no idea," Mom said. "Only a message that arrives every few months, touting her progress."

They offered nothing more. Only the bare minimum. More than I'd ever gotten in my life, yet still light years from what I'd needed.

I let the silence stretch long, the tension on both sides thick and palpable.

No apologies followed. Not for what had happened to Geneva—or me.

My inner darkness stirred, molten hot and filled with purpose. "I want access to everything you have on Geneva. Every note you've made, every communication you've received. Anna was right: You suspected I wouldn't join

EtherSphere One if that's what you'd wanted for me."

I took a deep breath, then fixed a hard stare at the two of them. "I won't be a lapdog. You may have shown loyalty to EtherSphere above all else, but I won't. What I want comes first." I'd never realized the importance of that fundamental requirement as starkly as I did now. "If EtherSphere One wants me as one of their agents, they'll have to earn that right. Now? I'm a free agent. I work for myself. Any assistance you want from me...is on my terms."

"Done." The words were spoken in unison from the two of them, as if that authority had been granted to them.

I turned away, sickened by the whole fiasco, bile rising into my throat. My head throbbed, my body...bone-tired. But curiosity stopped me, and I slowly spun back to face the screen. "What happened with the virus? To Anna and the prisoners? To Escobar's men?"

Common sense told me with EtherSphere's additional teams of agents watching Escobar's house, they already knew we'd bombed the hell out of it.

Mom straightened, business face back on. "Anna will be fine. The prisoners are all safe with local officials, their family members on the way. Alfredo Escobar's men were either killed by you and Alec or apprehended by local law enforcement. The only evidence they have of Miguel Escobar being on the scene is his blood stain on the cement."

I blinked, uncertain if I'd heard her correctly. "You stole his body?"

Dad gave a slight headshake. "Miguel isn't dead. Anna shot him up with the same Field Cocktail you received.

We need him alive. He's developed an antidote. But you destroyed all the notes for its formula."

Ahhh... "The clean rooms." They'd been developing more than the problem. They'd created the cure. For Ebola. Or at least their villainous strain.

After a short nod, Dad continued, "They'd masterminded more than an outbreak. They'd also activated sleeper agents across the States to hide bombs at key CDC installations and quarantine stations. We'd only been able to decipher that coded communication once you and Alec left with Escobar's men. We disabled the skeleton crew he'd left behind and were able to infiltrate their computer systems."

I gasped, not realizing anyone had been there when our plane crashed from the sky.

"No one was hurt," Dad continued. "They plugged in to the computer network, and we accessed their systems remotely."

On a hard nod, I huffed out a heavy breath. "Good. We're done here."

Without another word, I turned away once again. But this time I walked from the room. I continued on down the hallway, through Alec's living room, and stepped out onto his back deck that led toward the beach.

The sum total of everything weighed heavy on my chest, making it difficult to breathe. Countless betrayals stacked high, and I found it impossible to distinguish among them.

When my toes sunk into the damp shaded sand, I turned, sensing Alec's steady presence.

He stood only an arm's reach away, a pained expression etched into his features.

Overcome by sudden emotion, tears sprang into my eyes, further blurring the world. But I shook my head and pinched them shut, desperate to stem the rising tide.

Heat pricked over my skin seconds before his palms rubbed up my arms, over my shoulders, until he cupped my face in his trembling hands. Undeniably drawn toward him, I blinked open my eyes. Moisture glittered in his as he stared down at me.

"*Yes*, Devin," he whispered. "Yes. Don't say 'no' to us. Take the time you need. Process what you have to. But don't say you're done with *us*."

On a hard swallow, I lifted my hands to his. Not sure of anything other than my next breath, I gripped his wrists and tugged them away from me.

His gaze searched mine, dropped to my lips, then raised up to stare hard at me.

Before he did anything stupid, before I got sucked in and did something I would regret, I stepped back. My chest ached, heart slogging with every beat.

My thoughts drifted to the ocean engulfing me not even an hour ago. How I'd almost given up, let the depths swallow me whole, take away my suffering in this world.

But, no. Death was too sweet and easy. Far better to suit the dark world I'd cocooned myself in for all these years? Torture. To be denied the one thing I'd always wanted but never realized, never fully admitted to myself. The one thing I felt I'd never deserved. The one thing my sister never had a chance at.

Within reach, inches away, stood that one thing:

happiness.

But only if I wanted to continue the deception.

Excruciating torture, if I were to more accurately describe how my heart felt as it shredded from my chest.

"No." The word croaked from my constricted throat. "I'm saying it, Alec. What do we have? We have nothing. A life based on lies is hollow." I huffed out a sardonic laugh. "Trust me, I know."

When I took another step back, needing to increase the distance between us, he took a step forward. "Then we base it on something else. Something more."

I wanted to believe him. Every desperate part of me, body and soul, wanted there to be a way in our impossible situation. "On what?"

"On truth. On you. On me. On who we really are. Through it all, that's always been true."

The weight on my chest grew heavier, crushing the air from my lungs. He didn't understand. How could he…when I didn't?

"I don't know who I am, Alec. That's why I came down here." My voice caught, and I inhaled a shaky breath. "I don't trust anyone," I whispered. "I especially don't trust myself."

Because I'd deceived myself most of all.

This time when I took a step backward, then another, he didn't follow.

Gaze locked to mine, he stared at me, eyes boring deep into my soul as if he knew what lay there, even if I didn't. His hands dropped into the pockets of the wet cargo pants plastered to his legs. "You know who you are. Listen to yourself. *Really* listen. Then trust what you hear."

So simple. And yet, he held no judgment in his expression, only conviction—as if he already knew who I was, knew I would trust it once I discovered it.

"Good-bye, Alec." I stood there, memorizing every hard plane of his face and the tenderness in his eyes that he tried so doggedly to keep hidden from the world. And as I did so, something vital deep inside me began to rend apart.

I did nothing to stop it, grew certain I deserved it.

Then before the earth opened up and swallowed me whole, I turned away and trudged up the beach, devastated.

And, blessedly or not, he let me go.

Life held no promises of being easy. Maybe that was the point of its beautiful charade: The sugar coating made the bitter pill worth swallowing.

And maybe at the core of what I felt unraveling deep in my chest would be the person I needed to find: *me*.

CHAPTER 31

The standing breakfast order sat under metal-domed plates on a tray that was perched on the shelf inches away from the mocking *DO NOT DISTURB* sign that still hung in ridiculous innocence from the doorknob.

As if Anna and I hadn't been kidnapped from this very room.

As if resident royalty hadn't had his house bombed by me a mere hour ago.

As if my world, in spite of stupid signs and countless lies, hadn't imploded.

I ripped the sign from the handle, breaking its string and exploding a couple dozen colorful beads in every direction. With an infuriated growl, I threw the worthless laminated instruction over the balcony. "I've been disturbed!" I shouted both at no one in particular and the entire world.

Then as I stood there in a damp bra and underwear, I stared at the slot above the door latch. It waited patiently for a key card. A key card I didn't have.

"You've got to be kidding." I spun around. The door to the neighboring room was closed, its pretty little *DO NOT DISTURB* sign intact.

With zero deliberation, due to every random thread tangling in my mind in simultaneous chaos, I jogged down the curving tiled staircase and ran around the back. When the trunk of the coconut palm came into view, I took a running leap at its shaved surface and grabbed on to the side of the building for leverage.

My hip screamed in agony and the rough bark scraped my skin, but the pain only fired my determination. Nothing would stop me. From doing what, I had no clue.

After half-shimmying and half-climbing for five huffing seconds, my hand came within reach of the upper edge of the balcony wall. I gripped it while pushing off the trunk with my bare foot. Then with a grunt, I hoisted myself up, hiked a leg over, and leapt down onto the tiled floor.

"There. No stumble. I'm already doing better than you, Alec," I grumbled to myself.

Not that it had become a contest. But with every passing second, the world had a different cast to it. Now it held both darkness and color, shadows and light. Every facet and hue seemed more vividly defined with the contrast.

And I was about to make my mark on it.

On a slow exhale, I shoved open the french door. Then I scanned the room. Inanimate objects filled my vision. A lot of *fragile* objects.

The first sacrifice? My dead-calm gaze landed on Anna's

computer. The one that gave us away to Miguel. The one Alec had used as a penlight perch while examining blueprints. Right under my nose, evidence there all the time for me to find—if I hadn't blindly trusted.

I picked it up, opened the screen, then heaved it at the wall. The plastic shattered on impact, the device crumbling into several large pieces and countless gray splinters. A two-inch wide SHIFT key skittered across the tile until it hit my big toe. Then I stared at the tiny dent left in the ivory wall plaster.

"Not enough," I growled.

Not nearly enough.

With a wood-jarring yank, I pulled open the TV armoire, eyeing the barware. With a derisive snort, I skipped the sturdy shot glasses and reached with both hands for the wine glasses and tumblers. Launch after launch, glass shattered against the wall over the initial dent I'd made, adding divots and pock marks to my rage-driven mural.

The hotel phone began to ring, its red light tattling, as if calling me to the proverbial principal's office. I yanked the damn thing off the nightstand and threw it at the wall too, its thin cord jerking from the socket seconds before the clunking impact.

Frenzied to the point of no return, I plowed my way through the room, jerking paintings off the walls to whiz them away like Frisbees and lobbing ceramic lamps to smash to their deaths on the tiles. Even the TV hadn't been spared, toppling to the ground with a satisfying crack.

Breathing heavy, but unable to function without keeping

the momentum going, I ran into the bathroom. Then I stared at the mirror. A wild-eyed mess gawked back at me, hair plastered to my head, skin pallid, eyes red rimmed.

With a pang in my chest, I remembered Alec's reflection in that mirror the night we'd officially met and his snarky comments as I stitched him up. At the unexpected trigger, my gaze drifted down to my hip, to the dark-pink spiral scar that had formed because Alec had injected me with his Hail Mary Field Cocktail.

He'd saved my life.

For what?

"Argggh!" Angered beyond measure, I spun around. Scanning the open closet, I spotted the dozen ludicrous pairs of designer shoes Anna had toted down here. Grabbing the ones with metal heels, I overhand pitched them at the mirror. The first impact made a hole. The second one shattered a spider web of cracks across the image.

"Perfect."

Now the broken mirror reflected how I saw the world. Fractured.

Miserably unfulfilled, I shuffled back into the main room to survey the damage.

"Not enough," I muttered, disgusted. No amount of destruction would ever be enough to balance the damage I'd sustained on the inside.

Beaten and unable to do a damned thing about it, I let the bottled-up emotions well forth. Hot tears stung my eyes until they streamed down my face. The choking cramp at the base of my throat snapped into an agonizing gravelly wail.

My chest heaved for oxygen, unable to suck in enough air as I suffocated once again, drowning in the center of it all.

And as the deluge hit me like a burst dam, I collapsed on the bed in the middle of the shards of glass, overcome by body-racking sobs.

Hours later, after I'd cried my eyes and heart out in the destroyed hotel suite then collapsed from sheer exhaustion, I found myself absently sitting at the concierge desk, checking out.

"Your room is already covered under the credit card supplied by Ms. Johannsen."

"Good." Sounded more like the vacation had been covered on EtherSphere One's dime. "Oh, and things got out of hand in the room last night," I added in an offhand tone, implying we'd drank too much and had knocked a few things over. "Be sure to charge all the damages to that same card."

"Absolutely, Ms. Hill. We will take care of it all."

If only their five-star concierge abilities reached that far.

The thirty-minute drive back to the airport was uneventful. Only the illuminated Vegas-like billboards erected at five-hundred-foot intervals along the darkening jungle canopy on either side of the highway broke up the monotony.

Passing through the airport security checkpoint with my lone carry-on bag took longer than the ride due to the tourist group ahead of me, including a couple who insisted that a wide-brimmed sombrero and rainbow-netted hammock would fit into the overhead compartments.

While I waited my turn, two black eyes stared at me from behind the metal grid of a pet-carrier door, its expressive reddish-brown eyebrows blinking at me from its protective cage.

"Yorkie," the twenty-something girl holding the carrier supplied to a question I hadn't asked.

And yet, I felt a kinship to the little imprisoned Yorkshire terrier. Along for the ride, out of control of its destiny. Grateful for the walls around it casting it into shadow, yet instinctively wanting to break free—without worry of the inherent dangers of the world that put it there.

After clearing security, I wandered through a gauntlet of flashy designer products being hawked in the glaringly bright duty-free corridor, the only pathway to the departure gates. The food court greeting me at the other end didn't hold any appeal; out of pure necessity, I'd raided the breakfast tray to consume basic sustenance on my way to hotel checkout. A quick glance at the flight boards yielded no information; they only posted gate assignments within an hour of their departure times.

Weary from more adventure than I'd bargained for, and needing to be away from people, I found a vinyl seat amid a sea of empty chairs, dropped my bag beside me, and plopped down.

"Ow!" I growled, reminded with bright color dotting my vision that Alec's miracle Field Cocktail still had its limitations.

The low hum of distant conversations echoing against hard surfaces began to soothe me. Passengers with baggage in tow flowed from the duty-free area and stared up at the flight board, registered disappointment on their faces, then wandered off to get swallowed into the crowds of the food court.

A Margaritaville waitress walked into my line of sight, the long plastic strands of her lime-green grass skirt swishing over her short underskirt and tanned legs. When she waltzed behind the counter, my gaze rose to the giant replica seaplane suspended from the ceiling. The signature "Capt. Jimmy Buffet" was painted on the fuselage above the aircraft's name, *Hemisphere Dancer*.

Even though red-and-green Christmas lights dangled over the wings, the mock plane triggered memories of the real one just hours ago that Alec had flown—that we'd crashed. With a heavy heart, my mind wandered to the events of the past week.

But with every succeeding recollection of my time with Alec, the pain became less devastating, until some brought a smile. Dry comments he'd muttered while training me. The warm amusement in his tone when he'd call me "Pink." The intensity in his eyes as he'd held me in his bed that last time, moved deep inside my body with measured purpose, gazed at me as if I'd become his entire world.

There were moments when what we'd had between us seemed real.

My heart burned in my chest. I sucked in a deep breath, staring at the twilight world outside, but it didn't ease the pain. On a heavy sigh, I rubbed the heel of my hand on my sternum—to no avail.

Had I made a mistake by rejecting Alec?

I had no basis for comparison. No guideline or rule. Only the comforting familiar darkness I habitually fled to when needing to protect myself.

Through my tear-blurred vision, a couple sitting a few rows away at the neighboring gate caught my attention. Turned sideways in the connected chairs, they'd scooted together as far as the padded metal arm between them would allow. Her curly blonde shoulder-length hair to his dark shadow of stubble over his ears toward his temples. Her early twenties to his pushing forty. She had a clean, pretty, rounded face with thick, long eyelashes. He had a narrow scar slashing through one eyebrow and a countenance hardened by life. And yet, their stark differences didn't matter. Whatever their stories, despite anything that had marked them to this point, regardless of the endless cacophony of the airport around them, they only existed for one another.

But it wasn't how they embraced that deeply affected me. Nor was it the tender kisses every sixty seconds between furtive smiles and whispered conversation. With every shaky inhalation and slow exhale, through each firm press of lips and gentle nod of reassurance, it became evident they'd been through trials, still suffered through them.

It was the way they stared at each other with utter adoration that rocked me to the core.

I launched from my seat, dumping my purse from my lap and knocking my carry-on over as I drew in the first cleansing lungful of air in far too long. My pulse quickened as I pinched unshed tears from my eyes. A smile tugged at my lips as I scooped up my belongings.

Once I had fingers wrapped around each handle, I rushed forward, racing toward the duty-free corridor, intent on pushing back through the security area against the flow, even if alarm bells sounded and armed guards detained me.

But I never made it that far. Didn't even take ten full strides before I stopped dead in my tracks. There he stood under the trio of electronic flight boards.

Alec.

My breath caught. The bags I'd struggled to pick up in my chaotic rush, dropped onto the floor with a clatter. Frozen immobile, my lips parted as I gaped in disbelief.

Eyes narrowed, he stared at me. Determination etched into his features. A rogue lock of hair fell over his forehead as his gaze hardened with ferocity. His fists clenched, crushing paperwork held in the left one.

Then to put us both out of our tense misery, he lunged from his position, covered the few strides between us, and opened his arms wide seconds before he tackled me into an embrace and swung me around.

I squealed, holding tight to him as an unstoppable grin broke across my face.

After a second full rotation, when finally he put me down, my expression grew somber, smile faltering. What now? How did I bridge the yawning chasm between where I'd been all my life and where I desperately wanted to be?

Even though my feet touched the ground, my heart soared. The rest of my body lagged terribly behind: throat instantly parched, hands trembling.

He blew out a hard breath. "I'm pulling rank. You don't get to say 'no.'"

"Rank?" Utterly confused, my brow furrowed. "Since when do you outrank me?"

"I'm older. Clocked in more years alone." He lifted a shoulder, half-shrugging while his lips downturned for a split second, as if an explanation was inconsequential.

Inarguable statements.

I failed to utter any worthy response, head empty of every damn thought for once because emotion had overridden all else. Elation appeared to have a brainwave-cancellation effect.

He arched a dark brow in challenge. "Need more?"

"No."

His eyes sparked, nostrils flaring at my curt response.

"I mean, yes." Damn it all. I'd become a bumbling idiot.

Freaking out over how badly my hands were trembling, I took a step back and threw my arms outward, shaking out my hands with two quick snaps at the wrists. Then I sucked in a breath, afraid he would read my actions as a rejection, and I stepped closer to him.

"I'm sorry." I threaded my fingers through the side belt loops of his jeans, staring at the cotton weave of his black V-neck T-shirt that stretched over his chest. "I've never done this before."

"Done what?"

"Hey, you're wearing jeans." A first. Casual suited him well.

"Impeccable observation skills." His finger touched

beneath my chin, then gently lifted until my gaze met his. "Done what?" he repeated.

"A relationship."

"Neither have I." He took a measured breath, but stared at me with renewed intensity.

I swallowed hard, straightening my shoulders, preparing for whatever came next.

He cleared his throat. "I'm not the white-picket-fence guy. I'm definitely not the two-and-a-half-kids-and-a-dog guy. But if being with me makes your world less dark, if you'll have me, I'll be *your* guy."

Simple as that. All I needed to do was say...

"*Yes.*" The whispered word fell from my lips with conviction.

He didn't promise to eradicate the darkness. I didn't want him to.

Instead, what he offered fell into the realm of possibility: a brighter world filled with hope.

And I was done *lying to myself.*

I threw my arms around his neck, reveling in his solid heat as he embraced me. Our lips tentatively brushed, then molded together.

We stood in a crowded airport, and all of a sudden, I urgently wanted to be anywhere but.

A crinkle of paper rustled at my back.

Breathless from our heated kiss, I pulled back, examining what he held more closely. Two corners of white cardstock peeked out from a brightly colored slim rectangular folder. "What are those?" They appeared to be boarding passes.

"Two first-class tickets."

"Oh?" I arched a brow, amused. "Confident."

"Hopeful," he corrected.

"Where to?"

"Another home I own." He shrugged, his expression turning nonchalant.

"Which is located…" I drawled, well aware he was attempting to be both modest and vague.

"How do you feel about Switzerland?"

Stunned speechless, my lips parted even though no words came out. Until the warm, shining idea of it blanketed over me, different than the cold cloak of darkness I'd become accustomed to.

No longer lost on an undetermined mundane path, the million fractures once shattering me apart vaporized. Excitement pulsed through my veins at being on the brink of a new adventure. With Alec. On neutral ground.

A smile tugged at my mouth, seconds before I sealed my fate with a tender kiss. "Switzerland sounds perfect."

EPILOGUE

The absolute silence struck me.

Naked under thick bedding on a high mahogany sleigh bed, in a master suite perched on the cantilevered corner of Alec's home that overlooked the snow-covered Swiss Alps, the effect of the rare tranquility surrounding us began to take deeper hold.

A twelve-foot Christmas tree, decorated by his housekeeper while we'd flown over the Atlantic, occupied the left corner of the room, its solid colored lights reflecting off the nearest portion of darkening glass. A lush sweet scent emanated from the majestic fir, and if I let my imagination go, our lookout transformed into a magical treehouse.

Overwhelmed by the moment, I tugged Alec's arm, pulling him toward the foot of the bed with me. His deep laughter echoed off the polished concrete walls as we twisted on to our stomachs, ripping the bedding free from its tucked corners. Then we settled upside down on the bed with a mass of white sheets and down comforter tangled around us.

On a relaxed sigh, I entwined my fingers with his as we gazed through his wall-to-wall picture window at the mountain landscape painted with darkening shades of gray.

I leaned toward him, then pressed a tender kiss just below his shoulder, over the spiral-shaped scar caused by the wound I'd inflicted. "Merry Christmas, Alec."

He turned toward me, rubbing a hand down my side until his thumb gently grazed over my healing bullet wound. "Merry Christmas, Devin."

I arched up, brushing my lips across his, until we melted into a slow kiss.

When he pulled back, his brow furrowed. "I didn't get you a gift."

"*You* are my gift."

He was the one thing that remained true. Amid too many lies, after all the deception, Alec remained my rock. And through it all, the deepest part of me knew he always had been.

"This is my first real Christmas," I whispered. That I could remember, that meant anything beyond a young child tearing open shiny presents.

"Mine too," he admitted.

We'd both lost so much, had come so far, then conquered our greatest fears to be together. Yet the reward of being with him was so great, the arduous trials to get here had been worth it.

"What will you do now?" he asked.

"We have to do something?" I groaned, burrowing

against his side as I closed my eyes. "Thought maybe we'd stay here forever."

His low chuckle vibrated into me. "Sounds like a solid plan."

But then thoughts of Geneva trickled in. "Will you help me look for her?"

"Absolutely."

"What about your commitment to EtherSphere One?"

"Don't have one."

I frowned, easing back to look at his face awash in the soft glow of Christmas lights.

His head tilted down a fraction, his gaze penetrating. "My commitment's to you."

Understanding began to dawn. "You don't work for them anymore?"

"No." Anger flashed in his eyes. "After you spoke to the High Council, and my realization of all they'd done to manipulate you, I'd had enough. Their agendas no longer dictate my actions. *Mine* do."

"You're a free agent?"

"Just like you."

My heart warmed at the unmistakable support he'd shown for me—for us.

"What if we aren't able to find her?" he asked, his words softening as he spoke.

I understood the intention behind them. Thirteen years was a long time for my parents and EtherSphere One to come up empty on retrieving her.

"We will." I had no idea why I knew that fact deep in my

bones, but I did. "Maybe not tomorrow, or next week…but someday."

A vital part of me needed to know she'd been kept safe, had discovered love. And if she hadn't, that she knew it was out there—at least from me.

Just yesterday, on the beach in front of Alec's house, I'd claimed I hadn't known who I was.

His reply, filled with utter conviction, filtered back into my mind: *You know who you are. Listen to yourself. Really listen. Then trust what you hear.*

He'd been right.

When I stopped looking inside myself, no longer focused on my loss, I realized someone else's happiness depended on the course of my actions. Alec wanted to be a part of my life.

The darkness ceased to be what I turned to for comfort and safety. I unearthed something far greater: Love.

When I embraced that?

Then I discovered me.

I let out a slow grateful breath. My lips curved into a gentle smile, then I kissed him, heart burning with emotion. "Whatever the world has in store for us, I've already found all I need."

Alec mattered most of all. We did. In our blessed moments together, a profound peace washed through me. And the rest of the world faded away…

ACKNOWLEDGMENTS

Special thanks goes to Susana Córdova, our Spanish language advisor.

We would also like to express appreciation to the Belmond Maroma Resort & Spa for a magical five-star vacation that helped inspire *The Espionage Effect*.

Enormous gratitude goes to our readers, fans, and friends. Your support means the world.

ABOUT THE AUTHORS

Kat Bastion won several awards for her bestselling debut novel *Forged in Dreams and Magick.*

Kat and Stone Bastion's bestselling first novel *No Weddings* and the No Weddings series were named Best of 2014 by several romance review blogs.

When not defining love and redemption through scribed words, they enjoy spending their time mountain biking and hiking in the beautiful Sonoran Desert of Arizona.

Stay in touch with them on their social media pages:
@KatBastion
@StoneBastion
www.facebook.com/pages/Kat-Stone-Bastion
www.talktotheshoe.com
www.katbastion.com

Keep informed about new releases by joining their Email Subscription list:
www.katbastion.com/email-subscription

CHARITY SUPPORT AND AWARENESS

Your purchase of *The Espionage Effect* helps the victims of human trafficking because a portion of the net proceeds of all Kat and Stone Bastion's books are donated to charities who support them. These charities are creating legislation and prosecuting criminals, rescuing and restoring victims, and raising awareness in the effort to eradicate the tragedy of human trafficking.

Please visit the Charity Support and Awareness page on their website www.katbastion.com and blog www.talktotheshoe.com to learn about some of the organizations they donate to and to find out how you can further support them.

"A single act of kindness is the foundation of many miracles."
~ Kat Bastion, *Utterly Loved.*